Operation
Easy Street

A Jock Miles WW2 Adventure
By
William Peter Grasso

Novels by William Peter Grasso:

Operation Easy Street
Book 3 in the Jock Miles WW2 adventure series

Operation Long Jump:
Book 2 in the Jock Miles WW2 adventure series

Long Walk To The Sun:
Book 1 in the Jock Miles WW2 adventure series

Unpunished

East Wind Returns

Book design by Alyson Aversa
Cover photo courtesy of United States National Archives
Map data: Google

Author's Note

This is a work of alternative historical fiction. American and Australian forces did, indeed, fight and die to reclaim the Papuan villages of Buna, Gona, and Sanananda from the Japanese in late 1942 and early 1943. In these pages, we explore a different path to the eventual Allied victory—with a dramatically different pivotal event—while still reflecting the underlying tactical premises, bloody miscalculations, and terrible suffering of the actual campaign.

The designation of military units may be actual or fictitious.

In no way are the fictional accounts intended to denigrate the hardships, suffering, and courage of those who served.

Contact the Author Online:
Email: *wpgrasso@cox.net*

Connect with the Author on Facebook:
https://www.facebook.com/AuthorWilliamPeterGrasso

Dedication

To my son Joshua, whose literary knowledge and wisdom will always leave me in awe

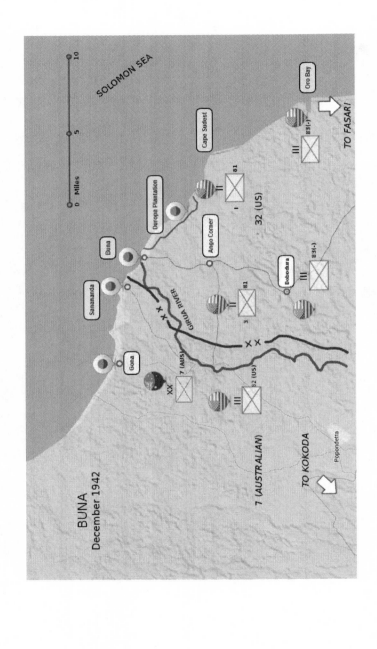

Late November
1942

Chapter One

I'm gonna die, Mama.

The sailor couldn't see any other outcome. He was trapped below deck of the mortally wounded aircraft carrier. One of the 500-pound bombs he was assembling had toppled off its cart when the first explosion rocked the ship. Like an inescapable vice, it fell just far enough to clamp his legs flat to the hangar deck.

They ain't broke but I can't move 'em a damn inch. Over two thousand men on this ship...and I'm gonna die alone. Everyone else must've gone over the side...or they're dead already.

I shoulda listened to you, Mama. I shoulda never joined the Navy. The bottom of the Coral Sea ain't a fit burial place for a Nebraska farm boy. I guess we lost the battle to the Japs for sure. I heard our pilots talking before they launched...they were scared. They said we were up against their whole damn navy.

Like a flickering ray of lost hope, his flashlight beam faded to nothingness, leaving an impenetrable darkness. Creaking and groaning like a giant, bellowing monster, the ship's bulkheads slowly collapsed one by one.

No vessel making sounds like that gonna be afloat much longer.

The sailor strained against the heavy iron sealing his fate, but it didn't budge this time, either. Frustrated and helpless, he pummeled the immovable object with his fists. A final shriek escaped his lips. Then a strange calmness washed over his body. He lay back against the cold steel deck and waited to die.

He didn't know how much time had passed before a beam of light appeared, bright and steady. It swept over the compartment that was his tomb and came to rest on his face.

Am I dead already? The light...Pastor always said there'd be a light. Go into the light.

"Take me, Lord," the sailor pleaded. "Take me now."

It wasn't God holding the light, though. It was just an NCO from a damage control party.

"You don't have to call me *Lord*, son," the NCO said. "*Chief* will do just fine." He glanced at the sailor's legs and asked, "Are you in any pain?"

"No, Chief, I surely am not."

"Then we'll have you out of here in no time. We've been ordered to abandon ship."

The rest of the damage control party, armed with pry bars and axes, materialized out of the darkness. In seconds, they freed the sailor. Rising unsteadily to his feet, he asked, "Chief, those Japs beat us pretty bad, didn't they?"

"Hear me good, son," the chief replied, "you may think we're in bad shape...but you should see the other guy."

Chapter Two

A few miles north of Port Moresby, Colonel Dick Molloy, US 81st Infantry Regiment commander, briefed his three battalion commanders. "Gentlemen," Molloy began, "General MacArthur feels we've been handed an opportunity we must pounce on immediately."

His battalion commanders grimaced at the word *immediately*. They weren't ready to fight—not yet, anyway. And they all knew it.

Molloy smacked his pointer against the big map of Papua. "MacArthur's really hot to claim the north coast of Papua while the Japanese Navy is still reeling from that whipping they just took in the Coral Sea."

His pointer pressing against a tiny dot on the map, Molloy added, "Our regiment, gentlemen, along with the rest of 32nd Division, is going right here—a tiny place called Buna."

The battalion commanders sat in stunned silence: barely one week after the bloody fighting for Port Moresby had finally ended, they were being thrown into action against the Japanese again.

Turning to Major Jock Miles, his newest battalion commander, Molloy said, "Now, Jock, I know you've only had First Battalion for a few days, and it's nothing more than a skeleton right now, barely at company strength. That's why I'll be holding you back until the final movement by air to Buna."

"When will that be, sir?" Jock asked.

"Looks like about ten days."

It could be ten months and it wouldn't matter a damn bit, Jock told himself. *I've got over two companies' worth of green GIs still coming on a boat from Australia...and I'll have to lead them into combat with no training and no time to get organized. I think I'm going to be sick...*

"I'm sorry for the tight schedule, Jock," Molloy added, "but I've known you since you were a shavetail, young man. I have no doubt you can handle it."

Jock's stoic expression belied his inner thoughts: *Gee, thanks, sir. I hope you're still that confident in me when the shit hits the fan.*

Molloy laid his pointer on the big map again, adding, "The Aussies have already pushed what's left of the Japs who fled Port Moresby back to here, about halfway across the mountains of the Kokoda Track. Those Aussie *diggers* are giving them hell, and our Fifth Air Force is giving them a pretty good pasting, too. Any Japs lucky enough to make it all the way to Buna will be in real bad shape."

So will any Aussies that make it, Jock thought. *They say the climbing is harder than the fighting.*

Molloy rolled steadily on. "And with the Jap Navy running back to Rabaul and Truk with their tails between their legs, there'll be little chance for them to land reinforcements around Buna. There won't be more than a few thousand exhausted Jap troops there, in poor defensive positions." He shifted the pointer to the extreme eastern end of Papua. "Plus, now that the Aussies have kicked the Japs out of Milne Bay, all of Papua will be under Allied control once we seize the Buna area. MacArthur says this operation will be a piece of cake."

A piece of cake: that was the last thing the battalion commanders wanted to hear. A collective voice in their

heads screamed what they didn't dare say out loud:
*Yeah...just like Port Moresby was supposed to be. And
we all know how well that turned out. Three weeks of a
bloody stalemate before MacArthur finally got his ass
off that cushy throne in Brisbane and sent enough troops
to do the job right.*

"There's one more thing," Colonel Molloy said.
"There's been a lot of bullshit talk that MacArthur's
given the Aussies a raw deal, sending them to chase the
Japs over Kokoda while we Yanks cool our heels here in
Port Moresby. So to show our Allies just how untrue
that is, this regiment has been assigned to support the
Australian Seventh Division on the Track. Colonel
Blevins, your Second Battalion will march across the
Owen Stanleys parallel to the Kokoda Track here"—his
pointer traced a path northward across the map—"along
what's known as the Kapa Kapa Trail. Since you won't
be slowed down by having to fight your way across,
you'll be able to cut off those Japs fleeing Port Moresby
before they get anywhere near Buna. Trapped between
you and the Aussies, they'll be finished off."

Lieutenant Colonel Blevins was less than enthused
with the assignment. This was painfully obvious even
before he opened his mouth. "Sir," Blevins said, "that's
almost a hundred miles on foot...and from what I can
tell from this map, we'll be climbing over peaks *ten
thousand* feet high! That'll take a month, at least."

"Not with good leadership, it won't, Colonel. A
week to ten days to get into a blocking position, at the
very most."

Blevins sputtered his next question: "How are we
going to be resupplied? The native porters can only carry
so much."

"The Fifth Air Force will handle that with air drops," Molloy replied. "Food, water, ammo, medical supplies…you'll get it all. Don't worry."

Jock couldn't help but feel bad for Colonel Blevins and 2nd Battalion. Suddenly, his battalion's assignment didn't seem so bad: *At least my guys get to ride over the mountains in airplanes.*

But that brought up a new question. "Sir," Jock asked Colonel Molloy, "our men aren't parachute infantry. These airplanes that'll take the rest of us to Buna…where are they going to land? It's nothing but swamps over there, isn't it? And if there are any suitable landing fields, won't the Japs be occupying them?"

"Negative, Major Miles," Molloy said. "Division has good intel from the Aussie coast watchers up that way. The areas we'll be using for landing strips are high and dry…and unoccupied."

Reading Jock's mind, Molloy added, "Let's hope they stay that way, gentlemen."

Chapter Three

It was like any other day since the Aussies began their march on the Kokoda Track. They'd been chasing the Japanese across this mountainous jungle hell for a week and were still nowhere near the halfway point to the north coast. At the moment, they were climbing another treacherous slope. On the peak, the Japs were dug in, peppering the lead elements of the long, narrow Aussie column below with rifle and machine gun fire. The diggers took cover anywhere they could, be it behind a scrawny tree trunk or sprawled flat on the ground, burrowing into hastily prepared fighting positions.

A captain scrambled through the brush—half-running, half-crawling—to his pinned-down men. He joined a corporal huddled behind a fallen log, which shielded them from the bullets sporadically thumping into its opposite side.

Struggling to catch his breath, the captain asked, "Can you see the bastards, Corporal?"

"Can't see a bloody thing, sir. They're up there somewhere...that's all we know."

All along the stalled front line, the captain's men returned fire blindly but to little effect. There was no let-up to the bullets raking their position from the peak.

"How many casualties, Corporal?"

"Two I know of so far, sir. One poor bugger's pretty bad, I reckon."

"Bloody shame," the captain replied. "Well, there's only one way to get those Japs off that peak..."

"I know, sir," the corporal replied with downcast eyes. "I bloody well know."

The corporal was already signaling the eight men of his section to move right. They knew the drill: they were seasoned troopers and they'd done this very thing before. When they were far enough off the trail, they'd turn uphill and hack their way through the thick jungle growth with machetes.

Once alongside the Japanese on the peak, they'd storm them with grenades and bullets in a flanking attack. Provided, of course, the Japanese didn't hear them coming.

The section was lucky: the jungle growth wasn't so thick on the route the corporal chose. There wasn't much hacking to do and not much noise to be made. The only problem the jungle caused was the constant snagging of web gear and uniforms on prickly vegetation. After a week in the steady heat, humidity, and frequent rain of the jungle, the damp fabric had already begun to rot. Each snag tore off another swatch of material, exposing more skin for the ever-present insects to feast on.

Their boots weren't faring well, either. It wouldn't be long before the sodden, rotting uppers tore away from the soles. The Aussies' only consolation: the uniforms and equipment of Japanese dead they came across on the Track seemed in even worse shape.

They were close enough to the peak now to hear Japanese soldiers screaming their usual epithets as they fired at the diggers downslope. Most were in Japanese and indecipherable. The rare ones in fractured English all boiled down to the same theme: *You Die! This be last day at Earth for you! You not go home Australia!*

Those taunts would have been comical if not delivered with such deadly purpose.

But the voices were close. Very close. The corporal lobbed the first grenade. Four more from his section quickly did the same.

As soon as the grenades detonated, the diggers charged, whooping like crazed drovers, firing their rifles from the hip. The section's Bren Gun laced a steady stream of lead that chewed up the ground all along the peak.

They never saw the Japanese soldiers until right on top of them. They were nestled in shallow fighting holes behind low parapets made of fallen trees. All the enemy soldiers seemed to be dead.

The diggers bayoneted each one just to be sure. They'd been fooled before by fakers lying among corpses who'd pop up and shoot you in the back once you passed. You only needed to be fooled once; after that, the bayoneting became routine and remorseless.

There were four Japanese. Only one of them wasn't dead before the bayonet plunged through his torso. They were all barefoot. Two still wore uniforms, badly tattered. The other two had fashioned tunics out of rice sacks.

"Only four?" the captain asked as he joined the section on the peak.

The corporal replied, "Where they were set up, sir, one man, with enough ammunition, could have slowed us down just as well."

The Aussie column could now slog forward once again, over the peak and down the backside of the mountain. They needed to make up time: an airdrop of supplies was scheduled for this morning. The drop zone was still several miles away, at the base of the valley between this mountain and the next.

They had only traveled half a mile when the drone of American C-47s echoed up the slope. "Well, fuck me right up the arse," the captain said. "The Yanks are early for once...too bloody early."

From their high perch, the Aussies watched as a dozen planes dropped their parachute-loads of supplies to the jungle below. For once, the targeting looked remarkably accurate: most of the containers seemed to land within easy reach of the Track. Usually, the loads floated down all over the surrounding jungle; the ground troops were lucky to recover a quarter of it.

This drop's rare display of precision would have been beautiful to watch—if it wasn't so frustrating.

Shaking his fist at the planes as they flew off, the captain said, "Thank you, you bloody wankers. Thank you for supplying the bloody Japanese instead of us."

Lagging miles behind the head of the Australian column, other men were fighting a different battle. Scores of diggers and native porters struggled like chain gangs with long, thick ropes, blocks and tackles secured to stout trees, and brute manpower to haul four 25-pounder artillery pieces up near-vertical slopes. Progress was sometimes measured in inches: each howitzer alone weighed over 3,000 pounds. Men could be killed, and a day's work undone in a terrifying moment, if a load slipped its restraints and careened backward down the trail.

They'd first tried using the pack mules for this task, but quickly gave up on it. The beasts would balk and gave up as much ground as they gained. The diggers had to put two mules out of their misery after the animals slipped, fell, and, still tethered to the tackle, were badly injured as a runaway load dragged them up the slope.

The Aussies were sure of one thing: all this effort was well worth it. They'd need those four guns—and the eight still well behind them on the Track—when they got to the north coast. Maybe sooner.

Chapter Four

The euphoria Jillian Forbes felt to be docking at Port Moresby again evaporated the moment she saw Jock Miles's face. He was standing on the wharf, slumped against his jeep, with what seemed like the weight of the world on his shoulders. Even from the pilot house of her ship, the Australian coastal trader *Esme,* she could tell there was bad news waiting to be told.

"What's wrong, baby?" she asked before even reaching the bottom of the gangway.

"Big change in plans, Jill," he replied. "We're not going to be here near as long as we figured."

She wanted to believe it was a cruel joke. They thought they'd have months together here in Port Moresby as 32nd Division regrouped and retrained. Even though she'd be captaining her ship as it sailed back and forth from Australia, shuttling supplies to the Allied forces, the young lovers would've still been together for a night or two on a fairly regular basis. "What? Where are you going?" she asked, expecting him to break into a sly smile any second, unable to play out the joke any longer.

He didn't smile. He didn't say anything.

"Jock, this isn't funny. What's going on?"

He told her about the plan to take Buna. She wasn't impressed. *Horrified* would better describe how she felt.

"You Yanks aren't ready to go anywhere," she said. "And you're a *battalion commander* now? When did that happen?"

"Right after I got my ass chewed for being AWOL the last time you were in port."

"My recollections of that night tell me it was well worth an ass-chewing, laddie."

Jock finally managed a smile. A big one.

"You bet it was, Jill. But dammit, nights like that are going to be hard to come by now."

"No kidding," she said. "In the next ten days, I'll only be back here twice at most. You *are* going to be able to slip away tonight, aren't you? Without getting nicked for being AWOL again?"

He snapped her a salute. "All taken care of, Captain Forbes. Command does have its privileges." Climbing into the jeep's driver's seat, he added, "Can you get away right now? They're holding supper for us."

She bounced into the passenger's seat. "Of course I can, silly boy. My lads have the unloading under control. Like you said, command does have its privileges."

Jillian was stunned by the sumptuous spread on Commander Shaw's dining room table. "Bloody hell, Commander," she said, "isn't there a war on? My crew and I have been living off nothing but bully beef for weeks...and you're offering a meal fit for a king!"

Trevor Shaw chuckled as he replied, "My dear girl, MacArthur insists on living like a king. We could exist off his scraps for months. That provides some small measure of consolation for me, shunted to the servants' house as he makes himself quite at home in mine. At any rate, Virginia's been doing a marvelous job looking after him. She's kept *The Great One* quite happy."

Virginia Beech's voice boomed from the kitchen, "It's easy if you remember the bloody wanker must have his luxury." She swept into the room toting another platter of seafood. "You ought to see *His Highness* in the mornings, prancing around the veranda in his dressing gown, downing crumpets and sipping his coffee while he reads his dispatches. Son of a bitch farts through silk while his lads live out there in the bush like filthy animals."

Jillian looked to Jock and asked, "Speaking of the lads, what are they eating right now?"

"At least they're getting hot chow and plenty of it," Jock replied. "Of course, it's not exactly being served on fine china like this…" His voice trailed off: it would be no time at all before he and his men would be in the swamps, subsisting on field rations again.

Jillian asked, "Where is MacArthur, anyway?"

"In Australia," Trevor Shaw replied. "A high-level meeting in Brisbane. He'll be back tomorrow." Ginny Beech added, "You didn't think he was out in the jungle, did you?"

Jock threw up his hands in surrender and said, "I can see I'm outnumbered here—the only Yank against three Aussies. So go ahead, bash us GIs all you like."

"Oh, we will, Jock," Ginny said. "We will."

"Speaking of Yanks," Jillian said, "where's First Sergeant Patchett? I figured if Ginny was here, he'd be around."

"Oh, don't worry, girlie…the old boy will be around, all right," Ginny replied, "but later, when I have some time for him." She pointed an accusing finger at Jock. "Didn't this wanker tell you? He's not *first*

sergeant any more. This man right here made him
Battalion Sergeant Major Patchett."

"Good on Patch!" Jillian said. "A promotion!"

"Don't get carried away, lass," Ginny said. "It's not
really a promotion, just a new title the major over there
stuck on him. No extra stripes involved. Leave it to the
bloody Yanks to give a man more responsibility without
something extra in his pay envelope. Not that their pay
envelopes aren't fat enough to begin with, compared to
our poor diggers."

Jock turned to Commander Shaw. "Sir, there's
something I really need to talk with you about."

The old coast watcher pushed his plate away and lit
his pipe. "Fire away, young man," he said. "I'm at your
disposal, as always."

Jock told them of the plans for taking Buna. When
he described 2nd Battalion's orders to advance over the
Kapa Kapa Trail, their jaws dropped and their eyes went
wide.

"You've got to be kidding," Ginny said.

"They're dead serious," Jock replied. "I take it there
are problems we Yanks don't know about?"

"That's an understatement, Jock," Shaw said. "Kapa
Kapa is a trail in name only. It's more like an imaginary
line through mountainous jungle—one you'll have to
hack through inch by inch."

Ginny added, "And if you're counting on native
porters coming with you, bloody well forget it. They'll
go as far as Ghost Mountain but won't cross it. As far as
they're concerned, it's a haunted, evil place. It won't
matter what you offer to pay them."

"It doesn't sound like a very timely plan, either,"
Shaw said. "You and your airlifted troops will be on the

north coast long before that unfortunate battalion emerges from the jungle...*if* they ever emerge. Are you sure those men are up to such a trek? The diggers have enough trouble crossing the Owen Stanleys...but the Yanks?"

"It's not my call, Commander. Ready or not, they'll be on the trail in two days."

Shaw and Ginny just shook their heads. "Poor buggers," she muttered.

"What about the landing fields they say are there?" Jock asked.

Shaw replied, "Dickie Bennett's been our coast watcher in the Buna district since before the first Japanese landings. I've known the man for years. If he says those fields are useable—and unoccupied—you can bet your life on it."

"Good," Jock said, "because that's exactly what my men will be doing."

Chapter Five

Jock would have loved to stand and watch *Esme* sail out into the Coral Sea until she was just a speck on the southern horizon. He couldn't, though: this was the morning the replacement troops for 1st Battalion would arrive. There would be a million details to attend to and not nearly enough time to do them. One last, lingering kiss with Jillian at the ship's rail and he was speeding off in his jeep, back to his battalion CP.

When he got there, Sergeant Major Patchett had everything under control. First Battalion's cadre—Patchett especially—seemed chipper and ready to face this challenging new day with a smile.

"I'm guessing every man jack in this outfit got laid last night, sir," Patchett explained.

Jock replied, "So the men's field trip to the Port Moresby *hospitality center* went well?"

"Well, indeed, sir. Well indeed. Ain't nothing like an evening with a fine Aussie lady…even the ones you gotta pay."

"Just so we don't lose anyone to the clap, Top…"

Jock fell into an awkward silence, worried he had just breeched military etiquette: Patchett wasn't a company first sergeant anymore. He was Jock's battalion sergeant major now.

"Don't you worry none, sir," Patchett said. "*Top's* still just fine, as long as it's just you and me talking private-like. *Sergeant major* is kinda formal between two dogfaces who been through as much together as we have."

"Got it," Jock replied. "But every other swinging dick better call you *sergeant major,* right?"

"Damn straight, sir."

A steady stream of confused, newly arrived GIs spilled from the deuce-and-a-half trucks shuttling between the Port Moresby docks and 1st Battalion's bivouac. By morning's end, some 300 men, all green privates—save for a few equally green sergeants and lieutenants—were distributed to fill the empty platoons of Able, Baker, Charlie, and Dog Companies.

It should have been pure chaos, like most mass movements in *this man's army.*

But it went smooth as silk. Until this morning, 1st Battalion may have been just a skeleton, but its key leadership positions were already staffed with the combat veterans of Charlie Company—men who Jock Miles had led into combat in Papua.

By mid-afternoon, the battalion was organized enough for its first formation. As Jock trooped the line with Colonel Molloy, Sergeant Major Patchett paced behind the rear rank, making sure the company sergeants tolerated no goofing off among their men. *Always a few dogfaces, too clever for their own damn good,* Patchett thought, *smarting off, thinking they blend in so good nobody can see them.* His studied eye caught one such incident in Baker Company. That unit's first sergeant found Patchett in his face immediately.

"I know y'all are brand spanking new to my battalion," Patchett hissed in the first sergeant's ear, "but let's get something straight right off. If you let them get away with that grab-ass on the parade field, how the hell do you expect them to follow orders in combat? You gotta stomp on that shit the minute you see it, Sergeant. Otherwise, it's gonna grow like a cancer and wreck your company. I guaran-damn-tee it. Do you understand what I'm telling you?"

"Yes, Sergeant Major, I just—"

"Didn't ask for no fucking explanation, did I?"

"No, Sergeant Major."

"Very fine. Now get your head out of your ass and carry on."

Colonel Molloy's inspection done, Jock dismissed the battalion formation. Their day was far from over: in one hour, they'd embark on their first tactical field exercise.

"It'll be a Chinese fire drill," Patchett assured Jock and Colonel Molloy, "so no live ammunition yet, that's for damn sure. We don't be needing no accidents."

Molloy asked, "When do you propose to do a live fire exercise, Major Miles?"

"The minute the sergeant major and I believe they're ready, sir."

"Good plan," Molloy replied, "but I'm more than a little concerned about the way you reorganized your cadre. Do you think it was a good idea to deplete Charlie Company of most of its combat-experienced officers and NCOs?"

"Yes, sir," Jock replied. "I believe it's better to spread the expertise around so all the companies have a relatively equal level. Otherwise, we get one very experienced company and three led by rookies."

Molloy pondered that for a moment, and then asked, "Sergeant Major, is that your opinion, too?"

"Absolutely, sir," Patchett replied. "I seen it too many times before. Get one company full of crackerjacks and the others full of jerk-offs...well, them jerk-offs will collapse the minute the shit hits the fan. Then we all end up getting overrun. But if they all fight about the same, we all got a better chance to keep drawing breath."

Molloy smiled: the sergeant major might have only limited command of the King's English but his experience had to be respected. "Very well, then," he said, "but I've got to drop a little bombshell on you both. Your battalion is still under strength by about fifty men, and, unfortunately, it looks like it's going to stay that way. By the time any more replacements are available, we'll all be bivouacking in Buna."

Jock knew what the expression on Patchett's face meant: *Should I bend over again, sir...or are you done fucking me?*

Trying to keep that same expression from his own face, Jock asked, "What about our heavy machine guns and mortars, sir? We'll still be getting those, won't we?"

"The S4 expects them within the week, Major Miles."

"That don't give us no training time for the weapons company hardly at all, sir," Patchett said. "Not if we're moving out in nine days."

As he climbed into his jeep, Molloy replied, "All we can do is our best, Sergeant Major. I'm counting on you two to do that for me."

As the colonel drove away, Patchett asked Jock, "Sir, I thought you said that man was in France in '18?"

"Yeah, he was, Top."

Patchett shook his head: "He don't sound like no one who been in a shit storm of lead...but let's hope he's better than that last paper soldier we had to put up with." Jock replied, "Trust me, Top. He is."

The first tactical field exercise went exactly as Sergeant Major Patchett expected: a Chinese fire drill. Radios broke down almost immediately in the tropical heat, causing coordination between units to break down just as fast. Among those with working sets, communications discipline was atrocious: several operators would constantly try to talk on the same frequency at the same time; knowledge of proper voice message format was sorely lacking; security procedures went out the window. Case in point: one squad leader in Able Company began identifying himself over the air as if answering a telephone. "McNally, First Squad," he broadcast rather than his proper call sign, *Rodeo One-One-Six*. Countless units reported their location's coordinates without bothering to code them.

An evaluator told one of Jock's company commanders, "They're making it way too easy for the enemy. A lot of your men just died because they told the Japs *who* and *where* they are."

Four of the battalion's nine rifle platoons got lost in the rainforest, unable to accurately dead reckon using map, wristwatch, and compass. Two of those platoons eventually found their way to the objectives and staged ragged mock attacks judged as "unsuccessful" by the evaluators.

A frustrated platoon leader told his evaluator, "These maps are all fucked up, sir."

In a deadpan voice, the evaluator replied, "It's not the maps, Lieutenant."

The other two lost platoons never found their objectives; they could barely find their way back to the assembly area when the siren signaled the end of the exercise. Ultimately, their evaluators guided them back to save time; too much had been wasted already.

Tactical dispersal was another area needing improvement. It wasn't uncommon for GIs to be bunched close enough to hold hands. In one incident, an evaluator encountered five GIs huddled—inches apart—behind the same fallen log while taking up a defensive position.

"You know what I see here?" the evaluator asked. "Five dead GIs. Did you ladies ever hear the expression *grenade gets you all?* Well, it just did. Here...put these around your necks." He handed each of the GIs a cardboard tag that read *KIA* in big black letters—for *killed in action.*

As the evaluator walked away, the GIs snickered among themselves like it was all some big joke. One lay prone and silent, pretending to be a corpse with eyes closed, hands crossed over chest, and a disdainful smirk on his face.

Chapter Six

Kokoda, the little mountain village that gave the track its name, was the halfway point in the 120-mile journey from Port Moresby to Buna. That distance was *as the crow flies;* it nearly doubled for men climbing up and down the towering peaks of the Owen Stanley Range. The head of the Australian 7th Division column had yet to reach the village. It was still some 20 miles away, a formidable distance for diggers still skirmishing for almost every yard.

General George Vasey, the division commander, watched with quiet despair as a stream of casualties trickled to a primitive aid station just a hundred yards behind the fighting. A few of the stricken could walk—or at least hobble—on their own. The others had to be carried by native litter bearers.

Most of the casualties weren't wounded; they were sick, weakened by malaria, bush typhus, or a host of other tropical diseases. General Vasey wasn't surprised he was losing men to sickness carried by insects and ground water; he just hadn't expected so many of them. General Blamey, the commander of all Australian forces in Papua and Vasey's boss, had estimated a casualty rate to disease of no more than 20 percent.

It's going to be twice that, at least, Vasey told himself.

There was no room for the newly sick and wounded under the aid station's tattered tarp. They'd stand, sit, or lie in the pasty mud and frequent rain, too tired to swat away the ever-present mosquitoes, waiting quietly until it was their turn with one of the three harried doctors.

Offering only triage and not treatment, a doctor's time with a sick digger would be over quickly. If deemed too sick to stay on the Track, he'd be marked for evacuation to Port Moresby. That journey would take several days on foot—without medical treatment and fully exposed to the conditions that made him sick in the first place. The trek would begin only if there were native bearers to spare after the badly wounded had been evacuated.

Sick or wounded, a digger might not survive the journey. Only an airplane could improve his odds.

A doctor said to General Vasey, "We've got to do better for the lads than this, sir. How long to Kokoda?"

"Two, maybe three days," Vasey replied, as if trying to convince himself.

"Is the airstrip there still serviceable?"

"As far as we know," Vasey said. "Let's bloody hope it still is when we get to it."

First Battalion's field exercise may have been every bit the Chinese fire drill Sergeant Major Patchett predicted, but it wasn't a disaster. Everyone expected there to be mistakes, and those mistakes were not the issue. What Jock Miles would do to correct them was.

"That wasn't the first time a platoon or squad got lost," Jock told the battalion's assembled cadre, "and it won't be the last. Those of us who've been here a while know Papua is not exactly studded with landmarks. But you'll learn quickly how to correlate terrain features with your map. Your company commanders all did, in no time flat. Learn from them."

Jock looked to the battalion communications officer and asked, "All the radios working again, Lieutenant?"

"Yes sir, they are," the commo officer replied. "User error, mostly."

"Very well, Lieutenant," Jock said, "and I'll expect all company commanders to educate their men on the care and feeding of those radios." Jock yielded the floor to Patchett: "Sergeant Major, you've got stuff to add, I'm sure."

"I sure do, sir," Patchett began. "First off, as far as those on-the-air fuckups went, I think a few good raps on the helmet should fix that. And if that don't work, make sure they write their fucking call signs in grease pencil right on their walkie-talkies so they can't forget. But most importantly, nobody got hurt...not so much as a stubbed toe. Believe me, that's something y'all can feel good about."

And they did: they all knew training accidents were endemic to the military. GIs could always find diverse ways to maim themselves. Even without live ammunition, their profession combined all the most dangerous elements of working with machines while existing in the wilderness.

"Now," Patchett continued, "we still got ourselves a li'l ol' morale problem. A whole bunch of these shitheads still ain't taking this soldiering business with the proper seriousness...because they ain't figured out how to take it serious yet. *Serious* is too damn terrifying."

He took a dramatic pause before continuing, "And they won't take it serious until that special something happens that makes a man change inside, like hauling off what's left of his buddy in a mattress cover. You need that *cat-list*."

There were strange looks being cast all around, men wondering if this was some army term they had somehow never heard before.

Jock broke the confused silence: "You mean *catalyst*, Sergeant Major?"

There was just a hint of indignation in Patchett's voice: "I believe that's what I said, sir."

"Just making sure, Sergeant Major," Jock said, in his best soothing voice. "Just making sure. Please continue."

"I just got one more thing to say, sir. I think we can stop fiddly-fucking around and move on to live fire training exercises first thing tomorrow. We're gonna need every minute to get our asses ready."

Jock replied, "I couldn't agree more, Sergeant Major."

Infantry may be *Queen of Battle*, but artillery is still king. As in any successful marriage, the king and queen have to learn to work together to achieve common goals. That's exactly what this portion of the live fire exercise was about: infantry and artillery coordination in the attack. The infantrymen of Charlie Company, under Lieutenant Lee Grossman, were dug in at the edge of the exercise area, watching as 75-millimeter artillery rounds landed on the hill some 50 yards in front of them. In another minute the fire would lift, and Grossman's men would assault the hill in a mock attack, firing live bullets at defenders made of burlap sacks and straw. None of the company's rookies had ever watched an artillery round impact so close before.

There were a few brief *ooohs* and *ahhhs*, but by and large, the men weren't impressed. *Disappointed* would be a better word. They were expecting hellfire and brimstone. All they got were some muffled *booms*, wispy puffs of smoke, and a few clods of earth flung into the air.

Surely nothing powerful enough to stop a horde of Japanese swarming down on them.

"You may not think it looks like much now, men," Grossman would tell squad after squad as he moved along the line, "but when we start doing this for real, we're going to be a hell of a lot closer to it—maybe right under it—so close you'll hear the shell fragments whizzing through the air. So close your ears will bleed."

His words only seemed to be making the men more disenchanted with their current lot in life, so Grossman would add, "You'd better believe that when the Japs are in your face, you're going to want that artillery. You're going to *need* that artillery, because without it, you'll be in real deep shit. Trust me on that one."

Yeah, trust me, Lee Grossman told himself as he reached the last platoon. *I've already been down that road a couple of times.*

Sergeant Major Patchett wasn't pleased by the interruption. He was trying to compile evaluators' reports on the live fire exercise for the lunchtime debriefing when the Headquarters mess sergeant burst into the command tent.

"We've got a big problem, Sergeant Major," the mess sergeant said, on the verge of panic. "We can't cook that chicken for lunch. We ain't got no grease!"

Patchett's slow boil began. Last night, he had plainly instructed the men would receive hot meals throughout their training at Port Moresby: *Three fucking squares a day, I believe my exact words were. The boys will have plenty of time to eat K rations once we're back in the field.*

But now, this mess sergeant was telling him his kitchen wasn't prepared to do that.

Patchett asked, "And when did you realize this, numbnuts?"

"Just now, I didn't—"

Signaling *stop* like a traffic cop, the sergeant major shut him up. "Don't want to hear no excuses," Patchett said. "You fucked up, plain and simple. Never checked your requisitions, did you?"

His eyes staring at his feet, the mess sergeant shook his head: *No.*

"So now you're telling me my hungry boys are gonna get dog squat for lunch? While you shitcan a couple hundred pounds of fresh chicken?"

"I ain't got nothing else to cook, Sergeant Major."

"Bullshit you don't. How much butter you got?"

"Plenty...but I need that for breakfast and—"

Patchett cut him off again. "That's right. You got plenty. *Fricassee* the goddamn chicken with some of that butter...and make it snappy. Lunch is in thirty fucking minutes."

"But—"

"And it better not be one second late, neither...or I'm looking at my new *mess private*. Or, even better, my new *rifleman*."

It was obvious to Jock: the men in his 1st Battalion still had that *li'l ol' morale problem*, just like Patchett had described. As they marched in from the live fire exercise, Jock could see it throughout every company. Most men grumbled, shuffling their tired feet as they walked, paying no attention to the steady cadences called by their sergeants. Some engaged in horseplay. Occasionally, there was a burst of snide laughter: a few jokers hidden deep in the ranks were, no doubt, passing witty comments attempting to satirize how *this man's army* was run by incompetent idiots who wanted to play *hurry up and wait* all day long. The men felt entitled to laugh: this whole war was nothing more than a cruel joke being played on them.

Their uniforms labeled them as soldiers; their manner labeled them as anything *but*. *Real* life was someplace else, thousands of miles across the ocean. They still thought they could play these silly army games just enough to get by: *keep your nose clean, keep your head down, and somehow you'll get home in one piece.*

They'd had the mantra *kill or be killed* drummed into their heads—but they still didn't want to believe it.

"They're just scared shitless, sir, that's all," Patchett said.

Jock hadn't heard his sergeant major walk up behind him.

"Scared shitless," Patchett repeated, "and them poor bastards don't know how to show it proper yet."

"I know, Top," Jock replied, "I know. Chow ready?"

"Yes, sir," Patchett replied. He didn't bother relating the incident with the mess steward; he knew Jock had enough on his mind.

Besides, Patchett told himself, *that's my job to take care of them nitpicky little details.*

A command echoed down from the lead platoon, and 1st Battalion's column of twos shifted right and became single file. Another battalion-sized unit was coming the other way on the narrow dirt road. The men in that column were in full field gear, heavily loaded with ammunition, horseshoe packs, and canteens. Full of somber purpose, they marched forward, their faces wearing the resolute expressions of men communally tasked with a difficult and deadly job.

"That's Second Battalion," Patchett said. "They're moving out to the Kapa Kapa." He paused, shook his head, and added, "Poor bastards."

"Look how different they seem from our guys, Top."

"A couple of week ago, they didn't look so different, sir. But they're *real* soldiers now. They've got bloody hands, just like me and you. They know what it's like to bury their own."

A faceless, sarcastic voice from 1st Battalion called out, "See you at Buna, suckers."

There was dead silence for a moment, until a voice from within its ranks—a voice cold, harsh, and certain—thundered 2nd Battalion's reply:

"You won't be seeing shit when you're dead, rookie...and that'll be real soon."

It was as if God himself had just spoken to the men of 1st Battalion. It took a few seconds to become obvious, but a change had swept over them: they shook off their slouched postures and stood ramrod straight. Any hint of indifference vanished from their faces. In those few seconds, the *cruel joke* they had considered this war to be evolved to a serious and inescapable reality.

Patchett took it all in with a smile. "I do believe we just had ourselves a *cat-list*, sir," he said.

Chapter Seven

The last of the American B-25s swept low over the mountain plateau that was the Kokoda airstrip. They released their bombs, hugged the treetops ringing the hardscrabble runway, and made their swift escape as the ground shook in a chorus of explosions.

On the high ground overlooking the airstrip, the Australians tried to take stock of the raid's effect. Looking through binoculars, the Aussie major said, "Well, at least they blew up the two bloody airplanes...not that they were causing us any trouble. They were probably broken down and left behind, anyway. And they were careful not to crater the runway."

A senior sergeant replied, "Those fucking machine guns are still alive, though, sir...both of them, one in each corner of the strip. Their parapets are still intact, too. They could put down some murderous interlocking fire on us."

"Yes, I can see that for myself, Sergeant," the major replied. "Shook the little buggers up, though, didn't they? They're jumping around like their pants are on fire. I still don't see any of that dug-in infantry on the perimeter we ran into this morning, though."

Yeah, the sergeant told himself, *when it cost us eight men for nothing, you silly bastard.*

He knew what the major's next words would be. He wasn't in the least bit eager to hear them. Setting down his binoculars, the sergeant drew a deep, anxious breath.

"There's only one way we're going to find out how many of those buggers are still alive," the major said.

Miserable at reading his commander's mind so well, the sergeant replied, "I know, Major. I bloody well know. But before we probe them again, can we at least wait until the twenty-five-pounders are ready to shoot? They say it won't be much longer until they're up on the ridge."

"We can't wait forever, Sergeant. We've got to have that bloody airfield."

The sergeant made no effort to stifle the pleading tone in his voice: "So give us a fighting chance to take it then, sir. Please...we need those guns."

There was no arguing with the sergeant's logic: artillery support could make all the difference between a successful attack and another slaughter at the hands of Japanese heavy machine guns.

Time...we can't waste any more bloody time, the major thought. *We're already days behind schedule.*

As he gazed into the distance, across that coveted airstrip, the major replied, "Thirty minutes, sergeant. We attack in thirty minutes, whether the bloody artillery is ready or not."

The closest artillery piece was still a hundred yards downslope from the ridge's crest. Muscles trembled as exhausted teams of men pulled on the long ropes hauling the 25-pounders up, struggling to get the four guns to clear firing positions. They knew the infantry desperately needed some fire support right now—and they were just as desperate to provide it.

But the laws of physics don't yield to desperation. With each pull, blocks and tackles groaned, ropes taut as wire blurred and buzzed, Australian soldiers and Papuan natives cursed their mothers for giving them life—all to gain mere inches of uphill progress.

At this rate, they'd never be ready to fire in time. They would fail their mates in the infantry.

A gunner shouted an idea: "Lieutenant…suppose all of us get on one rope and pull just one bloody gun into position? It'll be much faster…That one can be shooting while we haul up the other three. Better than nothing, no?"

The lieutenant knew a good idea when he heard one. So did everyone else: they all ran to the ropes of the gun closest to the ridge and started pulling with whatever might their wrung-out bodies could muster.

We could hide in this high kunai grass forever and the Japs would never see us.

The diggers took comfort in that fact as they crept toward the airstrip.

Of course, if they're around, we won't see them, either, until we're right on top of them. And this bloody kunai is sharp as razor blades. Let's try not to bleed to death from the slashing it's giving us.

The first Japanese soldiers they stumbled across were dead, scattered in the kunai, done in by an American bomb. Some bodies were intact but inert, their internals shattered by concussive force alone. Others were torn to pieces, shredded by fragments hurtling through the air like a thousand iron talons. The diggers couldn't see the bomb crater concealed in the tall grass until they crept right up to it. They slid in, welcoming the cover the crater afforded while they got their bearings.

They didn't all make it.

The kunai grass trembled as if gigantic, invisible scythes were trimming it to the height of a man's knee. The first digger struck by the bullets was dead before he hit the ground.

In a split second, three more would be hit but not die outright. They wailed as fate decided which of them to claim, making sounds the living never wanted to hear again but would never be able to forget.

The chatter of Nambu machine guns to their left and right...

Fuck! We're caught in their bloody kill zone.

Those lucky enough to be in the crater pressed tight to its rim, feeling the *thupp thupp thupp* of machine gun bullets burrowing into the churned-up earth all around them. There wasn't much else they could do...except stand up and die in the machine guns' fire. The sporadic *pows* of Enfield rifles and the *thumps* of light mortars posed an ineffectual counterpoint to the steady rhythm of the Nambus.

A digger tried to raise just his Bren Gun over the edge of the crater. Before he could squeeze off even one round, the weapon was shot away. The gun—and the hand that had tried to wield it—was now shattered and useless.

The wailing of the wounded and dying men in the kunai grass wouldn't stop. If anything, it grew louder...and there was still nothing the men in the crater could do for them.

An object flew into the hole...

"GRENADE," someone—or everyone—cried out.

The wounded Bren gunner stared at it in disbelief.
Two of the others tried to crawl inside their helmets.
The last man in the hole lunged for it...
He picked it up...
Started to throw it away...
And then stopped. He stared in disbelief at the
object for just a second and then pushed it away as if
toxic.

It was a digger's boot...with the severed foot still in
it.

"Bloody hell," was all he could say, over and over
again.

On the ridge a thousand yards away, a cannoneer
rammed the first round into the breach of the only 25-
pounder ready to fire.

The gunner lined up the target in his telescopic
sight...tweaked the elevation wheel...

Just a little bit more...There!

Satisfied, he jerked the firing lanyard.

The first artillery round of the battle for Kokoda
was finally in flight.

At first, the artillery round's impact to their right
front confused the diggers in the bomb crater.

A private asked, "Is that theirs...or ours?"

"Damned if I know," his sergeant replied.

The wounded in the nearby grass had stopped their
wailing. The diggers thought they could hear only a

single Nambu machine gun firing now, the one to their left front.

A second artillery round slammed in, hitting the same spot as the first.

The private said, "The Japs wouldn't be knocking out their own guns now, would they? That artillery's got to be ours."

"About bloody time."

The second 25-pounder was finally in position on the ridge. Its dog-tired crew began to lay their piece on the same target the first gun was engaging.

The lieutenant stopped them. "No, lads, not there," he said, binoculars pressed to his eyes. "You aim left, at the west edge of the runway. Target is the machine gun emplacement."

Peering down his sight, the gunner said, "Yeah...I've got it."

The Japanese machine guns were silenced, but the fight for Kokoda airstrip was far from over. The diggers had emerged from the bewildering blindness and point-blank combat in the kunai grass into the open spaces of the airstrip, pushing what was left of the Japanese defenders before them.

"Swing your company to the right, Captain," the major said. "Let's cut off their retreat and finish them before they vanish into the woods on the other side and the village beyond." Turning to his artillery liaison, the major continued, "Go with them and pick out targets in the village for your guns—anything that shows its ugly head."

"Very well, sir, but we've only got two guns in action so far," the liaison replied.

"And they've done a bloody brilliant job. Keep it up."

The men of 2nd Battalion, 81st Regiment had begun to wonder why it was called the Kapa Kapa Trail. It wasn't a trail at all—it wasn't even a footpath wide enough for two men in most places. GIs at the front of the column—the *point men*—couldn't walk 10 yards without having to hack a path with machetes through jungle growth clinging to the steep mountainsides. They'd swing those blades until they thought their arms would fall off. Then it was someone else's turn.

At least there was no shortage of drinking water; the frequent rain saw to that. All a man had to do was muster the strength to catch it.

Colonel Blevins, the battalion commander, was having a difficult time believing his native guide even knew where in this vertical hell they were. Puzzling over his map, Blevins said to the guide, "That stream we just crossed...it can't possibly be the one you say it is."

He pointed to another thin blue line on the map, farther down the "trail."

"I think it's this one," Blevins said.

The guide shook his head. "No, sir. No, sir," he replied. "It is the one I said it is."

"But that means we've only come about fifteen miles in the last two days."

"That's right, Colonel," the guide said.

Blevins blew out a sigh of exasperation. "We're falling way behind schedule. This can't be the right trail. Why is it so overgrown?"

"Because nobody uses it."

"Why not?"

"Because only the insects want to go where it goes."

Two days in this mountainous jungle hell and the GIs were already spent beyond recovery. They'd lost track of how many times they'd sunk in mud up to their waists or almost been swept away fording rapid streams. They'd left Port Moresby heavily loaded with weapons, ammunition, personal gear, and rations, but already men were faltering under their loads. Terrified to be left behind, they lightened up, discarding items that served no immediate purpose.

Mosquito netting was among the first items to get dumped alongside the trail: *It doesn't work anyway,* the GIs told themselves. *The fucking insects own this place.* Raincoats were abandoned, too: *You'll get soaking wet one way or the other in this jungle. If it isn't the daily rain, it'll be the chest-deep streams you have to ford.* In fact, the men had decided there was no point carrying any uniforms except the ones they were wearing.

And to hell with shaving kits...but keep your toothbrush: you'll need that to keep your rifle clean.

The 60-millimeter mortars began to vanish, too— first the heavy base plates; next, the bipods; finally, the tubes and ammunition.

You can't fire them with any accuracy in this dense jungle canopy, anyway...and the fucking things weigh forty-two pounds each.

It's not like we've seen any Japanese. We're the only ones stupid enough to be in this tropical shithole.

When told of the disappearing mortars, Colonel Blevins said, "But damn it to hell, that's all we had for fire support."

Before he could say, *Make them go back and find those weapons,* he stopped himself. There would be no point: the mortars would never be found now, hidden by that thick jungle. The column had to keep moving. The men detailed to the search might never find their way back.

He took cold comfort in one fact: *I guess it's a good thing I decided not to bring any pack howitzers. They would've just ditched them, too...and eaten the mules.*

On the spot, Blevins decided the heavy field radio set—three packs weighing 50 pounds apiece—would never leave his sight. Without that set, the airplanes that were supposed to drop supplies would never find them.

They'd wither and die faster than they already were.

December 1942

Chapter Eight

Everybody thought it, but no one dared to say it out loud: *the last supper.*

This could very well be the last time they'd all be together.

Beneath a canopy on *Esme's* foredeck, Jillian Forbes played hostess to Jock and the dozen American soldiers from Charlie Company she'd known—and fought the Japanese with—back in Cape York. Her ship's Aborigine cook had outdone himself: the GIs gorged themselves on the seafood feast.

There was something else the Yanks appreciated: anchored offshore, waiting her turn to unload her war cargo, *Esme* offered a respite from Port Moresby's ever-present squadrons of mosquitoes. Safe beneath the canopy, even the inevitable rain couldn't dampen their spirits.

"Just like old times, ain't it?" Corporal Bogater Boudreau said, shoveling still more food onto his plate. "Here we are again, with Miss Forbes bringing the vittles to us starving..."

He paused, searching for the right word.

Jillian finished the sentence for him: "*Wankers*, I think you mean to say. You poor, starving wankers."

"Yeah, that's it, ma'am," Boudreau replied. "That's us, for sure."

She laughed and planted a sisterly kiss on the top of the blond Cajun's head.

Sergeant Major Patchett popped open another bottle of Australian beer and downed half of it in one swallow. "That's mighty fine," he said. "I'm getting real tired of that Japanese *piss-water* them yellow bastards left behind."

He raised the bottle to toast Jillian: "Thanks so much, Miss Forbes, for bringing us the good stuff."

The sun was setting on the western Owen Stanleys. Once it slipped behind those jagged peaks, the gray filter of dusk would envelop land and sea once again, slowly dimming until darkness closed around them like a black curtain. There would be no party lights on *Esme's* deck: "Blackout rules, you know," Jillian reminded everyone.

Jock asked, "Jill, is this really your last trip to Port Moresby?"

"Afraid so."

"I thought maybe there'd be time for one more..." She shook her head.

"Where will you be sailing next?" he asked.

"Not sure," she replied. "There's been some talk of running supplies to the Aussies at Milne Bay—"

"What about Buna, Jill?"

She smiled, caressed his hand, and said, "Wouldn't that be lovely?" But the smile faded quickly. "There's just one little thing, Yank...you haven't taken the bloody place yet. I hear it's still lousy with Japs."

She took a long pull on her beer, trying to wash away the fear that after tonight, they might not be together again for months, maybe years...

Maybe ever.

"Sailing to Buna would be difficult, though," she continued. "Coming around the east end—through the Trobriand Islands—it's very treacherous. Nothing but reefs, Japanese airplanes—"

"And submarines," he said, like a raw nerve had been struck.

"No, not so much there, Jock. Too shallow and hemmed in for them. For big warships, too. But getting back to what I was saying, the only half-decent harbor near Buna is Oro Bay."

"How far away is it?"

"East, about fifteen miles, I think."

Fifteen miles of jungle, Jock thought. *Might as well be a thousand.*

It was time for the men to get back to shore. Tomorrow would be another full day of training, and these 12 combat veterans were among the teachers. Patchett gathered everyone for a last toast.

Raising his beer bottle, he said, "I've had better assignments in *this man's army*...but I've never been with better people."

Bottles *clinked* all around. No one felt the slightest hint of disagreement with Patchett's statement.

As the men began to climb into the longboat taking them ashore, a chill coursed down Jillian's spine. She turned to Jock and asked, "But you...you're staying the night, aren't you?"

He looked surprised as he replied, "Of course, Jill. Of course I'm staying."

They took their time making love. When they were finished, their damp, naked bodies still entwined on the sheets, Jock whispered, "We're getting awfully good at saying goodbye."

She squeezed him tighter. "We've had too much practice, Jock."

Nestled within the shading mountains, Kokoda was already in darkness, hidden from the sunset beneath the soft glow of a burnt orange sky. The Aussies had won the fight for the airstrip. This was no cause for celebration, though: they were still only halfway to their objective, the north coast of Papua. They hunkered down for the night, knowing today's victory would only ensure their chance to die another day.

Having the airstrip improved their situation dramatically. In the morning, once the mist cleared—and barring a blinding rainstorm—C-47 transports of the American 5th Air Force would land with their loads of supplies.

A digger said, "We won't be mucking about in the jungle, lads, looking for those bloody parachutes."

"And none of it will go to the Nips," another added.

His shattered hand swaddled in a blood-stained bandage, the wounded Bren gunner said, "I've got you all beat. I'll be taking my lunch in Port Moresby tomorrow. It's just a short airplane ride away."

Once past Kokoda, the Aussies would begin their downhill run to the coast. Often, it wouldn't seem like a descent: there would still be plenty of climbing out of valleys, but the peaks to be scaled would be lower. As the Owen Stanleys gradually yielded to swampy coastal plains, there would be more plateaus—and more airstrips to turn to good use.

But first, they had to evict the Japanese blocking their path at Kokoda Village.

"Level the bloody place," the major told his artillery liaison.

"But sir," the liaison replied, "that will take all the ammunition we have for the twenty-five-pounders...and probably more."

"So? The Yank planes are coming tomorrow. We'll get more."

A breathless sergeant from the recon platoon approached on the run. "Major, if I may?" he asked.

"What on earth is it, Sergeant?"

"Me and my lads think the Japs might have already pulled out of the village," the sergeant said.

"We'd be wasting the artillery ammo if that's the case, sir," the liaison added.

The major shot the liaison a look that made sure he'd shut up unless spoken to from this point on.

"What makes you think they're gone, Sergeant?" the major asked. He seemed dismissive of the reply before he heard it.

"We were able to get really close, right up the trail...almost into the village itself. It was getting dark, for sure, sir...but there was no sign of anyone. It's deserted. You'd think they'd lay machine guns across the trail, but no...Nothing. We even made some noise to try and draw fire."

The major didn't bother to deliberate more than a second or two.

"Level the bloody place," he said, and walked away.

It had taken the better part of the day for the Aussies to pull the last two 25-pounders into firing position. The effort cost them three more injured men: a block had fractured while hauling up the last gun. Ropes quivering with tension were suddenly released, whipping through the hapless diggers like horizontal guillotines, breaking bones and gashing flesh. Mercifully, nobody was run over as the gun slid downhill some 40 yards, accelerating and revolving end-for-end until it came to rest against a broad tree trunk. Save for a bent shield, the piece was undamaged.

Now, as darkness fell, the last gun was finally in place. Exhausted beyond caring, the artillerymen fell asleep wherever they dropped.

They stayed asleep for the 45 minutes it took the artillery liaison to climb to the ridge.

Shaking the lieutenant awake, the liaison said, "Get these lads shooting right bloody now, or you'll have a boot mark in your arse like the one the major just gave me."

He didn't want to wake up. "What? Shooting...at...uhh...what, sir?"

"The village," the liaison replied. "The bloody village. Come on, man...I'll help you work up the firing data. How many rounds do you have left?"

That was far more information than the lieutenant was able to process at the moment.

The liaison insisted: "A rough figure, man!"

"Fifteen...I think. Maybe seventeen."

"Good," the liaison said. "Prepare them all."

The native guide had begged Colonel Blevins to stop sooner along the Kapa Kapa Trail. He made an impassioned plea: "We must not stay on Ghost Mountain at night!"

"I can't stop while there's still daylight," Blevins replied. "We'll never meet the Aussies at this pace."

Only when dusk washed away the jungle's color did the colonel bring 2nd Battalion to a halt. The native guide wanted to flee, but he had taken an oath to support the Allies; he couldn't dishonor himself by going back on his word. Seeking shelter in the hollow of a tree, he pulled a GI blanket over his head. He didn't want to see what night on the mountain would offer.

It never grew dark. Twilight yielded to an eerie green glow: the jungle was alive with phosphorescence. The soft, chemical radiance seemed to emanate from everything: trees, vines, the vegetation and rotting logs covering the jungle floor. Devastated by exertion, the soldiers usually fell dead asleep at any halt. This time, they stayed awake, staring in uneasy wonder at the surreal light.

"It's perfectly normal," a GI said, "a natural process. Some materials store energy and emit it as light, just like the face of a wristwatch."

A squadmate sprawled on the ground nearby asked, "What are you, a fucking chemist or something?"

"I was studying to be one."

"Ahh, that's too fucking bad, pal...but I don't care if it's natural or not. It's scaring the living shit out of me. I thought Halloween was over already."

A sergeant stumbled by, making his way to the head of the column. "You ain't the only one scared shitless," he said. "The porters...it looks like they're all gone...high-tailed it back down the trail."

When the new dawn broke, the sergeant was proven right: the native porters—some 50 of them—had vanished. Unlike the guide, they'd taken no oath; they were just paid labor. The porters had no intention of spending a night on this place they called Ghost Mountain.

"Do you suppose they'll come back now that the sun's up?" Colonel Blevins asked his guide.

"No, Colonel, I don't think so."

That was the last thing Blevins needed to hear. There would be no one to tote the hundreds of pounds of ammunition, field rations, and pioneer equipment. No one but his own GIs—and he already knew how averse those GIs were to carrying anything that didn't support their immediate needs.

Blevins needed to sit down. He felt *strange*; he couldn't describe it any other way, as if whatever energy his worn-out, middle-aged body had left was being flushed into the ground.

If we ever get out of this jungle, he told himself, *my battalion will be useless as a fighting force...*

But who am I kidding? It's useless now. The only fighting we're doing is to stay alive.

Something was happening inside him. Pain began to shoot down his arms. He was sure some giant clamp was being tightened around his chest. Breathing caused excruciating pain.

Soldiers were gathering around him. They crawled up on hands and knees—*Are they too weak to stand, too?*—just staring, trying to understand. In the dim green light, their eyes seemed sunken in their skulls, just black holes where bright orbs once shined.

A shirtless GI—*The medic...I recognize him*—unbuttoned the colonel's shirt and pressed a stethoscope to his chest.

"His heart," the medic said, as he gently laid the colonel on his back.

Blevins was fascinated—and horrified—by the medic's ribs:

The spaces between them...they're all sucked in and hollow, like in those pictures of starving children...or that spear wound Christ suffered on the cross, only all over his chest. My boys are starving—they're eating three times the daily K ration and they're still starving. This jungle, these mountains—they suck the life right out of you...

And with one last, gasping breath, the jungle sucked the life out of Lieutenant Colonel Blevins.

The last shovelsful of dirt filled Colonel Blevins's grave. Major Henson, the man who was the battalion's XO just an hour ago, was now its commanding officer.

A senior sergeant told the new commander, "We should just turn back, sir. This has been a fucked-up deal from the git-go."

"Negative, Sergeant," Henson replied. "We have our orders. We're pushing on."

Chapter Nine

The view from the airfield at sunrise seemed conclusive: Kokoda Village was battered but still empty. The artillery had done its work in the night, expending their ammunition just as the Aussie major had prescribed. Six American C-47s arrived as promised, landing from the east as if borne on rays of the morning sun. Supplies were quickly offloaded; the sick and wounded filled the cabins for the flight back to Port Moresby. The Yank pilots—nervous to be on the ground in Papua's wild interior for the first time—didn't dare shut down their engines. They were airborne again just moments after their delicate human cargo was safely in place.

The materiel they delivered was short one notable necessity: "There's no artillery ammunition in the lot, sir," a lieutenant reported to the major.

"Get Port Moresby on the wireless immediately and make bloody sure the next lift brings some," the major said. "Fifty rounds at least."

"But that won't be before tomorrow, sir," the lieutenant replied. "At the earliest."

"Then let's hope to God we don't need any before then," the major said. "Now, why are you still here? Didn't I just give you an order?"

As the lieutenant scurried away, a captain asked, "Are we still going to clear the village this morning, sir? Even without the guns?"

The major seemed surprised by the question. "Of course we are," he replied. "Time waits for no man. Are you telling me the patrols haven't set out already?"

"Not yet, sir," the captain said. "The men are still eating."

The major's face flushed: "Eating, Captain? Now?"

"Yes, sir...you know how it is when we get a fresh food drop. The men eat and drink it immediately. It goes bad in no time otherwise."

The company of diggers grew more confident with each step. Now less than 50 yards of open ground away, the first mounds of rubble—like so many shattered totems—marked what was once Kokoda Village. No one—living or dead—could be seen.

"Looks like a piece of piss, men," the lieutenant leading the center platoon said.

He turned to say something to his platoon sergeant, but he never got the words out. The first burst of machine gun fire cut him down like a machete clearing jungle growth.

The second burst swept away the half of the platoon too slow in kissing the dirt.

All along the company line, diggers littered the ground. Some tried to burrow in and save themselves. For the rest, it was already too late.

As they lay immobilized, a smattering of deadly accurate mortar shells began to drop in their midst. Each *THUMP* of a round's impact took another bite from the already decimated company.

"THERE MUST BE AT LEAST THREE NAMBUS, CAPTAIN," a sergeant shrieked to the company commander. "I CAN'T SEE WHERE THE BLOODY HELL THEY ARE."

I can, the captain told himself.

On the far side of the village, behind a massive pile of shattered timbers the Aussie artillery left behind, was a well-fortified bunker.

Sure, the bloody Japs left...but the little bastards came back.

The captain crawled to his right platoon. "Go around them," he told the platoon leader. "Kick them in the arse. I'll call in the mortars."

He would have called for artillery, too—if they had any rounds to shoot.

The platoon crawled into the maze of tall, razor-sharp kunai grass and promptly became lost. The platoon leader had to stick his head up out of the grass to get his bearings—and nearly got it shot off for his trouble: a bullet snatched the slouch hat right off his head.

He didn't bother trying to find it.

Reoriented, the platoon tried its flanking attack. The machine gun fire that raked the diggers was every bit as savage as before.

"Our mortars, our Brens...they're aren't hurting that bunker a bit," the platoon leader said. "We've got to pull back."

The survivors escaped only by crawling back through the kunai, dragging their dead and wounded with them.

Far behind the fight and still high on the ridge, the artillerymen were rigging their impotent guns for the descent to the plateau below.

Gathering his section's gear, a gunner nearly threw his back out as he jerked on what he thought was an empty ammunition box. It barely moved; neither did the one beneath it.

"LADS," he said, "WE MUST'VE BEEN MORE COCKED UP THAN WE THOUGHT LAST NIGHT..."

He held open the lids of the ammo boxes as if revealing found treasure.

They still had four more rounds to fire.

It only took a few moments to have a gun ready to shoot again.

The first round was short.

The second was long.

The third and fourth blew the bunker apart like so many matchsticks.

As the diggers combed through the smoking remains of the Japanese position, a sergeant reported to the major: "We found eight Nips, half-naked, as usual."

"Are they all dead, Sergeant?"

"They are now, sir...also, three machine guns, two small-caliber mortars, and enough ammunition to hold us diggers off for another day, at least. Thank God for our bloody gunners...even if the silly bastards can't count for beans."

"Very well, sergeant," the major replied. "Now, let's get moving. We're still only halfway there."

Chapter Ten

Colonel Molloy took his pointer to the big map. "The Kapa Kapa is every bit as difficult as the Aussie coast watchers told us, apparently," he told his assembled commanders and staff. "Second Battalion has only made it to *here*"—the pointer made an aggravated *snap* against the paper—"as of last night's radio report."

Not even close to halfway, Jock thought. *Maybe we should've listened to those coast watchers a little better. MacArthur must be really pissed about now, with his "grand gesture of help" to the diggers turning to shit and all.*

"I think we can write Second Battalion off as being any help to the Australians," Molloy said, as his pointer now traced the Aussie advance along the map. "They're well past Kokoda Village now—to about here—on the Track's downhill run to the coast. They've occupied three more airstrips the Japs abandoned, too, so they're getting regular resupply and casualty evacuation from Fifth Air Force...but between all that mountain climbing and fighting Jap infantry tooth and nail for every mile, they're still in real bad shape. Any questions so far?"

There were none.

"Okay, then," Molloy continued, "we've got our airlift schedule to kick off *Operation Easy Street*, the conquest of Buna. Colonel Vann, your Third Battalion will fly over this coming Monday—three days from now. Major Miles, your First Battalion will go on Tuesday. Your respective areas of operation once we get there are marked on the map."

Jock had a question now. "Sir," he asked, "are you telling us it'll take an *entire day* to move one battalion by air?"

Colonel Molloy gestured to his Air Force liaison: "You want to answer that one, Major?"

"Certainly, sir," the liaison said. Taking the lecturing tone of a grade school teacher, he continued, "It breaks down like this, gentlemen: eight C-47s have been assigned to this movement. It'll take all of them just to move one company and its equipment. Each battalion has four companies. By the time you fly around the mountains, it takes almost three hours for a round trip between Port Moresby and Fasari—that's the airstrip our Aussie friends were nice enough to have the natives clear for us. Now, we get twelve hours of daylight..." He mimed adding columns of numbers in the air; the smile that crossed his face as he did it could only be described as condescending. "Are you with me so far?" he added.

"We can do the math," Jock said, "but I'm curious about the *allocation*. That's all we get? Eight airplanes?"

"There's a real big war going on, Major Miles," the liaison replied.

Yeah, Jock thought, *and I need some desk clerk with wings to tell me that.*

The air liaison continued, "Once you're on the ground, it's only forty miles over flat ground from Fasari to Buna."

Only forty miles...like this flyboy's ever walked— and fought—across forty miles.

Jock had another question. "Maybe I'm missing something here, but I thought we were taking a battery of seventy-five-millimeter howitzers with us. When do they get airlifted? And how will we move them from Fasari to Buna? Mules? Jeeps?"

Colonel Molloy's expression turned sour. "You're getting ahead of me, Major Miles," he said. "That's my next point in this briefing."

Standing in the corner of the tent, the captain commanding the artillery battery looked like he was going to throw up. Jock could feel the sting of bad news before it was even spoken: *I guess it's time to bend over and spread those cheeks, because here comes another shafting.*

"There's going to be a change in our fire support," Molloy said. "We're turning in the seventy-fives and replacing them with one-oh-fives. MacArthur figures we're in line for an upgrade in firepower...and the divisions struggling in the Solomons badly need the lighter pack artillery, and plenty of it, on the double."

So why does the chief cannon-cocker over there look like he's going to puke all over himself?

"This poses a bit of a transport problem for us, though," Molloy continued. "One-oh-five howitzers don't fit in a C-47...not unless they're completely broken down, airlifted piecemeal, and then reassembled. Unfortunately, it would take special tooling at each end of the trip to accomplish that...and that's something we don't have right now."

The air liaison added, "And each broken-down gun would take up an entire C-47. We just can't afford to waste airlift capacity that way."

"That's all great," Jock said, "but we're not going to give up the seventy-fives until *after* we've got control of Buna, right?"

Colonel Molloy shook his head. So did the artillery captain.

"The seventy-fives are to be at the docks by tomorrow, Jock," Molloy said. "MacArthur wants them in the Solomons within a week."

Jock couldn't believe what he was hearing. "So we land with absolutely no fire support? Not from Navy ships...not from our own guns. Just *nothing?*"

The air liaison replied, "The Fifth Air Force is all the artillery you'll need, Major Miles."

"Funny," Jock said, "but I've heard that line before. It was bullshit then...and it's bullshit now."

An hour after the briefing, Jock was still in a rage, swearing and throwing things around his battalion CP tent.

"NO FUCKING ARTILLERY," he said, kicking a footlocker across the dirt floor. "NONE AT ALL. CAN YOU BELIEVE THIS SHIT? DON'T WE EVER LEARN ANYTHING?"

He didn't notice Colonel Molloy enter.

"ATTEN-HUT," Sergeant Major Patchett said, hoping to silence Jock before he spewed another epithet their regimental commander might take personally.

Jock and the four battalion staff officers present snapped to attention.

"Begging your pardon, sir," Patchett said to Molloy, "but we were just hashing out a few of them *Problems of Command* training scenarios..."

The colonel laughed: *You've got to respect the loyalty of an NCO who'll flat out lie to cover for his commander.*

"I'll bet you were, Sergeant Major," Molloy said, "but I'm glad you're all here. I just gave Third Battalion this sermon, and now I'm going to give it to you. Let's sit down. Take a load off."

They grabbed whatever they could find—folding chairs, camp stools, storage chests—and formed a circle with Molloy at the head.

"Now, Major Miles," the colonel began, "I understand exactly how you feel: the battle for Port Moresby was a shambles because you didn't have the firepower to punch through the Jap defenses..."

"Amen to that, sir," Patchett muttered under his breath.

"And you think we'll be making the same mistakes at Buna all over again," Molloy continued. "Am I right, Jock?"

"Yes, sir. That's it, in a nutshell."

"Well, Major...I'd agree with you, if it wasn't for one thing..."

"What's that, sir?"

"It just might be different this time with our air support. When you were fighting for Port Moresby, they had to come all the way from Australia. I've heard the comments about how the Fifth Air Force did such a great job, for *five fucking minutes a day.* But this time, they're right over the mountains at Port Moresby and right down the coast at Milne Bay. That should make a big difference."

"I sure hope you're right, sir," Jock replied.

"But I've decided on one thing," Molloy said. "Until we know for sure what kind of fire support we're going to get—whether it's from Fifth Air Force, floating in our artillery and tanks on barges, or whatever it takes—I consider the mission of this regiment at Buna nothing more than a reconnaissance in force. We will not attack any fortified positions with our asses uncovered and left out to dry...not as long as I command this regiment. You have my word on that."

As soon as the colonel left the tent, Patchett said, "Maybe I was wrong about that man, sir...but it's all just fancy words until we see him in action."

Lieutenant Paul Hellinger peered over the tailgate of the deuce-and-a-half. Just as he feared, the bed was empty.

"Where's the rest of my mortars?" Hellinger asked the supply sergeant in charge of the truck.

"That's all there was, Lieutenant," the sergeant replied. He thrust his clipboard in Hellinger's face. "Sign here for what you got, sir...in triplicate, please."

The paperwork done, the truck drove off, leaving nothing but dust and empty promises in its wake. Paul Hellinger watched it go, a forlorn young man trying to come to grips with a failure not of his own making, but his to bear nonetheless. He shuffled the useless sheaf of requisitions in his hands. He wasn't a combat veteran yet, but he didn't have to be one to know some lousy sheet of paper merely requesting a weapon was no substitute for the real thing.

"Something wrong, Paul?" The voice belonged to Lieutenant Lee Grossman, commander of Charlie Company.

"Yeah, Lee...something's wrong. Real wrong. I was supposed to get four 81-millimeter mortars. I only got two...and it's only four stinking days until we move out. Some *weapons company* I'm running, eh?"

Grossman asked, "You tell Major Miles yet?"

"No...I just found out. But to be honest, I'm not looking forward to telling him...not one bit."

"Why's that?"

Hellinger wasn't sure where to begin. "Well, for starters," he said, "I'm the new kid on the block. I don't know him...not like you guys do, anyway. I'm not sure how to approach him. Plus, he's a West Pointer and—"

"Oh, hell, I wouldn't worry about that, Paul. I know some of those ring-knockers from the Academy can be real assholes...like this is their club and we don't really belong. But Jock Miles isn't like that. You couldn't ask for a better CO. Give it to him straight. Just don't ever try to bullshit him."

A dark thought crossed Grossman's mind: "Paul...your paperwork...it was in order, wasn't it? I mean...you didn't make some clerical mistake that's causing us to get the short end?"

Hellinger held up his handful of requisitions. "Nope...the paperwork's okay, Lee. I checked it a hundred times. Supply just didn't deliver."

"Then just deal with it...that's all he's going to tell you to do," Grossman replied. "Being short a couple of mortars is a bad deal, for sure...but it's not your fault. Hell...we're already short artillery support. But we've been in deeper shit than this, believe me. We'll figure a way out."

Chapter Eleven

Colonel Dick Molloy didn't imagine General Hartman had summoned him for a friendly chat: *I can smell the ass-chewing coming a mile away.*

The look on the general's face didn't change Dick Molloy's mind. Ordering his CP tent cleared so they'd be alone, the general began, "At ease, Colonel. You and I need to have a little talk. I think your outlook on things may need a little…"—he took a second to search for the right word—"reorienting."

Molloy decided this might be a good time to just shut up, stand at parade rest, and speak only when spoken to.

"I've heard some rumors," Hartman continued, "that you've been telling your men this Buna operation will be a *reconnaissance in force.* Is that true, Colonel?"

"Yes, sir. I believe I did use those words."

Hartman kept pushing: "You *have* read the operations order, have you not? You are aware Buna is an *offensive* operation?"

"A reconnaissance in force can be a great asset to an offensive operation, General."

The general's face began to turn red. "It can also turn into an excuse to make a lot of noise but take no ground. The mission of Operation Easy Street is to *seize* Buna, not *recon* it, Colonel Molloy."

"I understand that, sir. But until we know exactly what we're up against—"

Hartman cut him off. "We already know what we're up against, Colonel. MacArthur's intelligence estimates are quite clear: there will be only a few thousand exhausted, disorganized Japanese troops in the Buna area. The terrain there is flat and wet—unsuited for defensive positions. Between the Aussie division and our own, you don't think we can handle that in short order?"

Molloy couldn't keep the ironic smile from his face. "Sir, I believe you were the victim of General MacArthur's last intelligence estimate, right before you tried to take Port Moresby. That was supposed to be a cake walk, too."

He watched Hartman bristle but the spoken truth was impossible to evade. The general needed a moment to compose his thoughts. Suddenly, he seemed very old—and very tired.

Finally, Hartman said, "Colonel, you're a West Point man. You do still remember the priorities of command they taught you there, don't you?"

"Yes, General. Of course I do."

"Repeat them for me, please."

"The first priority is my mission, sir. The second is my men. The third, the materiel under my command."

It was Hartman's turn to smile. "Very good, Colonel," he said. "Don't you ever forget that...the mission always—and I mean *always*—comes first."

"I understand, General...but I remember something else, too: you won't accomplish your mission if your men are outgunned and slaughtered."

Hartman's smile faded. Once again, he seemed to be searching for the right words. This time, nothing came.

"Dismissed, Colonel," was all the general said.

No one was surprised when the argument quickly escalated to first punch. Sergeant Mike McMillen's left hook sent the C-47's crew chief sprawling to the ground.

"Enough of your flyboy bullshit," McMillen said, standing over his stunned victim. "We get the whole damn cabin for our stuff...six thousand pounds' worth...says right here on the load manifest. You don't get to kick any of it off to haul your Air Force crap."

The C-47's pilot, a young lieutenant who looked barely out of his teens, jumped down from the airplane's loading door to break up the fracas.

"I want to press charges against this man," the crew chief said to his pilot. "He assaulted me, Lieutenant, plain and simple."

"Go ahead...press all the charges you want," McMillen replied. "I'm a lot better off in the stockade than where I'm going."

Another voice rang out in the pre-dawn darkness: "At ease, Sergeant McMillen." When the men who had gathered around saw it was Major Miles speaking, they snapped to attention. The crew chief quickly picked himself up off the ground to do the same.

Ignoring the young pilot eager to get his attention, Jock said to McMillen, "What's the story here, Sergeant?"

McMillen reiterated what had just happened while pointing emphatically to the load manifest in his hand. "We can't let them cheat us out of cargo space, sir. We need every ounce of this shit," he concluded.

Jock now put the pilot in his sights, asking, "Was this your bright idea, Lieutenant?"

"Oh, no, sir. I'm sure it's all a big misunderstanding."

The crew chief glared at his pilot like a man betrayed.

"I'm sure it is, too, Lieutenant," Jock said. Looking to the crew chief, he added, "Are you injured, Sergeant?"

"No, sir. I've been sucker-punched before."

"Very well," Jock said, "then there's no need to set the wheels of military justice in motion just yet. Lieutenant, I hope this isn't an example of the cooperation you *winged heroes* of Fifth Air Force are prepared to extend...cooperation we're depending on in a big way."

"Oh, no, sir. Not at all, sir."

"Good. We're in agreement. You two—shake hands."

Swallowing their pride, McMillen and the crew chief did as they were told.

"Now," Jock said, "let's quit fucking around and get this airplane loaded...and every last piece of our gear rides. Is that clear, Lieutenant?"

"Yes, sir. Absolutely clear, sir."

As the men went back to work, Jock pulled McMillen aside and said, "That was good work, Mike...but don't push your luck with the quick hands. Next time, I might not be there to bail your ass out."

McMillen asked, "You're not gonna tell Lieutenant Pop on me, are you, sir?"

"No, Mike, you're going to tell your company commander yourself."

McMillen did a two-step of frustration as he said, "But he'll want to take it out of my ass, sir. He'll probably bust me. Maybe you could—"

"Sorry, Mike. That'll be his call."

The run-down building, just down a dusty street from the harbor, looked like any other sailors' pub in Australia, right down to the sign over the door that read, *No Boongs Allowed*. Jillian Forbes could have recognized the place in the dark. This establishment, in Cooktown, on Cape York's eastern coast, seemed to be the only game in town if you were in the market for alcoholic refreshment.

Behind her, two of *Esme's* Aborigine crewmen were pulling a cart. "Wait here," she told them. "I'll get the grog out to the street; then you roll it back to *Esme*. Just make sure it stays covered, and don't let a constable see you. We don't have enough money on hand to buy lager and post your bail, too."

One of the men patted the canvas tarp folded on the cart. "No worries, Miss Jilly," he said.

Jillian expected to be the only female in the crowded pub who wasn't a prostitute. When she stepped through the door, though, she got a surprise: seated at a table in the corner was a woman of late middle age. Dressed in men's clothes yet unmistakably female, with a cap trimmed with faded gold braid on the table before her, this tall, sturdy *sheila* radiated an aura that said, *Screw with me at your peril.* Her gnarled hands told of a lifetime of hard work...

At sea, no doubt, Jillian surmised.

Sizing up Jillian's workaday trousers and shirt in a quick glance, the woman called out, "Are you lost, *schatzi*? You may still be young and pretty but no man will pay for you dressed like that."

The men in the pub—merchant seamen all—must have agreed, because they laughed out loud. So did the women slithering through the ranks of sailors, plying their trade.

That accent...she's not Aussie, that's for sure, Jillian thought. *She sounds German...maybe Dutch.*

The older woman said, "You'd better come and have a drink with me, *schatzi*, before the sharks in this sea eat you alive."

Jillian strode over to the woman's table and said, "I beg your pardon, ma'am, but nobody eats me alive."

"Oh! A feisty one, she is! You must join me for *two* drinks, then."

"Just let me take care of a little business, and then I'll be glad to."

Stacking the cases of beer on the wooden sidewalk outside the pub, the barman scowled when he saw the two Aborigines waiting with their cart.

"You didn't say this was for no boongs," he said to Jillian.

"That's right, mate. I didn't say," Jillian replied. "What's wrong? You don't want my money?"

The barman spit on the ground, narrowly missing the stacked bottles. Then, he stomped back into the pub. Jillian followed him in and made straight for the older woman's table.

"Buying spirits for the blacks, I see," the woman said, pouring Jillian a glass of whiskey. "Can't that be a bit dangerous for an Aussie, schatzi?"

"Nothing I can't handle," Jillian replied. "I suppose introductions are in order. I'm Jillian Forbes. I captain the coastal trader *Esme*."

"Good for you! My name is Beatrix Van Der Wegge. I'm master of the good ship *Java Queen*."

"So you're Dutch, Beatrix?"

"Yes. I've been in the East Indies all my life. Where have you been running?"

"Port Moresby and back. But the next run is to Milne Bay."

"Mine, too! We'll be sailing together," Beatrix said as they clinked glasses. "Jillian...what do they call you for short?"

"Mostly, they don't. But the blacks call me Miss Jilly, and my man—and *only* him—calls me Jill."

Beatrix took hold of Jillian's hands, examining them closely. "Hmm, you're not afraid of hard work, I see. You mentioned *your man*...but there's no ring on your finger."

"We're not up to that yet. He's a Yank soldier—a major—in Papua at the moment."

Releasing Jillian's hands, Beatrix said, "A Yank and an Aussie...a very dangerous coupling. Take my advice, schatzi...never get attached to any one man. Especially not a soldier."

She held up her own hand, wiggling her fingers to show she wore no ring, either. "I've rid myself of three husbands already, one way or the other, Jillian. When you're young, it's all tongues and naked skin and sweat and sticky bedclothes. But once you're old and drier than a nun's nasty, they just become a nuisance, wagging their little willies in your face all the time."

"Regardless—," Jillian began to reply, until a drunken sailor stumbled and nearly upset their table.

"STEADY ON, YOU MONGREL," Jillian commanded, while Beatrix coolly appraised her and the intruder.

The drunk staggered back a step, trying his best to shape alcohol-soaked facial muscles into a look of indignation. The best he could manage was a twisted grimace.

"The both of you can go fuck yourselves," he said, "or fuck each other...or whatever it is you do. I don't take me no orders from someone who squats to pee."

He couldn't react quickly enough to Jillian's movements. In an instant, she was face-to-face with him, one hand holding her long, sharp seaman's knife firmly against his groin. Her other hand held him by the throat. He didn't—no, couldn't—move.

"You know, laddie," Jillian said, "I can fix it so you squat to pee, too. Would you like that?"

He shook his head.

"All right, then," Jillian said, pushing him away.

He tumbled hard on his backside as the rest of the patrons roared with laughter.

"Well, schatzi," Beatrix said, "that was quite an impressive display. Here, have another drink. That imbecile spilled your last one."

As they clinked glasses once again, Beatrix said, "I believe this is the start of a beautiful friendship."

Jillian downed the whiskey in one swallow. "You know," she said, "I never got to ask what they call you for short."

Beatrix gave a tight-lipped smile and replied, "They call me *captain*."

Chapter Twelve

Corporal Bogater Boudreau could see it coming: the man sitting next to him on the C-47—the BAR gunner in his squad—was about to throw up.

"C'mon, *mon frère*...suck it up," Bogater said, snapping open a paper airsick bag with a flick of his wrist. "If you heave, the whole damn plane's gonna start in. It'll smell like a flophouse shitter in here in no time flat."

Bogater was right: in a few minutes, the plane's cabin reeked with the odor of vomit as the stomachs of GI after GI succumbed to the rough ride.

Standing at the cockpit entryway, Lieutenant Theo Papadakis, Able Company's commander, said to the pilot, "For cryin' out loud, pal...can't you do something about these air pockets? My guys are puking their guts out. They're gonna be useless once we're on the ground again. Hell of a thing if we have to fight our way off the airstrip."

"First off," the pilot replied, "I can't do anything about the turbulence. It's from the mountains. Only two ways to avoid it—fly real high or fly all the way around—and we can't do either one right now. And as far as having to fight your way off the airstrip—you won't. We were in and out of there all day yesterday with your other battalion. We didn't see a lousy Jap anywhere."

Theo Papadakis took small comfort in that fact. "But they're out there somewhere," he said.

"Just remember the rule," the pilot said. "If you puke, you clean it up."

Someone tapped Papadakis on the shoulder. It was Mike McMillen, one of his platoon sergeants.

"Lieutenant Pop, you got a minute?" McMillen asked.

"I've got until this fucking airplane touches down again."

McMillen related the story of his fight with the crew chief.

"You mean that guy over there?" Papadakis asked, pointing to the crewman fast asleep against the cabin's aft bulkhead.

"Yeah, him," McMillen replied.

"I was wondering who lumped up his face like that. You say you did that with one punch, Mike?"

"Yes, sir. It was only one, I swear."

"Then I'd say you did a good job, sticking up for your platoon and all, Sergeant."

"But I don't want to get you in Dutch with Major Miles, Lieutenant. You know...letting it slide and all."

"Don't worry about Major Miles, Sergeant. He's got bigger things to worry about...and so do I. Do you know what a reprimand is?"

McMillen looked confused as he replied, "I suppose...it's...umm..."

"Let me make it real simple, Mike. You just got one. Case closed."

They had only been there a few hours, but already the men of Jock's battalion had devised a nickname for the airstrip at Fasari: *So Sorry*. It seemed to fit: the field was nothing but a flat expanse of ground which natives had cleared of the high kunai grass and a few inconveniently placed trees. The soil was muddy but firm enough, despite the frequent deluges of rain. When airplanes were absent, the only clue to its purpose was the long streamer at the top of a high pole serving as a wind sock. There was barely enough room for the flight of eight C-47s to land and, squeezed wing tip to wing tip, unload their cargo.

In short, a sorry excuse for an airfield.

By mid-afternoon, the three rifle companies of 1st Battalion were on the ground, going through the motions of providing perimeter security for an airstrip yet to be threatened by enemy soldiers. There was always the prospect of marauding Japanese aircraft but they hadn't appeared, either.

Now, they thought the sun was taunting them. This evening, it seemed to be in a bigger hurry than usual to hide below the horizon, giving relief from the broiling heat of day but plunging them into immobilizing darkness. Jock and Colonel Dick Molloy tracked that merciless orange star as they stood on the airstrip, awaiting the final airlift of the day, the one that would carry the weapons company and complete the movement of Jock's battalion to *So Sorry*.

"At least we'll get a later sunset," Jock said. "The mountains don't block the setting sun here on the north coast like they do at Port Moresby."

Molloy didn't seem to be listening as he scanned the empty sky. "The rain's slowed them down," he said. "If the Air Force doesn't show up soon…"

There was no point completing the sentence. Everyone knew the rest: once the sun went down, the planes wouldn't be able to find the place, let alone land. Jock's battalion would face their first night back in the field—and many more, perhaps—shorthanded and undergunned.

The long shadows of dusk had begun their slow creep across the airstrip when the first whisper of airplane engines echoed off the mountains. In a few moments, the C-47s drifted into view, the setting sun glinting off their windshields. As the line of aircraft turned one by one to the runway's heading, Jock grimaced:

"There are only seven planes, sir," he said. "There should be eight."

Once on the ground, the transports—with engines still running—wasted no time unloading. Sergeant Major Patchett jumped from the lead aircraft and ran straight to Jock and Molloy. "One of the planes had to turn back," Patchett shouted over the rumble of 14 idling engines. "Motor trouble, they said."

Jock asked, "Did they make it back to Port Moresby?"

"Don't know, sir."

"What was on that plane, Top?"

"The two heavy mortar sections, a shitload of ammo, and Lieutenant Hellinger."

"Son of a bitch," Jock and Dick Molloy said, their words in almost perfect unison.

Jock blew out a chestful of frustration and added, "What the hell's going on here? It's like the gods and MacArthur are conspiring to take away all my firepower."

Dick Molloy found that ironic—and funny. He asked, "The gods and MacArthur…is there really any difference, Jock?"

First Battalion bivouacked at *So Sorry* for the night. At first light, they hit the narrow, coastal trail leading to the regimental assembly area—a village called Dobodura—some 40 miles away and eight miles inland from Buna. The men had come up with a more easily pronounceable nickname for that place, too: *Double-Dare.*

"The Aussies say it's a good place for an airstrip," Colonel Molloy told Jock just before the battalion set out. "I got a message last night saying the native labor has already been lined up to start the land-clearing operation. *Double-Dare Airfield*...that has an audacious ring to it, don't you think?"

They weren't sure how far they traveled down the trail that first day. Division's schedule for the forced march showed the battalion arriving by sundown of the second day on the trail.

"Ain't no way, sir," Melvin Patchett said. "This ain't much of a trail...it's a damn footpath, and it ain't exactly no straight-line footpath, neither, like them dumbasses at Division sketched it on the map. All these twists and turns are adding the miles like crazy...and with getting slowed down by rain every couple hours and all, we'll be lucky to drag our sopping wet asses into *Double-Dare* by sunset of Day Three."

Jock replied, "Yeah, maybe...but at least we aren't running into any Japs."

"Not yet, anyway," Patchett said, "but I'm kinda surprised we ain't caught up with Third Battalion. They only got less than a day's head start on us...and we know what a bunch of route-step fuckups they are."

It was early in their second morning on the trail. Lieutenant Lee Grossman's Charlie Company was leading 1st Battalion. A new corporal was out in front of the column as *point man*. First Sergeant Tom Hadley was right behind him, grading his every move.

It all happened so quickly. In one swift motion, the point man went to ground, his finger tightening on the M1's trigger.

Hadley was practically flat on top of him, whispering, "What've you got?"

"Something up ahead," the point man said, "it looks like a foot."

"It doesn't *look* like a foot, numbnuts. It *is* a foot. And it's wearing a GI boot."

Hadley began to low-crawl forward.

"It could be a trap," the point man whispered.

Hadley didn't stop. He couldn't hear the words, anyway.

Lieutenant Grossman scuttled up and joined the point man on the ground.

"What's going on, Corporal?" Grossman asked.

It was First Sergeant Hadley who answered the question: "GET THE MEDIC UP HERE! RIGHT NOW!"

Lieutenant Grossman and the medic joined Hadley, who was hunched over two prone, semi-conscious GIs.

"These guys aren't wounded," Hadley said. "They're sick...they're burning up. Is this what dengue fever looks like?"

The GIs moaned as the medic tried moving their arms and legs.

"Yeah, could be dengue," the medic said. "Or maybe bush typhus."

"I can't believe Third Battalion just left them here like this," Hadley said.

One of the sick men was trying to say something:

"Fell...behind...might...not know...not know...we're gone. Help me..."

"Yeah, sure, buddy," Hadley replied. "Just take it easy." He asked Grossman, "Sir, what do you say we get some of the native porters to carry these guys back to *So Sorry*?"

"Yeah, by all means," Grossman replied. "Just figure out how to redistribute the loads those porters were carrying. Do not leave anything behind. And for cryin' out loud, Top, let's get this column moving again, on the double."

Chapter Thirteen

First Battalion made it to Dobodura—*Double-Dare*—on the morning of the third day.

It wasn't the last glimpse of the glistening blue Solomon Sea before the trail turned inland that caught the attention of the GIs, or the barren swampland stretching for miles that offered a soldier little in the way of cover or concealment.

What did catch their attention was the aid station overflowing with casualties.

"What the hell?" Lieutenant Theo Papadakis said to no one in particular. "Somebody's been blowing smoke up our asses. Looks like there's plenty of Japs around here. Those GIs didn't wound themselves. Third Battalion must've took a hell of a beating here last night."

Another disquieting sight: natives digging row after neat row of holes—unmistakably graves.

Jock Miles had just sat down to rest his soggy, aching feet when he was set upon by Lieutenant Colonel Horace Vann, 3rd Battalion commander, and the Australian coast watcher for Buna District, Dickie Bennett. Both had the haggard look of men too busy—or too terrified—to sleep.

Colonel Vann said, "My lead company had advanced halfway down the trail to Ango Corner, Jock. They were unopposed and had no problems until the sun went down. Then the Japs came out of the woodwork. My men got hit with everything—artillery, mortars, machine guns. I swear, those Japs were rising out of the swamps like ghosts. I took over fifty dead or wounded—almost half of King Company."

Jock asked, "Your other companies, sir...did they have any contact?"

"No," Vann replied, "they were here, guarding the darkies clearing this airfield, and in Dobodura village. They heard it all, but they never got hit."

Dickie Bennett was obviously biting his tongue. Finally, he could hold back no longer. "You've got it all wrong, Colonel. Your men of King Company got spooked," he said. "The Japs were doing their *firecracker reconnaissance* trick—a handful of sappers running around throwing firecrackers to see if you'll start shooting and give your positions away. Your men did...and they paid for it."

It was Horace Vann's turn to bite his tongue as Jock thought, *Vann's only been here a day but already there ain't much love lost between these two. That ain't good.*

Bennett poured more gasoline on the fire: "If me and my blokes fell for that every time the Japs tried it, we'd have been dead a hundred times over by now."

"All right," Vann said, "that's enough out of you, Mister Bennett—"

The Aussie interrupted with a surly, "That's *Lieutenant Commander* Bennett, Colonel."

"Fine...*Commander.* Thanks for all your help, but I've had enough of your fucking snide comments, okay?"

Bennett stormed off. The words *that ain't good* repeated in Jock's head. He asked Vann, "Do you have radio contact with Regiment yet, sir?"

"Nope. Haven't been able to raise them. My radios are as waterlogged as this swamp. Do you know if Colonel Molloy's in the area yet?"

"Should be, sir. He and his headquarters group were at the ass end of my column."

"Well, then," Vann replied, "me and my boys are sitting right here until he shows up and figures out what he wants us to do. I'm not crippling another company doing some *recon in force* when we have hardly any *force* at all. If you're smart, Jock, you'll keep your men right here, too. At least for now."

Lieutenant Papadakis approached and said, "Able Company's ready to move out, Major Miles."

Jock slung his Thompson submachine gun over his shoulder. "Very well, Lieutenant," he replied. "Let's go."

Unmistakably annoyed, Colonel Vann said, "That's a bad idea, Major Miles. Your men should stay here and reinforce my battalion. You and I are all alone out here. The Aussies are still up on Kokoda, the rest of our division will take days to trickle in, and the Japs are like the insects...they're everywhere."

Jock kept walking.

Vann called after him, "Stay here, Jock. It's the smart thing to do."

"I never said I was smart, Colonel."

Theo Papadakis asked, "What was all that fuss with Colonel Vann about, sir?"

"Don't worry about it, Theo," Jock replied as he spread the map on the ground. "Take your company and start moving to the coast. Find a good, dry place for a camp between Cape Sudest and the east end of Duropa Plantation."

"Will do, sir."

"Just be careful, Theo. There aren't a lot of places to hide in those swamps."

Papadakis laughed and said, "Those swamps...that dumb Cajun Boudreau can't wait to get ass deep in them. Says it feels just like home on the bayou."

"Use Bogater wisely," Jock replied. "He's the best scout in this battalion...probably the whole damn division."

"I will, sir. I promise."

"Keep me posted on the radio what you find, Theo. I'll send the other companies up after you. By nightfall, the whole battalion should be settled in."

"I promise one more thing, sir," Papadakis said.

"What's that, Theo?"

"I promise my men won't be shooting at no firecrackers."

Jock started to laugh, but the racket of automatic weapons fire—definitely *not* firecrackers—erupted from the head of Able Company's column. The shooting ended quickly.

When Jock and Papadakis arrived, GIs were pulling the bodies of two dead Japanese soldiers—a private and a lance corporal—from the swamp and onto the trail.

"ANYONE HIT?" Papadakis asked.

"Just these Nips," a sergeant replied. "Probably scouts, but the fucking idiots shoulda known better than to be snooping around like that in broad daylight."

"Funny thing, though," Jock said. "These Japs are awfully well dressed. Their uniforms and gear look right out of the box. And they're fit and well fed, too. They sure don't look like sickly, rag-tag survivors of the Port Moresby evacuation…like we've been told to expect."

Theo Papadakis asked, "You think they're getting reinforcements over the water from Rabaul, sir?"

"They're getting them from somewhere, Lieutenant, that's for sure."

"I like the way you've set up your men so far, Jock," Colonel Molloy said. "If you can push the Japs out of that plantation, we'll be money ahead. We can come at Buna Mission—and Buna Village—from two directions."

Jock wished he felt more optimistic about that prospect. The Duropa Plantation—the little he could make out of it through binoculars from the tree he climbed for a better view—looked like a narrow, deep fortress of closely spaced coconut palms. The sea guarded its long, northern flank; a seemingly impassible swamp guarded the southern flank. *We might take it*, Jock thought, *and be money ahead, like the colonel said, but I'll bet we spill gallons of our blood doing it.*

Molloy's radio operator rushed up with a report. "*Revelation Six* reports they're in position, sir," the radioman said."

Revelation Six: Lieutenant Colonel Vann of 3rd Battalion.

"Very well. Thank you, Simmons," Molloy replied.

Alone with Jock again, Dick Molloy said, "About damn time Vann's in position…especially after that cavalcade of fuckups he presided over last night. It's just poor combat discipline that a company got chewed up like that. For cryin' out loud...*throwing firecrackers?* Have you ever come up against that, Jock?"

"Heard about it, but no, sir, never came up against it."

"You think your men will handle it better than Vann's did?"

Jock really wanted to answer in the affirmative, but he knew better. "Hard to say, sir," he replied. "You never know what's going to happen that first time."

"Yeah," Molloy said, "ain't that the hell of it? I appreciate your candor, though. Speaking of candor, what do you think of that Aussie coast watcher we're working with?"

"He's got a temper, sir...and I don't believe he thinks too highly of us Yanks. But he's all we've got right now. At least he was right about the airstrip at *So Sorry* being wide open."

Chapter Fourteen

Sergeant Mike McMillen was pissed off and didn't mind saying so: "We're going to be spending Christmas in this sewer. You all realize that, don't you?"

The men in Able Company's 1st Platoon were already miserable enough. They didn't appreciate their sergeant dumping coal in their stockings two weeks in advance. In fact, they didn't want to be reminded of Christmas at all. This waterlogged, mosquito-infested, disease-ridden tropical hell called Buna had taken them as far from the Yuletide spirit as anyone could imagine. What was worse: they were about to go patrolling again—farther out this time—in search of the Japanese they knew were there, somewhere, but had yet to see.

"Let me walk point again, sir," Bogater Boudreau said to Lieutenant Papadakis. "I don't trust none of these touch-holes up front, anyways. They'll get us all fucking dead."

"You sure?" Papadakis replied. "You did it yesterday. It's not your turn again for a while."

Actually, Theo Papadakis would be thrilled to have Bogater Boudreau on point today, or any other day for that matter. He didn't trust any of those *touch-holes*, either. At least not yet.

A strange sound greeted Jock and Sergeant Major Patchett as they slogged their way to Colonel Molloy's HQ at *Double-Dare*: a jeep's engine.

"What in tarnation is that thing doing here?" Patchett asked, more annoyed than surprised. "All I can say is it better be loaded to the brim with stuff we need...like food, medicine..."

Jock caught first sight of it as it wound its way along the trail. "Well, Top," Jock said, "looks like all that jeep's bringing is General Hartman."

Patchett laughed. "I hope he's got enough gas in his tank to get his ass back outta here, 'cause he probably ain't gonna like what he sees one bit."

The sergeant major couldn't be more right. The first words out of General Hartman's mouth were, "Why haven't you pushed into Buna, Colonel Molloy?"

Not the least bit flustered or intimidated, Dick Molloy turned to the map. "We're not in a position to do so yet, General," he replied. "The rest of the division is only just arriving in the area. As of this morning's report, the Australians estimate they're still three days out on the Kokoda Track. As a result—and per your orders, sir—I've had to shift my regiment's Third Battalion west, well into the Aussie area of operation, to try and cut off any Japs retreating from Kokoda to Buna, Sanananda, or Gona."

Hartman scowled. "Something your Second Battalion on the Kapa Kapa should have done some days ago, Colonel."

Molloy tried not to let his irritation at the general's studied indifference to reality boil over into anger. "I've had no radio contact with Second Battalion, sir," he said. "Neither has the Air Force at Port Moresby. In all honesty, we sent them off on a mission that was ill-fated from the start. I'm not sure if or when we'll ever see them again."

Hartman scowled again. "It could have been done, Colonel. It *should* have been done."

Without skipping a beat, Molloy continued, "Nevertheless, sir, that leaves me with just two battalions—now less than seven hundred men due to combat casualties and sickness—trying to secure a front almost eighteen miles long. That's one man for every one hundred thirty-five feet. I'm afraid I'm in no position to attack anything at the moment."

General Hartman stepped to the map and said, "That's a ridiculous mathematical analogy, Colonel. Now, what about Miles and his First Battalion? What are they doing way over there by the coast?"

Molloy replied, "We believe the best way into Buna Mission and Buna Village is through Duropa Plantation, sir, it's—"

"Nonsense," Hartman interrupted as he stabbed a point on the map repeatedly with his finger. "It's painfully obvious the best way into Buna is straight up the road from Ango Corner. Didn't you bother to do a map recon, Colonel?"

"We've done much more than that, sir," Molloy replied, "and quite painfully, too. Colonel Vann's battalion took nearly fifty casualties at Ango Corner a few nights back."

He let his words sink in before adding, "As far as the maps go, they're almost useless. Almost nothing on the ground jives with them. For example, that road you mentioned is little more than a footpath, flanked by swamps. And we still haven't received the low-level recon photos we requested from the Air Force."

"You're giving me nothing but excuses, Colonel," Hartman said. "We need results...and we need them quickly."

"Well, sir," Molloy replied, "if it's results you want, we just may get some very soon. Major Miles, are your men going into Duropa Plantation today?"

"As we speak, sir," Jock replied.

"Then I wait with bated breath, gentlemen," the general replied.

Outside the tent, all was not well with Hartman's jeep. The odor of burned-out clutch hung heavy in the air.

"Damn thing won't move, sir," his aide said. "We must've damaged the transmission slipping and sliding all over that jungle trail."

A broad smile of satisfaction spread across Sergeant Major Patchett's face. "Maybe he should've come in a tank instead," he said to Jock. "We could've used it...but then again, the piece of shit probably would've broken down in about a mile, anyway."

It could all seem so normal, so ordinary—like an idyllic stroll in a tropical sylvan paradise. The handful of combat veterans in Able Company knew better, though; the neat row after row of coconut palms defining the Duropa Plantation formed perfect lanes of fire. The few rays of sunlight filtering through the palm fronds seemed to be spotlighting the killing zones. Instinctively, the veterans slid close to the nearest line of palms. They wanted to be no more than a step from the best source of cover available: a stout tree trunk.

The rookies hadn't learned that lesson yet. They walked, cautious yet oblivious, in the middle of lanes wide enough for a jeep, passing from one pool of sunlight to another. They were unable to draw visual cues from their more experienced comrades for one very simple reason: they couldn't see most of them. The dense stand of palms limited visibility in every direction but one: straight ahead.

It seemed unnatural when the first chorus of gunfire rang out...

And even more bizarre when bullets—like invisible tripwires—began to cut GIs down.

It didn't matter whether a GI had been in combat before or not: no one could tell where the Japanese shooters were. They were close—the racket of their weapons made that clear—but invisible.

For the rookies, it was hard to decide which was more frightening: the deadly chatter of Nambu machine guns or the screaming of the wounded.

A terrified private clung to Bogater Boudreau's back as they took cover behind a tree trunk. The private had already dropped his rifle; his free hands were trying to cover his ears.

"What'd you think was gonna happen?" Bogater told him. "This ain't some cowboy movie where you get shot and then you lay down and go to sleep. Now pick up your fucking weapon and return fire, dammit."

"Where, Corporal? I can't see where they are! Can you?"

Bogater slammed a fresh magazine into his Thompson. "Shoot anywhere, numbnuts. It don't matter where. Just shoot." He squeezed off another unaimed burst and then tried to stick his head out for a better look.

The solid *thup thup thup* of bullets hitting the other side of the tree trunk changed his mind in a hurry. He seemed to be asking the heavens when he said, "Am I the only son of a bitch trying to fight back around here?"

Crawling flat on his belly, Theo Papadakis slid past the private to get to Boudreau.

"I can't see where the hell those bastards are, Lieutenant Pop," Bogater said.

"I think I saw something," Papadakis said. "Looks like there's a couple of places out there where the ground rises up a little. That don't look right, considering the land around here's flat as a board."

The lieutenant spoke quietly but his words seemed determined, as if he was calculating the odds. It was difficult to hear him over the close-in noise of Japanese machine guns and the wounded crying for God and their mothers.

Bogater asked, "You think they're bunkers, sir?"

"Fuck yeah I do."

"How far, Lieutenant?"

"Forty, maybe fifty yards."

Boudreau had already pulled the safety pin from the hand grenade. Papadakis shook his head like it was a very bad idea. "No!" he said. "All that's gonna do is bounce off a tree and come back at us."

"What choice we got, sir?" Bogater asked. He flung the grenade side-arm around the tree trunk, putting as much might as he could into the awkward motion.

Thup thup thup...more bullets hit the tree. Bogater snatched his throwing hand back with a grimace: "Shit...got me some damn splinters."

Two Mississippi, three Mississippi, four Mississippi—the grenade bounced off the ground and detonated not even halfway to the bunker.

"Well, that didn't do shit," Bogater said. "Where's the fucking thirty cal, sir? The mortars?"

"Too late for that," Papadakis replied. "We're gonna pull back and regroup before we all get fucking killed. We've got too many men down already."

The tally for Able Company's morning probe was grim: five men dead and twelve wounded, eight badly enough to be evacuated by native litter bearers back to the airfield at *So Sorry*. If they survived that trip, they'd get a plane ride back to Port Moresby. Hopefully.

Among the badly wounded was the lieutenant leading 1st Platoon.

"Can I just move up Sergeant McMillen to acting platoon leader, sir?" Theo Papadakis asked Jock. A muscular but small man, Papadakis looked positively miniscule as he grieved his company's losses.

Jock looked at Sergeant Major Patchett to gauge his reaction. He was relieved when Patchett gave a slight, almost imperceptible nod.

"Sure, Theo," Jock replied. "Do it."

As the rest of the company commanders gathered in the CP tent for the briefing, Patchett told Jock, "We've got another problem, sir. Ain't enough field rations showed up in that last air drop to feed two companies, let alone a battalion. We're gonna have to ration the rations."

"Shit," Jock said. "How are we fixed for sixty-millimeter mortar ammo?"

The battalion supply officer replied, "We're not flush, that's for sure, sir. Fifty-two rounds total, assuming the companies are leveling with me. That breaks down to forty HE, eight white phosphorous, four illum."

Fifty-two rounds between twelve tubes, Jock thought, *a little better than four rounds a tube, against Japs dug in like moles. That ain't good.*

Patchett said, "Maybe we can get Third Battalion to farm out a couple of their eighty-ones."

Jock shook his head. "Even if Colonel Molloy agreed to it, the Third is already headed west across the Girua River, into the Aussie zone. They'd come up with a million excuses to make sure we never got those mortars."

"Yeah," Patchett agreed. "We'd do the same to them, I reckon."

"Damn right we would," Jock said, "and who knows...they may need it where they're going, too."

Jock took a count of the attendees and said, "All right, gentlemen, we're all here, so let's get down to it. Believe it or not, we learned a few things this morning. It appears the Japs—despite those fine intelligence estimates to the contrary—have constructed rather formidable field fortifications. The good news is: they're above ground."

The faces of Jock's officers couldn't lie: they didn't see the good news in that at all. The only news that might be classified as *good* involved the Japanese fleeing the field of battle completely.

It fell to Lee Grossman to ask the question on everyone's mind: "Why's that good news, sir?"

"Because if they're above ground and we can pinpoint where they are, maybe the Air Force can flatten them for us," Jock replied. "Of course, if we had some artillery or tanks, we'd do it ourselves. Theo's been closest to those bunkers so far, so I'll let *The Mad Greek* describe them."

Theo Papadakis took center stage, exhausted but still looking every bit the scrappy fighter he had long since proven to be. "They just look like big lumps on the ground...ten, maybe twenty feet wide in front," he began. "They don't seem to be very deep front to back, though. You really can't see them until you're right on top of them...the jungle's grown over them real thick already. I think they'll stand out a little more if you can view them from the side. Their humped shape will probably be more pronounced that way."

Lee Grossman asked, "Can you see the firing ports?"

"Nope...and that smokeless powder they're using doesn't give them away, either," Papadakis said. "Your only hope is to see a little bit of muzzle flash...but you've got to be too damn close already to see that. One more thing, the way they're laid out, they look to be mutually supporting. We got caught in a shitstorm of interlocking fire."

The morning's losses had taken their toll on Theo Papadakis; he was trying hard not to get choked up. It was obvious he wouldn't be able to fight off the tears much longer, though.

Jock came to his rescue. "Okay, very good, Theo. Thanks. Now listen up, gentlemen...this is what we're going to do." He pointed to Lieutenant Tony Colletti, Baker Company's commander, and said, "Tony, take your company and retrace Able's steps into the east end of the plantation. Get their attention and draw their fire. Use a few grenades, if you have to, and pull that *firecracker recon* the Japs are so fond of."

He turned to Lee Grossman next. "Lee, once Baker Company's got their attention, your Charlie Company will advance on the plantation's east end from the south—out of the swamps—and see what the Japs look like from that direction. Everybody pool your mortars— we'll set them up at the jumping-off point just east of the plantation. Sergeant Major, you'll coordinate the mortar fires. We'll all only be about a mile apart, at most, so we should be able to communicate with the walkie-talkies just fine."

Theo Papadakis raised his hand. "What do you want Able Company to do, sir?" he asked.

"Your company's in reserve, Theo," Jock replied. "Be ready if we need our asses bailed out."

Papadakis seemed hurt by that answer. "But, sir—" he began to protest.

Jock put a hand on his shoulder. "You and your men earned a break, Theo. And hey...if we screw up, it may not turn out to be much of a break at all." He looked at his wristwatch and said, "Okay...it's oh-nine-fifteen. I want an ops order written and distributed within two hours."

The battalion operations officer grimaced—*that's cutting it mighty close*—but nodded in acceptance.

Jock continued, "Everybody remember: this is still a recon. We're not looking for a serious engagement, unless we see a golden opportunity...and I mean *really* golden. Then, I'll make the call whether we change missions or not. Don't anybody go freelancing on me. Let's plan a jump-off time of thirteen hundred. Any questions?"

Patchett had one: "Where will you be, sir?"

"I'll be with Charlie Company...in the swamp," Jock replied.

Chapter Fifteen

The swamp's mud was threatening to suck the boots right off the feet of Charlie Company's GIs. At the best spots, they were ankle deep in soft, silty soil. At the worst, they were waist deep in fetid water.

"This is like living in a fucking sewer," Lee Grossman grumbled, "and the rats here shoot back. It's a shame we don't have any boats."

Jock replied, "Why, Lee? You don't mean you'd try to sneak up on them from the seaward side, do you?"

"Hell, no, sir. That'd be suicide. I'd use the damn boats to get through this swamp."

"Staying dry is the least of our worries, Lee, considering there's next to no cover here. And if this high swamp grass thins out, we're out of concealment, too."

"Concealment? No problem, sir. We'll just hide behind a cloud of these mosquitoes."

The GI carrying Grossman's walkie-talkie said, "These fucking mosquitoes...I just know I'm getting malaria."

Another GI replied, "You've got it already, you dumb shit. We all do. Any day now, we'll start shaking with chills...and then burning up with fever. That Atabrine shit they want you to take ain't gonna help you none."

"Enough of that talk, you men," Grossman commanded. "Let's stay focused."

Talking softly so his words wouldn't carry, Jock said, "You know, Lee, I'm afraid they may be right."

Lieutenant Tony Colletti was pleased with how things were going so far. His Baker Company had entered the coconut palm forest of Duropa Plantation as silently as thieves. He told himself, *No way in hell we're going to get cut up like Theo's company did. Poor Theo...he's taking it real hard. He had a charmed life when he was a platoon leader, but that's all over now. He's tough, though—he'll make it.*

Two scout teams—two men each—were some 50 yards ahead of the rest of the company, inching from tree to tree so as not to expose themselves for more than a second or two. Behind the scouts, the company's three rifle platoons were ready to lay down supporting fire as necessary.

"We've got to be at least as far in as Lieutenant Pop's guys were," a scout said to his partner. "Can you see anything?"

"Not a damn thing," the partner replied.

Huddled low against a tree trunk, the scout called Lieutenant Colletti on the walkie-talkie. *"Panty Raid Zero-Six,* this is *Panty Raid Three-Seven,* over."

He cringed as his company commander's hushed voice crackled in the earpiece: it seemed loud enough to be heard a mile away.

"This is *Three-Seven...*you want us to try the firecracker trick?"

"Affirmative, *Three-Seven.* Do it now. *Six out.*"

He never even got to pull the safety pin from the grenade. A loud shout rang out from his right flank. A GI was screaming, "HALT! HANDS UP!"

The reply contained no words—just the thunderous roar of weapons discharging.

The two scouts were lucky; their tree of salvation had dense, above-ground roots which wrapped around them like a mother's embrace.

They needed it: bullets were whizzing past their position in every direction, it seemed.

Both scouts knew his partner's first thought: *What fucking idiot tried to capture somebody?*

They knew each other's second thought, too: the Nambu machine gun trying to saw down the tree shielding them couldn't be more than 20 yards away.

Their third thought wasn't a thought at all, but an instinct: *We need mortars! Now!*

Each was so eager to make that call for fire, they nearly fought over the walkie-talkie.

It took almost a minute for the first mortar rounds to arrive.

That minute seemed like a hundred lifetimes to men pinned down under fire.

Only a few rounds landed anywhere near the bunkers, doing no more than assaulting the eardrums of the Japanese inside.

The rest burst in the dense palm canopy above the scouts, raining invisible shards of steel all around them.

The scouts yelled as one into the radio, "TURN IT OFF! TURN IT OFF! TURN IT OFF! YOU'RE KILLING US!"

"Oh, shit," Lee Grossman said, as the sounds of the fight in the plantation rippled across the swamp. "I guess

Baker Company got their attention, all right. Sounds like somebody's getting their ass riddled in there but good."

"We still can't see shit, though," Jock said. "We've got to get closer."

"Mortars on the way, sir," the radio operator said.

Jock spied through a tall clump of swamp grass as the mortar rounds began to burst in the trees.

"Shit," he muttered, "the rounds aren't even making it to the ground. That's all we need...tree bursts, with our own guys underneath. Shit."

The radio operator had another news flash: "They're canceling the mortars, sir."

"Good," Jock replied. "Get *Panty Raid Zero Six* for me."

The radio conversation was brief. When it was done, Jock told Grossman, "Baker's holding in place. Let's you and me try to get up to that next bunch of swamp grass. Maybe we can see what we need to from there. Make sure the rest of your company stays put."

It was a 30-yard slog to that next patch of grass.

Thirty yards had never seemed so far...but they made it.

Nobody was shooting at them.

"I make it as about a hundred yards to the southern edge of the plantation," Jock said. "What do you think?"

"That looks about right, sir," Grossman replied. "And not a stitch of concealment the entire way. Our asses will be hanging out if we try to cross it."

"I can tell there's a line of bunkers facing east, shooting at Baker Company," Jock continued, "and about where that line is...but I can't make the individual bunkers out."

Grossman nodded in agreement and asked, "You think there are any facing this way?"

"I'm betting there are, Lee...I just can't tell exactly where. Not until they start shooting."

Grossman asked, "You want to do a little *firecracker recon*, sir?"

"Yeah. You've got First Platoon on the left flank, correct?"

"Correct."

"Good. Let them do it. Have Hadley pull the company back first."

"While we stay and watch, sir?"

"That's what I've always liked about you, Lee. You catch on fast."

As the rest of 1st Platoon followed First Sergeant Hadley out of the swamp, three men stayed behind. Rather than throw the grenades into the swamp water, where their submerged detonation might or might not draw the attention of the Japanese, the three came up with a different concept for the *firecracker recon*. They stuck two grenades in the thick mud of a grass thicket and tied a long cord to their safety pins.

The cord was played out as far as it would go—only about 20 feet—but that was enough. It was then tugged firmly.

The three GIs ran like hell, surprised and terrified by how much noise they made as they sloshed through the swamp.

The grenades exploded with a dull *thud* and a great geyser of mud and brackish water.

A fusillade of rifle and machine gun fire erupted from Japanese bunkers facing the swamp. It was aimed precisely where 1st Platoon used to be.

The rounds struck nothing but the swaying swamp grass. The GIs were long gone.

"They fell for it," Lee Grossman said, his words more a sigh of relief he wasn't in the bullseye.

"It's just like the other bunkers," Jock said. "I can tell where they are but I can't actually see them."

"So what do we do now, sir?"

"We figure out map coordinates for the bunker complex, Lee. Then we get the Air Force to pummel the shit out of it. Something's bugging me, though."

"What's that, sir?"

Poking his head through the swamp grass for another look at the Japanese positions, Jock said, "We don't see any Japs. Not one...and we can see a lot of that plantation from here. They can't stay in those bunkers forever...and there can't be many Japs in—"

He stopped talking, grabbed a startled Lee Grossman by the web gear, and yanked him down.

In the swamp, *down* meant under the stinking water.

It was the only place to hide from the machine gun suddenly traversing toward them. Its bullets swept just inches over the water's surface before swinging away.

There was no need for words when they surfaced: they knew they had to make their escape.

Grossman couldn't talk, anyway. He was coughing up the swamp water he swallowed.

They were crawling along the swamp bed on hands and knees, heads just above water, weapons slung but dragging through the foul stew.

They could sense the machine gun tracking back their way...

No way I'm going under that fucking water again, Grossman thought.

He saw what he thought was a patch of solid ground. He hurled himself onto it.

It wasn't solid at all: he sank into it—flat, face down—like a cookie cutter into soft dough.

The dough held him like a giant suction cup and wouldn't let go.

Bullets trimmed the swamp grass all around like an invisible lawnmower making one broad pass...until their path swung away again.

Jock popped out of the water. It took him a few moments to find his partner, squirming, semi-submerged and stuck like glue in the muck.

Prying on Grossman's helmet, he freed the man's face so he could breathe again. The dank air of the swamp had never smelled so sweet as it rushed back into Lee Grossman's lungs.

He didn't seem to be hit. Using the stock of his Thompson like a spade, Jock liberated the stuck man limb by limb.

The second Grossman was free they were on the move, leaving behind a man-sized, perfectly detailed impression of a soldier in the Buna swamp.

The two scout teams weren't sure how they made it out of the plantation. All four men were wounded, the jagged tears in their flesh from American mortar fragments and splintered trees, not bullets. The battalion surgeon treating them couldn't understand how they hadn't been killed.

"We must've crawled under the fucking ground, Doc," one of the scouts told the surgeon. "All I remember is clawing through dirt."

The mystery of *HALT! HANDS UP!* still needed to be sorted out; that colossal mistake wouldn't be unraveled until Baker Company was back at the assembly area. There, the answer came quickly.

The shout had come from 3rd Platoon on the right flank. A mortified PFC was immediately fingered by his squadmates for the mistake.

"Two Japs popped up right in front of me and started to run away," the PFC tried to explain to his company commander. "But they vanished, just like that. I had to do *something*, sir."

Doing a slow burn, Lieutenant Colletti said, "You picked the wrong *something*, Hallstrom. You weren't on fucking guard duty. You were on a recon patrol. Did these Japs even see you?"

"We looked right into each other's eyes, sir."

"All right...so what do you mean by *vanished*, Hallstrom? Where'd they go?"

"I don't know, sir. They just dropped out of sight. Gone...just like that."

"All right," Jock said as the debriefing wound down, "let's sum up what we've learned today. We know pretty well where the Jap bunkers are on the eastern edge of the plantation as well as its southeastern corner." His fingers retraced the red lines already drawn on the map.

"We also learned our mortars aren't worth a shit in the palm groves," he added. "We were damn lucky they only wounded four of Tony's men. How are those guys, Tony?"

"They'll be okay, sir," Lieutenant Colletti replied. "They can stay and fight."

"That's good news," Jock said. "Now, I've already called in the Air Force. They gave an ETA of sixteen hundred, give or take a little. A spotter plane will mark the targets with smoke. We'll have to guide him in so he puts the smoke in the right places for the attack planes. We'll set up an OP here"—his finger marked a spot on the map—"near the coast on the far edge of the swamp, with the big radio."

Sergeant Major Patchett had been quiet throughout the briefing, but now he was sketching on a pad of paper like a madman. "Begging your pardon, sir," he said, "but I think I've got something here."

"Let's have it," Jock replied.

"Well, gentlemen," Patchett said, "y'all been talking about how you actually ain't seen no Japs, except those two that Lieutenant Colletti's man tried to capture. And even those two *vanished* like ghosts. By the way, Lieutenant"—he nodded to Colletti—"I trust you're gonna reassign that man, before his own platoon does him in?"

"Already taken care of, Sergeant Major," Colletti replied.

"Very fine, sir," Patchett said. "That man just made hisself a mistake…a real fucking stupid one…but he won't be making it again, I guaran-damn-tee it. Now let's be getting back to these *invisible* Japs. I don't believe they're invisible at all. They just done like both sides did in France in '18—they dug a network of communications trenches linking their bunkers. They're probably not too deep, or they'd fill up with groundwater like every other hole in these parts, but them Japs can use 'em to move around, bring supplies, visit the latrine...all without their heads ever popping up above ground. And the jungle will hide those trenches just like it hides those bunkers."

Patchett passed the pad he'd been drawing on to Jock. "I sketched out a few ideas how we can use them trenches to our advantage."

The other officers gathered around; the drawings diagrammed an attack plan brilliant in its simplicity.

"So," Jock said, "we take a corner bunker...and then work our way down the trenches, one bunker at a time."

"And all the while," Patchett added, "the Japs can only get at us from one direction—down that narrow little trench from the next bunker. Keeps everything real *linear*, sir."

Chapter Sixteen

The only thing that came from the sky around 1600 was the rain. The Air Force radioed their regrets: there would be no air raid on Duropa Plantation today.

"They'll try to be back first thing tomorrow," Jock said.

"Maybe it's just as well, sir," Patchett added. "We wouldn't have much daylight for a follow-up attack if the flyboys came now, anyway."

When the chills and shakes hit him a few hours back, Lieutenant Colonel Vann had insisted he was all right and 3rd Battalion was to push on. Now, the fever was upon him and he could barely stand, let alone slog through swamps. Pushing on was impossible.

"I'll be all right," Vann told his staff. "I'll catch up in a bit."

His staff thought that much too optimistic. They'd seen enough malaria to know the symptoms on sight: each platoon had already lost half a squad due to illness, and sick call kept growing slowly but steadily. They knew their commander's fever wouldn't break for hours.

"Major Raddatz," Vann said to his executive officer, "get the men into the ambush position along the Sanananda Road. You've still got time before dark."

But not much time, Herman Raddatz thought as he studied his map in the fading light of dusk. *We should've crossed flowing water at four points—one river and three creeks, according to this fucking map—but by my*

*count, we've forded five already and we still haven't
stumbled across anything a civilized person—let alone
that annoying Aussie Bennett— would call a road.*

The road, Dickie Bennett had told them, was on dry
terrain and wide enough to accommodate a truck. It was
the final leg in the Kokoda Track. Any Japanese fleeing
Kokoda to the north coast would be on that road. Maybe
they'd be on it tonight.

Dry terrain had Raddatz scratching his head,
though. Every step the men of 3rd Battalion took seemed
to go deeper into swampland.

The only thing Herman Raddatz was sure of was his
exhausted men had been walking all day, trying to cover
the eight miles between Dobodura—*Double-Dare*—and
Popondetta, a village straddling the Sanananda Road his
men had promptly nicknamed *Pompano*, like the city in
Florida. Or the fish, perhaps.

We should have been there by now, Raddatz told
himself, *but we've got no choice except to keep going.*

By the time the sun was about to set, 3rd Battalion
had come to some sort of swamp thoroughfare, a north-
south path, high and dry, that appeared heavily—and
recently—used. Whether it was wide enough for a
vehicle or not depended on one's definition of a vehicle:
a bicycle would fit; maybe a donkey cart. But that was
about it. If they were anywhere near the village of
Popondetta—*Pompano*—they couldn't tell.

Racing the darkness, Major Raddatz used one rifle
company to set up a roadblock, another to lay the
ambush along the trail, and the third to close the trap

from behind once their quarry was stalled by the roadblock in the kill zone.

"When the Japs come down this road from Kokoda," Raddatz told his staff, "they're dead men."

They waited half the night. Most of 3rd Battalion had long since dozed off at their ambush posts.

The small band of Japanese stragglers, silhouetted by the light of a full moon, were more than halfway down the gauntlet before the Americans realized they were there. "Wait," a sergeant whispered to a wide-awake GI about to fire, "let them get all the way to the roadblock."

"But I've got 'em dead to rights, Sarge!"

"Take it easy, Killer...they could be the lead element for a battalion still way down the road. Or a division. Don't give us away just yet. Let them get all the way in."

At the roadblock, the company commander watched as the stragglers approached. "Only four or five of them, by my count," he said to his men. "Capture them. Don't shoot unless they want to fight. Try to keep it quiet...in case there are more coming."

The five Japanese surrendered without a fight. Hands up, they knelt until pushed face-down on the road by their captors.

"Look at them," the company commander said to Major Raddatz. "They're in rags...and barefoot." One by one, he lifted their heads and shined a red-filtered flashlight into their faces. In the dim light, it might as well have been skeletons staring back at him. "These guys look like death warmed over."

No one noticed the secret smile on the face of one prisoner as he was rolled over to be searched. Quickly, deftly, he pulled the grenade from beneath his tattered shirt and—with a *CLANK*—armed it by striking the primer against the helmet of the GI bent over him.

"What the hell?" the GI said—and then he saw the small, round object rolling slowly toward the circle of officers.

"GRENADE!" the GI yelled as he pulled the Japanese soldier in front of him for cover.

It was too late.

The blast seemed little more than that of a large firecracker to those far enough away.

To those closer, it didn't matter.

Major Raddatz was dead. Two junior officers in the circle were, too. The company commander was mortally wounded. So was the Japanese soldier who dealt the grenade.

The other four Japanese were quickly bayoneted to death by a mob of GIs who *whooped* like cowhands as they thrust their blades through flesh and bone.

For good measure, the Japanese soldier who had already stepped through death's door was bayoneted repeatedly, as well.

Bloodlust knows few limits.

A few hundred yards to the west—on the actual Sanananda Road—two battalions of exhausted and sickly Japanese soldiers stole through the darkness toward the north coast. They could sense they were close to the end of the harrowing journey that began in Port Moresby. They could already taste the fresh coconut milk that would slake their bottomless thirst; that was the only thing keeping them on their bleeding and swollen bare feet.

None of them were the least bit interested in the sound of an explosion from across that forbidding swamp or the barely audible screams and cries which followed: the horrific sounds of men facing—and dealing—death.

Chapter Seventeen

There was good news over the radio at first light: the attack planes from 5th Air Force were in the air. They'd be over Duropa Plantation within the hour. Jock was trying to rub from his eyes the two hours of fitful sleep he'd managed to get. Sergeant Major Patchett looked like he'd bagged a solid eight hours as he bustled around the battalion CP. Jock knew better; Melvin Patchett had probably never gone to bed. He seemed to be the only human on the planet who didn't require sleep.

Jock asked, "How's sick call looking, Top?"

"We've got ten more, sir...mostly malaria, Doc says."

Jock did the math in his head: between the combat casualties, the sick, the still-missing mortar platoon, and the fact they had been short some 50 men to begin with, his battalion was at 60 percent of full strength—about 250 men.

And it's only been five days since we flew in here...

A strange sound drifted in from outside the CP tent: *hoofbeats.* Colonel Molloy and Dickie Bennett were approaching on horseback.

"We're on our way to Third Battalion over near Popondetta," Molloy said. "These mounts seem like the best way to travel...until we get some jeeps here, at least."

Dickie Bennett asked, "Would you like one for yourself, Major Miles? My boys pinched quite a few from the bloody Nips."

"No, thanks, sir...I'm not much of a horseman."

Patchett laughed and said, "Which one of you Yankees is, sir?" He stopped laughing when he remembered Colonel Molloy was from Ohio...and he was an ex-cavalryman. "With all due respect to both you gentlemen...just making a little joke."

"No time for jokes, I'm afraid," Molloy replied. "I've got some bad news. The plane carrying your mortar platoon—the one that never showed up at Fasari. Well...the Air Force spotted it, crashed up in the mountains. Survivors don't look very likely, they said."

Patchett's jaw tightened. His voice flat and emotionless, he said, "That's a tough break, sir."

Jock could only mumble, "Dammit."

But there was no time to grieve. He asked Colonel Molloy, "Are you going to stay a while and see what the Air Force can do, sir?"

"That's my plan, Major."

They made their way on foot to the designated observation post—the *OP*. As they walked, Molloy asked Jock, "You copied the radio traffic from Third Battalion, didn't you?"

"Yeah...Colonel Vann's down with malaria and some of his staff are dead. Sounds like a pretty shitty ambush when you lose as many as you kill."

"My thoughts exactly," Molloy replied. "That's why I'm headed over that way. I've got to see for myself what's going on with that unit...even if it takes all damn day on horseback to get there and back."

Jock asked, "Are you going to replace Colonel Vann, sir...him being sick and all?"

Molloy shook his head. "With who, Jock? We won't see any replacements for weeks...maybe months. If Vann can function at all, he's my best bet for the time being."

Patchett broke into their conversation. "Begging your pardon, sirs, but we've got the spotter plane on the big radio. He's about four minutes out. Major Miles, you want to call the shots here?"

"Yeah," Jock replied, "but I want to do it with Lieutenant Papadakis and Corporal Boudreau. They've been closest to the target."

The two men he'd just named were poised for the task. Jock walked over and gave each an encouraging pat on the back. Bogater Boudreau asked, "How come we can't just mark the target with *Willie Peters* from our mortars, sir? Seems kinda silly to have some air-machine do what we can do for ourselves."

"Not really, Bogater," Jock replied. "By the time we got the mortars adjusted on target, we'd have smoke all over the place. Wouldn't be very precise for the bomber pilots. Besides, when there are friendly aircraft in the area, we don't lob high-trajectory fire through their airspace. Don't want to shoot down our own guys." He paused, and then added, "Plus, we don't have a whole lot of white phosphorous rounds to play with at the moment."

Boudreau thought that over, finally nodding as if it all made perfect sense.

"Let's try to get it done in one pass," Jock said. "That slow little bird is too vulnerable to keep coming back over those Japs."

Papadakis asked, "You sure got a lot of sympathy for those flyboys after all that aviating you did over Port Moresby, don't you, sir?"

"Yeah, Theo. Some of them, at least."

"Don't sweat it, sir," Boudreau added. "It'll be just like tossing apples into a barrel."

The faint *purr* of the spotter plane's engine was on the breeze now, growing louder by the second.

"There she is, sir," Boudreau said, pointing out over the water. "Maybe that's the same L4 you were flying in." Bogater cradled the microphone in his hands like it was their key to salvation.

"Maybe," Jock replied, eyes glued to the little plane. "Turn him...wait...wait...NOW, Boudreau."

Within seconds, the L4 banked sharply toward land while diving lower to skim the waves.

"Smart," Jock said.

"Why's that, sir?" Papadakis asked. "Is he harder to hit flying low like that?"

"No, Theo...but he won't have so far to fall when the plane gets shot out from under him. Vector him left five degrees, Boudreau."

The plane settled on its new course.

"Perfect," Jock said. "All we've got to do now is watch."

Patchett nodded with satisfaction, too. "Even if his smoke rounds burst in the treetops, that should still get the job done."

Jock asked, "You mean *mark the target with a burning coconut tree,* Sergeant Major?"

"Whatever it takes, sir," Patchett replied.

They could hear the Nambus firing from the far side of the plantation. "They ain't using tracers," Patchett said. "Can't tell if they're hitting that flying bag of sticks or not."

"He's still airborne," Jock replied. "That's all that counts."

The L4 was just above the plantation's treetops.

"NOW, NOW, NOW, OVER," Bogater screeched into the microphone.

Four smoke grenades tumbled in rapid sequence from the little plane.

Two of them actually made it all the way to the ground. The other two nestled in the treetops, setting them ablaze just as Patchett foresaw.

"Close enough for government work," the sergeant major said.

The radio squawked with a new voice: the attack flight leader.

"We've got the smoke," the leader's voice said. "Heads up...here we come."

As the L4 made its escape across the swamp—and heading straight for the OP—Jock and company didn't need tracers to see the Japanese machine guns were slicing the plane to ribbons.

Each man made his unique sound of distress as the L4's tail section suddenly swung up and away from the fuselage, detached itself, and began a fluttery, spiraling descent to the swamp a hundred feet below.

Minus its tailplane, the rest of the airplane nosed over and—like the projectile it now was—plunged straight down for a heart-wrenching second, its engine roaring until the swamp silenced it with a final, sickening *THWOOSH* and a mighty spray of muddy water.

It had come to earth just yards in front of the OP's cowering occupants, an upside-down crucifix—or an olive drab angel with broken wings, its head jammed deep into the mud.

The pilot—still inside, strapped to his seat—was obviously dead, the grotesque twist of a broken neck unmistakable.

The strike of the attack bombers was almost anticlimactic.

Peering into the tangle of bomb-blasted coconut palms, Theo Papadakis asked, "Think the Air Force did us any good?"

"Let's go find out," Jock replied, "and we'd better do it on the double...while those Japs are still shell-shocked."

This time, Charlie Company led the advance into the plantation. Their objective was simple: take the bunker anchoring the southeast corner; it seemed to have taken quite the desired pounding from the bombers. Boudreau even thought it might have suffered a direct hit with a 250-pound bomb. With any luck, the occupants of that bunker were dead—or at least too dazed to fight.

Once the bunker was taken, the other two companies would exploit the success by attacking the next ones in line down the communications trenches. The bunkers would fall like dominoes—hopefully—and that cleverly built defensive wall would be breached.

It didn't take long to realize that wouldn't be the case. Far from it: the fire from the southeast bunker—

and every other bunker facing the approaching GIs—
was just as withering as the first two ventures into the
plantation.

Never getting closer than 200 yards to the objective,
Charlie Company pulled back, dragging its dead and
wounded through the merciless swamp as best it could.

Once back at the assembly area, Melvin Patchett
flung his gear on the ground as he summed up
everyone's feelings: "Fucking Air Force is useless as tits
on a bull."

General Hartman took the news of 1st Battalion's
failed attack as a personal insult. Berating Jock Miles, he
asked, "How could that be, Major? Clearly, you don't
have a very good grasp of your enemy's situation.
You've played right into his strength time and again."

Jock was beyond being intimidated or insulted.
"Sir," he began, "until we have a means of putting large-
caliber direct fire on those bunkers, be it from naval
gunfire, tanks, or our own artillery, we will not breech
them. They're too well built. The Air Force just dropped
a couple of tons of high explosives on them, and it looks
like they bounced right off."

"I just cannot accept that, Major," General Hartman
replied. "Were the targets marked for the bombers?"

"Well marked, sir. The spotter plane pilot gave his
life doing it."

"That's a shame," Hartman said, "but don't get all
down on the Air Force just because one strike didn't kill
every Jap. Give them a chance."

"It's not a question of killing *every* Jap, sir. I don't think they killed *any* of them. And every second we wait for the Air Force to live up to its promises, more of my men die."

"Well, Major...we can't sit on our hands and wait for someone else to win the battle for us. MacArthur won't hear of it...he'll hang me out to dry so fast your head will spin. I'll be discussing a new plan of attack with Colonel Molloy the minute he returns from Popondetta."

Chapter Eighteen

Dickie Bennett didn't believe in sugar-coating bad news. He told Horace Vann point-blank, "You're in the wrong bloody place, Colonel. You don't really think this piddling goat trail is the Sanananda Road as I described it to you? In great detail, I might add."

He considered capping the insult with *you stupid Yank wanker*, but in a rare surrender to tact and cooperation, decided not to do so.

Maybe it's just the malaria making him bloody stupid, Bennett speculated. *Looks well enough at the moment, though.*

Colonel Molloy told Vann, "Get your men saddled up and over to Popondetta. Expect to link up with the Aussies coming down from Kokoda within twenty-four hours."

Horace Vann didn't mind those instructions one bit. He knew of the beating Jock Miles's 1st Battalion was taking at Buna. He'd gladly stay well out of the way and act as greeters for the Aussies.

"Something else, Horace," Molloy said. "Get the Aussies to loan us a couple of their artillery pieces. Don't wait for it to have to go through MacArthur's channels. Just get us those fucking guns right away."

The word passed through Colonel Vann's battalion quickly: they'd set up their ambush in the wrong place. The five Japanese they'd captured—and then killed— were probably as lost as they were; that sarcastic Aussie coast watcher with Colonel Molloy seemed quite sure of it.

The men of 3rd Battalion weren't terribly upset with that turn of events, though. Their collective thinking: *If we can stay out of the Japs' way, that's just fine with us.*

Another issue wasn't *fine* with them, however: their commander was sick with malaria and, as a result, occasionally unable to perform his command duties to the fullest.

But he was staying at his post.

That meant only one thing to the men in the ranks: if they got sick with malaria—or any of the other tropical diseases that laid a man low sporadically, only to recover until the next, unpredictable attack—they'd be expected to stay at their posts, too. Parading to sick call with the slightest hint of chills or fever would only get you paraded right back to your company.

Forget about being evacuated to Port Moresby...or even Australia. You're stuck in this tropical sewer for the duration...

On half-rations, yet.

Half-rations sounded like a pretty good deal to the gaunt, exhausted diggers who stumbled out of the mountains and into Popondetta the next morning. Compared to the little 5th Air Force had been able to supply the last few weeks, half-rations would be a grand feast.

What didn't sound like a good deal: the Japanese they were pursuing had slipped right through what should have been an impassable American roadblock.

General Vasey, the Aussie division commander, vented his frustration on the first American officer to greet him: Lieutenant Colonel Horace Vann.

"Are you bloody kidding me?" Vasey said. "You stopped a grand total of five Nips? And you want to nick some of my artillery, to boot?"

"Buna has turned into a hell on earth, sir," Vann replied. "The bulk of the Japanese defenders seem to be holed up there...and they're very well dug in. The Jap strongholds in your area of responsibility—Sanananda and Gona—appear to be held much more weakly."

Vasey snickered. "That sounds like another of MacArthur's brilliant intelligence assessments. They may have been weakly held once but not anymore. Not since you Yanks let in the whole bloody lot I chased from Port Moresby."

"We need those guns, General," Vann insisted. "If Buna falls, the pockets of resistance you face will crumble quickly."

Vasey mulled it over for a moment. Finally, he said, "I've brought twelve pieces over the mountains, Colonel. I'll loan you four of them. If I don't, your General MacArthur will just order it, anyway. Consider it a gesture to promote *Allied cooperation*—something I haven't seen bloody much of from your camp."

"We greatly appreciate the gesture, General," Vann said, "and he's *our* General MacArthur, sir. We're all in this together."

"Bloody unfortunate," Vasey replied. "Perhaps I'd be more willing to believe we were in this together if I had seen just one Yank walking the Kokoda Track. Just do me a personal favor, Colonel."

"What's that, sir?"

"The gun crews I loan you...make sure the lads get to enjoy a fair share of your half-rations, please."

It took a full day for the four Australian artillery pieces, drawn by horses and mules every bit as hungry and exhausted as the men driving them, to arrive at 1st Battalion's CP near Duropa Plantation. The diggers couldn't believe their luck when the first words out of Sergeant Major Patchett's mouth were, "Let's get you boys fed. We fixed y'all a nice, hot supper here."

Nice, hot supper: that meant C ration cans warmed in a 55-gallon drum full of water boiling over a fire. In this primitive setting, it was better than a dinner at the Ritz. The diggers nearly ripped the scalding cans of stew open with their bare hands.

The Aussie lieutenant in charge of the gun sections asked Jock, "Do you Yanks eat like this all the time, sir?"

Jock laughed. "No, I'm afraid not. We just set some aside because we heard company was coming."

The lieutenant seemed embarrassed as he asked, "Some of your lads didn't eat, then, sir?"

"No, we all ate. Just not very much."

In truth, the GIs didn't look anywhere near as malnourished as the Aussies—*But give us a little more time,* Jock told himself.

Their stomachs content for the moment, Jock and the Aussie lieutenant—*Leftenant* Fairburn, as the Aussies pronounced the rank—raced the setting sun to complete their recon of firing positions. Fairburn grew more uneasy as they waded ankle-deep in swamp water.

He asked Jock, "You say there's some dry ground ahead, sir, closer to the target? We can't shoot from this muck. The guns will just slide and sink."

"Yeah, there's dry ground...and a treeline, too. Should give you some concealment from air attack."

"Has there been much air activity from the Nips, sir?" Fairburn asked.

"Not yet, Lieutenant. Not yet."

When they reached the place Jock had in mind, Lieutenant Fairburn didn't look pleased. As he gazed across the vast expanse of swamp into the distant plantation, he asked Jock, "It has to be direct fire on those bunkers, sir, like we were engaging tanks?"

"Affirmative," Jock replied. "We need that dead-on accuracy. Lobbing indirect fire at them is just too chancy. Hell, the Air Force just bombed the crap out of the place...but those bunkers are still there."

"Well, sir...if this is the closest we can get, then it's too bloody far for direct fire," Fairburn said. "It's well over two thousand yards. Anything over fifteen hundred yards and it's indirect fire. You really think those bunkers are that tough?"

"We don't *think*, Lieutenant. We *know* they're that tough. I tell you what...rest your men and your animals tonight. Set up your guns here at first light and we'll see what you can do. Maybe we can pull a rabbit out of a hat together."

In the harbor at Milne Bay, Jillian smiled as a small but familiar vessel glided alongside and tied up to her anchored freighter *Esme*. It was *Andoom Clipper*, one of her fishing boats out of Weipa, Queensland. Old Robert, the Aborigine elder and Jillian's right-hand man in Weipa, was at her helm.

Beatrix Van Der Wegge downed the last swallow of after-supper whiskey and asked, "You're not really going adventuring in that little tub, are you, schatzi?"

Jillian replied, "Why not? It's perfect for the job. That's why I volunteered her."

Beatrix said nothing in reply but her scowl made it obvious: she didn't agree.

Old Robert didn't look too pleased as he came aboard *Esme*, either.

"Try not to get this one sunk, too, Miss Jilly," he said. "We need it to catch fish so our *country* can eat."

Jillian put on a display of mock indignation. "Well, it's very bloody nice to see you too, Robert," she said.

Without a hint of contrition in his voice, Old Robert replied, "I mean no disrespect, Miss Jilly, but we really do need the boat." He paused, looked down at his feet, and added, "We need you, too. When are you going to come home? What happened to the woman who wanted nothing to do with their war?"

Jillian exhaled loudly, an exasperated puff whose meaning Robert knew all too well: *She'll come back to Weipa when she's good and ready...*

His mind finished the sentence with a note of personal dread: *if she gets to come back at all.*

"I wish everyone would stop worrying," Jillian said. "It's just a little survey mission, trying to find suitable harbors closer to Buna—"

Beatrix interrupted, "More likely, trying to get closer to that Yank of yours, schatzi."

Jillian ignored her, adding, "A small, fast, inconspicuous boat is just what we need—better than one of those patrol boats that keep getting shot up all the time."

Old Robert laughed without smiling. "Inconspicuous? She's fifty feet long. Only a canoe would be inconspicuous when the Japanese planes come," he said. "Even then..." His voice trailed off, as if he didn't want to think about how vulnerable a boat like *Andoom Clipper* would be when an airplane—Japanese or Allied—strafed her.

"To hell with both of you," Jillian said, turning her back to them to watch the sunset.

Both Beatrix and Old Robert wanted to believe those words were offered in jest. But they were having a rough time convincing themselves.

Chapter Nineteen

The nights, at least, were quiet at 1st Battalion's perimeter. Only the hushed sounds of nature fell on the GIs' ears: the hiss of inevitable rain, the rustle of wind, the calls of animals. There had been no combat in the dark; the sickly, starving, yet still deadly Japanese troops were content to stay in their fortress-bunkers. Jock and Colonel Molloy had discussed using the cover of darkness to surprise and overwhelm the nearest enemy positions, but no plan had been formulated. It was hard enough trying to fight an enemy you couldn't see in broad daylight. Trying to seek him out at night only seemed like a prescription for confusion, massive casualties, and certain defeat.

"Maybe we'll get lucky in the morning with this Aussie artillery," Colonel Molloy said before trying to catch an hour or two of sleep.

Melvin Patchett wasn't so sure about the *getting lucky* part. "It's still gonna take some fancy shooting from them cannon-cockers to blow them bunkers apart," he said to Jock, "and that's gonna be pretty hard and all with just throwing a few rounds their way. Maybe it'll make their ears bleed…but hell, their ears should already be bleeding from our Air Force's little visit."

As his words faded, quiet should have prevailed once again…but the night stillness was abruptly pierced by the continuous shrieking of a man. The terrible cries seemed to be coming from Charlie Company's area. As Jock and Patchett hurried closer, the wailing subsided to sobbing and a torrent of tortured, unintelligible words. Their source: a distraught young private in the grip of his first sergeant, Tom Hadley, who was carefully burning a leech from the man's body with a cigarette.

"McCurdy's just gone a little swamp-crazy, sir," Hadley said. "I'll get him calmed down and—"

"The hell you will," Private McCurdy said, a big man coming apart at the seams before their eyes. "I can't take it no more...these bugs...the snakes...fucking crocodiles...the crotch rot...everything's wet and falling apart"—he held up a sodden GI boot with the sole half-detached—"and I know I'm sick." He put the palm of his hand to his forehead. "Look...I'm burning up."

Hadley put his own hand against McCurdy's forehead. "You're not burning up. You're no sicker than the rest of us."

"But I'm starving to death, First Sergeant," McCurdy whimpered.

"We're all a little hungry," Hadley replied as he gave Jock and Patchett a searching look, its meaning evident even in the dim moonlight: *What the hell do I do now?*

Patchett nodded to Jock, a gesture that meant *let me handle this, sir.* He pulled Hadley aside and, speaking softly, said, "Don't fret none that you're new to this top sergeant game, Tom. You'll learn how to be their mama when you need to be. You're doing just fine for now."

Hadley didn't looked convinced he was *doing just fine*; he was out of ideas how to deal with Private McCurdy.

Patchett stepped over to McCurdy. "I just want y'all to remember something," the sergeant major said, his voice as soothing as a country preacher comforting the bereaved. "Sure, ain't none of us had a decent meal since Grant took Richmond...and we've been living in stinking water up to our asses for what seems like a month of Sundays...but the same goes for them Japs over there, only worse."

Hadley and McCurdy had the same confused look on their faces. His voice high-pitched and trembling, McCurdy asked, "How do you figure that, Sergeant Major?"

"It's just a natural fact, son. Mother Nature can't be no kinder to them yellow-ass bastards than she is to us. In fact, they gotta be suffering worse than we are 'cause they been here longer than us."

McCurdy wasn't buying it. "So why are they kicking our asses?" he sobbed. "They're killing us left and right."

Patchett's tone changed from soothing to evangelical. "Why, son, we're just getting started. We'll get our ducks in a row real quick here, and then your Charlie Company will go right through them Japs like shit through a goose, just like it did at Port Moresby."

Hadley rolled his eyes. *Bullshit*, he thought. *Nobody had walked right through anybody at Port Moresby.*

"I wasn't at Port Moresby," McCurdy said. "I'm a replacement."

"Then you're a lucky man, Private McCurdy," Patchett replied. "Your chance to make history has finally arrived. Now, the question is, are you gonna seize that chance like a man? Or are you gonna keep sniveling like some little nancy-boy?"

McCurdy had been in *this man's army* long enough to know there was only one answer to that question. His body gave a shudder of resignation—and then he picked up his helmet and began bailing water from his fighting hole.

"It's just going to fill back up," McCurdy mumbled as he flung the water away. "It always does. More water, more fucking bugs. Some fucking foxhole..."

"A foxhole's something you hide in, son," Patchett replied. "You're standing in a *fighting hole*. Besides, the exercise'll do you good...take your mind off your troubles."

As he and Jock began to walk back to the battalion CP, Patchett said, "We gotta keep a handle on this shit, sir. If it can start in an outfit as squared away as Charlie Company, it can happen anywhere. If we let it take hold, it'll spread like wildfire."

Tom Hadley hurried to catch up. "Something else I've got to tell you, sir," he said to Jock. "Lieutenant Grossman...he's in a real bad way."

They found a groaning Lee Grossman, his pants around his ankles, lying across the narrow, water-filled slit trench that functioned as the latrine. The Charlie Company medic was holding on to him, trying to prevent his weakened, spasming body from doubling over and sliding butt-first into the trench. Even in this pungent swampland, you could smell what was wrong with Lee Grossman from a long way off.

"Good lord," Patchett said, "the man's squirting like a fire hose."

"It's dysentery," the medic said. "Worst case I've ever seen."

"I've seen worse, son," Patchett replied. "Plenty worse. Saw a whole company come down with it once..."

He didn't finish the sentence because the rest of it would have been *and half them sumbitches died.*

Instead, Patchett said, "But I've gotta ask…how the hell did a company commander, of all people, get laid low like this? I figured some dumbass private would be the first one drinking water he shouldn't."

Too busy to consider an answer, the medic said, "Who knows, Sergeant Major? Who the hell knows?"

I think I know how he might have gotten it, Jock told himself. *That head-dunking I gave him in the swamp a couple of days ago to duck those bullets…*

Shit. You save a man's life…but the saving might kill him anyway.

Patchett asked the medic, "You give him any sulfa yet?"

"Not yet, Sergeant Major. Dehydration's the biggest danger right now. I'm waiting on this shit-blast to finish, then I've got to get the lieutenant rehydrated and up to Doc at battalion so—"

Patchett cut him off. "Save it, son, we all know the drill." Looking to Jock, he asked, "What do you want to do about Charlie Company's command, sir?"

"I'll bet Lieutenant Grossman's already taken care of that," Jock replied. "Am I right, Sergeant Hadley?"

"Yes, sir," Hadley said, "Lieutenant Havers has already stepped up to acting company commander."

"Very well," Jock replied. "Get Lieutenant Grossman to the battalion aid station as soon as you can. Doc will want him shipped back to Port Moresby, I'm sure."

Despite his pitiful state, Lee Grossman heard every word. He managed to sit up and, his voice a dry, harsh croak, say, "No, sir...no evacuation...please...I'll...I'll be okay."

Jock tried to offer a comforting hand to Grossman but the medic stopped him. "Better not, sir," the medic said. "It's a mess around here right now...fecal matter everywhere...and dysentery's highly contagious."

Shrugging off the medic, Jock said to Grossman, "We'll see, Lee. We'll see. Right now, you just rest. Don't worry about a thing."

Turning to Hadley, Jock added, "First Sergeant, fill in this latrine as soon as they're done here. Dig a new one for the healthy men and another for the sick. Keep them far apart. Make sure any man who touches a shovel washes up real good."

"Good plan, sir," Patchett said. "Couldn't have put it better myself."

As they once again began their walk back to the battalion CP, Jock added, for Patchett's ears only, "The last thing in the world we need right now is a whole bunch of our men dying from the shits."

"Amen to that, sir," Patchett replied.

"And where'd you pick up this *nancy-boy* stuff, Top? Are you trying to learn the King's English from your Aussie girlfriend, too?"

Patchett smiled. "Among other things, sir."

Chapter Twenty

The Japanese sergeant took comfort in one—and only one—fact: *Our officers are very brilliant men.*

They designed this network of fortifications we cower in—these bunkers of logs, steel, and earth. So efficiently laid out, so resistant to enemy detection and fire even sick, starving, and exhausted men like us can stop our adversaries in their tracks.

All we have to do is point our weapons out the firing slits when ordered and pull the triggers. The enemy drop like flies. They never see us. We see only fleeting glimpses of them just before they fall.

Not long ago, this beautiful patch of land was a coconut palm plantation.

Now, it's a killing field.

My men and I were never at Port Moresby, never fought our way triumphantly over the mountains only to flee back. We've been in Papua only a month.

We're lucky: it takes longer than a month for a man to starve to death.

But it only takes a moment to lose your mind when the bombs and shells start to fall.

Already, two of my men are locked in that moment forever. Call it shell-shock, combat fatigue—whatever you wish...

Insanity is the same no matter what name it hides behind.

The sunrise began to cast its rays through the firing slits, slicing across the interior of the bunker like the beams of searchlights, blazing a row of neat rectangles along the rear wall.

A new day, the Japanese sergeant told himself. *I wonder if the enemy will—*

The muted *poom* of artillery fire answered his unfinished question. He and his men had barely an instant to exchange looks of panic before the rounds came screaming in.

Jock had watched the Australian artillery at work long enough. He put down his binoculars and told Lieutenant Fairburn, "Okay...one more volley at that corner bunker, then cut it off."

Patchett's face registered agreement. He asked, "How many rounds will that leave us, Lieutenant?"

"Six per gun, Sergeant Major," the Aussie replied.

Patchett grimaced as he calculated: *Six rounds times four guns...twenty-four rounds total. Just barely enough if we need to exploit a success...or cover a retreat.*

"Get Able and Baker Companies moving," Jock told his radio operator. "Let's take a bunker or two from these bastards while their heads are still spinning."

Lying flat on his belly, Lieutenant Theo Papadakis felt he could reach out and touch that corner bunker— the one Charlie Company had failed to take in their attack two days ago. Crawling forward with the lead squad of his company—Able Company—Papadakis was close enough to see the bunker for what it was: a long, low earthen mound, overgrown with vegetation, with narrow firing slits carved just above ground level.

Although the artillery fire had shattered wide swaths of coconut palms and heaved up mounds of earth all around, the bunker didn't seem to be damaged at all. But no shots had come from it.

They were only 50 feet away.

"I'm gonna put a grenade through one of them shooting holes, sir," the squad leader whispered to Papadakis.

He pulled the safety pin...rose to a kneeling position, his arms splayed like a baseball pitcher delivering a killer fastball...

And that was as far as the sergeant got. The Nambu machine gun opened up from the bunker and cut him down.

The grenade fell to the ground at Papadakis's feet, its safety lever gone, its fuze burning. If he hadn't felt it bounce off his boot, he might never have noticed: his head, like everyone else's, was pressed tight to the ground, hiding from the machine gun bullets.

Four to five seconds until detonation, a voice in his head recited like a drill instructor. That clock had started ages ago.

Four to five seconds...

Had that interval of time ever seemed so long...or so short?

Pivoting his prone body, he grabbed the grenade and flung it with all the awkward strength he could muster toward the bunker.

It exploded halfway there—still in midair— claiming nothing and no one as its victim, leaving only tiny vortices of uplifted dirt and shredded vegetation where the fragments struck.

Theo Papadakis pulled the walkie-talkie to him. "ONLY ONE NAMBU FIRING," he shrieked to 2nd Platoon on the left. "IT CAN'T COVER OUR WHOLE FRONT. GET AROUND AND BEHIND IT…NOW!"

Second Platoon's leader—Lieutenant Squibb—was thinking the same thing even before his company commander's voice spilled from the radio:

If we can get behind this fucking bunker, that could be all she wrote for the Japs. One Nambu shooting through one little slit ain't got enough field of fire to stop us all.

He ordered his men forward.

Squibb was startled when the point man of the lead squad—moving on the dead run—suddenly dropped from sight.

What the fuck? Nobody shot him, did they?

The point man wasn't shot. He was lying in the mud at the bottom of a shallow trench, alive but in much pain.

"My fucking knee, Lieutenant," the point man moaned to the platoon leader. "I think I tore it up. Where'd this fucking hole come from, anyway? Better not be some Jap latrine."

It wasn't a latrine. They'd found their first communications trench: furrows that allowed the Japs to crawl from bunker to bunker unseen and under cover. In one direction, the trench sketched a beeline to their objective: the bunker guarding the southeast corner of the plantation.

In the opposite direction could only be another bunker—one sitting on the southern edge of the plantation. That bunker hadn't fired a shot at them yet, as near as they could tell.

Now or never, Lieutenant Squibb told himself. Motioning for his men to follow, he dashed to the corner bunker.

From inside, the Nambu kept on playing its staccato rhythm of death.

There was an opening on the back side, framed with timbers...

This must be the way in...

He made a grenade his calling card:

Fire in the hole, you sons of bitches!

There was a muffled, uninspired *thud* as it detonated inside the bunker.

Why do grenades always sound so damn disappointing when they go off?

But the Nambu stopped firing.

The lieutenant stepped through the entrance into the dim interior of the bunker. He was surprised—it seemed so much smaller inside than out, its roof so low he couldn't stand straight.

Claustrophobic...that's the word.

The stench greeting him made him lurch backward—a nauseating mix of spent gunpowder, excrement, decay...and death.

Unable to see much—and not wanting to—Squibb slammed his eyes shut and emptied the magazine of his Thompson into the bunker's interior. The sound of his weapon firing in that hellish echo chamber assaulted his body like the blows of a mallet.

Fumbling in his web gear for a new magazine, he opened his eyes...

Shit! They ain't dead!

But they weren't fighting back, either.

He tried to guess how many...*a dozen, two dozen?*

They squirmed like a tangled mass of worms in the muck of the bunker's floor...

Half-naked, sickly, swimming among their own dead, their skin ghastly white canvases for the brushstrokes of blood and mud, trying to get away...

But with nowhere to run.

It looks like that painting of asylum inmates I saw once.

Their mouths were moving but made no sound. Nothing Squibb could hear, anyway—his ears rang like sirens from the blast of his Thompson in these close quarters.

It's like they're begging...but for what? Life? Or death?

He leveled his Thompson but couldn't pull the trigger. Bile was burning its way up his throat.

He lurched for the exit.

Outside the bunker on all fours, the meager contents of his stomach now a small, mucousy puddle on the ground beneath him, Lieutenant Squibb heard the weapons of his GIs finishing what he had been unable to do.

It took Theo Papadakis just seconds to run to the bunker Squibb's 2nd Platoon had just seized. That run ended with him hugging the bunker's front face for dear life: there was withering fire from deeper in the plantation raking its rear side.

These fucking bunkers are laid out in depth, he realized. *The next row is killing us.*

Now what?

He could hear men—his men—shouting from inside the bunker. He slid down to a firing slit and yelled: "SQUIBB…YOU IN THERE?"

"Yessir, I'm here. What do we do now?"

Wish I had a quick answer to that question, Papadakis thought.

"We're pinned in here, Pop," Squibb said. "I've got about half my platoon with me, the rest are in the commo trench to the south. We can't go near the exit…bullets are coming through there like fucking sideways rain. I think I've got at least five men down already."

Papadakis asked, "Does your radio work?"

"Don't think so. I've been trying to call for artillery, mortars, anything. No one's home."

"I'll call it for you," Papadakis replied. "How far out there you figure the next line of Japs are?"

"No fucking idea, Pop. Take a guess."

"Okay, I'll do it. Sit tight."

Jock had the artillery on the way within seconds of Theo Papadakis's call.

Studying the attack diagram, Jock picked up the mic and said, *"Trenchfoot Six,* this is *Dry Rot Six.* Can you move down the commo trenches to the adjacent bunkers, *over?"*

"Not real sure, *Dry Rot,"* Papadakis replied. "I've got guys in the south trench but they're pinned down. Looks like the next bunker—behind this one—finally woke up, *over."*

"Are there other trenches? *Over."*

"Not that I can see...but I can't see a whole lot right now. My head's up my ass. We're getting creamed here, *over.*"

The four Aussie howitzers let fly their first salvo.

Patchett mentally clicked off the ammo count: *Twenty rounds left.*

The artillery rounds screamed over Able Company's heads and impacted about 50 yards deeper into the plantation.

Cutting it a little close there, Papadakis told himself.

But the Japanese fire seemed to wane.

"Repeat," Papadakis said. "I say again, repeat, *over.*"

Four more rounds screamed over Able Company. *Sixteen rounds left...*

The Japanese fire thinned to sporadic rifle shots.

"Okay," Papadakis said, "I think I've got an opening. I'm gonna hook up with *Mildew Six* on my left and push toward the south, to that next bunker, *over.*"

"Roger, *Trenchfoot.* I'm committing *Green Mold* to exploit on your right, *over.*"

"Roger...and thanks. I could use some cover from *Green Mold* on that flank. Better give me one more volley from the cannon-cockers, too, *over.*"

Jock asked, "You sure you need that? We're tight on rounds, *over.*"

"I'd feel a whole lot better if I had it."

"Twelve, dammit," Patchett mumbled as the Aussies let the rounds fly.

Charlie Company—call sign *Green Mold*, with Lieutenant Havers now in command —was the battalion reserve for the attack. Major Miles had just committed them to exploit Able Company's gain; Havers was scrambling like a chicken with his head cut off to put his company into action.

Tom Hadley, his first sergeant, took Lieutenant Havers aside. "Are you sure you want to do it this way, Lieutenant?" Hadley asked. "You're sending in one platoon at a time. That's asking for trouble. All the platoons should attack at once...you know, *massing of force* and all that."

"We need to be cautious, Tom," Havers replied. "Let's probe first to see what we're getting into."

Hadley bristled; he didn't know Havers very well. Certainly not well enough to be on a first name basis:

And his tone—like I should be grateful he's lowering himself to be my buddy. Pretty snobby for a rookie C.O. fresh out of the box.

Worse, several GIs had overheard the way the new company commander casually addressed him. That sort of informality could cripple a unit's chain of command in no time flat. If he'd learned anything at all from Melvin Patchett, it was to never let a slip of discipline go uncorrected—not even for a second.

"With all due respect, sir, it's *Sergeant Hadley.* Even *Top* would be okay...if you don't mind."

Without looking up from his map, Havers replied, "Sure, *Sergeant.* Whatever you like. Now let's quit screwing around and get this show on the road."

Chapter Twenty-One

Able Company owned the bunker in the southeast corner. Theo Papadakis—*Trenchfoot Six*—left Squibb's platoon to defend it. With his other two platoons, he moved south along the commo trench toward the next bunker. Tony Colletti—*Mildew Six*—and his Baker Company would distract the Japanese in that bunker by feigning a frontal attack from the swamp. Once Colletti had the attention of the Japanese, Able Company's two platoons would slip around and behind the bunker...and take it, too.

It was the best chance they'd had so far.

But the battalion radio net began to tell another tale: *Trenchfoot Two-Six*—Squibb's platoon at the corner bunker—was being overrun. The Japanese counterattack was coming from their right flank—exactly where Charlie Company—call sign *Green Mold*—was supposed to be covering.

"We're dropping the ball real bad, sir," Tom Hadley told Lieutenant Havers. "Able Company's getting the shit kicked out of them because we ain't where we're supposed to be. We've got to push forward—right now—with the whole damn company on line."

"You heard what First Platoon said after they got pushed back," Havers replied. "The Japs are already there in force. We can't cut them off now."

"In force, my sweet ass, sir. Couldn't be more than a platoon or two of Japs doing the counterattack. If it was, we wouldn't *have* a First Platoon anymore. They'd all be dead...instead of milling around here with their thumbs up their asses like the rest of us."

Lieutenant Havers didn't seem to be listening. "Our only chance," he insisted, "is to go around and behind the Japs hitting Able Company—"

"That ain't gonna help anybody, sir," Hadley said. "It'll be too little, too late. If we're gonna pussyfoot around, we might as well save our energy and just call in the artillery and mortars on them."

Havers smirked and shook his head. "You do remember Battalion cautioning that we're low on artillery and mortar ammo, don't you, Sergeant?"

"Yeah...but as long as we've still got it, using it's better than getting everyone killed, sir. I'm pretty sure Battalion would want it that way."

"Negative, Sergeant...we'll do like I said. Let's get the company swung around to sweep from the north, platoons in column. Third Platoon will lead."

"No, sir...not in column. We've already made that mistake enough today. We need platoons on line...more firepower up front that way."

"Sergeant, did I not make myself clear?"

"Please, sir...at least two platoons up and one back, then?"

Havers shook his head. "Negative. I want my platoons in column. No more discussion. Now let's get moving."

It all fell apart so quickly. Theo Papadakis and his company were no longer on the offensive, seizing ground from the Japanese. They were the defenders now, in a desperate fight for their lives.

He'd lost contact with Squibb's platoon at the captured corner bunker.

Worse, he was taking brutal fire from that direction—the one direction from which, just a few moments ago, he'd felt safe.

Something's fucked up with Charlie Company, I'll bet, Theo told himself. *There should be nothing but GIs behind us, not Japs.*

Something else I'll bet...that never would've happened if Lee Grossman was running Charlie, instead of that greenhorn Havers.

He was taking brutal fire from another direction, too. It had to be coming from bunkers deeper in the plantation.

The wails of his wounded men—a growing chorus singing a song of mortal fear—wove around and through the constant racket of gunfire.

Most of the men still able to fight were sprawled in the mud at the bottom of the commo trench, crammed shoulder to shoulder. The rest scuttled behind trees, darting back and forth, not sure in which direction to seek cover from the crossfire.

It no longer mattered how well Tony Colletti's Baker Company was keeping the Japs in the next bunker occupied. Theo Papadakis—and what was left of his Able Company—would never be able to seize it now. They'd never get there alive.

Papadakis keyed the walkie-talkie and said: "ALL TRENCHFOOT UNITS, THIS IS SIX...PULL BACK. REPEAT, PULL BACK."

He didn't realize how loud he had spoken until he looked down the trench: he was the only man still there.

The rest had heard and heeded his command long before their platoon and squad leaders could relay it.

Charlie Company's sweep from the north progressed at a snail's pace—it had covered only a few hundred yards so far. Surprisingly, it had met no resistance.

"We're not moving fast enough, sir," Hadley told Lieutenant Havers. "At this pace, Christmas will be come and gone before we make contact."

Havers replied, "You're mighty eager, aren't you, Sergeant? Didn't your mother ever teach you *haste makes waste?*"

Tom Hadley remembered another expression his tough-as-nails mother—a West Virginia miner's wife— had often told each of her many sons, something quite different than the lieutenant's cliché: *Son*, she would say, *don't fuck up.*

He decided to keep that piece of wisdom to himself. They were already past the point of prevention and well into the *fuckup.*

Over the chatter of distant gunfire, another sound made itself known: the dull *poom poom poom* of cannons firing from a mile or more away.

They weren't the Aussie cannons—their sound was coming from the opposite direction. The wrong direction.

Within seconds, the whine of incoming shells drowned out every other sound—even the beseeching voices of the combat-experienced men like Tom Hadley, who were screaming, "INCOMING! HIT THE DECK!"

The rounds' impact shook the ground like an earthquake, shattered some trees, and loosed the bladders and bowels of Charlie Company's rookies. As the rain of debris from the explosions subsided, First Sergeant Tom Hadley made a decision: it was time to take command of this idiot circus before they got wiped out to the last man.

"CHARLIE COMPANY, PULL BACK," Hadley roared. "MOVE IT! ON THE FUCKING DOUBLE!"

A few yards away, several green troopers huddled on the ground, paralyzed with fear.

"GET UP AND RUN," Hadley bellowed at them.

"Fuck that," one of the troopers said, his trembling voice at least an octave higher than normal. "We need to take cover."

"NO, DUMBASS," Hadley replied, kicking the speaker firmly in the backside, "WHEN THE ROUNDS ARE COMING DOWN ON YOUR HEAD, YOU TAKE COVER. WHEN THEY'RE NOT, YOU RUN LIKE HELL OUT OF THE KILL ZONE."

The dull *poom poom poom* sounded in the distance once again...

And this time, every man who still could ran like hell.

It wasn't much of a run to the rally point, only a few hundred yards. Once there, Charlie Company's men would have been content to keep running all the way to the airfield at *So Sorry*, but First Sergeant Hadley corralled and quickly reorganized them. A headcount was not encouraging: there were fifteen wounded, six of them stretcher cases that had been dragged out of harm's way by their comrades. The lieutenants who led 1st and 3rd Platoons were among the badly wounded.

There were eight men missing. Among them were the other two company officers: the leader of 2nd Platoon and the company commander, Lieutenant Havers.

Dammit, Hadley told himself, *that puts me officially in charge. Those junior officers don't last too long, do they?*

He called four names: "Wozniak, Simms, Mukasic, McCleary...saddle up. You're coming with me."

PFC Wozniak raised his hands to the sky as if beseeching heaven and asked, "Why are we so fucking lucky, Top?"

The first sergeant grabbed him by the web gear, jerked him to his feet, and replied, "Because, wiseass, I need experienced people. I ain't got time to wipe some rookie's ass right now. Come on...we're going to go find our missing guys."

Corporal Bogater Boudreau had long since run out of ammunition for his Thompson. But it didn't matter—as long as he was stuck in that corner bunker, he had a seemingly inexhaustible supply for the Nambu machine gun.

And them dumbass Japs keep walking right up and let me cut 'em down. They ain't figured out it's a GI behind this gun—and it's pointing right at them.

But this little ruse de guerre of mine is about played out. Maybe it ain't such a swell idea to be rear guard after all.

And I don't remember volunteering to do this alone...but I'm the only son of a bitch in here who's still drawing breath.

He was expecting the grenade that sailed through the bunker's entrance.

A pile of dead Japanese provided ample cover.

But the explosion finished off whatever hearing Bogater had left.

As he pulled himself from under the shelter of the corpses, he tried without success to shake off the awful ringing in his ears.

But I'd rather be deaf than dead any day, the Cajun told himself as he picked up a Japanese rifle and dropped the two soldiers who entered the bunker with one shot each. Each squeeze of the trigger made nothing but a muted, mechanical *clank* in his crippled ears, more felt than heard.

Pretty good shooting...considering you gotta cycle the fucking bolt on these Jap rifles after each shot. Ain't they heard about semi-automatic yet?

But it's time to get the hell out of here.

Hoisting a Japanese corpse before him like body armor, he burst out of the bunker.

Nobody fired at him.

He didn't stop to wonder why. He dropped the lifeless shield and ran.

That's when Mother Nature decided to open her faucets once again.

The deluge took the sprinting Bogater Boudreau by complete surprise: *Usually, you hear it coming, that shisssh of rain sweeping across the jungle is hard to miss...*

Trouble is, I can't hear nothing but that high C note in my ears...and now, with this rain pouring down, I can't see shit, neither...

Where the hell am I?

He wasn't the only man lost in the rain.

Out of the curtain of falling water walked another soldier.

He might have been 100 feet away...

He might have been 10.

They saw each other at the same time, hesitated for just an instant as they processed whether *friend or foe.*

Both decided *foe.*

Both squeezed their rifle's trigger.

Neither weapon fired.

"Fucking Jap piece of shit," Boudreau spewed as he cycled the Arisaka's bolt.

Damn. It's empty.

Never taking his eyes off his adversary, the Cajun searched his trouser pocket for another clip.

Don't tell me I lost the son of a bitch...

The Japanese soldier found his new clip with little fanfare. He loaded it into his rifle with a chop of his open hand...

Slammed the bolt home...

And caught the stock of Boudreau's rifle squarely against the side of his head.

Just like Babe Ruth swinging for the fences, Bogater told himself. *I believe I killed the little bastard. Split his head open like a melon dropped off a truck.*

"So sorry about that," he said out loud, "but, you know...it's *kill or be killed, mon frère.*" Snatching the loaded rifle from lifeless hands, he added, "Tell you what...I'll trade you."

Now all I gotta do is figure out which way's east...

The Japanese artillery was silent now as First
Sergeant Tom Hadley and his four-man detail searched
for their company's missing along the plantation's edge.
The sounds of the fight for the corner bunker—so
tumultuous a few minutes ago—had dwindled to
sporadic gunshots that seemed more like afterthoughts
than signals of battle.

"How come the Jap artillery shut off?" PFC
Wozniak asked as he tried to wipe the rain from his face.

"They're probably just as low on ammo as we are,"
Hadley replied. "Shut the fuck up and stay alert."

They entered a grove where the trunks were scarred
as if they were the artifacts of some demonic whittler.
There were more signs of the artillery's handiwork, too:
the drops of viscous pink painting the terrain—some
small, some in fist-sized globs mixed with scraps of
olive drab fabric—the detritus of a life's sudden and
violent end refusing to be flushed away by the
downpour.

"Well," Hadley said, his voice flat, "looks like we
found at least one of them. Okay, split up and spread
out. See if you can at least come up with dog tags. But
keep on your toes, dammit—this is still Indian country."

Under a pyramid of broken trees, Tom Hadley
found Lieutenant Havers.

He was still alive...barely.

A broken but stout tree branch, sharpened like a
spear when sheared from its lofty home, had run the
lieutenant through.

Now, its tip impaled in the ground, it held Havers face-up in mid-fall, his lifeblood slowly trickling down its shaft in rivulets of deep red to mingle with the rainwater puddling below.

He's as good as dead, Hadley knew, *just like my big brother was when that boiler blew up and ran a pipe right through him. Take that branch—that spear—out of him, and he'll bleed out in a second or two.*

"Get me the medic," Lieutenant Havers commanded.

The tone of Havers's voice—so demanding, so entitled, so full of the patrician arrogance Hadley had endured as a boy from the offspring of bankers, lawyers, and coal mine bosses in his West Virginia town— dissolved whatever compassion he might have had for his dying commander.

Just like that asshole platoon leader who got himself killed up on the mountain back at Port Moresby—who was it? Oh, yeah...Lieutenant Wharton. Shit, I damn near forgot his name already.

"The medic," Havers demanded. "Where the hell is he?"

"He'll be along in a minute, sir," Hadley lied. "Let me help you out in the meantime...Sorry, sir, but this is going to hurt a bit."

Before Havers could sputter another word, Tom Hadley wrenched the branch—with Havers still attached—sideways and out of the ground.

Then, his foot firmly against the lieutenant's chest, he yanked it out of Havers's body...

God forgive me.

It was all over quickly: the arrogance in the lieutenant's eyes faded, replaced by a blank stare that seemed focused on some other dimension.

In his last seconds of life, he seemed to be saying something, an inaudible whisper Hadley felt sure he understood:

Fuck you, Tom.

As he took one of the dog tags from Havers's neck, Tom Hadley remembered an old poster he had seen on a barracks wall back in the States. It said: *Death Comes Quickly...Treat Immediately.*

Chapter Twenty-Two

General Hartman was red-faced with annoyance. They could imagine smoke pouring from the general's ears as he said, "In other words, gentlemen, you've failed again."

Jock and Colonel Molloy winced for just an instant before placing the appropriate expressions of contrition on their faces. They well understood how the army game of blame assessment was played: it was their fault the attack on Duropa Plantation had failed, and that's all there was to it.

"Major Miles," the general continued, "I'm going to put a stop to this *attack through the plantation* obsession of yours. It's getting us nowhere."

The general stepped to the map and, stabbing a finger repeatedly into the shaded area representing Buna Village, said, "You're going to shift your focus to a direct attack on Buna."

Colonel Molloy decided this was the time to speak up. "But that's an attack across nothing but swamp, sir, it's—"

"It's *what,* Colonel?" Hartman interrupted. "I hope you weren't planning to say it's *suicide.*"

"No, sir," Molloy replied. "I was going to say *extremely difficult.*"

What Molloy wanted to add but didn't: *and extremely unlikely to succeed.*

It was obvious from Hartman's expression he didn't care how difficult Dick Molloy or Jock Miles thought it would be.

"I'm going to tell you gentlemen what MacArthur told me," Hartman said. "Take Buna...or don't come back alive."

Jock and Colonel Molloy exchanged a fleeting, worried glance: *this is crazy talk.* If MacArthur actually said those words, he was nuts. If General Hartman believed them, he was nuts, too...

Because it ain't the generals who do the dying.

"May I make a suggestion, sir?" Molloy asked.

"By all means, Colonel," Hartman replied, his tone not in the least bit cordial.

"This campaign has, so far, taken a frightening toll on Eighty-First Regiment. Major Miles's battalion is—after only a week of combat—down to fifty percent of its fighting strength—"

"Much of that is from sickness, not wounds in action," Hartman interrupted.

"That makes no difference, sir," Molloy replied.

"I'm well familiar with your regiment's casualty figures, Colonel," Hartman said. "Get to the damn point."

"Those casualty figures *are* my point exactly, sir. One could say we already are, to a very great degree, *not coming back alive.* Now that the other two regiments of this division have finally joined us here on the north coast, it would be greatly appreciated if they could help in assaulting this stronghold which, to our collective shame, we greatly underestimated."

General Hartman couldn't have looked less sympathetic.

"And while we're talking about reinforcements, sir," Molloy continued, "where do we stand with getting the artillery and tanks we've been begging for?"

Finally, there was a slight smile on Hartman's face. "Molloy, I'm glad you brought those topics up together," he said, "because they're joined at the hip. We can't bring in tanks and artillery vehicles until we have a nearby harbor. It looks like the best candidate is a place down the coast called Oro Bay, about fifteen miles east of here. From there to here, we'll need to build a wide road through the jungle, complete with bridges to cross the many rivers and streams along the way. Now, gentlemen, I'm going to share something with you that I do not—and I repeat, *do not*—wish to become general knowledge, lest it cause panic among the troops. MacArthur suspects that since we're putting so much pressure on Buna, and the Aussies on Gona and Sanananda, the Japanese are—despite their weakened naval position—about to risk landing seaborne reinforcements of their own. Perhaps as much as a *division.* Therefore, I must ensure that all our coastal installations—the airfield at Fasari and the one under construction at Dobodura, any port we may establish, and any roads connecting them all—are well protected. I've assigned that vital task to Eighty-Third Regiment."

Molloy asked, "What about Eighty-Second Regiment, sir? What'll they be doing?"

"MacArthur feels it's best that they augment the Aussie division. It's time we finally gave our steadfast allies a bit of a helping hand."

Jock and Colonel Molloy exchanged another quick glance, one of frustration this time. They were both thinking exactly the same thing: *As usual, politics is dictating tactics...and we're going to take our lumps for it. Again.*

General Hartman had one more point to make: "You gentlemen already know MacArthur's position on the artillery—as long as you have the support of our Air Force, they're all the artillery you need. Learn to employ it better. Now, do you two gentlemen have any further questions?'

Neither Jock nor Colonel Molloy said a word.

"Good," Hartman said. "You're dismissed. Go and bring me a victory."

As they walked from Hartman's CP tent, Jock said, *"Learn to employ it better*, my ass. Colonel, I don't believe the general's been paying attention."

Through clenched teeth, Molloy muttered, "Affirmative, Jock. *Operation Easy Street*, my aching ass. Hasn't been a damn thing easy about it."

Andoom Clipper was making good time as she sailed along the Papuan coast. "Fifteen knots, on average, I reckon," Jillian Forbes said to the US Army captain standing beside her on the bridge. Easing her helm left to glide past the shallows of a reef, she added, "We'll make Oro Bay before sundown."

The captain—Marcus Concavage, US Army Engineers—had nothing to say in reply.

Jillian found the whole situation amusing: *Leave it to the Yanks to send an army man for a navy job. Look at that frown on the wanker's face…I don't think he believes we'll be there when I say we will. Bloody hell, it's only a day's sail. He's been a nervous wreck ever since he came on board. Wound a bit tight, I'd say…*

And he's not happy about a sheila driving the boat, that's for bloody sure.

Something else was bothering Captain Concavage, too. Pointing to the Aborigine man ministering to the *Clipper's* engine, he said, "I'm still not sure why that *abo* needs to be on board, Miss Forbes."

"Like I told you back at Milne Bay, Nigel is the best engine mechanic I know," she replied. "Far better than I am at keeping her running. Surely you can appreciate that, Mark."

She watched him tense as the familiar form of his name rolled off her lips. She'd done it intentionally; after spending all morning trying to foster a more comfortable working arrangement with this stick-up-the-ass Yank, she'd gone for broke.

"*Captain Concavage*, please, Miss Forbes. I can't let my men think it's okay to abandon proper military etiquette and discipline just because we're…"

He didn't seem to know how to finish the sentence.

She glanced down at the rest of her passengers: a US Army survey team—one old, fat sergeant and two privates barely out of their teens. They lounged on the main deck among piles of gear, their shirts and boots off.

Military discipline, my arse, she thought. *Looks like his lads think they're on a bloody vacation cruise.*

She asked, "Because we're *what*, Mark? In mixed company? In the middle of nowhere?"

"Yes," Concavage replied, "all of those things, I suppose, Miss Forbes."

"You know, Mark, this isn't the first time I've worked with the US Army."

She didn't bother to add *and that last lot was a hell
of a lot tougher and far more interesting than you and
your wankers.*

"Regardless, Miss Forbes. I must insist we address
each other properly at all times."

"Fine, Captain Concavage. In that case, I must insist
you refer to me as *Captain* Forbes."

"But, that's not..."

Again, Concavage floundered, not knowing how to
finish his sentence.

"I'm a licensed ship's master. That earns me the
title of *captain.*"

The Yank seemed wounded; he hadn't seen that
parry coming.

"Get used to it, Mark," Jillian said.

There were almost two hours of daylight left when
they reached Oro Bay. Captain Concavage's team
wasted little time: in minutes, sounding lines were over
the side as Jillian gently maneuvered *Andoom Clipper*
around the potential harbor. By sunset, the initial survey
was complete. Oro Bay was deemed a suitable harbor
for the coastal and inter-island freighters that made up
the bulk of the Allied transport tonnage around Papua.

"I'd bring my *Esme* in here any day," Jillian said,
well satisfied with the day's work.

A delicious thought crossed her mind: *I'm only
about fifteen miles from my Jock, I think. Close enough
to walk.*

The heavy radio, with its hand-cranked generator,
was ferried ashore in the *Clipper's* pram. Soon its

message was acknowledged by Milne Bay and Port Moresby: this was the place to build a harbor.

As he savored a cup of hot coffee from the *Clipper's* galley, Concavage said, "Once we get the landing ships the Navy's promised, we can even bring in tanks and all sorts of heavy vehicles."

"You don't have to wait for the bloody Navy," Jillian replied. "Beatrix's ship, the *Java Queen*, used to carry railroad cars. Tanks won't be a problem for her. All you blokes need to do is come up with a lighter big enough to float them ashore. Shouldn't be much of a challenge for Yank geniuses like you."

Looking bewildered, Concavage asked, "Beatrix? You mean there's another ship captained by a girl?"

"A woman, Mark," Jillian corrected. "She's a woman. Just like me."

Chapter Twenty-Three

Jillian awoke to the clanking of tools. The sky was already turning pink at its eastern fringe; the sun would rise very soon. Nigel was fussing with the *Clipper's* engine.

"Everything all right, Nigel?" she asked.

"I suppose, Miss Jilly," the mechanic replied. "Better safe than sorry."

Jillian glanced at the narrow beach. The pram was still there, just where the Yanks had left her last night. Captain Concavage and his team had spent the night on shore with the equipment they'd shuttled from the boat so far. They'd come back for the rest first thing this morning, and then she'd be free to weigh anchor and return to Milne Bay. There'd been no point continuing the risky process of unloading in the darkness; she wouldn't dream of trying to sail back through those hazardous waters at night, anyway. She went below to make coffee.

At first, the chattering of the old, dented coffee pot on the burner masked the sound from outside, until it became too loud to be ignored:

Airplane engines...and they don't sound like Yanks or Aussies, either.

Jillian rushed out to the deck. The first thing she saw was Nigel cradling the hunting rifle they kept on board: *pirate insurance*, they called it.

The second thing she saw was the jagged-V formation of six Japanese planes in the dull gray sky— single-engined fighters—low over the water, no more than a mile offshore.

One by one, they peeled away, forming an accelerating column that descended straight to the anchored *Andoom Clipper*.

"GET IN THE WATER, NIGEL," Jillian shrieked.

She dove overboard, propelling her body as deep into the watery darkness as she could.

Just when she thought her lungs would burst, she heard the *swoosh* of bullets piercing the water's surface...

And then the explosion—its shattering roar amplified by the water—that shoved her still deeper like a giant hand.

Melvin Patchett seemed lost in thought. Jock asked, "Something on your mind, Top?"

Picking up the operations order from the field desk, Patchett waved it like a flag and replied, "Much as I like this little plan you and Colonel Molloy cooked up, sir, I think I know what's gonna happen. Y'all are asking to get yourselves relieved...maybe even court-martialed."

"It's worth that risk, Top."

"But the general specifically said he wanted a full-blown regimental attack on Buna, didn't he? This ain't nothing more than that *recon in force* business all over again...and it's kinda light on the *force* part. Most of our battalion's still going to be on the edge of the plantation, sitting on the balls of their asses, marking time."

"Consider them my reserve, Top. In the meantime, we can say they're there to block those reinforcements everybody's so damn sure the Japs are going to land. And what's the difference, anyway? We don't have a snowball's chance in hell of just walking up the road into Buna without serious armor and artillery support."

"You don't have to convince me, sir…but it just looks like we ain't even *pretending* to do what General Hartman ordered. Not by a long shot."

Melvin Patchett's voice took on the fatherly tone Jock hadn't heard directed at him in quite a while. "I know what y'all are trying to do, sir," he continued, "and I surely do appreciate it. So do the men who won't be dying in this shithole quite yet. But we like having you around, Jock Miles…and Colonel Molloy, too. I guess I misjudged that man—turns out he's all right. Now, we don't want the brass thinking you both slipped into *casualty avoidance mode*. Don't ever forget that MacArthur knows your name…and in your case, that's a bad thing. He'd make an example outta you in a fucking heartbeat."

"Thanks, Top," Jock said. "I appreciate the sentiment. I really do. But those are my orders…at least until we get the firepower to do this job right."

Patchett shrugged, and then replied, "As you wish, sir. Now, speaking about *casualty avoidance mode*, are you good with having Charlie Company commanded by an NCO?"

"What do you mean? I can't think of a better man for the job than Tom Hadley, Top. Can you?"

"No, sir, I sure can't, neither. But it's a natural fact that an outfit run by sergeants is gonna be a lot less likely to take the initiative…especially when that initiative involves bloodshed. That's why *this man's army* thinks so highly of its officers. They don't seem to mind getting people killed as much…present company excepted, of course, sir."

"You really believe that's true?"

"I guaran-damn-tee it, sir."

A sly grin crossed Jock's face. "Then maybe we should offer Hadley a battlefield commission, Top."

An equally sly grin was on Patchett's face now. "And I would strongly advise him to refuse it, sir. He don't need hisself no gold bar. Besides, if I buy it one of these days, you just might need him to fill my shoes. That's a damn sight more important than minting yourself another mustang."

She thought she'd never make it to the surface. The need for oxygen, the convulsive panic, the growing certainty these were her last moments on earth, all rolled together into a darkening maelstrom...

But suddenly, her watery grave began to lighten; the surface was just above...just an arm's length...an inch...

A burst of air filled her lungs—a life-saving infusion that quickly had her choking on the fumes of burning diesel. She was adrift in a field of shattered wooden planks that once formed the proud hull of *Andoom Clipper*.

Between her and shore was a spreading pool of floating fire. She couldn't tell how long or wide the pool was.

"NIGEL," she yelled, "NIGEL...WHERE ARE YOU?"

There was no answer.

She did a quick inventory of her physical state: *Now that my lungs have stopped aching, I think I'm all right.*

The offshore breeze was pushing the pool of fire slowly toward shore.

If I stay behind it, I'll make it to the beach...eventually. It's not far...I've swum a hundred times farther than that before. Please tell me Nigel's not hurt. But if he stayed on the boat...

She tried not to think about it. Tasting the still-unburned diesel coating the surface of the water around her, she thought, *If this lot starts to burn...*

But the flaming pool began to diverge into smaller pockets, dwindling and snuffing themselves out as the floating diesel was burned off. After minutes that seemed like they'd never end, Jillian was ashore.

The pram hadn't moved: *Why aren't the Yanks trying to help? You'd think they'd at least want to try and salvage their equipment, some of which is still bobbing around out there in the bay.*

Where the bloody hell are they, anyway?

Jillian walked into the trees, where she thought she'd seen the Yanks' campfire glowing last night.

Pretty stupid of them to light a fire when you don't know who's around. It's got to be here somewhere...

She found it. The fire was snuffed out.

So were the lives of Concavage's three men.

They were dead in their bedrolls, each man's throat cut.

That explains why there was no noise...

But where the bloody hell is Marcus Concavage?

She heard the crunch of vegetation being trampled. It sounded very close.

Able Company was the unit Major Miles picked to probe along the road leading to Buna Village. That didn't bother Theo Papadakis even as he told himself, *It's not much of a road, actually, more of a dangerously exposed goat trail on a strip of dry ground just a little above swamp level, with occasional dense stands of trees—perfect places for the Japs to pull off ambushes.*

What did bother Lieutenant Pop was the unit on his left flank: Colonel Vann's 3rd Battalion:

I wouldn't trust those useless sons of bitches to mind my dog, let alone cover my ass. They're supposed to be probing along a trail about a mile west of us. But they're moving so damn slow we keep getting way ahead...and I end up with nobody protecting my left flank at all. But we've got to maintain contact with them—I think I'll detail Bogater Boudreau and his squad to that job.

When Boudreau finally found some of 3rd Battalion's men, they were huddled at the edge of a grove, taking cover behind the stoutest trees they could find.

"Get down," a sergeant hissed at Boudreau, "there's a sniper in those trees up ahead."

Bogater replied, "So? Shoot the son of a bitch."

"No," the sergeant replied. "If we don't shoot at him, he won't shoot at us."

"Oh, for cryin' out loud," Boudreau said, as he turned to one of his men. "Curly, swap me your M1 for a minute."

"You looking for a Purple Heart, pal?" the sergeant asked.

"Don't need one, Sarge. I already got two," the Cajun replied. "Give me that damn M1, Curly."

"Ahh, c'mon, Bogater," Curly replied. "Let me do it."

"Nah...you city boys can't shoot for shit." Offering his Thompson in trade, he insisted, "The rifle, please...that's a fucking order, Private."

Binoculars in hand, Boudreau asked, "All right...which tree is this dead Jap in? Oh, never mind. There he is."

"You'll never hit him," the sergeant said. "He's at least three hundred yards away."

"More like two hundred, Sarge, and I can shoot the eye out of a bayou gator at two hundred yards."

Boudreau's first shot splashed against the tree trunk, so close it made the sniper flinch.

"Hmm...a little left," the Cajun said and squeezed the trigger again.

The shot knocked the sniper from his perch. His body dangled lifelessly from its tether, high in the air.

"There," Bogater said, "just let the bastard hang. Now then, Sarge, where's your C.O.? We gotta get you boys moved up about half a mile. First Battalion's got its *derriere* sticking out in the wind with y'all dug in way back here."

Crouching at the edge of a grove, the men of Able Company could see the rooftop of Government House, the long, one-story building that had once been the Australian district headquarters at Buna Village. Just to its east was a cluster of similar buildings that comprised

Buna Mission. Jock, having joined the company for this probe, asked its commander, "How far do you figure to Government House, Theo?"

Papadakis replied, "A mile, sir...maybe a little more."

"Yeah, that's what I figure, too," Jock said. "I can't believe we haven't run into any Japs yet. Not that I'm complaining..."

About a half mile up the trail was one more grove, a broad island of cover and dry ground jutting from this unforgiving swampland. To get to that grove, you had two choices: you either walked down the road in plain sight, like lambs to the slaughter, or you slogged through the swamp and took what little concealment the swamp grass offered.

"Spread your platoons wide and use the swamp, Theo," Jock said.

Without a hint of reservation, Lieutenant Pop replied, "Roger, sir."

They could hear the steady *thrum* of aircraft engines growing closer. Spotting the first flight—a quartet of American P-40 fighters streaking toward the village at low level, Jock said, "Even better...while they're hitting Buna, maybe they'll distract the Japs enough to mask our advance. Get your men moving, Theo...and pray those flyboys do us some good for once."

They were halfway to the next grove when the Japanese machine guns concealed there opened up on Able Company. They had no place to take cover except the noxious water of the swamp.

"It's like hiding in a fucking toilet," Papadakis said. "I'm calling in the Aussie artillery, sir. We need—"

"No, hold up, Theo," Jock interrupted. "They can't shoot with the Air Force overhead."

Half-crawling, half-swimming the few yards to his radio operator, Jock asked, "You got those planes up on the net?"

"Yes, sir," the radioman replied, handing Jock the walkie-talkie.

"Good," Jock said. "Let's give them another chance to see if airplanes really can be as good as artillery."

Tracers were rising up from anti-aircraft guns within Buna Village, spraying the sky with speeding balls of brilliant light as the gunners zeroed in on the P-40s. Jock's conversation with the flight leader was brief.

"They'll be more than glad to come over and help us out," he told Papadakis. "They're getting their asses riddled over the village. Do all your platoons have yellow smoke?"

"Yes, sir."

"Good. Have each platoon pop one to their front. That should be enough to get the pilots oriented...hopefully."

Papadakis sounded wary as he asked, "So they hit the Japs and not us?"

"Yeah, exactly," Jock replied. "How are your casualties?"

"We're okay so far...two wounded in Third Platoon...not badly, though, sir."

"Let's try and keep it that way. The Japs fucked up, Theo...they've got our range all wrong. Most of this stuff's going over our heads."

"Yeah," Papadakis replied as he scanned the grove with binoculars. "I swear to God, sir...that fire's coming from a bunker just like the ones on the plantation."

"Wouldn't that be hot shit," Jock said. "You've got to hand it to these little bastards. They built up one hell of a fortress on real short notice."

Theo Papadakis had to laugh. "Yeah," he replied, "it's amazing what you can do when there's someone's sword up your ass."

Their spirits plummeted when the P-40s made their first pass at the grove. It was a strafing run with their .50-caliber machine guns.

"That's all they've got?" Papadakis said, genuinely disappointed. "Machine guns? No bombs? Shit...we've already got fucking machine guns. Look how much good they did us so far."

Jock's radio came alive with the flight leader's voice.

"They're coming around for another pass," Jock said. "I told them to strafe closer to the near edge of the grove this time."

"Might as well," Papadakis replied. "I guess the Air Force likes it here. Nobody's shooting at them."

"Yeah," Jock said. "You must be right about those Japs being in a bunker. Their machine guns don't seem to be able to shoot *up*, only *out*."

Papadakis had a new concern: "What about the Jap artillery, sir? Why do you figure they ain't opening up on us? We're in range...and they don't give a shit if they hit one of our planes or not."

"I'm betting they're as low on ammo as our guns," Jock replied. "They're saving it until they really need it."

"Like when they had to blow the shit out of Charlie Company at the plantation, sir?"

That was a memory Jock didn't wish to relive right now. "Yeah, Theo," he replied. "Something like that."

The four planes flew a low circle in trail and lined up for their next run. The third began to trail grayish smoke, which quickly turned oily black. As it closed on the grove, tongues of bright orange flame burst from the stricken P-40.

Already close to the treetops, she snapped over on her back...

And plowed into the ground, snapping tree trunks and digging a furrow through the grove like a meteorite come to Earth.

Just like that, the firing from the Japanese bunker stopped.

Able Company wasted no time racing toward the grove.

When they got there, a startling find awaited them:

It had, in fact, been machine gun fire from a bunker pinning them down.

But the bunker had been cleaved open by the crashing P-40, its engine an unyielding projectile of nearly a ton traveling over 200 miles per hour.

Now, the bunker was just so many mangled logs, charred and torn bodies, and upturned dirt.

From the grove, Jock had a concealed yet unobstructed vantage point for observing Buna Village.

"Dig your guys in here, Theo," Jock ordered. "Let's hold on to this patch of turf for a while."

Chapter Twenty-Four

They're lost, Jillian realized. *We're walking in bloody circles.*

The two stumbling Japanese soldiers holding her captive seemed to be getting weaker and more confused with every passing minute.

They're sick...and wounded, too, she told herself. Look at those bandages...they're filthy. Festering. Bloody hell...if I'd realized that, I would've just taken my chances and run. But those bayonets...they look sharp enough even a child could drive one right through you.

There was no question of running now. Ropes wrapped around her torso had her arms—with wrists lashed together—pinned tightly behind her back. A noose had been fashioned from another rope and slipped around her neck. One of the soldiers had a grasp on the other end of the noose rope and used it to pull her along.

Like a dog on a leash, I am.

The soldiers' movements grew more lethargic; their eyes became glassy.

Maybe they'll stop walking, lie down, and slip off to sleep. I could work these ropes against one of those bayonets...maybe take back my knife from that one's belt...

A sharp tug on the noose nearly jerked her off her feet. They were changing direction. The soldiers suddenly seemed more confident, with a tepid burst of renewed energy. The smell of meat cooking drifted through the air. In a few moments, Jillian realized why:

a small camp of lean-to shelters was nestled among the trees ahead.

In the camp were four more Japanese soldiers. One was a lieutenant, complete with sword.

I still remember the rank insignia from their little stay at Weipa.

The soldiers were busy boring holes into coconuts—the task seemed to be causing them great difficulty—and then pouring the milk down their throats.

Old women can crack open coconuts with ease. What's wrong with this lot?

They must all be sick.

Seated on the ground nearby were four nuns in full habits, the black cloth torn, tattered, and filthy. No bonds held them in place. They seemed to be patiently waiting their turn to drink. One appeared to be middle-aged: *Mother Superior, probably.* Jillian put the ages of the other three as very close to hers: *mid-to-late twenties, I reckon.*

Not far away stood Marcus Concavage, lashed to a tree, looking battered and in shock. His vacant stare seemed focused a million miles away; he didn't notice Jillian being brought into the camp. He didn't seem to notice much of anything.

Using the free end of the noose rope, the soldiers tied Jillian by her neck to a tree not far from the Yank captain. Almost choking her, they pulled the rope tight, leaving her stretched in an awkward and painful *parade rest*, body rigid, hands joined behind back.

Concavage still seemed oblivious.

"Marcus," she whispered, "what in bloody hell happened to you?"

He didn't seem to hear her. He just kept staring straight ahead, gazing into some alternate reality only he could see.

The Japanese lieutenant put six coconuts on the ground and motioned to the older nun. She gave one to each of her charges, set one aside for herself, and carried the last two to Jillian and Concavage.

"Do you speak English, my dear?" the nun asked with a thick Irish brogue.

"I bloody well do," Jillian replied.

"Ahh, wonderful...an Australian," the nun said. "Here...drink."

She held the coconut to Jillian's lips. It was difficult to regulate the milk's flow: Jillian's head, lashed against the tree as it was, could not tilt back to catch all of the refreshing liquid. A good deal of it ran down the front of her bound torso.

"That's all right, Sister," Jillian said. "I'm not very thirsty. I was sipping coffee on my boat not that long ago."

"What's your name, child?

"Forbes. Jillian Forbes. What do I call you?"

"Sister Benedicta. Was anyone else with you, Jillian?"

"My mechanic...Nigel...I'm afraid..."

"That's all right, dear girl. He's in the hands of our Lord." The sister pointed to Concavage. "Do you know this poor man?"

Jillian explained how they came to be at Oro Bay. When her story was done, she asked Sister Benedicta, "Are you their...prisoners?"

"Technically, I suppose," the nun replied, "but it seems to be a somewhat more *symbiotic* relationship now."

"What the bloody hell do you mean, Sister?"

She pointed to the wild pig roasting on a makeshift spit. "They supply the food, and we provide the medical care." Benedicta winked when she said *medical care*. "We're nursing sisters, don't you know?"

"How do you converse with them?"

"The lieutenant—that beastly young man; that murderer—studied in Paris for a few years, so with my schoolgirl French, we get by. It's a shame those studies didn't impart some western civility in him. Actually, I think he's quite homesick for Japan."

"He's more than homesick—he's got some jungle disease or another. They all do. And all their wounds are infected. You can smell it."

"Of course they're infected, child. We've seen to that."

Jillian looked at the nun with a mixture of awe and respect. "Then maybe you could see to getting me untied, too, Sister? This is all a bit overdone, don't you think? What is it with these bloody Japs and their fondness for ropes?"

From their vantage point in the grove, Theo Papadakis and the men of Able Company watched as the attack planes pummeled the Japanese at Buna Village. The hail of bombs and bullets went on all morning and well into the afternoon; six waves of aircraft came and went, the waves separated by an hour or so. By the third wave, Lieutenant Pop's men—as well as the airmen overhead—noted the lessened volume of anti-aircraft fire. By the fifth wave, there was none at all.

"Them anti-aircraft guns...they probably ran out of ammo," Sergeant Major Patchett said.

Papadakis replied, "They'll just get more and use it against us when we attack." He didn't sound defeatist, merely resigned and girding for the next struggle.

Melvin Patchett frowned, raised an eyebrow, and asked, "More? From where, Lieutenant?"

"You heard the rumors, Sergeant Major...they're bringing in supplies and reinforcements during the night...on barges and submarines."

Patchett pointed to the planes darting overhead and said, "Don't you think the Air Force would have spotted them, Lieutenant? Even if they showed up here at night, it's a long ways to anywhere, and boats don't move that fast. They'd get caught out in daylight somewhere."

Papadakis wasn't convinced. "What about submarines? You can't see them when they're underwater."

"They ain't gonna be underwater if they're anywhere near shore around here. It's too damn shallow. And I ain't no sailor, Lieutenant, but from what I hear about them pig-boats, they ain't hardly got room for their crew inside, let alone passengers or cargo."

Still unpersuaded, Theo Papadakis shook his head and replied, "I don't know...they just seem to have this shit figured out better than us."

It was Patchett's turn to shake his head. "Lieutenant," he began, "I'm sure as hell hoping you ain't been pumping them fairy tales to your men. Major Miles and me got enough trouble keeping the damn rumor mill under control. With all due respect, sir, we sure as hell don't need no officers greasing them wheels. Besides, that little ol' plane crash taking out that bunker over there just might be the *cat-list* we've been looking for."

Papadakis looked confused: "The *what*?"

"*Cat-list*, Lieutenant...You know, something that lets something happen that couldn't happen before."

"Oh, yeah," Papadakis said. "That."

Patchett added, "Y'all enjoy the night in this nice, dry hunk of tropical paradise...and tomorrow—once the rest of the battalion gets here—we just may find ourselves a way to take that li'l ol' village over there."

It might've been a *nice, dry* night in the grove if it hadn't rained steadily until midnight, soaking everyone to the bone once again. The offshore breeze that followed the storm blew in something the GIs didn't want to hear: the faint, puttering sound of engines coming from the seaward side of Buna. Unmistakably nautical.

"See?" Theo Papadakis said. "Rumor, my ass, Sergeant Major. I told you the Japs were bringing stuff in at night."

Melvin Patchett's acknowledgement was simple yet irritated: "Shit."

Jock Miles's reply was slightly more expansive: "Dammit. No wonder we keep hitting a brick wall."

Whatever those vessels were, their stay was brief; the sound of engines drifted away quickly. The night became still and quiet—you might dare call it peaceful.

Each man in Able Company's perimeter—officer and enlisted alike—allowed himself a brief interlude to imagine he was not at war, not stuck in this soggy hell called Buna. Thoughts drifted to home, to loved ones, to happier times...bittersweet memories that fortify a soldier's will to keep going while leaving his heart torn and aching with loss.

It was a coincidence Jock Miles checked his watch—*0310 hours*—at the exact moment the explosion shattered that peace. It came from west of Able Company's position in the grove.

"Third Battalion's getting hit," Patchett said, his ears sorting the racket of gunfire that came on the heels of the blast. "I ain't hearing nothing but Jap weapons. Ain't those fools gonna fight back?"

The radio frequencies came alive with screaming voices from Colonel Vann's 3rd Battalion begging for fire, begging for reinforcements...

Or just begging for salvation: "THEY'RE EVERYWHERE! THEY'RE EVERYWHERE!"

But in Able Company's perimeter, there was no attack. None of Lieutenant Papadakis's men had fired a shot.

"Negative contact for my platoons, sir," Papadakis said to Jock.

Very good, Jock thought, *they're not panicking...not even in the dark.*

Another explosion rumbled from 3rd Battalion's direction.

"Just a mortar," Patchett said. "Small-caliber stuff. Gotta be Jap."

A new voice shrieked from the radio—Colonel Vann himself:

"I'M PULLING MY BOYS BACK. WE'RE
GETTING FLANKED."

The pitch of Vann's voice raised with each terrified
word.

"Flanked? How?" Patchett said. "We're snug up on
his right, the Aussies are on his left."

The next voice to spill from the radio was cool and
composed. It belonged to Colonel Molloy: "Negative,
negative, *Mudbath*. Stay in position. Artillery on the
way."

"Artillery...swell," Jock mumbled. "How many
rounds did they have left?"

"Twelve," Patchett replied. "And those idiots over
in Third Battalion didn't even shoot their own mortars
yet, neither."

Colonel Molloy was back on the radio. This time,
he was calling Jock. His message was terse: "Proceed
west with all available resources, engage enemy forces
in unknown strength attacking *Mudbath*."

"That's a new one on me," Patchett mumbled. "A
company going to rescue a battalion."

They listened as the first volley of Aussie artillery
impacted to the west.

"Eight rounds left, I reckon," Patchett said. "I bet
they're gonna shoot up every last round before this
thing's over."

"Okay, here's the plan," Jock said. "Theo, take Able
Company west...probe carefully, now...and engage
whatever Japs you find."

Papadakis asked, "Should I leave a platoon here to
hold the grove, sir?"

"Negative, Theo. Take all your firepower with you."

Papadakis didn't like that idea. "I don't know, sir," he replied. "If we leave, we may never get it back."

"That's the chance we've been ordered to take, Theo."

Patchett asked, "Where are you gonna be, sir?"

"I'm going to Third Battalion CP...maybe between me and Colonel Vann, we can sort this thing out."

"Very well, sir," Patchett replied. "Where do you want me?"

"Get with our staff...make damn sure that when Baker and Charlie Companies get here, they go where we need them..."

"Wherever in hell that may turn out to be," Patchett said, finishing Jock's sentence perfectly.

"Theo, one more thing," Jock said. "Don't walk into our own artillery. Your job's going to be hard enough."

Chapter Twenty-Five

The first person Jock ran into at 3rd Battalion CP was Colonel Molloy. "I'm sorry I had to pull your guys out of that great position," Molloy said, "but General Hartman ordered me to do it. I tried to change his mind, but—"

"I understand, sir," Jock replied.

"No, Jock, you don't understand the half of it yet. Hartman's convinced we've got the whole damn Imperial Japanese Army storming our front. I say that's bullshit...this is just more of their night probing, trying to get us to panic...and it sounds like that's exactly what Vann's people are doing. Again."

Jock asked, "Are the Aussies helping out on the other flank?"

Molloy laughed. "Fuck no," he replied. "They're smarter than that...and they're determined not to let our confusion become their problem. They say if we pull back, they're withdrawing all the way to *Pompano*."

Moving along swamp trails was hard enough in daylight. At night, it was inviting disaster. By the time they had walked half a mile, most of Able Company's men had fallen off the trail into swamp water at least once.

One terrified private swore he landed on a crocodile.

Bogater Boudreau tried to shake some sense into the man. "If you did," the Cajun corporal said, "you wouldn't be standing here to yack about it. Trust me on that, *mon frère*."

"But I felt it! It moved! I—"

Bogater wasn't buying it. "Do us all a big favor, McConnell, and shut the fuck up. Look at the bright side...now that you're all wet, nobody can tell you pissed your pants. Get moving."

Boudreau addressed the rest of his squad: "If I see one more fucking flashlight come on, I'm gonna shove it up your ass until your belly button glows. All you gotta remember about crocs and gators is stay away from the teeth. The rest of it can't hurt you much. And if one's in your way, shoot it in the fucking head."

Able Company had advanced a few hundred yards farther when a machine gun began raking the trail.

The first two men in the column were erased in the blink of an eye.

The third man, Theo Papadakis, found himself in swamp water up to his chin.

He knew what and who it was slicing up his company:

That ain't no Nambu! It's a fucking thirty cal! Our own guys are shooting at us!

He grabbed the two men closest to him in the water.

"Follow me," Papadakis told them as he pulled them forward.

One of the men, a private crouched so low in the water the helmet on his head looked like a floating turtle, asked, "Where the hell are we going, Lieutenant?"

"That's our own guys shooting at us," Papadakis replied. "We're going to make them stop. Now follow me. That's a fucking order."

"But what about the crocs?" the private asked, on the verge of tears.

Papadakis replied, "What are you more afraid of...a croc or a machine gun? Come on, dammit."

It didn't take long for the trio to slog alongside the machine gun emplacement. The gunners, focused on the trail, never saw them coming.

Theo Papadakis stood up, covered in muck like some comic book swamp monster, and bellowed: "HEY, SHITHEAD! WHO THE FUCK DO YOU THINK YOU'RE SHOOTING AT?"

The gun went silent.

He was startled to see three Japanese faces—just as startled—staring back at him in the glow of a parachute flare.

But the gunners were only startled for a moment. They began to swing the machine gun toward Theo Papadakis.

His grenade dropped right in their midst...and blew them to kingdom come.

Theo and his two men crawled out of the swamp water and onto the dry ground. They found the US-issue Browning .30-caliber machine gun toppled on its side.

"Some sons of bitches in Third Battalion gave up a thirty," Papadakis said.

"Maybe they got it taken from them, sir," a sergeant said, "and they're dead."

Theo Papadakis shook his head. "Knowing those useless bastards," he said, "they gave it up and ran like scared little girls."

Able Company pressed on. They had yet to encounter a trooper of 3rd Battalion.

And they encountered no more Japanese.

"If we go much farther," Papadakis said, "we're going to have to start talking Australian again."

There was a commotion ahead—men scared out of their minds, running and yelling in American English:

"HURRY UP, LOUIE...HELP ME WITH GEORGE...BEFORE THE BASTARDS CATCH UP WITH US."

Four GIs—Louie, George, and their two buddies—ran right into Theo Papadakis and a group of his men.

"Hey, wait a minute...calm down," Theo said, corralling the petrified GIs. "Where the fuck are you guys running to? And where are your weapons?"

"We're getting out of here, Lieutenant," came the reply, "and you should to, if you know what's good for you. They're coming."

Papadakis asked, "Who's *they*?"

"Who do you think? The fucking Japs."

Growing weary of all this, Theo rubbed his head and said, "You know, we've been all over your position. We've seen exactly three Japs...and we killed them."

"But they're everywhere, Lieutenant!"

"They're everywhere...and nowhere," Theo Papadakis replied. "Everywhere and nowhere, dammit."

A flare popped overhead, casting the swamp in its ghostly, flickering light.

There was no one to see in the flare's glow but themselves.

Once dawn broke, four facts became unmistakably apparent:

The Japanese casualties littering the alleged battlefield could be counted on one hand.

Third Battalion was in hopeless disarray. It would take a day or longer to re-establish their position opposite Buna—provided the Japanese let them.

The casualty count for 3rd Battalion boiled down to zero killed, zero wounded, and two missing.

"The crocs probably got them," Jock mumbled.

Finally, Jock's 1st Battalion, through no fault of their own, had suffered the worst. While they were rushing to aid 3rd Battalion—aid it was now obvious hadn't been needed—the Japanese had reoccupied that choice position in the grove in force.

Probably with fresh troops that landed last night, Jock feared.

Able Company, with the help of the just-arrived Baker Company, tried to retake the grove. Both companies were exhausted before they began, Able from the night's needless adventure, Baker from the all-night march from the plantation to rejoin the battalion. As the casualty reports began to trickle in, Jock ordered, "That's enough. Call it off. Pull back and regroup."

With great disgust, he summed up the night's action: "That was a big step backward."

As if the fiasco never happened, General Hartman found something else on which to vent his displeasure. Lining up Jock and Colonel Molloy in his sights, he began: "You both deliberately ignored my orders. Explain to me, Colonel Molloy, why only one of Major Miles's four companies was where I ordered them to be?"

"Three companies, General," Molloy said. "There are only three companies in First Battalion."

"Why the hell is that, Colonel?"

"Because his weapons company was decimated by a plane crash before it ever got here. Perhaps you recall, sir."

Hartman looked confused, as if this was all news to him. But he recovered his air of disapproval quickly. "Regardless, Colonel. Where were the other two companies?"

Molloy replied, "Two are here, sir, and they did the bulk of the fighting last night. The third, Charlie Company, is still at the coast, near the plantation."

Hartman's face turned a furious red. "And what the hell are they still doing there, Colonel?"

"They're holding that terrain until Eighty-Third Regiment relieves them," Molloy said. "I believe that was your intent, sir, to protect our flank against the Japs reinforcing by sea." He paused, hoping the logic of his statement would sink in, before adding, "Was it not?"

General Hartman's face grew slack as the feistiness drained out of him. He seemed struggling to remember something...

His own words, probably, Jock thought as he watched the confrontation in silence. *I think the old man's losing it.*

Molloy asked, "By the way, sir, where is the Eighty-Third, anyway? We thought you said they'd be here yesterday."

"There's been a small change of plans," Hartman replied. "I've ordered them to secure Oro Bay. The engineers will be there within days to build the road to Buna."

He hesitated, sensing how inadequate his explanation seemed, before saying, "Didn't my staff advise you?"

"We've been pretty busy with the Japanese, sir," Molloy replied. Making a great play of conciliation, he added, "Perhaps we overlooked the message."

Molloy knew differently, though, telling himself: *There was no message, General, because neither you nor any member of your staff can find his ass with both hands.*

But news of the road sounded like a dream come true. In a hopeful, polite tone, Molloy asked, "And with this road, we can expect our artillery and armor support soon?"

Sounding more like a naïve cheerleader than a division commander, Hartman replied, "You betcha, Colonel...and then we'll really show those Japs something!"

But the stern general in him quickly resurfaced, pushing the enthusiasm aside. In harsh, adult tones, Hartman said, "But you will not sit on your asses and wait for it to arrive, gentlemen. You will continue to attack the Japanese with everything you've got..."

His voice faded. This time, at least, he didn't add *or die trying.*

Chapter Twenty-Six

It had been four days since Jillian became the unwilling guest of the sickly Japanese detachment. Sister Benedicta was true to her word: the Japanese lieutenant had been persuaded to ease Jillian's bonds. She was still bound by the neck to a tree, but the noose rope was looser now, allowing a foot or more of movement. Her hands were still bound behind her back, but not as strictly as before, helping to ease the ache in her shoulders and numbness in her hands. The ropes binding her arms to her torso were gone.

She was allowed brief periods to deal with bodily functions. The long tail of the noose functioned as a leash; the soldier holding it would turn his back as one of the nuns helped Jillian, her hands still bound, through the process. On this particular toilet break, Sister Benedicta provided the assistance.

The nun said, "I must ask you, when is your womanly time of month due? I've saved some wadding for you."

Jillian scowled; her period had been the last thing on her mind.

"Why do you care?"

"They must not know you are bleeding. In the primitive religion these savages practice, menstrual blood is considered poison."

Jillian smirked as she replied, "Oh, so they're Christians, then."

"Do not make a joke of this, child," the old nun said. "They will beat you...maybe kill you. We

witnessed several young women from our mission killed
by them in that way."

"Why? Just because they had their periods?"

"Yes, and the Japanese found them handling their
food."

Jillian mulled that over for a moment. Growing up
around the missionaries at Weipa, she was used to
religious hysteria...

*But right now, I suppose it's better to be safe than
sorry.*

"All right then, Sister. If you must know, it was due
last week. I'm usually regular as clockwork but—"

"Oh, goodness," Benedicta said as she hurriedly
crossed herself. "Have you sinned with a man?"

"I certainly have...but we were real careful."

"Perhaps not careful enough, dear girl."

Wanting desperately to change the subject, Jillian
asked, "What if I just ran away right now? That tosser
can hardly lift his rifle, let alone chase me."

"I'd ask you not to do that, Jillian," Benedicta said.

"Why not?"

"Because if you escape when in our charge, they
will kill us. That was the deal I had to make to help
you." Her brogue sounded as somber as a funeral march.
"The Lord has helped my sisters and me survive the
captivity of these...these *creatures*. Don't undo his good
work so carelessly, I beg you."

Jillian had watched and marveled at how Sister
Benedicta and her nuns were, slowly but surely,
sickening the Japanese soldiers. She had been told of
their cache of coconuts—well hidden beneath fallen
fronds, empty and long drained of their sterile milk—

which they repeatedly used to "cleanse" the wounds of the steadily deteriorating men.

The milk in those coconuts wasn't fresh; it wasn't even milk—it was water from a nearby stream.

Everyone who'd spent any time in this corner of the world knew never to drink or wash with water from the streams, creeks, and rivers of Papua. They were nature's sewers, chock-full of disease-causing organisms.

It can't be much longer before these wankers are too weak to move.

"But suppose I *wasn't* in your charge," Jillian said. "If you could somehow get my knife to me and—"

"I'm afraid that's a very dangerous undertaking, too, Jillian."

"All right...slip me something that's sharp. *Anything.*"

Benedicta nodded. "Perhaps I can manage that."

"And for God's sake, Sister, you and the other nuns come with me. Once they're too weak to catch food, you'll starve."

Sister Benedicta shook her head. "We're doing God's work, child, and it's not done yet. He will provide."

Pointing to the delirious Marcus Concavage, bound to a nearby tree, Benedicta asked, "What about the Yank? Would you take him, too?"

"I don't think that would work out, Sister."

It must've been hours since the sun went down; Jillian slumped against the base of the tree that was her prison. Concavage was babbling nonsense: something

about his mother and the Christmas pudding he couldn't
have.

That poor tosser is so off his nut. Could he possibly
know it's nearly Christmas?

There was a soft swishing noise—the sound of a
nun's habit as she walked.

Something was pressed into Jillian's hand. It felt
smooth and cool—and very sharp on its edge. Like a
rock. Or a piece of glass.

Out of the darkness, Sister Benedicta's voice
whispered, "I believe this is your chance, child. God
bless and be with you."

It took a long, frustrating while to free her hands
with the crude tool, and then just seconds to slip out of
the noose. She'd watched the sun's path every day of her
captivity; she knew which way to walk to get back to the
coast.

I can't be far from Oro Bay...but I don't fancy
stumbling for hours through the pitch black jungle, with
all the goodies it has to offer: snakes, crocs, venomous
spiders, wild pigs, falling into hidden ravines...maybe
even more Japs. And I have nothing for a weapon...but
what choice do I have?

Maybe the Yanks will be there already.

As she made her way, walking in circles became her
biggest fear. She was relieved to find the rare break in
the jungle canopy, allowing her to observe the stars and
stay on course.

Jillian had no idea how many hours she had walked
when the sounds of vehicles rumbled out of the
darkness. A few more minutes of walking and she heard
the voices of Americans.

"HELLO," she called out. "I COULD USE SOME HELP, YANKS."

The surly reply: "OH YEAH? HOW ABOUT IDENTIFYING YOURSELF, LADY?"

"MY NAME IS JILLIAN FORBES. I'M MASTER OF THE MOTOR VESSEL *ESME*."

"AND I'M THE FUCKING KING OF ENGLAND."

"NO YOU'RE NOT. YOU'RE SOME BLOODY YANK TOSSER WHO'S TOO STUPID EVEN FOR GUARD DUTY. YOU'RE SUPPOSED TO CHALLENGE ME FOR THE PASSWORD, NUMBNUTS."

A hushed conversation ensued among the still-unseen Yanks.

"YOU DON'T EVEN KNOW WHAT THE PASSWORD IS, DO YOU, YOU WANKERS?"

A different voice spoke up: "JUST COME FORWARD WITH YOUR HANDS UP, LADY. NICE AND SLOW."

Jillian did as she was told and was soon surrounded by a squad of Yanks. Each of her arms firmly in the grasp of a GI, she was marched off, a prisoner once again. It didn't take much walking until the waters of Oro Bay came into view, shaded in the soft light of dawn. Half a dozen freighters were at anchor, unloading their cargoes of men and materiel onto lighters and whaleboats. She knew all the ships on sight, including Beatrix Van Der Wegge's *Java Queen*.

She recognized the small boats, too: *They were in the salvage heap at Milne Bay.*

Soon, Jillian was inside a tent, standing before a US Army colonel. He knew her name; he just wasn't convinced she was the person attached to that name.

"I told you," Jillian said, "my papers went down with *Andoom Clipper*."

"Then how do I know you're not a spy?" the colonel asked.

Beatrix's voice boomed from the tent's entryway: "If you Yanks were any dumber, you'd need help dressing yourselves. Of course she's Jillian Forbes. Who else could she be?" She threw an arm around Jillian and asked, "What happened, schatzi? Did you lose your boat?"

Jillian told her story. As the telling came to a close, she asked, "I suppose you've found the bodies of those three lads from the survey team?"

The colonel nodded, and then asked, "And their captain...you say the Japs have him?"

"Yes, and he's gone completely crackers."

"I see," the colonel replied. "And these nuns? They're..."

He wasn't sure how to finish the sentence.

Jillian helped him out: "They're killing the Japs for you. Just slowly."

The colonel leveled a jaundiced eye and said, "Kind of odd that just you escaped, though. Why are you so lucky, Miss Forbes?"

"Maybe because I'm not doing the Lord's work, Colonel. Just MacArthur's."

The colonel's display of suspicion had finally ground to a halt; Jillian and Beatrix left the tent, triumphant. As they walked toward the beach, Beatrix said, "You gave us quite a scare, schatzi. Pity about your little boat, though...and your poor mechanic, too." Jillian stopped walking and flopped down on a supply crate. "Hold on a minute," she said, grasping her mid-section. "My stomach...something's not right."

"Good lord, schatzi! You're not preggers, are you?" The sudden wetness between Jillian's thighs provided the answer. Her words came out like a sigh of relief: "Definitely not...but I'll need to borrow some trousers from you. I've bloodied mine, I'm afraid."

Now it was Beatrix who breathed a sigh of relief. "I can't tell you how wonderful it is not to have that little problem anymore," she said, wrapping her overshirt around Jillian's lower body. "Actually, schatzi, I would have loved for that to have happened right in front of that idiot colonel, just to see the look on his face. Men can be so squeamish about these things."

When she stopped laughing, Jillian added, "I should count my lucky stars *Aunt Flo's visit* held off until now. I'm told Japanese men can be a lot worse than squeamish."

A lighter slid up on the beach carrying a small tracked vehicle—a *Bren Gun Carrier* in Aussie parlance—armed with the machine gun for which it was named. The soldiers called them "tanks," but Jillian wasn't impressed. As they rumbled off a makeshift ramp onto shore, they didn't seem to her like armored vehicles at all: *They look like cheese boxes on treads.*

"I carried four of them this trip," Beatrix said. The Aussies are going to drive them up to their lads fighting near Buna. If they manage not to break down, they'll be there in a few hours."

Buna was all Jillian needed to hear. As soon as she was in fresh pants from Beatrix's foot locker—a little too roomy but nothing a belt couldn't handle—she quickly found the Aussie lieutenant in charge of the vehicles. "Do you think you could give a sheila a ride to Buna?" she asked. "I've got a Yank I'd like to see up there."

"I don't know, ma'am," the lieutenant replied. "It could be a dangerous trip...and you're not military."

Jillian could feel the blood rising to her face as she said, "Not *military*? I'm military enough to drive a boat that brings you and these bloody *kiddie cars* you call tanks to this hell hole...and I've tangled with the Japs a few times already without any help from you and your lot. So how about it, sport?"

He didn't doubt her determination. She looked ready to throw the first punch.

The lieutenant gave a quick look around to ensure none of the brass were watching. Reluctantly, he said, "Well...all right. Climb in, ma'am."

Beatrix called after her, "Don't stay too long, schatzi. We need *Esme* in the convoy again."

"I'll be back in a jiffy," Jillian replied. She pointed to the sky and added, "Be careful, now. There's nowhere to hide from the bloody Jap airplanes."

There was nowhere for the Japanese to hide from the American and Australian airplanes, either. Huddled in their bunkers, their bodies were safe from all but the improbable direct hit of the bombs.

But their minds were not:

The planes come day and night now
Like an invasion of locusts
Kill one, kill two...it makes no difference
They are millions
Every bomb blast shakes our squalid world
like the earthquakes of home
Pounding our souls flat like the blows of a
thousand hammers
Making us certain of our demise
Shattering our courage to face this
unwelcome inevitable
The blasts come in clusters of ten,
twenty...sometimes more
Multiples of terror
We are helpless
We are hopeless
A crowd of deaths—all different, all the
same—argue over which will claim us

The Japanese soldier closed his notebook. His only hope was someday someone might read it—and learn the truth.

Chapter Twenty-Seven

New and different sounds—unrecognizable at first—began to mix with the constant rumble of bombs dropping on Buna. Soon the sounds grew loud enough to be identified: the creak and growl of tracked vehicles. Men scrambled from the CP tent to have a look.

"Sounds like tanks," Patchett said, with an exuberance he rarely displayed. "We must be getting them bastards after—"

His words stopped dead. The exuberance died with them.

"Shit," he said as the vehicles came into view, "it's just some Aussie Bren Gun carriers. What the hell do they think they're gonna do with those pieces of shit in these parts?"

"Yeah," Jock said, "they'll just stall in the swamps. And they aren't heavy enough to flatten a bunker, anyway. I'd trade all three of those things for one fucking—"

It was time for Jock's words to stop dead. One of the carriers had groaned to a halt. A most unlikely passenger popped out.

"Hooooleeeee sheee-it," Patchett said, eyes wide, jaw dropped, like he had just seen the ninth wonder of the world.

Jock muttered, "How in the hell..."

The woman walked toward them as if her presence was the most natural thing in the world. "You wankers got something to eat?" she asked.

It took a while for Jillian and Jock to unravel from the embrace and kiss. GIs in every direction stopped and stared in disbelief: *Something's bizarre about this little scenario. This ain't supposed to be happening here.*

One GI was unwise enough to make a lewd comment about what the lady was about to do to one of the major's body parts. Bogater Boudreau put him flat on his back with one punch.

"Don't you never say nothing like that about Miss Forbes again," Bogater said, his foot on the man's neck, "or there'll be a line of guys in this battalion waiting their turn to kick the shit outta you."

Jock wouldn't let go of her, even after the crush of the embrace was through. He needed the physical reassurance this wasn't a cruel dream. He asked, "What the hell are you doing here, Jill?"

As she related the story, he wished he hadn't asked.

He had never feared more for her safety than at that moment.

Gently, he tried to trace the fading ligature marks on her throat. She grasped his hand to guide it away; when she did, he saw the flesh on her wrists for the first time. Raw, chafed, and bruised, it looked so much worse than the faint coil pattern pressed into her neck.

Even though he was keeping a respectful distance, Patchett couldn't help but wince when he saw the wounds, too.

"Never mind, both of you," she said. "It's over now."

Her face broke into a devilish smile: "Are you tossers going to feed me, or what?"

She polished off the first C ration meal in short order and asked, "Got any more?"

"Go easy, Jill," Jock replied, feeling worthless for having to say it. "We're real short. We haven't had a food drop in days. Once the airfield up the road at Dobodura opens up, it'll get better."

She hoped he was right about that. He'd lost so much weight; he seemed to be shrinking before her eyes.

"Those Bren Gun carriers I rode in with," Jillian said, "do you think they'll be any help? We started out with four, but one broke down after a couple of miles...and the one I rode in was on the verge of overheating any minute."

Jock's embittered silence was the only answer she needed. She slid closer and wrapped her arms around him.

"It's got to get better, Yank," she said, her voice a soothing whisper. "We'll have all sorts of goodies pouring into Oro Bay before you know it."

Jillian wanted to look deep into his eyes but couldn't; there was no depth to them anymore. They had drained to shallow pools of exhaustion and torment. But something else was floating there, too. She tried to tell herself otherwise, but the evidence was staring her in the face: he was losing hope. It wasn't just Jock: she could smell the despair on every GI she saw.

Even Jock's attempt at a smile couldn't disguise it.

"Can you spend the night, Jill?"

She wanted nothing more than to say yes, to stay, to give him any measure of comfort she could manage.

But she knew she couldn't. She had to get back to her ship.

"I can't, Jock," she replied.

"But how will you get back?"

"I'll hitch another ride. There are enough blokes driving on that trail now. It'll be a main road before you know it."

"But what if there's no one, Jill?"

"Then I'll walk. It's not far."

"What do you mean, *not far*? It's fifteen miles back to Oro Bay."

She gave him the smile you'd shine on a fearful child needing reassurance. "You forget where I'm from, Jock," she said. "To us, fifteen miles is—like you Yanks say—*around the corner*."

"But there might be more Japs…"

Jillian's smile didn't fade as she replied, "After that last encounter, I think I'm more afraid of nuns than Japs."

"I ain't fucking doing it, Tom, and that's all there is to it. You've got me confused with somebody who gives a shit."

Acting Company Commander Tom Hadley looked the new buck sergeant, a Philadelphia wise-ass named Frank Bustamante, dead in the eye.

"Then you're busted, *Bustamante*."

Hadley took a moment to enjoy his statement's alliterative flair before adding, "And you're under arrest."

The buck sergeant laughed out loud—but there was a rising panic in his voice as he asked, "For what, Tom?"

"Failure to obey orders, inattention to duty, insubordination, you name it." Hadley motioned to one of the corporals and said, "Take *Private Bustamante* up to battalion. Tell the sergeant major I'll send the charge sheet along later."

Frank Bustamante made a cocky show of seeming unconcerned. "You can't, Tom. You ain't an officer and you ain't really the fucking company commander. You're just acting."

PFC McCleary, the company's resident scholar, looked up from his well-worn copy of Kafka and said, "He *can*, Frank. If he can order you to put your ass on the line he sure as hell can take your stripes. It's quite logical."

"And actually," Hadley added, "all I was asking you to do is have another look for our missing guys."

"Fuck that," Bustamante replied. "I ain't gonna get my ass shot off looking for corpses. Put me in the stockade, Tom...I don't give a shit. I'm better off there, anyway."

A look of mock disbelief on his face, Hadley said, "Who said anything about the stockade, *Private*? Short of men as we are right now, you think we're going to ship you off to a nice, cozy jail cell back in Port Moresby? Allow me to repeat your own words: *fuck that*. Actually, I'm thinking you'll be staying right here, doing your duty alongside your brothers in arms, while a different disciplinary measure is employed."

"And what the fuck would that be, Tom?"

"Forfeiture of pay," Hadley replied.

Frank Bustamante's face looked truly stricken now. "You can't do that," he moaned.

"He can, Frank," PFC McCleary said, this time without bothering to look up from his book.

"Oh yeah? If you do, Tom, you'll be taking food out of my mother's mouth."

Hadley asked, "How's that?"

"I allot all my pay to her. You take that money, she don't eat."

"Geez, too bad about that, Frank," Hadley replied, without a hint of sympathy.

Still moaning, Bustamante asked, "What am I gonna tell her?"

As he walked away, Hadley replied, "Tell her she should've had a smarter son."

PFC McCleary offered Bustamante one final piece of wisdom: "You know, Frank, if you really wanted to help out your mom's piggy bank, you should've gotten yourself killed. That ten grand life insurance payout would've done her a lot more good than the measly thirty bucks a month."

It was late afternoon before Tom Hadley made it to the battalion CP.

"No luck finding your missing men?" Jock asked.

"No sir," Hadley replied. "The patrol got a little deeper into the plantation before they started taking fire, though. Looks like the Japs might have abandoned some of the outer bunkers."

"About time," Jock replied. "We've only dropped about a million tons of high explosives on them. Any of your guys hurt?"

"Two men wounded, sir. Doc's patching them up right now."

"So they can stay, Tom?"

"One can, sir. Not too sure about the other."

Jock shuffled some papers on the field desk. "I see you're going to court-martial Bustamante."

"Yes sir."

"Good. Sounds like he's got it coming. It's a shame, too, him just getting his third stripe and all. You'd think he'd know better."

"I think he was just trying to test me, sir."

"Well, Tom, I'd say you passed that test. But I've got one little problem...you really want to bust him *and* hit him with forfeiture of pay? Isn't that a little steep?"

"I know it might sound that way, sir," Hadley replied. "That's why the paperwork to stop his pay is going to get lost somewhere between here and division."

A wry smile crept across Jock's face. Melvin Patchett, at his field desk a few feet away, was smiling, too.

"So," Jock said, "you're just going to let him stew for a while, thinking his pay's getting docked."

"Yessir. I figure having a pissed-off guy on the line is better than having no one."

After Hadley left the tent, Jock turned to Patchett and said, "Top, I'd say you trained that young man real well."

Chapter Twenty-Eight

Night is different, Sergeant Mike McMillen thought as he stared into the dark, moonless void beyond Able Company's perimeter. *Everything changes in the dark. Shadows you wouldn't pay a damn bit of attention to in daylight become monsters wanting to eat you...or maybe just Jap soldiers trying to stick you in the gut.*

A match's flame becomes bright as a flashlight. A flashlight becomes a beacon.

You can hear better...or at least hear more of everything. Jungle rain sounds like a toilet that won't stop flushing—and I can hear that fucking creek running like it's right in front of us, but it's a hundred yards away.

The sound of some moron coughing can be heard for a mile. The crack of a branch is like a gunshot.

And the battle raging seven or eight miles away sounds like Armageddon, waiting to swallow you up.

Within seconds, a fire ignited in the distance, an orange dome of brilliant light...

Another fire flared, and then one more.

Suspended in the darkness, the three blazes were funeral pyres on a black canvas.

Mike McMillen had a pretty good idea what was burning. So did the man crouched next to him, Sergeant Major Patchett.

McMillen asked, "That's where the Australians are, ain't it?"

"I reckon so," Patchett replied.

McMillen asked, "You think that's those Bren Gun carriers going up?"

"Hell yeah," Patchett replied, "every last one of them, it looks like. Damn fool Aussies were using tracers. Didn't anyone ever tell them those things work both ways?"

"You think the Aussies were trying a night attack?"

"Doubt it," Patchett replied. "More likely it was the Japs doing the attacking. Stay on your toes, Mike. If them Nips feel like roaming around in the dark, they may come visit us, too."

"We're ready," McMillen said.

"You'd better be. Oh, and Mike...Merry Christmas."

"Oh, yeah. You, too, Sergeant Major."

The Japanese came to visit in less than five minutes. The night instantly devolved into the swirling, deafening, and incomprehensible melee of combat.

Silhouettes raced through the darkness, appearing and disappearing like pop-up targets in a shooting gallery.

Some men yelled in rage and bloodlust.

Others screamed in mortal agony as their lives were stolen away.

And still others cowered in their fighting holes, too terrified to fight...

Too terrified to even move.

Mike McMillen dropped into such a hole. The two GIs in it were curled into tight balls, as if each wanted to be back in his mother's womb.

McMillen smacked them both across their helmets with the butt of his Thompson.

"FIRE THOSE FUCKING WEAPONS RIGHT FUCKING NOW," McMillen said.

He could see the whites of their frantic eyes, shining like marbles in the darkness. No words were necessary; the eyes told him all he needed to know.

"I've done this drill too many times before, assholes," he said, thrusting an M1 into each man's hands. "Just pull the fucking trigger. I don't give a flying fuck where the rounds go. Pull it...NOW."

One of the GIs summoned the courage to speak: "But, Sarge, I don't know where—"

McMillen cut him off. "No fucking *buts*. Shoot the goddamn weapon. If nothing else, it'll keep their heads down. That's all you gotta do."

Each man did as he was told, flinching when his rifle fired as if he'd never pulled that trigger before.

"That's it," McMillen said. "Now keep it up. I'll be coming back to check on you two douchebags real soon...and I better find this hole filled up with empty clips when I do."

It seemed like everything was happening at either light speed or slow motion; there was no in-between. The normal rhythms of life had vaporized into the warm night air.

Light speed: the Japanese soldier racing toward Able Company's CP.

Slow motion: Theo Papadakis cutting him down— cutting him nearly in half, actually—with his submachine gun.

Light speed: the shock wave and lethal fragments of an enemy grenade tearing through the CP.

Slow motion: knocked down and stunned by the blast, Theo Papadakis dragged himself along the ground. He found the CP's field telephone.

He couldn't believe how difficult it was to turn the crank.

Even more unbelievable: the phone still worked.

It was Major Miles who picked up at Battalion. Papadakis's words wheezed out of him: "Fire mission, target Roger Peter Three, shell HE..."

It was too hard to hold the phone anymore. He dropped it, leaving Major Miles's anxious voice still hissing in the earpiece.

For a few, brief moments, life returned to its normal cadence. The sound of men talking, yelling commands, curses, even promises of death to every Jap within the sound of their voices could be heard clearly...

So could the staccato chatter of weapons firing...

And the *crump* of mortar shells—the fire mission he had just called was spraying its deadly mayhem across *Roger Peter Three*, a registration point for mortars and artillery just outside the perimeter.

Then, as if someone forgot to wind the clock, the mysterious whirlpool of combat spun down to slow motion again. To Theo Papadakis's ears, the sharp cracks of gunfire became little more than the *clanks* of a tinker's hammer. Those *clanks* faded—and died.

The fight's over, Theo told himself.

I hope to hell we won.

He tried to wipe his eyes clear with his hand but only made them worse. It felt like he was dragging a wet rag across his face.

Even in the dark, he could tell why: great flaps of skin were dangling from his hand like a torn glove.

No wonder I couldn't crank the damn phone...
What a great Christmas this is gonna be.

And then his world went blacker than the night.

Chapter Twenty-Nine

With sunrise came the reckoning. Jock toured the aftermath of last night's battle with Melvin Patchett at his side.

Patchett's eyes, tough and unshining like ovals of suede, took in the scene at the perimeter near Roger Peter Three, one that was all too familiar. He summed it up simply:

"We took an ass-whupping, sir."

"But we held, Top," Jock replied. There was no hint of boast or pride in his words, just exhaustion and resignation.

"Yeah," Patchett said, the word clipped and dry. His eyes panned the field of battle once again and added, "But we paid one hell of a price." He summoned Sergeant McMillen to join them.

"Mike," Patchett said, "you sure all these Japs are dead?"

"Absolutely, Sergeant Major. I saw to it myself."

"Did you have to shoot any of them all over again?"

"Just one."

"That's damn good," Patchett replied. "We don't be needing no more surprises from them sneaky bastards today. How many Jap dead do you count?"

"About fifty-seven, Sergeant Major, near as we could count the ones that ain't all in one piece. Looks like at least two were captains. Three stars sitting on two stripes—that's a captain, right?"

"Sure is," Patchett said. "That means we got hit by more than one company. Probably a battalion."

"Oh, that's just swell," McMillen replied, his voice as sarcastic as he could make it. "By the way, are the natives going to bury all these Japs, just like back at Port Moresby?"

"That's the plan," Patchett said, "but if they don't, maybe we can tear Eighty-Third Regiment away from their *essential duties*, like guarding that airfield that don't need to be guarded."

Jock asked, "What's the word on Lieutenant Pop, Mike?"

"Touch and go, sir. That hand of his is tore up real bad and he's hit in a couple of other places, too. Lost a lot of blood."

Patchett's mind was focused elsewhere: "You notice the same thing I'm seeing, sir? A lot of these Japs died of gunshot wounds. You better believe they were flat on their asses before the mortars ever hit. Otherwise, they'd be chewed up like them other poor bastards scattered in pieces all over the place."

"Yeah, I see that," Jock replied, and then asked McMillen, "What do you make of that, Mike?"

"I tried to keep my whole platoon shooting, sir."

"How successful do you figure you were with that?"

"About fifty-fifty, sir."

"Then you did way above average, Mike. Damn good job."

"Damn right," Patchett added.

"Thanks, sir," McMillen replied. "I heard a rumor that when Third Battalion got hit the other night, only a handful of guys expended any ammo at all. I didn't want that to happen in my platoon."

Jock nodded in agreement. The rumor sounded just about right, based on what he'd seen at 3rd Battalion that night.

"I'm noticing something else, sir," Patchett said. "This is the second time we're seeing actual dead Japs...and this bunch is looking awful well fed, just like the first. These uniforms ain't much wore out, neither."

They all knew what that meant, but Patchett felt obliged to spell it out: "Them sounds we hear from the beach at night—wherever they're coming from, they're bringing fresh meat by the boatload. You don't suppose *His Majesty MacArthur* finally got some intel right?"

"It would be about time," Jock said. "It's about time for something else, too. I'm putting Lieutenant Pop in for a Silver Star. If he hadn't managed to call in the mortars—wounded like he was—we probably would've been overrun."

"Damn right again, sir," Patchett replied.

Something near the edge of the swamp caught Mike McMillen's attention. "Ahh, shit," he said. "Look at that fucking Jap. Where the hell was he hiding?"

Fifty yards away, a Japanese soldier—one leg mangled and useless—was trying to low-crawl away through the swamp grass. If he had a rifle with him, it was submerged in the swamp water.

"Berman," McMillen yelled to a bespectacled private, "put that poor son of a bitch out of his misery."

Hesitantly, Private Berman took a shot with his M1. It missed by several feet.

"Oh, for cryin' out loud," McMillen said. "Never mind, *four eyes*. I'll do it...before he gets away."

Mike McMillen brought the Thompson's stock to his shoulder and took aim.

"God forgive me," he muttered, and let a short burst fly.

The man stopped crawling.

Without saying another word, McMillen walked toward his victim.

"Careful, Mike," Patchett called after him. "Make sure he's good and dead."

"I know the drill, Sergeant Major."

When he was 20 feet from the man—close enough to ensure the head shot wouldn't miss—he fired one more time.

Then he turned—forgiven or not—and slowly walked back to the perimeter.

A runner approached and handed a report to Patchett. He scanned the page in silence.

Jock asked, "How bad, Top?"

"Real bad, sir. Able Company got hit worst. Ten killed, a dozen wounded, four of them evac cases."

Patchett ran through Baker and Charlie Company's casualty lists. Jock took some small comfort: those numbers could have been much worse.

Patchett flipped the page, read for a moment, and made a *tsk-tsk* sound.

"The Aussies got their clocks cleaned real good, too," Patchett said. "Them Bren Gun carriers? Cross 'em off, just like we suspected."

Then the sergeant major told his commander something he knew all too well:

"Technically, sir, this battalion ain't anywhere near combat effective strength anymore. And this whole regiment certainly ain't. Probably the whole damn division, neither."

Trevor Shaw put down his book and patted the cushion next to him, beckoning Ginny Beech to join him on the villa's veranda. Being MacArthur's host and housekeeper were providing far greater challenges than either of them had imagined. They needed to grab moments of relaxation whenever they could.

From inside the house, they could hear MacArthur ranting.

"*His majesty* is in quite a snit," Ginny said as she took a deep drag on her cigarette. "He's worked up about the bloody wankers in Washington telling him what to do again."

"And here I thought he was giving that poor bloke in there with him bloody hell," Shaw said.

"Oh, no," Ginny replied, "General Freidenburg hasn't gotten a word in edgewise yet. I'm not sure he even knows why he's here. Probably thought he was getting invited to Christmas dinner."

Actually, General Robert Freidenburg had a pretty good idea why he was there. He had a map case full of his ideas for Operation Easy Street, ready to show MacArthur. But the supreme commander wasn't ready to hear them quite yet. As his head tracked *The Great Man* pacing back and forth across the drawing room, Freidenburg felt like he was at a tennis match.

MacArthur suddenly stopped, turned to his guest, and said, "Do those fools in Washington really think they can tell MacArthur *anything* about how to run a war, Robert?"

A rhetorical question, for certain, Freidenburg told himself. *I'll just purse my lips and shake my head, like*

I'm agreeing with him. Surely, those stupid bastards in Washington know by now they can't tell him a damn thing.

MacArthur continued, "I will not—repeat, *will not*—consider bypassing Buna, like George Marshall is suggesting, just to keep the casualty figures down to something they can stomach. I will not stop fighting until I raise the stars and stripes over Buna Village. They can't have their war and not expect to spill some blood, too. Now show me what you've got, Robert."

Freidenburg spread his maps across the table. "Our mistake," he began, "was not realizing that the Japanese strong points at Buna, Gona, and Sanananda are essentially *islands*, with the sea on one side and swamps on the other. We need to stop treating their capture as if it's a land attack and employ an amphibious assault."

MacArthur said nothing, just stroked his chin as he studied the maps.

"Of course, sir," Freidenburg continued, "we lack the transport equipment to stage an amphibious assault across vast swamps—we can't truck the necessary boats over land. But we could certainly stage an amphibious assault from the sea."

"But what of naval fire support, Robert? We can't sail capital ships through those treacherous waters."

"That's very true, sir," Freidenburg replied, "but do we really need capital ships? Corvettes, frigates, and all sorts of gunboats are already sailing as far west as Oro Bay. It's only fifteen miles more to Buna and twenty-five to Gona. In conjunction with Fifth Air Force, those vessels can sail close to shore, giving us all the firepower and anti-aircraft cover an amphibious landing needs."

"What about landing craft, Robert?"

"The Australians have retained quite a few from the Milne Bay landings, sir. Many of them are already at Oro Bay, being used as lighters to unload transport ships. Not enough to land an entire division in one wave—but when have we ever had that luxury?"

Deep in thought, MacArthur stepped away from the maps. He began pacing once again but more slowly this time. It didn't take more than a minute for his *eureka* moment to strike.

"Robert," the supreme commander said, "I'm placing you in command of Thirty-Second Division, effective immediately. Relieve Hartman and turn his fiasco around."

Freidenburg fingered the three stars on his collar. "But, sir," he said, "I'm a *lieutenant general.* It would be a demotion to command a division."

"Nonsense, Robert. Not only will you command our Thirty-Second Division, I'm putting you in overall charge of the Aussies, as well. You will be the theater commander, in complete charge of Operation Easy Street. A job certainly befitting three stars. Who knows? Perhaps it will be the path to your fourth star."

Or, Freidenburg thought, *I'll be your perfect scapegoat if this plan doesn't succeed.*

"I'll arrange an airplane for you to leave within the hour," MacArthur said. "You will personally hand-carry the orders relieving General Hartman of his command. For security reasons, I will not broadcast such information over radio channels."

Salutes were exchanged and Freidenburg headed for the door.

"Good luck, Robert," MacArthur said. "I'll bet you never expected to be taking supper at Buna tonight, did you?"

"No, sir, I certainly didn't." He wished his reply had sounded more enthusiastic.

"And Robert...one more thing."

"Yes, sir?"

"I'll tell you the same thing I told Hartman: take Buna, or don't come back alive."

Chapter Thirty

Jock and Colonel Molloy could tell their fate right away. When they stepped into the division CP tent—General Hartman's headquarters—no one would look them in the eye.

"We're getting shit-canned, Jock," Molloy mumbled. "Merry Christmas, dammit."

General Hartman got straight to the point. "Gentlemen, I'll put it bluntly: MacArthur's breathing down my neck for results, and I'm just not getting them from you. Colonel Molloy, I'm relieving you as commander of Eighty-First Regiment. Your XO will take over until a permanent replacement is decided on. You are to report to General MacArthur's headquarters at Port Moresby for reassignment immediately."

Dick Molloy said nothing; he remained braced at *parade rest*.

"Now, as for you, Major Miles," Hartman continued, "I'm having you reassigned to Eighty-Second Regiment. Since that regiment is fighting with the Australians, I believe you'll fit in there just fine, as fond of Aussies as you apparently are."

Shit! Does anyone not know about me and Jillian?

Hartman asked, "Do either of you have any questions?"

They replied, "No, sir," in near-perfect unison.

"Then you're dismissed. Pack your bags, gentlemen."

Dick Molloy was packed and ready for his drive to Fasari in less than an hour. The jeep driver assigned to take him was delighted: he'd have plenty of time at *So Sorry* to grab a hot Christmas meal at the airfield mess, a luxury the GIs stuck in Buna could only dream about. No doubt, the supply sergeants at the airfield, not wanting to waste a precious cubic foot of cargo transport, would want to fill his jeep with materiel for the trip back. They'd done that every trip he'd made, so far.

Maybe it'll be stuff I can squirrel away and sell to some poor suckers.

They were driving on the coast trail only a few miles out of Buna when Colonel Molloy yelled, "STOP."

"What's the deal, sir?" the driver asked as he slammed on the brakes.

"There are men in the brush alongside the road, Corporal," Molloy replied.

Gunning the engine, the driver threw the gearshift into reverse and said, "But they could be Japs! We gotta get the hell outta here!"

"They're not Japs, Corporal. They're GIs. Now stop…that's an order."

A man—an American soldier—stumbled onto the trail before them. Each step seemed an agonizing task. He collapsed to his knees and began to crawl toward the jeep.

Dick Molloy met him halfway. He tried to help the man to his feet but it was no use. He was little more than a skeleton draped in skin, which was hollowed and sunken everywhere there was no bone. His uniform was filthy and in tatters, his boots disintegrating about his feet. On his collar, he wore the gold leaf of a US Army major.

Molloy gently cupped the man's unshaven chin, raised his head, and looked into his empty eyes. Somehow, despite all the severe changes in appearance, Dick Molloy recognized this man.

"Major Henson," he said.

There was a glimmer of recognition in those empty eyes for a moment, and then Ralph Henson replied, his voice a tortured whisper, "Colonel..."

"Unbelievable," Molloy said. "You men of Second Battalion made it off Kapa Kapa after all. How many are you, Ralph?"

Henson seemed to be searching the heavens for the answer before he said, "A hundred...give or take."

My God, Dick Molloy thought. *One hundred...out of the four hundred fine men who I sent on that trek. What a waste...I am the stupidest son of a bitch who ever wore this uniform.*

In time, Colonel Molloy would remember their journey hadn't been his idea: he'd been ordered to send a battalion over Kapa Kapa Trail.

He would mourn forever the loss of those 300 under his command nonetheless.

"Corporal," Molloy called to his driver. "Empty all my gear out of the vehicle."

Molloy began to load as many of the bedraggled troopers of 2nd Battalion as would fit into the jeep. When it could hold no more, he told the driver, "Take these men to the field hospital at Buna. I'll stay here and round the rest up as they straggle in. Come back on the double with as many vehicles as you can find."

"But sir," the driver said, "wouldn't it be better to take them to *So Sorry?*"

"Too far," Molloy replied. "Take them to Buna."

"But your orders, Colonel! You're supposed to be—"

"Fuck the orders. Take them to Buna NOW, Corporal."

The driver looked at the starving men—only inches from death—piled into the jeep. He began to feel guilty he'd wanted to make these starving suffer the much longer journey…just so he could snag a hot meal.

No—*guilty* was too kind a word. He felt like a piece of shit.

"Roger, sir," the driver said. "I'll be back in a flash."

Lieutenant General Robert Freidenburg was on the ground at Fasari three hours after his meeting with MacArthur. The 25-mile-long road to Oro Bay was still under construction by Army engineers but usable. Good speed could be made along the road in dry weather, and it hadn't rained yet today. The jeep carrying General Freidenburg made the trip in less than an hour.

"Your gunboat is ready, General," Freidenburg was told as he arrived at Oro Bay, "but are you sure you don't want to *drive* to Buna, sir? You can be there over the coast trail in about an hour. The boat will take three times as long."

"Negative," Freidenburg replied. "I need to see the overwater route for myself. Consider it a reconnaissance."

The Australian crew of the gunboat—eight men with a *leftenant* in charge—seemed less than thrilled to be spending Christmas Day making this voyage into hostile waters. General Freidenburg tried to lay their fears to rest: "The aerial photos show no evidence of shore batteries at Buna. We'll take a good look around for ourselves before I go ashore at Cape Sudest. An American unit will receive me there."

None of the Aussies bothered to say their collective opinion out loud: *Good luck, chum. Yank intelligence hasn't been worth a bloody fart so far.*

Once out of the general's earshot, one enterprising seaman wanted to start a betting pool on whether they'd encounter Japanese coastal batteries or not. The wager was a non-starter: none of his fellow crewmen would bet against the gunfire. It didn't matter to them what this Yank with the stars on his collar said.

The general found the motoring toward Buna quite congenial: plenty of sunshine, delightful sea breezes. The steady throb of the gunboat's engines was comforting. Sailing less than a mile offshore, he scanned the beaches with binoculars and made copious notes.

"This looks like perfect terrain for amphibious landings," Freidenburg told the boat's skipper.

The *leftenant* replied, "Then how come nobody's tried one yet, sir?"

"Call it *a failure of imagination*, young man," Freidenburg said.

The general checked his map. "I'm estimating five minutes until we're off Buna Mission. That puts us right—"

"BLOODY HELL," the *leftenant* cried as he jammed the boat's throttles full forward.

A string of rail-thin geysers—like the spurts of decorative fountains—stitched a path straight as an arrow across the water's surface.

With one slight correction by the Japanese gunners on shore, the geysers zeroed in on the gunboat. They had her range now.

More guns joined in, throwing shells toward her in shallow arcs, slicing into her wooden hull like a team of skilled carpenters.

The *leftenant* swung the helm hard to starboard.

It only helped for a moment. The boat was quickly zeroed in once again.

"THIS ISN'T SMALL ARMS FIRE," the *leftenant* yelled. "TWENTY MILLIMETER, AT LEAST. THEY'LL CUT US IN BLOODY HALF."

He began to order his crew to return fire, but there was no point...

He had no crew anymore.

They—and the deck guns they manned—had been swept clean by Japanese shells into the sea.

The *thuds, clanks, snaps* and *groans* of the boat's dissection drowned out her engine's soothing throb.

General Freidenburg was still onboard, huddled behind the twisted steel of what had once been a gun mount. As the boat turned, he skittered on all fours to put the scant safety of the metal between him and the gunners on shore.

At least the bloody Yank knows how to take cover, the *leftenant* told himself.

He'd turned her 180 degrees now, gotten farther offshore...

But she was dying fast.

She's shipping too much water...her engines will die any second.

And the Japanese gunners had found her range again.

The *leftenant* yelled to the general, "I'M GOING TO TRY AND PUT HER AGROUND NEAR CAPE SUDEST."

Now low in the water, she'd sink without any further assistance from the Japanese...and soon.

The gunboat went under still a hundred yards from shore.

General Freidenburg and the *leftenant*, buoyed by life jackets, paddled to the beach. A handful of GIs met them in the low surf and pulled the exhausted and shaken men ashore.

"What's your name, First Sergeant?" the general asked one of the soldiers holding him up.

"Hadley, sir. Thomas P."

"What's your unit, Sergeant Hadley?"

"Charlie Company, First of the Eighty-First, sir. I'm acting C.O."

Freidenburg gave him a curious look and asked, "Why's that, son? Where are all your officers?"

"They're all dead or wounded but one, sir...and he's got the shits real bad."

"Hmm, I see."

"Can I ask you something, sir?" Hadley said.

"Go ahead, son."

"With all due respect, sir, what the hell were you trying to do out there in that boat? Didn't the Air Force tell you Buna is a fortress? Anti-aircraft guns work pretty darned good against everything else, too. They sure cut that boat of yours to shreds."

"Couldn't be helped, son," Freidenburg replied. "I needed to do a little recon."

The *leftenant* tried not to burst out in sardonic laughter as he thought, *Or maybe you were just demonstrating a "failure of imagination," you bloody tosser. "Couldn't be helped," my bloody arse. Tell that to my dead crew.*

One of Hadley's men handed the general a canteen. He drank it down with gusto.

"Well, Hadley, Thomas P.," the general said, "You've done me a good turn. Now what can I do for you?"

Hadley replied, "Well, for openers, sir, you can get us our battalion commander back. That might take a lump or two of coal out of our Christmas stockings."

Chapter Thirty-One

General Hartman looked at the orders General Freidenburg had just handed him and smiled. More than anything, he marveled at the economy of the English language:

I'm relieved of my command: fired, sacked, shit-canned, kicked upstairs—whatever you wish to call it.

At the same time, that same word has a different meaning: I'm relieved to be relieved.

In fact, you can say I'm thrilled. This unholy donnybrook is out of my hands now.

Robert Freidenburg found Hartman's idiotic grin ridiculously inappropriate.

Where's this man's sense of dignity? His military bearing?

He wondered if the outgoing commander was of sound mind. All the more reason he needed an answer to a question vexing him ever since he washed up on shore:

"General," Freidenburg said, "I've been told you've just fired the commander of the Eighty-First as well as one of that regiment's battalion commanders. I must ask you: why?"

"Quite simple, sir...their performance was deficient."

The answer earned a *harrumph* from Freidenburg. *That sounds odd coming from a man being fired for exactly the same failing,* he thought.

After giving a quick situation briefing—and a most superficial one at that—to the new division commander, Hartman was eager to depart. He wasn't worried at the moment about the stigma that would undoubtedly be attached to his firing. He could taste the hot food and cold beer of Port Moresby already, perhaps even the safety and comfort of an Australian posting.

The moment Hartman left the tent, Freidenburg told the division G1, "Rescind those relief orders for Molloy and Miles immediately. There's going to be enough chaos around here...I don't need multiple changes of subordinate commands going on at the same time, too."

"But sir," the flustered colonel replied, "Colonel Molloy is probably back in Port Moresby already."

Freidenburg was about to say *then get him back,* when Dick Molloy walked into the Division CP.

After salutes and introductions, Molloy said, "I have some surprising news, sir—Second Battalion of the Eighty-First has finally come off Kapa Kapa Trail...what's left of it, anyway."

At 82nd Regiment HQ—an island of Yanks in the middle of the Australian Seventh Division HQ—a field telephone rang. The sergeant taking the call turned to Jock Miles and said, "Major...hope you didn't unpack yet."

Jock wasn't in the mood for beating around the bush. "Why, sergeant?" came from his mouth like a growl.

"Because you're going back to the Eighty-First, sir. Your orders just got rescinded."

Leaving should've been no problem at all. He hadn't even met Colonel Triplett, the regimental commander, yet and had been assigned no duties in his command. It was only 12 miles back to his old unit; Jock would've walked it—even lugging all his gear—but nightfall would catch him before he was halfway there. Wandering around in the dark was a good way to get yourself shot. He needed a ride, but all of the Eighty-Second's vehicles—scarce as they were—were busy at the moment. He flopped down on his pack outside the headquarters tent and laid in wait to snare a jeep.

He didn't remember dozing off. It seemed dreamlike, though, when something began tapping him on the shoulder rather firmly. When he opened his eyes to see what it was, a reflex shot through his body; he transitioned from repose to standing at attention in less than a heartbeat.

An American bird colonel and an Aussie general hovered before him, looking less than amused.

"You must be Major Miles," the colonel said. "I'm Colonel Triplett. This gentleman to my right is General Vasey. Do you know who he is, Major?"

"Yes, sir. He commands the Australian Seventh Division."

"Very good, Miles," the colonel said. "Now I've just been told you won't be staying with us. Damn shame, too…we could use replacement officers. But before you go, the general would like to pick your brain for a few moments…or will that cut into your beauty sleep?"

Hmm, Jock thought, *first he refers to me as a "replacement" officer, then the "beauty sleep" crack. I'm not a replacement—replacements are rookies and I ain't a rookie. And everyone knows a smart soldier catches his sleep whenever he can. Keep the insults coming, Colonel. It'll be a pleasure not working for you.*

Jock kept his annoyance to himself and replied, "I'm at your disposal, sir."

"The bunkers, Major," General Vasey said. "They're nothing like the defenses we defeated coming across Kokoda. These are some very tough nuts, and we haven't cracked one yet. We hear you've had some success at taking them. Please share with us how you did it."

"I wouldn't call what I've had *success*, sir," Jock replied. "A platoon got behind one once and went in through the back door. Couldn't hold on to it, though. The Japs counterattacked in force and kicked them out. The other time...well, that was just a fluke."

"What kind of *fluke*, Major?"

"A plane did it, sir. It—"

Growing impatient, Vasey interrupted, "You mean a plane bombed it?"

"No, sir. I mean the plane crashed into it. The engine block went through that bunker like a hot knife through butter."

"I see," said the general. "That way doesn't seem bloody practical at all, does it?"

Jock shook his head. "Without big guns or tanks, sir, those bunkers are still going to be here long after we're dead and gone."

Colonel Triplett cast a disapproving glare Jock's way. "That sounds a bit defeatist, Major. Not something I'd expect to hear from an American officer. With an attitude like that, you'll never succeed in taking Buna."

Jock replied, "I really don't think it's a question of attitude, sir."

"I'm inclined to agree with the major," the general said. "I can't wait to hear how your General Freidenburg intends to proceed with this bloody cock-up, now that MacArthur's made him *my* boss, too."

Vasey didn't sound pleased with that turn of events. Not one bit.

"I wouldn't worry about it, sir," Colonel Triplett said. "Bob Freidenburg will have *Easy Street* straightened out in no time."

It was late the next day—the day after Christmas—when Jock finally got back to 1st Battalion. As he threw his gear down inside the CP tent, Melvin Patchett greeted him with a bemused smile: "Couldn't find no work, I reckon?"

"Afraid not," Jock replied. "You're still stuck with me, I guess."

"Worse things could happen, sir," Patchett said as he shook Jock's hand with genuine enthusiasm.

"Have we seen anything of our new general yet, Top?"

"Not since Hadley and his boys fished him out of the drink. But there's a big briefing at Division for all you mucketymucks tomorrow at 0800."

"Is Colonel Molloy back yet?"

"Actually, sir, the colonel didn't get too far at all...and you ain't never gonna believe who he brought back with him."

"I heard a rumor," Jock replied. "He found Second Battalion, right?"

"Yep, he sure did. About a hundred of 'em's all that's left. Seventy-five percent casualties and they never ran into even one Jap. Didn't do the Aussies they were supposed to help a bit of good, neither." His voice dropped to just above a whisper as he added, "Damn shame. The ones who made it here look like they already got one foot in the grave. Another of *The Great MacArthur's* master plans turned to shit."

Theo Papadakis limped into the tent, grinning from ear to ear. His wounded hand was concealed in a mitten of bandages. "Great to have you back, sir," the *Mad Greek* said.

"Theo!" Jock said, truly surprised to see his Able Company commander. "I figured you'd be at the hospital in Port Moresby by now, with nurses catering to your every whim."

"Nah, I'll save that shit for the badly wounded, sir."

Jock gave him a good once-over: Lieutenant Pop was one tough son of a bitch, but at the moment, he looked anything but fit for combat duty.

"I know what you're thinking, sir," Papadakis said, "but I can manage. Besides...my guys need me. *You* need me." He held up his bandaged hand. "Don't worry about this. It ain't my shooting hand."

"But you're beat up all over, Theo...your leg, your—"

"I'm fine, sir...and a lot better off than Lee Grossman is. At least I can get off the crapper now and then. If you'll excuse me, I've gotta check my perimeter before it gets dark."

With Papadakis gone, Jock asked, "Grossman's still here, too?"

"Yep," Patchett replied. "He insists he's gonna be fit as a fiddle any day now. I can't get rid of these officers of yours no how."

Patchett began briefing Jock on what he had missed the past two days. "Basically, sir, it don't look like we'll be doing much of anything until our new division commander gets his britches dried out." Sweeping his hand across the local map, Patchett continued, "We've been using the time to harden our position—we strung out what little barbed wire we could get our hands on along likely avenues of approach, laid in some more mortar registration points across the battalion front, got our fields of fire marked right down to the last rifleman, and rigged a whole shitload of noisemakers. You can see them all marked on the map."

"Yeah...looks good, Top. How's our sick call doing?"

"About the same...a handful of new cases every day. Guys with malaria are, for the most part, going right back to duty, riding out the fevers and the chills as they come. Of course, they're useless as tits on a bull during those times, but we ain't got the transport to evacuate them, anyway. The Atabrine supply is getting pretty low, but Doc's expecting a fresh shipment real soon."

Jock asked, "Are the men actually taking the Atabrine now?"

"Most of 'em are, sir. They're getting used to that yellow tinge it gives the skin." Pointing to his own sallow face, he added, "I tell 'em it blends in with the jungle better, anyway."

"What about quinine, Top?"

Patchett laughed. "Ain't got none. Ain't seen none."

Jock didn't see anything funny in that. "So we're still below combat strength," he said, "and getting worse by the day."

"Affirmative, sir," Patchett replied. He paused, and then added, "But we're still in better shape than those poor bastards who come off the Kapa Kapa."

Chapter Thirty-Two

The Japanese planes came just after midnight, twin-engined bombers droning high in the sky. They scattered their bombs far and wide with no precision, blasting barren swampland more often than any Allied position. It even appeared some of the bombs fell into the Japanese positions near the plantation and Buna Village. The only serious damage done to the Americans was on the airfield under construction at Dobodura: the longest runway—almost finished after laborious clearing and leveling by hand—was now pockmarked with bomb craters and useless. It would take a week or more of backbreaking work to make it right again. Until it was, no transport planes with supplies for Buna could use it; Fasari—some 40 miles away—would remain their closest suitable airfield.

The night bombing served another purpose: it ensured all the Allied troops were wide awake when the Japanese ground attacks began a few minutes after the planes flew away.

Sergeant Mike McMillen was surprised—and well pleased—to find every man in every fighting hole of 3rd Platoon firing his weapon. "Keep it up, you guys," he'd tell the occupants of one hole before scurrying to the next.

The company's mortars were pumping a steady stream of shells toward the enemy. A few of those would be illumination rounds. Any second, their flares would pop, throwing harsh light and crazily dancing shadows across the battleground as they drifted down on tiny parachutes. When they did pop, McMillen figured he could get a fair estimate of how many attackers they faced:

All you see is their motion..

You get a second to count the ones in the open when they first get lit up. You'll see their shapes plain as day—until they freeze.

One or two of them, and it's probably just a squad—or maybe just a few sappers—probing you for a weak spot.

Four or five, it's a platoon.

More than that, you won't be able to count them all before they stop moving and you lose them. You're looking at a company—or better.

Something seemed odd to McMillen about the sound of this fight: *The wounded screaming their fucking heads off—it's a lot more than usual...*

And most of the screaming seemed to be in Japanese.

The flares popped. Mike McMillen could see what all the screaming was about:

Japs caught in the barbed wire, getting their asses riddled. More than I can count...a lot more.

Struggling to free themselves from the wire, they stayed in plain sight—their thrashing silhouettes backlit by the cruel beacons floating down—until bullets and mortar fragments finally ended their misery.

Turkey shoot, McMillen told himself.

At the company CP, Theo Papadakis was starting to get the same impression: *This seems to be going a whole hell of a lot better for us than the last time they attacked.*

His mangled and bandaged hand hung at his side, a grim reminder of that night. In his other hand, he held his Thompson by its trigger grip, its butt against his hip.

One of the field telephones rang. The voice from 2nd Platoon said: "We've lost contact with Baker Company on our right."

"Stand by," Papadakis said. He put down his Thompson and cranked another phone—the one to Battalion—with his one good hand.

"We've got Baker Company on the line right now, Lieutenant," Melvin Patchett told him. "They're saying they lost contact with *you*."

"I'm gonna check it out," Papadakis replied. "I'll be on the radio."

Thompson in hand, walkie-talkie slung over his shoulder, Theo Papadakis set out toward the break in the treeline marking the boundary between Able and Baker Companies.

Fucking guys are probably five feet away from each other but too scared to know it, he hoped. *They should be right around here...somewhere...*

Two fresh illumination rounds popped over the swamp, casting jiggling shadows through the trees before him.

He thought the silhouettes popping in and out of those moving shadows were scrub.

Then he remembered there was no scrub as tall as a man in this wooded position.

The flare's light hung still for a moment, long enough to catch the shape of the helmets...

They were definitely not GIs—and they were maybe 30 feet away...

There was no point in challenging with the password.

He squeezed his trigger instead. He didn't let go. The magazine was empty in two seconds.

One silhouette was still standing.

Theo Papadakis dropped to one knee, propped his Thompson against his bent leg and, with his good hand, pulled another magazine from its pouch.

Then, with his bandaged hand supporting the weapon against his leg as best it could, he tried to ram the magazine home.

The weapon slipped and fell to the ground.

Out of the darkness, there was a sharp, metallic *clack-clack*—like a rifle bolt being cycled...

And then a single shot.

Theo Papadakis felt nothing. He expected a flash of hot, searing pain as the force of the bullet's impact knocked him back.

But he hadn't moved an inch. All he felt was the *thup-thup* of his heart pounding. All he heard were the sounds of the fight still raging far in front of him.

His good hand found the Thompson and brought it back against his leg. This time, he rammed the magazine in and managed to pull the charging handle.

In any other time, the reloading mishap would've seemed brief: it only took a few seconds to resolve. But in combat, those few seconds seemed like hours.

And the silhouette was still there, unmoving...

Definitely not shooting.

Bogater Boudreau's voice came from Lieutenant Pop's left: "I've got it, Lieutenant. Don't shoot me."

The flare's light was fading fast, but Papadakis could make out another shape with a GI helmet— Boudreau, he was pretty sure—blend with that unmoving silhouette. Then they were both gone with a soft *plop* of an object hitting the ground like a sack of potatoes.

Bogater's voice floated out of the darkness again: "His gear was just hung up on that tree, sir. Between you and me, we killed him at least twice. What're you doing out here, anyway, banged up like you are?"

"You guys said you lost Baker Company."

"Yeah...some damn fool over there tripped on the commo wire, sir. Pulled it right out the phone. It's all fixed now. Don't worry yourself none over it."

"Don't worry myself none? Are you fucking kidding me, Bogater? Japs walked right through a gap in our line."

"Looks like we just fixed that, too, Lieutenant."

Charlie Company held the right flank of 1st Battalion; Charlie Company's right flank was the Solomon Sea. They could hear the fight raging at Able and Baker Companies to their left, but so far they'd had no contact with the Japanese this night. Not so much as a stray gunshot came their way.

On paper, elements of the 83rd Regiment—the unit guarding the coast trail from Fasari—were covering Charlie Company's rear.

In reality, Tom Hadley and his men knew better. The GIs covering the coast trail—soon to be the *coast road*—had grown quite fond of high-tailing it back to the relative comfort of Oro Bay each night, leaving nothing but weakly staffed listening posts behind.

Tom Hadley had long ago decided his company would cover their own back door. He'd expressed his reason bluntly: "What's an LP going to do for us when the Japs show up? Say goodbye as those long bayonets run them through, that's what. That ain't what I call *protecting our rear*."

He knew full well there was nothing stopping the Japanese from coming ashore in boats behind his company at any number of places along that 15-mile stretch of coast from Buna to Oro Bay. If they came that way, he had no intention of getting caught with his pants down.

And if they came that way, it would be at night.

That's why he wasn't surprised when one of the positions on the backside of the company's perimeter called for illumination rounds. "Something *clanged* a couple of the noisemakers out there, Tom," the voice on the field telephone said. "Let's see what the hell it is."

At the battalion CP, Jock got the phone call from Hadley just as the first flare popped behind Charlie Company's perimeter. The roar of gunfire filtered through the dense woods almost immediately.

Jock asked, "How many Japs, Tom?"

"Too many to count, sir," was the reply.

"Do you need help?"

"I'll get right back to you on that, sir."

It was nearly five anxious minutes before Tom Hadley was back on the line. By then, the shooting had died out all across 1st Battalion.

"They're either dead…or they ran away, sir," Hadley reported. "Nobody's screaming for mama or the medic, so I guess we're all okay."

Melvin Patchett blew out a big sigh of relief. "If them reports stand the light of day," he said, "we made it through a large-scale attack with just a couple of wounded and no dead. Didn't give up an inch of ground, neither."

As his grease pencil *screeched* across the manpower status board, Patchett added, "I'm real pleased, sir. Our boys handled that real calm-like, and I believe they're gonna be real proud of themselves when the sun comes up."

Jock nodded; he was thinking the same thing.

"Hey, Top," he said, "you think we just had ourselves a *cat-list*?"

"Maybe so, sir," the sergeant major replied. "Maybe so."

Morning broke and the casualty reports from last night's action were confirmed: only a handful wounded in 1st Battalion, none seriously. There were no deaths. The Japanese they faced hadn't been so lucky. Some 50 of them were dead, and the GIs were still counting.

The morning brought more good news: for the first time since leaving Port Moresby, they had mail.

"Best Christmas present we could give these boys is a letter from home," Patchett said to Jock, "even if Christmas was two days ago." Then he added, "You ready to head up to Division, sir? Don't want to keep our new general waiting."

The morning's good news stopped as soon as General Freidenburg opened his mouth. He sounded totally serious in his plan to throw an amphibious invasion at the Japanese stronghold of Buna. Dick Molloy was the only one of the three regimental commanders not too shy to voice his disbelief.

"Begging your pardon, sir," Molloy said, "but didn't you just get blown out of the water off Buna?"

"As I told you already, Colonel," Freidenburg replied, "that was merely a reconnaissance...and it told me everything I needed to know."

General Vasey, the Aussie division commander, sneered at those words. *Merely a reconnaissance,* he told himself, *that cost Australia a ship and her crew. Thank God their sacrifice was so helpful to this Yank wanker.*

Freidenburg continued, "When we stage our assault, it will include proper and effective suppression of enemy fire by sea and air..."

The general paused. He could tell from the look on Colonel Molloy's face he was not convinced. Plenty of other faces in the tent weren't convinced, either.

"Something you'd like to say, Colonel?" he asked.

Molloy replied, "I was just wondering about this *effective suppression* you speak of, sir. The Air Force has been pounding the daylights out of the Japs ever since we got here, and it hasn't done us a bit of good yet. As to naval gunfire, what caliber guns are we talking about, sir, if I might ask?"

"We'll have the use of several frigates, corvettes, and gunboats from both our Navy and the Australians," Freidenburg said.

"So the biggest guns we're looking at are four inches...maybe five inches, tops?"

"That's correct, Colonel."

Trying to keep his voice calm, Molloy replied, "Sir, we've been firing Aussie artillery pieces of that caliber at the Japanese positions for two weeks now...and we haven't made a dent in them yet. Shooting from boats isn't going to make it any more effective...unless those boats are cruisers or battleships with guns twice that size. And from what I hear, the big ships aren't interested in coming into these waters just yet."

There was a murmur of agreement from the other officers. Robert Freidenburg got the distinct impression he was losing this crowd. But he was a *general, by God*—and generals always got their way. The blinding reflection off those three silver stars on his collar never failed to silence the most vocal of subordinates.

"Gentlemen, gentlemen," the general said, "there's been much talk in Port Moresby about how your troops are demoralized and won't fight. That's because they've been led in a manner that is less than, shall we say, *inspirational*. We're going to change all that—right here, right now. Nothing brings *inspiration* like a plan that's truly different—and what could be more *different* than the failed strategy you've been employing than a dynamic amphibious assault?"

He paused to read the faces of the silent men before him: *They're bending to my will—they have no choice, of course—but they're not fully on board yet. I think it's time to puff them up with some bullshit.*

General Freidenburg continued, "Speaking of inspiration, gentlemen, last night I witnessed something truly inspirational. The First of the Eighty-First did a positively crackerjack job against those Japanese probes..."

"Probes?" Patchett whispered loud enough for Jock and Colonel Molloy to hear. "More like battalion-sized attacks, wouldn't you say?"

But the general was still talking: "And seeing the outstanding job that battalion did inspired me to make a decision. Major Miles, you and your men will have the honor of spearheading the amphibious assault on Buna."

That was the last thing Jock wanted to hear; he was sure his face showed it. But for some reason, Patchett had a big grin on his face. He leaned toward Jock and whispered, "The man can make an ass-screwing sound like the sweetest blow job you ever got, can't he?"

"Dammit, Top," Jock said, "he's watching us. Knock it off."

"That's why I'm grinning like a fucking idiot, sir. He thinks I'm telling you how proud our outfit is to get shit on like this. *Spearhead*, my ass."

General Vasey had a question. "Sir, will my Australian troops be involved in these amphibious landings in any way?"

"I'm afraid not, General," Freidenburg replied. "We don't have the boats for it."

General Vasey grinned broadly and made no attempt to hide it. That was the most *inspirational* thing he'd heard in a long time.

Freidenburg wasn't finished with the Aussie commander, though. "You and I will discuss the role of your Australians in the coming operation at the conclusion of this briefing," he said.

The briefing was turned over to the division staff officers—the G2, G3, and G4—responsible for the assault's planning. It quickly degenerated into the usual litany of half-baked estimates and wishful thinking. The only bright spot revealed: the amphibious assault couldn't be scheduled any sooner than 10 days from now. It would take that long to gather enough assault boats at Oro Bay.

"Plenty of time to whip your troopers into fighting shape," the G3 assured everyone.

"Happy Fucking New Year," Patchett mumbled when the assault date of January 6, 1943, was announced.

It was 1100 hours when the briefing finally lumbered to a close. Before dismissing his officers, General Freidenburg said, "Gentlemen, I have it on good authority that your previous division commander was told to *take Buna, or die trying.* I suspect he might have expressed that same mandate to all of you."

Nodding heads throughout the tent confirmed his suspicion.

The general continued, "Well, I'm here to tell you…I don't plan to *try* and I certainly don't plan to *die.* I just plan to win."

As they walked from the HQ tent, Patchett muttered, "Now how fucking *inspirational* was that for a way to close a briefing?"

General Vasey's private talk with his new field commander, General Freidenburg, got off to a rocky start when Freidenburg, with complete sincerity, said, "George, I'm sorry your Aussies won't be part of the amphibious assault."

"I'm *not*, General," Vasey replied, "not in the least. We climbed over the bloody mountains to get here, pushing the Japs back the whole way, while you Yanks rode in leisurely and unopposed on your bloody airplanes. After all that mountaineering, we don't need a bloody swim, too. You're bloody welcome to it."

Freidenburg thought, *Maybe that's why they call him "Bloody George." And here I thought it was because he was such a tough fighter.*

The American general bristled as he said, "Need I remind you, General, it's those American planes that keep you supplied."

"And for that, we are most grateful to our generous ally," Vasey replied. "But what we need most—tanks and more artillery, bigger artillery—your airplanes can't provide. That can only come from the sea."

"And the American regiment fighting with you, General Vasey—the Eighty-Second. I trust you're most grateful for them, too?"

"Of course we are, sir…they make wonderful ammo mules and road guards. And they're very happy to leave the actual fighting to us."

Chapter Thirty-Three

Jock and Patchett had just made it back to their battalion CP when the sound of rifle fire pierced the quiet midday. It didn't sound like a fight was in progress—more like a solitary soldier taking target practice, dispensing well-aimed rounds at a leisurely pace.

"That's an M1 doing the shooting," Patchett said. "Sounds like it's coming from over at Charlie Company."

More curious than alarmed, the two men headed off in that direction.

When they came to the source of the gunfire, it took a moment to sort out what was going on.

A weeping Private McCurdy was standing a few yards beyond the treeline that was Charlie Company's perimeter, M1 in hand, in plain sight of any Japanese sniper who happened to be in range. Across a swampy clearing, tangled in the plantation treetops some 200 yards from McCurdy, was a decoration that hadn't been there earlier that day: a Japanese fighter plane, upside down, its lifeless pilot dangling from the cockpit by one leg still trapped inside. McCurdy would take his time lining up the dead pilot in the rifle's sights, wiping the tears from his eyes before squeezing off another round.

His last shot had been a hit; the pilot's body was still rocking back and forth like a pendulum.

"First Jap son of a bitch I've actually seen in this shithole," McCurdy announced as he pushed another clip into the M1, "even if he was dead from the git-go."

At the shooter's feet was an ammo box still brimming with bullets.

"I could do this shit all day," he added.

A dozen GIs from McCurdy's platoon—men responsible for defending this sector of the perimeter—had left their positions and clustered like grenade bait, watching in aimless silence from a respectful distance. Tom Hadley, the acting company commander, was among them.

"Sergeant Hadley," Jock said, "stop that man from what he's doing immediately. Get him back under cover before he gets his ass blown off."

"We tried, sir," Hadley replied, "but he took a shot at Sergeant Matthews."

Matthews stood next to Hadley, looking none the worse for wear but with eyes full of anger. It seemed likely he would have already shot McCurdy if not for the continuing intervention of Tom Hadley. Now that their battalion commander and sergeant major were on the scene, no one except Private McCurdy was in a hurry to commit a court-martial offense.

McCurdy popped off another shot at the Japanese pilot's body.

It missed.

Patchett asked Hadley, "Ain't that the lad who got all girly over some leeches on him about a week back? You were burning them off him, weren't you?"

"Yeah, that's him," Hadley replied. "Looks like he's really gone off his rocker this time."

Jock asked, "Do you know what brought all this on, Sergeant Hadley?"

"Mail call, sir. McCurdy just found out his wife had a baby. His sister sent the damn letter. Only trouble is, he isn't the father. Even counting for the two months it took the letter to catch up with us—the baby couldn't be his by about three months."

Before Patchett could say, *You want me to handle this, sir?* Jock was already striding straight for the shooter, who was lining up his next shot.

But McCurdy heard the footsteps approaching from behind. He spun around, pointing the rifle straight at his battalion commander...and then he faltered, if just for an instant. You could see the uncertainty flash across his face: there was all this *serious authority* closing in on him.

That gold leaf on his collar...

McCurdy's aim wavered. He knew he was already in deep trouble, but if he pulled the trigger now, he'd open the door to a whole new realm of retribution.

But he didn't care. He'd already made himself an easy target for the Japanese. He couldn't see any difference in whose bullet ended his miserable life.

In for a penny, in for a pound...

The muzzle of the M1 rose, inches from the major's heart...

With a lightning-quick jerk of his hand, Jock snatched the M1 from McCurdy's grasp.

It happened so fast: the private's trigger finger squeezed hard but the trigger was already gone.

Jock's voice sounded like the judgment of the heavens when he said, "We don't desecrate the dead around here, Private. And we don't shoot each other, either."

Grabbing McCurdy by the web gear, he disarmed him of his bayonet as he pulled the man back inside the perimeter. "Turn him over to the MPs at Division," he told Hadley. "And get the rest of your men back in position right fucking now, before the Japs join us for lunch." Turning to Patchett, he added, "Sergeant Major, a word in private?"

They walked out of sight behind a thicket. Jock squatted, his back against a tree. He seemed to be gasping for breath.

"You okay, sir?" Patchett asked. It was then he noticed Jock's hands shaking.

"I...I will be...in a minute, I think. Cover me, will you?"

Melvin Patchett stood guard, watching as his commander passed through the three stages all sane men endure when conquering mortal danger: first, the decisive action that recognizes no fear; second—the stage Jock was in now—the sudden remembering you are mortal after all, and what you just succeeded in doing could have ended instead in a variety of tragedies. Soon would come the third stage: pushing as much as possible of what just happened from your mind so you can get on with the business at hand, knowing full well the memory had taken up permanent, life-altering residence in your psyche.

Patchett waited the few moments it took for Jock to pass into that third stage before saying, "Well, I'm here to tell you, sir, they're gonna be calling you *B-B* from now on."

"*B-B*? What the hell does that mean?"

"*Brass balls*, sir. I can hear 'em clanking together now, matter of fact."

"Cut it out, Top," Jock said as he pulled himself to his feet. "C'mon...let's find Hadley and have a word with him before we head back to the CP."

Hadley found them first. He asked, "Permission to speak freely, sir?"

"Sure, Tom. What is it?"

"I just wanted to say, sir, that what you did...well, that was really impressive."

"No, Tom, it wasn't impressive...just necessary. By the way, you did a pretty good job keeping that situation from getting too far out of hand."

Hadley shrugged and replied, "The way I figure it, sir, we had enough of our guys killing each other back on Cape York."

Jock and Patchett were halfway back to their CP before either man spoke; Hadley's parting words had brought back some painful memories of the ordeal on the Cape. It was Patchett who finally broke the ice: "How do you want McCurdy's charge sheet to read, sir?"

"Make it so they've got no choice but to give him a Section Eight, Top. He doesn't belong here...never did. But he doesn't need to rot for the rest of his life in Leavenworth, either. Life's dealt him a shitty enough hand already."

Patchett mulled that over for a few seconds before nodding with satisfaction. "Sounds good to me, sir," he said. "But, you know, just before he saw you coming, I was pretty sure he was fixing to turn that weapon on hisself."

"Nah," Jock replied, "he may be fucked up...but he ain't *that* fucked up."

Patchett looked skeptical. "I don't know, sir," he said, "and I can still hear them balls clanking."

Over in 3rd Battalion—Colonel Vann's command—
two GIs had decided to become *that* fucked up. Posted to
a stinking, water-logged, mosquito-infested hole that
served as a listening post on the trail between Ango
Corner and Buna Mission, the PFCs took the assignment
as their golden opportunity: a guaranteed ticket out of
this deadly tropical hell.

"If we're wounded so we can't pull duty, they've
got to evacuate us," the first PFC—the more
accomplished *shithouse lawyer* of the two—said. "And
nobody's ever going to be able to tell how the wound
happened."

"And even if they suspect you did it yourself," the
other PFC—a *lesser genius*—added, "they can't prove
nothing, right?"

"Absolutely correct," the *lawyer* said, swept away
in righteous logic. "Just make sure you break a bone.
That's the way out of this shithole forever. Flesh wounds
won't get the job done." He pulled the Nambu pistol he
found after last night's attack and asked, "Are you
ready?"

The *lesser genius* nodded. They began to lay down a
theatrical volley of fire with their M1s. It was a
deception aimed at nothing in particular, since there
were no Japanese anywhere to be seen. The *lawyer*
threw a grenade for good measure.

As soon as it burst, he pointed the Nambu at his
lower leg, closed his eyes...

And pulled the trigger.

He expected it to hurt. But he wasn't prepared for
the blinding pain as the bullet scorched a path along his

tibia and into the thick muscle behind. It was like being stabbed with a blowtorch.

He hadn't expected so much blood, either.

There was nothing theatrical about his screaming. He meant every agonized word:

"MEDIC! MEDIC! HELP ME. OH GOD, HELP ME..."

The Nambu pistol had fallen to the ground. The *lesser genius* decided not to pick it up. Watching the *lawyer* writhe on the ground was fast changing his mind about the wisdom of self-inflicted wounds:

It wasn't supposed to hurt that bad.

Struggling to get his words out, the *lawyer* moaned, "Come on! Do it already! Before help gets here."

The *lesser genius* shook his head and tossed the Nambu into the swamp. He'd take a pass.

He would've been better off if he hadn't. When he raised his head from the hole to hail the approaching medic, a sniper's bullet struck his helmet at the perfect perpendicular, punching cleanly through thin steel as if it was no sturdier than an eggshell, spraying his brains out the other side.

They weren't back at the battalion CP more than a few minutes when Melvin Patchett said, "Sir...you gotta take a look at this."

Approaching the CP tent was a ragged, stumbling column of GIs, perhaps two dozen in number. New fatigues hung on their skeletal frames as if they were department store mannequins. Their heads didn't seem wide enough to fill their helmets. They didn't seem fit enough to put one foot before the other.

"Detail, halt," the sergeant-in-charge commanded, his reedy voice weak and barely audible. On his next command—"At ease"—the men of the detail collapsed to the ground. The only things keeping them from falling flat on their backs were the bulky packs they wore.

As the sergeant walked toward Jock, his steps were so uncertain it looked like even odds he wouldn't make it.

"Sergeant Overton reporting, sir," the man said, offering a wobbly salute.

These men don't look strong enough to stand up in a stiff breeze, let alone fight the Japanese, Jock thought. *Where the hell did they come from?*

Then it hit him: they were survivors of 2nd Battalion. The men of the Kapa Kapa.

Jock asked, "Who on earth sent you men down here, Sergeant?"

"Orders from Division, sir. They said you needed replacements."

Jock's silent reply: *Yeah...and you ain't them.*

"Get these men under shelter, Sergeant Major," Jock told Patchett. "I've got to find Colonel Molloy."

Over the telephone line, Dick Molloy's voice was anything but enlightening. "I didn't know anything about it, either, Jock. Just see if you can find something for those men to do. Maybe they can man some observation posts or something."

"They're so wrung out they can hardly stay conscious, sir," Jock replied. "Putting them in an OP just risks getting us all killed. And it's hard enough to keep the men I already have fed. I don't need more useless mouths."

Even the poor acoustics of a field telephone couldn't mask Molloy's frustration. "I know, Jock...I know," he replied. "But we'll figure something out."

"I'm not so sure, sir. We've got enough going on here already. We don't need to be playing convalescent home to troops who should have already been evacuated—just to make Division's manpower figures look better down in Port Moresby."

Another thing the phone couldn't mask: the tone in Molloy's voice that meant he considered this conversation over. "Tell me something I don't know, Major Miles," he said.

And then the colonel rang off.

The rest of 2nd Battalion's survivors—some 75 in number—were still languishing at 81st Regiment's aid station. Even by the relaxed standards for *combat-ready troops* General Freidenburg had imposed, these men still weren't fit for duty. It would take a considerable amount of nutritious food and uninterrupted rest to rehabilitate them. Neither commodity was readily available at Buna.

They may have been physically weak, but their minds still worked just fine; the ordeal of the Kapa Kapa hadn't blinded them to the realities of the stalemate they had finally joined. One of those realities was on full display in the person of a new arrival, his stretcher lying on the ground outside the triage tent.

"That guy over there," a corporal who survived the Kapa Kapa said, "I heard the docs talking about him. His leg…that's a self-inflicted wound, they say."

"Oh, yeah?" his fellow survivor—a sergeant— replied. "Let's go have a word with him."

They staggered over to the stretcher, looming over the recumbent, immobile GI with the heavily-bandaged shin.

"Hey, bud," the sergeant said, "I hear tell you shot yourself."

"That's a bunch of crap," the *shithouse lawyer* replied. "They dug a Nambu slug out of me."

Shaking his head, the corporal said, "That dog ain't gonna hunt, fella. They say the angle that bullet went in, a fucking Jap would've had to be holding hands with you. And I hear there are Jap weapons laying all over the place out there."

"You don't know shit, my friend" the *lawyer* said. "While you assholes were fucking off in the jungle, I got wounded in combat. Leave me the hell alone."

"I ain't your friend, Private," the corporal said. "You know, we learned something while we were *fucking off in the jungle*, as you say…a little something about emergency first aid. Let us show you how we cleaned out wounds…"

The two survivors proceeded to urinate all over the *lawyer*. He couldn't escape—all he could do was squirm on the stretcher. That wasn't enough to stay dry.

"You'd best close your lying mouth, now," the sergeant said, enjoying himself as he redirected his stream at the man's face.

When they were finished, they buttoned up and started shuffling back to their tent. The sergeant had one thing to say in farewell:

"Fucking coward. I hope they shoot your worthless ass for good this time."

Chapter Thirty-Four

Aside from the daily bombing raids on Buna by 5th Air Force, it had been quiet all along 81st Regiment's positions for the third day running. As a new day dawned on Charlie Company, 1st Battalion—Tom Hadley's outfit—the men were starting to get used to this new level of inactivity. But they knew it couldn't go on forever: higher headquarters was cooking up a new way to get them killed, they were sure.

But until those plans—whatever they were—came into play, the men were very happy to cool their heels. "I could get used to this," a GI named Joey Rossetti said, sprawled in a low hammock he had rigged between two trees from a supply-drop parachute.

His buddy Jimmy Quigley—seated on an ammo box that was gradually sinking into the soggy ground—warned, "You'd better not get used to it. When you drop your guard, that's when a bullet's gonna find you." He took a long swig from his canteen cup and then plunked it down on the crate the two troopers used like a coffee table.

"Cut the crap, Jimmy. When your number's up, your number's up, and you can't do nothing about it." Joey sat up in the hammock and lit a cigarette. "Hey, ain't tomorrow night New Year's Eve? You got any plans?"

"Oh, sure. I suppose I'll do the usual stuff—take my girl out dancing, watch the ball come down in Times Square, then take her home and put it to her like usual."

"You can't," Joey said. "I heard there ain't no ball this year. Blackout, you know."

"No problem. I don't need no lights to get laid."

"Nah, you can't do that, neither. She's screwing some 4-F now."

Jimmy Quigley took another long drink from the cup, set it back on the crate, and—laughing at himself—sighed, "Fuck me..."

There was a sharp *CLANK*—when their eyes fell on the *coffee table* again, the canteen cup was gone.

What the hell?

It only took a second for them to crack the mystery of the vanishing cup: *SNIPER!*

They flung themselves to the ground and began crawling for cover.

Along the way, they came across the cup; its journey had ended in a thicket a few feet from the *coffee table*. There was a neat bullet hole punched in each side, the holes aligned as if drilled by a master machinist.

The whole company got the word in no time flat. Complacency vanished; every man was jumpy. Crouched in a fighting hole, Tom Hadley and a trio of his best sharpshooters peered across the swamp to the treeline marking the plantation's eastern edge. Treetops still supported the upside-down Japanese plane and its dead, dangling pilot. Even using binoculars, no one could pick out the sniper.

"He's got to be up in those trees on the edge somewhere," Hadley said. "If he was any deeper in the plantation, his field of fire wouldn't be worth a damn."

"Why don't we just rake the treetops with the thirty cals, Sarge?" a sharpshooter asked. "We're bound to hit him that way."

Without a hint of uncertainty, Hadley replied, "No. Our machine guns are in perfect defensive positions. We need them to stay hidden right where they are. If we start using them as tree-trimmers, we'll give their positions away. Then we'll have a lot more than some sniper to worry about."

"So what're we gonna do, Sarge? If we ever needed a tank, it's—"

Hadley interrupted, "We ain't got a damn tank. But I just got an idea."

His men didn't like the sound of that.

"What kind of idea, Sergeant Hadley?" another sharpshooter asked. "Don't tell me you want to send out a patrol, so we can get picked off one by one."

"No," Hadley replied, "better than that. I'll be right back. In the meantime, everybody keep their asses down. Don't do anything stupid."

Esme was sailing with the sunrise out of Milne Bay, rounding East Cape for a day's run up Papua's north coast to Oro Bay. It would be the vessel's first trip there—and her captain's second. From her bridge, Jillian took in the stockpiles of military hardware being amassed in and around that harbor. The sheer amount of it all made her think:

It'd take weeks for the mob of us coastal traders to move all that stuff up to Oro Bay...and the big ships from Australia just keep bringing more and more. Too bad they can't make that bloody trip. It would save us all so much time.

Her ship's load was like all the others she had carried since signing on to the Allied merchant navy: the hold was crammed with ammunition and rations; lashed to the deck were a few light vehicles—jeeps and light trucks the Yanks called *three-quarter tons*—and 55-gallon drums of gasoline and oil. She couldn't carry the tanks Jock and his men needed so badly; the vehicles already on board taxed the lifting ability of *Esme's* small deck cranes to the limit. Beatrix Van Der Wegge's *Java Queen* was the only ship in the coastal trader fleet that could handle the tanks. On her reinforced deck, she had space for three, plus the sturdy cranes to lift them.

There were half a dozen light tanks lined up on shore at Milne Bay: *Stuarts*, they were called. Jillian didn't find them particularly awe-inspiring: *Sixteen tons of armor plate wrapped around a puny gun. A steel coffin on treads.*

But she knew the Yanks at Buna were desperate for them. Unfortunately, the bigwigs in charge of logistics considered construction equipment far more important at the moment. So the Stuarts sat, while bulldozers and earth-moving trucks were loaded onto Beatrix's *Java Queen*.

Esme was steaming west in the Solomon Sea now, making 15 knots for the 12-hour run to Oro Bay. Her ship's company had been enhanced by four, courtesy of the Royal Australian Navy: the crew of the Oerlikon 20-millimeter cannon freshly mounted to her foredeck. Jillian patted the ship's wheel as she thought, *You're really a warship now, old girl. Maybe the next Jap plane that tries to sink us will get a right thrashing.*

The gunners had been disgusted, at first, to learn they were assigned to a ship captained by a woman. One young seaman even had the gall to spit on Esme's deck. Two facts changed their minds, though. First, they learned their skipper had just escaped several days in

Japanese captivity. Her first mate hadn't hesitated to embellish the story: "Captain Forbes has already killed—single-handedly—a bunch of Japs both at Cape York and Papua. More than all of you lot put together, I reckon."

The first mate could tell from their faces he had reckoned correctly: the most combat any of the gun crew had seen, most likely, was brawling in a Brisbane pub, where bruised prides were the only casualties.

"In other words," the first mate continued, "the captain's not to be trifled with or her ship subjected to any disrespect."

Second, there was a significant cache of Australian beer on board, some 60 cases destined for an American unit at Buna as a New Year's surprise. "But if you behave yourselves like good lads," the Aussie gun crew was also told, "a case of that delicious brew can be yours."

Tom Hadley returned to Charlie Company in short order, riding the hood of a jeep towing two .50-caliber machine guns on a common wheeled mount. He pointed to a spot at the edge of the treeline and called to the driver, "Set up over there, pal."

The jeep sloshed to a stop at the appointed spot. The three men crewing the weapon disconnected it from the vehicle, manhandling it the last few feet into position.

"There," Hadley said, "you've got a great field of fire. This will only take a minute. Then you guys can high-tail it back to Division."

"Okay, great," the buck sergeant in charge of the twin .50s said. "Now what is it that you want us to do, exactly? We're an anti-aircraft unit, you know? We're not trained to do ground combat."

"That's just why I called on you guys," Hadley replied. He pointed across the swampy clearing to the far treeline and asked, "See? What's in those trees over there?"

"It's a fucking wrecked airplane," the buck sergeant said.

"Right. Now shoot it down. And while you're at it, take the tops off the trees fifty yards to either side."

"Are you shitting me, Top?" the buck sergeant asked.

"Wouldn't dream of it," Hadley replied. "But if I were you, I'd make it snappy. We've had a little problem with snipers around here."

The twin .50 mount came complete with a steel shield to protect the gunners. At the word *sniper*, its entire crew scrambled to huddle behind it.

"Oh, what the hell," the buck sergeant said as he swung the sights onto the suspended airplane and pressed the trigger button.

Tom Hadley covered his ears and smiled: *The racket of a couple of fifties alone is enough to scare you to death.*

The gun crew did what was asked of them. It was all over in less than 20 seconds. The machine guns sat silent and smoking, their ammo drums empty.

"We're getting the fuck out of here," the buck sergeant said as he hurled himself into the driver's seat.

"Thanks a bunch," Hadley replied. "Come back anytime."

The men on the perimeter were breathless with excitement. As Hadley walked up, a GI told him, "You should've seen it, First Sergeant. *Three* of those Jap bastards fell out of the trees. One of them was hiding in that fucking airplane. Only trouble is, before those fifties showed up, one of them got Jimmy Quigley. He tried to take a peek and they shot him dead, right through the neck."

"Shit," Hadley said as he surveyed the now-altered far treeline. What had once been tall coconut palms looked like well-chewed toothpicks. The wrecked airplane no longer dwelled in the trees; it was in pieces on the ground.

"Major Miles on the horn, First Sergeant," a runner reported.

When Hadley picked up the phone, Jock asked, "How'd the landscaping go, Tom?"

"Pretty good, sir. I don't think we'll be having much trouble with snipers for a while. Those fifty cals did the trick."

"I'm glad they're good for something," Jock replied. "As far as I can tell, they haven't hit an airplane yet...and they can't get close enough to try and split those bunkers open, either."

Esme was halfway to Oro Bay when a lookout shouted, "PLANES OFF THE STARBOARD QUARTER—ABOUT A MILE AND CLOSING."

Jillian fixed them in her binoculars. It didn't take but a second to realize they were Japanese fighters—two of them, low in the sky...

And they'd be upon the ship in much less than a minute.

We're a bloody sitting duck. Not much room to maneuver in these waters.

Easing the ship's wheel to port, Jillian said, "Let's show them her skinny arse, lads."

The planes flashed along her starboard side, their bullets splashing wide off her bow.

The Oerlikon gunner tried to track them as they sped ahead and broke hard left.

But he couldn't keep up. His tracers arced far behind the nimble fighters, never closing the gap.

"LEAD THEM, YOU WANKERS," Jillian implored from the bridge.

But the gun crew down on the foredeck was too far away to hear.

Jillian eased the wheel back to starboard: *Can't get too close to shore...too many shallow spots.*

The fighters lined up for another pass. This time, they came straight for her port side.

No leading necessary for the Oerlikon gunner this time...

Just a difficult head-on shot at their minute front profiles.

The deck gun's tracers seemed to float all around the attackers like helpful beacons guiding them to the ship...

But never hitting them.

With the *THUNK THUNK THUNK* of a rivet gun gone amok, Japanese bullets slammed against the weathered steel of *Esme's* hull and deckhouse.

The bullets left only dents.

Jillian allowed herself to relax for a moment: *What's that the Yanks say? Close, but no cigar?*

But all that bloody petrol lashed to the deck...I ought to dump it in the sea right this minute.

The planes sprinted away, making safe distance from the ship before beginning their turn to strike her once again.

With nothing to lose—and no hits yet to his credit—the Oerlikon gunner began firing with planes still a long way off.

He tried to find the range as the tracers—short of their mark—bounced crazily off the water.

"BRING IT UP, LAD...BRING IT UP," the gun crew yelled at their mate on the trigger.

He did.

Like magic, both planes suddenly pulled straight up and over, reversing direction and racing away with engines screaming.

If the planes had been hit, no one could tell. All they knew was the Japs were leaving in a hurry.

Everyone on board wanted to slap the gunner on the back and give him a hearty, *You did it, lad! Well done!*

But then they saw the real reason the Japanese planes were fleeing: a quartet of American fighters—P-40s by their silhouettes—were diving down from high overhead, giving chase.

For the Aussie gunners, the thrill of bagging an enemy aircraft would have to wait. The relief of the fight being over would have to suffice for now.

"It's about bloody time," Jillian said. "The Yank Air Force is finally doing what it promised."

Chapter Thirty-Five

It had only cost a few cases of beer to bribe the GI truck driver. Just like Jillian figured, he'd be glad to take her and the rest of the golden brew up to Buna.

These Yanks will do anything for some grog.

It was late afternoon when the truck pulled up to 1st Battalion's CP. Melvin Patchett was the first out of the tent. He was surprised—and delighted—to see her, especially after he saw what was waiting to be unloaded. Within a few moments, he had a detail carrying the cases of beer into the CP *on the double.*

"Young lady," Patchett said, "are you trying to corrupt us fine American boys with all this Australian mother's milk?"

"I doubt I could corrupt you Yanks any worse than you already are," Jillian replied as she gave him a big hug. "Where's the major?"

"Up at Regiment. I'll give them a ring and—"

"No, don't," she said. "I want to surprise him."

"That you will, dear girl. That you will."

When Jock stepped into his CP some 30 minutes later, he was afraid he was dreaming: there was the woman he loved, perched high on a stack of beer. He stood there, dumbfounded; no words would come out.

"Nice to see you too, Yank," she said, enjoying his stunned surprise as she jumped down to her feet. "I thought I'd bring the lads some New Year's spirit."

The next thing she said made Jock, Patchett, and everyone else in the tent burst out laughing: "I'm not going to get you in any trouble, am I?"

Jock replied, "What kind of trouble could be worse than what we're already in?"

He began to pull her by the arm out of the tent.

"Sergeant Major, I'm going to take a walk up to Cape Sudest with Miss Forbes," Jock said. "Charlie Company can fetch me if you need me."

"No problem, sir," Patchett replied. "Take your time. But just one thing…" He handed a helmet to Jillian. "Best put this on, Miss Forbes. Snipers, you know."

She glanced at Jock for a clue if Patchett might be joking. The look on his face told her the sergeant major definitely was not.

They stretched out among some big rocks at Cape Sudest, not far from a Charlie Company outpost. "Good cover here," Jock said. Their hideaway afforded a splendid view of the sea and the setting sun. It was a fine place to share a K ration supper.

There was quiet, too: not a bomb, artillery round, or gunshot to be heard.

Buna could almost be a lush, tropical paradise—if only your mind could forget it was also a burgeoning cemetery.

It had only been a week since Jillian last saw him. He had been gaunt then—much too thin. Now he looked even worse.

"Your skin…it's all yellow," she said.

"It's the Atabrine, Jill. Supposed to help prevent malaria."

The exhaustion she had seen in his eyes the last time was still there. The despair was gone, though, replaced with what she could only believe was *acceptance*:

Bloody hell! He thinks he's already dead...and he's accepting it. I've heard about this before: soldiers can only function if they believe they're already dead. Otherwise, any sane man would be running as fast as he could to get away from the madness.

They always knew every time together could be their last. But this time, there seemed an ominous certainty about it.

His gaze fixed out to sea, he said, "They want us to make an amphibious attack..."

She wasn't surprised. She had seen the growing collection of barges and landing craft at Oro Bay—far more than were necessary to unload the coastal traders.

"When, Jock?"

"A week or so."

"How's that going to work?"

"It's not, Jill. It's a fool's game. We're going to die in record numbers. The Japs will win."

They watched in silence as clumps of driftwood washed ashore, the waterlogged planks smashing to pieces as they crashed against the rocks.

"We're going to end up just like that," Jock said, "just broken pieces floating in the water." He said it so matter-of-factly; if she hadn't seen his face, she might have thought he was making an idle observation instead of a dire prediction.

He seemed too tired to think and plan beyond moment-to-moment necessities of survival anymore.

But she wasn't too tired. Her mind reeled feverishly, searching for anything that might reverse the inevitability of failure—and death.

Maybe this will do it...

"We've got tanks for you down at Milne Bay," she said. "Isn't that what you need?"

"Tanks at Milne Bay don't do us a damn bit of good here, Jill."

"But we can bring them to you!"

"Can you do it by tomorrow?"

They both knew the answer to that question was beyond their control.

"They're making us bring the bloody construction equipment first," she said.

"Of course they are," Jock replied with a sneer. "What's more important than building their fucking airfields?"

She watched as more driftwood shattered against the rocks...

And it gave her an idea:

"Jock, it's a fool's game, you say...and I'm sure you're right. But suppose you staged an amphibious attack that was really just a diversion—a decoy for the real attack?"

"But the diversion, Jill...the men trying to pull it off will get slaughtered."

"Suppose it didn't have any men—the whole thing was a ruse. Would that work?"

There was a light in his eyes that hadn't been there a moment ago. He had no idea exactly what she was suggesting, but the possibility there was something— *anything*—they could do other than the guaranteed disaster General Freidenburg wanted was enough to spark a ray of hope.

"It's simple," Jillian began. "There's a whole bloody fleet of old barges and whaleboats at Oro Bay that are useless and in the way. Most of their engines still run. We're supposed to take them out and scuttle them...but what if we towed them off Buna—at night, of course—lashed their tillers down and set them straight for shore? We could fill them with explosives and gasoline drums on very long fuzes..."

"You mean *fireships*? That's a centuries-old tactic, Jill. Do you really think it would fool them?"

"Why not? You told me your blokes got fooled by firecrackers, didn't you?"

Jock had to laugh at himself. "Point taken," he said.

Jillian wasn't finished. "We could even cut palm fronds to look like men's silhouettes and nail them into the boats. That should get the Japs soiling their trousers, don't you think?"

"And while they're distracted with all that," Jock added, "we can push in from the land side. We could probably get halfway to Buna Village before they realized what the hell was going on."

"So what do you think, Yank?"

"I think we'd better go talk to Colonel Molloy right now."

Jock and Jillian were sure the colonel was going to say no. Molloy sat in silence, staring off into space, as they described their plan. Once they were finished, he still had nothing to say. They stood before him in the awkward silence—anxiously hoping for his approval—for what seemed like an eternity.

When he finally spoke, his words were steeped in tones of rejection.

"What bothers me most," Colonel Molloy said, "is your plan's reliance on civilians. They'll be preparing the boats for the fake assault, they'll bring them into position, they'll launch them toward shore. I can't risk the lives of my men for a plan that rests so heavily on non-military personnel not under my command."

That was the wrong thing to say to Jillian Forbes. The air began to charge with the energy of her response before she spoke a word.

"Colonel," she began, "you seem to have forgotten your whole operation depends on the *civilians* you think so little of. Who do you think brings all your supplies? It's *civilian* sailors like me. Whatever those bloody little airplanes of yours bring in doesn't amount to a trickle compared to what comes over the water."

Molloy began to wish he had chosen his words more wisely.

Jillian continued, "And who's been carting those supplies through jungles, down rivers, and over mountains for you...when they're not carrying the litters of your wounded and burying your dead? Or have you inducted all those natives into your army?"

She waited for him to absorb those blows before adding, "No, wait...then you'd have to actually pay a generous wage—like the rest of you wankers get—instead of the pittance you throw at them."

"Miss Forbes," Molloy said, "I don't mean to imply I'm not appreciative of your—"

"Good," she cut in. "Then let us *civilians* help you even more…before Buna becomes nothing but a Yank graveyard."

Molloy went silent again. But this time, he didn't seem to be contemplating *yes or no*. It was more like *how and when*?

Jock asked, "I suppose it's too much to ask that the other two regiments help us out this time?"

"You suppose correctly, Jock," Molloy replied. "That would involve coordinating through Division…and General Freidenburg would put the screws to this scheme the second he heard it. He'll see it as someone trying to step on his toes…and he'd be right. Better he knows nothing about this *fireship* scheme until it's all over."

"Yeah, I guess so," Jock said. "But speaking of coordinating, how will we maintain communications with you civilians?"

Glaring at him like he was an idiot, Jillian replied, "We do have wireless on our ships, you know."

Before Jock could say anything, Molloy asked, "But what about message security, Miss Forbes? All messages have to be coded…and I can't release our codes to you."

"You don't have to," she replied. "We'll let you use our merchant navy codes." She pulled a small notebook from her pocket. "Copy it quickly, please. I need it back."

Molloy's concerns didn't stop there. "But General Freidenburg's assault is laid on for the sixth of January—less than seven days from now," he said. "We couldn't possibly pull this off before then…could we?"

"Colonel, we could have those boats off Buna as early as tomorrow night," Jillian replied, "the first of January. We civilians aren't bogged in all your military red tape."

"Well, we're not going to do it tomorrow night, that's for sure," Molloy said. "How much time do you need to get your men ready, Jock?"

"We could go in forty-eight hours, sir."

"Very fine," Molloy replied. "If we set it for oh-one hundred on January third, is that agreeable to you, Miss Forbes?"

"Absolutely, Colonel."

"Good," Molloy said. "It's set, then. One more thing, Miss Forbes...you're positive there are half a dozen Stuart tanks awaiting shipment at Milne Bay?"

"Without a doubt, Colonel."

She could see the question in his eyes. It was breaking her heart the answer couldn't be *yes*.

"I can't stay, Jock," Jillian said. "I've got to get back to my ship...and get the wheels turning on our little plan."

"I know," Jock replied. "We've both got a lot to do."

He could feel the distance already growing between them although they were still close enough to touch.

Within minutes of their arrival at Jock's CP, Patchett had a jeep waiting to take her back to Oro Bay. As she hopped into the passenger's seat, Jock said, "Don't even think about being anywhere near Buna—

offshore or onshore—when we launch this attack, Jill. I mean it."

The kiss she gave him tried to convey so much: hopes, dreams, reassurances, confidence—anything but the nagging fear growing within her that somehow she was creating the circumstances of his death.

"I wouldn't worry, silly boy," she replied, trying her best to dodge the issue. "I've got a ship to look after."

"I'm serious, Jill. Don't."

Colonel Molloy wasted no time tracking down General Freidenburg. He was at one of the airfield construction sites near Dobodura, admiring the repair work in progress on the bomb-damaged runway.

The general said, "These coloreds do some fine work as long as they're closely supervised. Wouldn't you agree, Colonel?"

The urge to reply with *sho-nuff, massa,* was very strong, but sarcasm wouldn't help Dick Molloy a bit right now. Instead, he replied, "Yes, sir, but there's something I must discuss with you."

"Go ahead, Colonel," Freidenburg said, his eyes never drifting from the natives hard at work on his airfield. "I'm all ears."

"General, are you aware there are six Stuart tanks at Milne Bay, just waiting to be shipped up here? And there's a ship on hand capable of carrying them to Oro Bay?"

Freidenburg acted surprised to hear that.

Maybe he knows, maybe he doesn't, Molloy thought. But he learned something a long time ago: generals always knew everything they *wanted* to know.

"Stuarts! How do you know that, Colonel?"

"An eyewitness told me, sir."

"Even if that's true, Colonel, it would be a week or more before they could be here and—"

"Negative, sir. I'm told they could be here in two to three days."

The general appraised Molloy with the cold, dead eyes of a shark. His voice soft yet menacing, he replied, "Do not interrupt me again, Colonel. As I was saying, a few tanks that may or may not be at Milne Bay will not be necessary after your men storm Buna Village from the sea. It might be different if tanks could be part of that amphibious assault, but we don't have the landing ships for that. Do I make myself clear?"

The only thing that was clear to Dick Molloy: General Freidenburg was every bit as obtuse as the man he replaced.

**January
1943**

Chapter Thirty-Six

First Sergeant Tom Hadley was delighted to no longer be acting company commander of Charlie Company. He greeted Lee Grossman, the real company commander, by handing him a bottle of beer. "Happy New Year, Lieutenant," Hadley said. "Here…have a brew, sir. Everybody gets one…and you sure as hell look like you need it."

"Better not," Grossman replied, gently rubbing his belly. "This gut's going to be tender for quite a while. Doc said mine was the worst case of dysentery he'd ever seen. I damn near died of dehydration."

"Well, on behalf of every swinging dick in the outfit, it's good to have you back, sir," Hadley said. "But with all due respect, you do look like you got rode hard and put away wet. You sure you're up to this? We're going back into the plantation tomorrow night, you know."

"Tom, I've had my ass dangling over a slit trench for the better part of two weeks. It's time I did my bit again. Let's start with you filling me in on who's in charge of what in this company now."

"Begging your pardon, sir," Hadley said, "but before we do that, the men would like to give you a little *welcome back* present."

As a crowd of GIs watched, two privates approached, each concealing something behind his back. Once standing before Lieutenant Grossman, they dropped to one knee and produced the hidden objects. Each man held out a roll of toilet paper. On the side of both rolls were written the words *Reserved for Company Commander's Use Only.*

"We figured these might come in handy, sir," Hadley said.

For a moment, the men thought their C.O. had not found their gift funny at all. But after an awkward, silent moment, he took the offered rolls, tucked them under his arm, and—with a big smile—said, "Thank you very much, men. I'm sure I'll be putting this generous gift to good use...and real soon, too."

The men were surprised to hear a sound they didn't think existed anymore; it was the sound of their own laughter.

Less than a mile away, in a stinking, squalid bunker, the Japanese soldier wrote:

> *The lieutenant killed himself today*
> *As if the failure of the Empire was solely his*
> *And his alone*
> *Maybe the hunger drove him crazy*
> *Or the diet of lies we have been forced to live*
> *on*
>
> *They said our victory was certain*
> *But the boats no longer come, bringing fresh*
> *troops each night*
> *All clean and strong*
> *Ready to be sacrificed*
> *Or just join the ranks of the starving*
>
> *The dead feed us now*
> *Ours...theirs...it makes no difference*

The lieutenant killed himself today
Already there is not much left of him

Chapter Thirty-Seven

Sergeant Major Patchett's grease pencil squeaked as it made the last of the day's entries on the unit manpower board. Totaling the columns yielded a bleak picture: barely 200 combat-able men—less than half of a full-strength battalion—would be attacking the Duropa Plantation later that night. Zero hour for the attack—3 January at 0100—was just six short hours away.

Patchett had been meticulous not to include the survivors of the Kapa Kapa in his tally. They were not combat fit. *Hell,* Patchett told himself, *the bunch of us who wasn't on the damn Kapa Kapa ain't all that fit ourselves. But we gotta draw the line somewhere whether you fish or cut bait.*

The men from the Kapa Kapa would *cut bait.* They'd man the battalion and company CPs, handling the phones and radios, freeing able men for the assault. They'd even man the fighting holes providing headquarters security; with any luck at all, that task would prove to be more convention than necessity.

But they wouldn't be making that walk in the dark into the plantation.

One of the Kapa Kapa men manning the phones called out: "Major Miles, Regiment says the boats are leaving Oro Bay now."

"Excellent. Right on time," Jock replied.

Already in his field gear, Jock slung his Thompson and stepped from the tent into the gray light of dusk. Patchett did the same, telling himself, *Time to do a little fishing.*

They *would* be making that walk into the plantation.

The captain of the ocean-going tug, *Mieke*, was not a happy man. Hendrik Jansen had allowed his cousin, Beatrix Van Der Wegge, captain of *Java Queen*, to badger him into this voyage on two conditions: first, he would go no closer than two miles to the shore at Buna Village, rather than the one mile that crazy Australian girl Beatrix was so fond of wanted; second, Beatrix would forgive one-half of the 10,000 gulden in Netherlands East Indies currency he was in debt to her.

He had begun to have second thoughts on the incentive of the second condition: *If the fucking Japs win, that Dutch money is worthless, anyway. I'd be off the hook.*

It was too late for Hendrik to back out now, though. His blacked-out tug—and the 25 barges and whaleboats it was slowly towing from Oro Bay—was drawing close to Buna. *Full of fake men, dynamite, and gasoline to boot,* he thought. *We'll be lucky if we don't all get blown to bits. And I'm already in trouble with the Yank Navy.* Indeed he was: he was supposed to be picking up another load of barges at Milne Bay this very night.

Jillian spun the dials on *Mieke's* radio direction finder, plotting the bearings to the Japanese transmitters at Lae and Rabaul as well as the Australian Navy station at Milne Bay. She smiled as the three radio vectors intersected on the chart quite close to her celestial plot. "About a mile to the release point," she told Hendrik. "Twelve more minutes on this heading and speed."

Somewhere in the darkness to the south lay Buna Village.

"Let's get the skiffs ready," she said.

Twelve minutes later, *Mieke's* throttles were cut and she coasted to a stop. Her two skiffs were lowered into the water. The starter ropes for their small outboard engines—short lengths with a knot in one end and a wooden handle on the other—were wound onto the flywheels and given mighty pulls. The outboards came to life with a steady *putt-putt* which had never before seemed so loud.

"The Japs are going to hear these bloody engines all the way to Rabaul, let alone Buna," the Dutchman with Jillian in the first skiff said.

"If we do this right, Ruud," Jillian replied, "we'll be long gone before they suspect a thing. For all they know, these are their boats. They won't risk lighting us up with a searchlight...not right away, at any rate."

In a most unconfident tone, Ruud said, "I hope you're right, missy."

Jillian and Ruud—plus the two crewmen in the other skiff—went about the business of maneuvering the unmanned boats for their blind southerly run to shore. Six big barges would be in the lead, towing columns of three boats each. Engines roared to life, tillers were lashed amidships. Very long fuzes for the explosives were lit.

That left one boat—a big whaleboat loaded with barrels of gasoline—as a free agent. It was the fastest boat of the lot and its engine the loudest of all: a corroded muffler had seen to that. They'd set this one to sail southwest—toward shore but diagonally away from the other boats. Hopefully, its noise would divert the attention of the Japanese, making the arrival of the other two dozen boats at a different point on the beach all the more alarming.

The big whaleboat's engine was cranked and Jillian steered her to the southwesterly course. Lashing down the tiller, she said, "Light her fuze, Ruud...and let's get the bloody hell out of here." They jumped into the skiff and cast off from the floating timebomb.

The roar of the whaleboat's unmuffled engine drowned out the *putt-putt* of the skiff's outboard motor for a good 15 seconds—until that roar sputtered and died.

"Go back," Jillian said to Ruud on the skiff's tiller. "We've got to start her again."

"Forget it," the Dutchman replied. "I'm not getting my ass blown up for you or some Yanks."

"That son of a bitch won't blow for a good ten minutes," she said, "and a lot of good blokes are depending on us to make this work. Turn this fucking boat around. Now."

The helmsman laughed and replied, "I don't take orders from you, missy."

She didn't bother answering. He was seated on the side bench, one arm casually draped over the outboard motor's tiller, his long legs spread wide apart.

She kicked him squarely in the balls.

As he writhed in pain, she grabbed him by his feet and levered him over the side.

"Best inflate your life belt, Ruud," she called to the man now struggling in the water. "I'll be back for you when I'm done. Don't go too bloody far."

It didn't take but a few minutes to figure out what was wrong with the whaleboat's engine in general terms:

Plenty of fuel but no bloody spark. The battery's going to give out if I keep trying to crank her, too.

Fumbling in the sparse illumination of her blackout flashlight, she got to the heart of the problem: *The bloody ignition lead is so corroded, it fell right out of the distributor.*

Using her pocket knife, she stripped clean the ignition wire and distributor terminal.

Now, how do I hold them together?

Her bootlace did the trick: a few sturdy wraps around the lead and post, secured with a sound knot, and the circuit was restored.

If only the bloody battery has enough life for one more crank...

It didn't. Pushing the *start* button resulted in nothing but a few anemic clicks of the solenoid.

I'll have to pull-start her.

She glanced at the fuze, sizzling its way around the whaleboat: *Looks like it's about half burned down. Maybe five minutes left.*

Five minutes—*at most*—until the fuze set off the dynamite and gasoline drums, blowing this boat to matchsticks and setting the sea on fire.

Jillian needed a starter rope. There was one in the skiff—the one they used to crank her outboard.

She held it in her hands, examining it closely:

It's too short. It'll never turn over this big motor enough to get her started.

The only other rope was the long, stout length tying the skiff to the whaleboat's beam—and it had plenty of extra hanging from the cleat.

She cut it, knotted one end and wrapped it around the crankshaft's start pulley.

It fit perfectly.

She grasped the rope with both hands and tugged with all her might.

The rope slipped through her hands; the crankshaft didn't budge.

I need a handle on the free end of this bloody rope...something to give me more grip.

Her eyes fell on the skiff's bilge:

The oar!

She tied the rope to the oar's handle. They formed a "T" she could grab firmly with both hands.

Jillian pulled...

She was rewarded with a partial turn of the crankshaft—one *pumff* of a cylinder's compression stroke...

And that was all.

The burning fuze rounded another turn in its path to the dynamite caps.

Four minutes...maybe. I need more leverage!

Jillian tried straddling the engine block, squatting as low as the machinery allowed. She pulled again...

This time, two *pumffs*...and then silence.

More bloody leverage!

She climbed onto the engine itself, struggling for a precarious foothold among the manifolds and wires.

Jillian wound the rope's slack around the oar's handle, making a short, tight lead to the pulley, squatted low...

And sprung to a standing position with every ounce of strength in her being.

She went flying as the rope played out from the pulley.

Tumbling backward, she ended up wedged in a sitting position between the engine block and deck, her backside stuck into the bilge.

But the loud mechanical throbbing between her knees could only mean one thing:

Success. The engine was running.

The whaleboat was moving again, heading with purpose toward shore—and the Japanese.

The fuze was in the final leg of its long, circuitous run to the dynamite.

Three minutes, tops.

She leaped into the skiff and cast off from the vessel about to find its destiny as a *fireship.* The raucous sound of her unmuffled engine grew fainter.

Jillian couldn't find the starter rope for the outboard.

Bloody hell! It's still on the other boat!

She tried to fit the rope she had fashioned for the whaleboat's engine into the outboard's flywheel:

Too thick!

At least she still had the oar.

In the moonlight, she could see the faint outline of *Mieke*, 200 yards—maybe more—to the north. She kept rowing.

Somewhere in between—hopefully—was Ruud.

At least without this bloody kicker running, I'll be able to hear the wanker sobbing.

Ruud must have heard the slap of the oar, because he began to call her name, mixed into a continuous string of curses.

"KEEP IT UP, WANKER," she called out, "IF YOU DON'T MIND DROWNING."

Jillian edged the skiff toward the sound of his voice. Soon, she could catch glimpses of his head, wet and glistening in the moonlight, as it bobbed not far off in the low swells.

Reaching him, she thought the wiser of offering a helping hand to climb back into the skiff.

The bastard will just pull me in for spite.

She threw him the rope instead.

Ruud sloshed over the side, an animated silhouette, eyes glowing with rage.

His profane tirade began anew, first in Dutch: "*Stomme kut! Stomme hoer!*"

And then in English: "I swear to God, I'll fucking kill—"

The brilliant orange flash lit the sea and everything on it for an instant. A split second later, the sound of the whaleboat's detonation assaulted their ears.

Ruud's face was no longer just a dark shape with luminous eyes. In the flare of the explosion, Jillian could watch as his anger and hate changed abruptly to shock and fear.

There was good reason for the sudden change: he could see the seaman's knife in her hand, reflecting the fire's light as if it, too, was ablaze.

He remembered Hendrik's warning: *Mind Beatrix's words...that crazy woman will gut you like a fish if you cross her.*

At first, they thought the fire spreading across the water's surface was throwing brilliant sparks.

Then they realized what they were seeing was actually tracers bouncing off the water all around them.

Large-caliber tracers, at that, aimed at the pool of fire spreading from where there was once a whaleboat.

"We've certainly caught the Jap's attention now," Jillian said, pumping the oar through the water as if competing in an Olympic event.

Ruud's arm was over the side, the palm of his hand paddling frantically, adding whatever propulsion he could.

The skiff drew closer to *Mieke*. They could hear the *THUNK* of rounds striking the tug's steel hull.

They were so near—but *Mieke* was beginning to move away, her propellers churning the sea beneath her stern.

A loud *CRACK*—and all at once a whirlwind of stinging splinters, a splatter of something warm and wet. The sea began to flood in where the skiff's bow used to be only a moment before.

The last thing Jillian heard was the inflation cartridge on her life belt hissing like an enraged viper.

Chapter Thirty-Eight

Charlie Company lay poised on the eastern edge of Duropa Plantation. The sea to their right, the rest of the battalion to their left, they were ready—and waiting—to push west toward Buna. When that first whaleboat exploded in the night, it didn't seem very impressive at all. Lieutenant Lee Grossman began to doubt the wisdom of this whole attack, asking, "That's it? That's the whole damn diversion?"

The whaleboat's fiery demise—several miles away, well out to sea and over so quickly—seemed to have little effect other than to rouse a robust Japanese response. Judging by the amount of Japanese firepower raking the sea, the weary, disheveled men of Grossman's company were thanking their lucky stars they were on land right now—even if it wasn't exactly *dry* land—and not out on that water, trying to storm the beach in flimsy wooden boats as General Freidenburg would have them do in a few days.

But if the attack they were about to launch succeeded, there'd be no need for dying in the little boats. At the moment, though, this attack seemed just as stupid as the general's plan.

The GIs' thinking didn't change for a few minutes—until the main body of the *fireships* erupted in a thunderous succession of explosions, showering flaming gasoline onto a broad stretch of beach just a mile or two ahead.

"Now *that's* more like it," Grossman said.

Tom Hadley, his first sergeant, was even more expressive: "It's like we're staring into a red-hot furnace..."

Indeed, the rows of coconut palms between them and the beach could resemble a furnace's grill in a man's imagination.

Understanding the power of the flames within that furnace required no imagination at all.

Hadley squinted into the distance for a better look. "Looks like those bunkers along the beach took a dose of burning gas, sir."

That sounded like a good bet: the Japanese heavy weapons firing out to sea had stopped. All that could be heard now was the irregular *poom...poompoom* of their ammo cooking off.

"I think it's now or never, guys," Lieutenant Grossman said. "Let's get moving."

Within minutes, the men of Charlie Company were deeper into Duropa Plantation than they'd ever been...

And they hadn't taken a round of enemy fire.

The blaze's orange light shone from the beach like a beacon guiding the GIs forward—without lighting them up like targets for the slaughter.

The first line of bunkers—the bunkers that had stopped them cold on each of their previous attacks into the plantation—were backlit by the flames. The GIs could make out their shapes clearly.

Carefully, they skirted the silent bunkers and then approached them from the rear—close enough to hurl grenades through their entryways.

When the dust from the grenades' explosions settled, they stormed inside—and found no one...

No one alive, anyway.

But the grenades hadn't killed a soul.

The corpses, stacked like cordwood in corners, had been dead for a long time.

Some were missing limbs.

All seemed to be stripped of flesh somewhere.

The corpses weren't all Japanese. Tom Hadley noticed that right away.

Some of the bodies had dog tags—*GI dog tags*—around their necks. Hadley reached out for one.

"Careful, Sarge...they might be booby-trapped," a squad leader said.

The first sergeant paid no attention. He read the name on a dog tag.

Then another.

Hadley looked stricken. They could barely hear him when he mumbled, "Son of a bitch!"

Then he said it again, much louder this time.

There was no need to ask Hadley what was wrong. Everyone knew.

They needed to get out of that bunker, to get some fresh air...

Even if that air stunk from the fumes of the inferno on the beach.

Better that than the stench of death.

Lee Grossman arrived to find most of the GIs around that bunker hunched over, puking the meager contents of their stomachs.

Grossman asked Hadley, "What the hell is going on, Tom?"

The first sergeant had trouble putting the words together. Finally, they spilled out in an anguished torrent: "Miserable fucking bastard lowlife animals..."

Lee Grossman wasn't sure who or what he was talking about.

Hadley saved him the trouble of asking: "OUR GUYS, SIR! THE GUYS WE COULDN'T FIND…THOSE BASTARDS, THEY WERE EATING THEM!" His voice dropped: "No wonder we couldn't—"

Tom Hadley's words were cut off as he surrendered to his own nausea.

Grossman struggled to put the terrible visions out of his mind. There was a more immediate problem: huddled in distraught clusters, his men seemed anything but alert:

Do they need to be reminded we may be just yards from the enemy?

An eruption of heavy gunfire far off their left flank, where the rest of the battalion was, reinforced his thinking:

There are still Japs around here somewhere…and plenty of them.

Another problem: when the blaze on the beach died down, they'd all be night-blind for a while.

We're not done here and we don't have much time. I've got to get them moving, right now.

But he didn't need to say a word to make that happen.

GIs who were disoriented and doubled over with nausea just a moment ago had—*on the double*—fallen into combat formations. At First Sergeant Hadley's forceful direction, they were stalking deeper into the plantation.

A sense of rage hovered over the company now, subdued yet powerful enough to overcome the illness, exhaustion, and misfortune they had suffered.

It was powerful enough to channel the unspeakable horror they had just witnessed—a horror among horrors that would stay with them forever—into one purpose: retribution for the desecration inflicted on their buddies.

Every man—even the lowest private—felt the same: *Dying was one thing...shit, we're all gonna die...but even a man you killed deserves respect after he's gone.*

We've had it just as bad as you, you little bastards...maybe worse.

But no matter how bad things got, we never ate the dead.

We're better than you, you fucking cannibals...and now we're going to show you just how much better.

Sergeant Major Patchett appeared out of the darkness just as the last platoon of Charlie Company was moving out. He smiled with satisfaction as he watched them go; an old soldier could tell a good unit from a worthless one at a glance.

"I've got to show you something," Grossman told him.

Inside the bunker, Patchett retraced the steps Hadley had taken, reading each dog tag.

"Son of a fucking bitch," the sergeant major said, and then spat on the ground. "Better get Major Miles over here."

They stepped outside the bunker. Patchett said, "No wonder your boys were looking real sharp, Lieutenant. It's a damn shame, too, but I reckon we got ourselves the *cat-list* for certain now."

The light from the fires had dimmed to a faint glow far in the distance.

"I can't see a fucking thing, Top," a platoon sergeant said to Tom Hadley.

Hadley replied, "So what? It just means they can't see us, either."

Charlie Company had reached the second line of bunkers without even realizing it.

The first clue came from a trooper who had walked right into a bunker's stout wall of logs and earthwork.

He heard voices from inside—excited voices—and they weren't speaking English.

A few feet to his left a Nambu machine gun began firing, its muzzle sweeping wildly back and forth, spitting tracers into the darkness in an arc too narrow to touch him.

Surprising even himself, the trooper climbed on top of the bunker and—almost casually—dropped a grenade into one of its vent holes.

The grenade exploded. The Nambu stopped firing.

He slid down the backside of the bunker and walked in.

There were just two Japanese soldiers inside.

One was motionless on the ground.

The other was screaming his head off...

Probably calling for his mama.

Two rounds from an M1 silenced the screamer as First Sergeant Hadley rushed in.

"You okay?" Hadley asked.

"Yeah," the trooper replied. "Just fine. Gotta ask you something, though, Top."

"Go ahead."

"You shot guys before, right?"

"Yeah...a couple I know about, anyway."

"Did it bother you any?"

"A little bit," Hadley replied. "Still does."

"Funny, but it ain't bothering me at all right now...not these fucking bastard cannibals."

The trooper fired another round into each of the dead Japs.

"All right, that's enough," Hadley said. "You only have to kill them once. Save your ammo. You're gonna need it."

Farther south—to Charlie Company's left—Able and Baker Companies were still stuck at the first line of bunkers. The automatic weapons fire they faced was murderous. They pulled back to regroup as Jock called his company commanders together.

Despite his still-healing wounds, Theo Papadakis was as feisty as ever. He was frustrated, too: "How come Grossman's not hitting hardly any resistance at all, while we're still fighting the whole damn Imperial Japanese Army?"

Tracing his fingers along the map spread on the ground, Jock Miles said, "It's simple, Theo. The Japs facing Lee's company pulled back to defend the beach when the *fireships* hit, just like we hoped they would. The ones facing you and Tony didn't. But they've still given us an opening we can exploit."

Tony Colletti, Baker Company's commander, asked, "So how far has Charlie advanced?"

"Looks like they're about a mile into the plantation," Jock said. "Is that right, Lee?"

"Yes, sir," Grossman replied. "Near as we can figure in the dark."

"Shit," Papadakis said, "that's almost to Buna Mission. Another half mile and you're in Buna Village. Are you guys finding any more bunkers?"

"Again, it's hard to tell in the dark, Theo," Grossman replied, "but we're past the second line now, and we haven't come up against anything else."

Practically jumping up and down with eagerness, Papadakis said, "Let's go, then! We can bypass all this shit in our sector and follow Lee and his boys right into Buna Village. We'll be there by sunrise. Wouldn't that surprise the shit out of the Japs when we join them for breakfast?"

Nobody laughed. No one wanted to hear jokes about *eating* right now. Not after what Charlie Company had found earlier.

"Anyway, I've told Lee to stop and dig in where they are," Jock said.

Papadakis couldn't believe what he was hearing: "Why? Why stop now, sir?"

"Because," Jock replied, "all those Japs that pulled back, thinking we were going to hit Buna Village from the water? Well, we've got to be ready for them when they decide to return. A lone company could get cut off real easy."

Papadakis wasn't giving up. "But ain't that what Third Battalion is for, sir? Protecting our flanks...and our asses?"

"Sorry, Theo," Jock replied, "but I've seen enough of Colonel Vann's people under fire. So have you. I'm not going to trust them to protect us."

"Amen to that, sir," Melvin Patchett said.

Jock continued, "Now, Theo...this is what I need you and Tony to do. We've had a lucky break. For the first time, we've broken their line of defense. Move your companies through the area Charlie has cleared and take out the bunkers in your sectors *from behind*...while it's still dark and they can't see you coming." He sketched a line on the map. "Don't go any farther into the plantation than this line. Link up with Charlie Company on your right. We need to stay close together so if a counterattack comes our companies don't get cut up piecemeal. Do I make myself clear?"

Papadakis and Colletti nodded in unison.

Patchett added, "Shouldn't be no big thing taking those bunkers in the dark. You know exactly where they are...damn fools have been firing tracers at you all night."

Tony Colletti had one more question: "If we can pull that off, sir...have we gained enough to make that amphibious landing the general wants unnecessary?"

Jock replied, "That's a real good question, Tony."

Chapter Thirty-Nine

Beatrix Van Der Wegge couldn't sleep, even though it was the dead of night. She and her ship were stuck at Milne Bay: *those idiot Yanks in charge of supply have proven their incompetence once again. Bloody fools could fuck up a free lunch.*

Beatrix decided to drown her frustrations in whiskey. She should have been at Oro Bay already—and on the tug, *Mieke*, with Jillian.

But the Americans at Milne Bay had ruined all that. After spending last night loading her ship with the usual complement of heavy construction vehicles, her manifest and sailing orders were cancelled at the last minute. *Java Queen* was to be unloaded. Her new cargo would be three of the Stuart tanks that had languished on the wharf for days.

When she asked the reason for the change, the pencil-pushing American lieutenant had pointed skyward and replied, "Orders from upstairs, ma'am. Some general must've changed his mind."

The unloading and reloading would take until tomorrow morning. *Java Queen* would then be on her way. By this time tomorrow night, the tanks would be at Oro Bay.

Beatrix poured herself another glass and thought, *It's a shame I have to leave Jillian all alone with my cretin of a cousin and his barbarians. But no worries…she can handle herself anywhere.*

It was 0500 before Lee Grossman got back to Charlie Company. He didn't have much trouble finding it in the dark; all he had to do was follow the sounds of one vicious skirmish after another being waged.

But the gunfire wasn't coming from his company's perimeter. Once safely within its bounds, Grossman asked the first platoon sergeant he could find, "Where's First Sergeant Hadley?"

The platoon sergeant pointed toward the sound of the gunfire. "He's over by the beach, sir, I guess. He heard boats coming—"

Worried and impatient, Grossman interrupted, "What *boats*? Not our decoy boats?"

"No, sir. Not ours…theirs. Lots of them. He took a thirty cal, one of the mortars, and all the ammo they could carry with him."

"Damn it," Grossman said. "I told him to stay put."

"We got your message, sir," the platoon sergeant said, tapping the walkie-talkie slung over his shoulder. "We *are* staying put…we're dug in here real good. But the first sergeant was worried the whole battalion was about to get flanked, so…he did what he did."

A few hundred yards away, nestled in a grove at the edge of the sea, were Tom Hadley and the detachment of men he'd dragged with him. He wasn't sure how many GIs he took: *Ten, I think…couldn't really tell in the dark. One of them's already dead. And I'm not even sure where we are…we might even be in Buna Mission. I guess we'll find out when the sun comes up…if we're still alive.*

The Japanese barges were still coming—down to a trickle now, but the clatter of their engines still unmistakable. The machine gunner had become proficient at estimating their range from sound alone—he'd had a lot of practice in the past hour.

The mortar crew had the whole length of beach before them zeroed in. Whenever a landing barge *scrunched* to a stop on the sand, the men scrambling to get off were met by the blast of a high explosive or white phosphorous round. Here, the mortar had found a decent field of fire; back within the plantation, the thick overhead canopy all around yielded almost no good firing points for the high-angle weapons.

The other two riflemen on Hadley's team were tasked with making sure no Japs snuck up behind them.

Hadley tapped a man each from the machine gun and mortar crews: "Go back and get more ammo, some batteries for the radio, and more water."

"We ain't had time to get thirsty yet, Top," a GI replied.

"Not for you, zipperhead…for the thirty cal's barrel. It's gonna melt if we keep shooting her this much."

Tom Hadley wasn't sure how many Japs they'd killed, or if any had managed to slip away from the killing zone of the beach. It was still too dark to tell. The moon had finished its duty for this night; the sunrise was more than an hour away. The only light was from the scattered flames of burning wooden barges, set alight by the mortar's white phosphorous shells.

In that dim light, Hadley's detachment could see the surf slapping against what seemed a seawall of corpses.

Sunrise brought a number of surprises.

For Tom Hadley and his men by the beach, there were two big ones: by rough count, there were over 100 dead Japanese littering the shore, and they weren't just *near* Buna Mission—they were *on the edge of its grounds*. A few hundred yards away, Japanese troops were scurrying in and out of the Mission's houses.

They were practically out of ammunition—again—for their GI weapons. But just before sunrise, they had scooped up all the Japanese weapons littering the beach they could carry. They were better armed now than when they first took up this position: three Nambu machine guns, a host of Arisaka rifles, and boxes full of ammunition and grenades were ready for action.

Hadley assessed their chances: *So long as an artillery or mortar round doesn't land right on top of us, we can hold out for a long time.*

Just how *long* this time would be was a big question mark; the sporadic fire of Japanese small arms—some of it to their rear, between them and the rest of Charlie Company—had broken out since first light. If there had ever been a chance to return to the company perimeter, it was long gone. The enemy was all around; *Combat Team Hadley* was an island in a dangerous sea.

The extra walkie-talkie batteries had come in handy: they still had communication with the rest of the company and could coordinate fire against the Japanese probes.

General Freidenburg didn't like surprises. When he awoke, the trucks were waiting to shuttle 81st Regiment to Oro Bay in preparation for his amphibious assault. But the 81st was nowhere to be found. He flew into a rage.

The general sprayed spittle all over his staff as he fumed, "How dare that son of a bitch colonel fuck up my simple plan so totally?"

By the time Dick Molloy's jeep slogged the six miles to the division CP, General Freidenburg was ready to pluck that eagle right off his collar.

Then Colonel Molloy stepped to the map and explained exactly where his troops were—and the deception that had enabled them to get there.

"Let me get this straight, Colonel," Freidenburg said. "You took it upon yourself to *fake* a night amphibious assault...and the Japs fell for it?"

"Yes, sir," Molloy replied. "We've broken their defensive ring. Most of the Japs have been squeezed into the village itself. Major Miles's First Battalion has done an amazing job. Now, since I still don't have the tanks or artillery I've asked for, I need the Air Force to rain holy hell on Buna Mission and Buna Village right now."

General Freidenburg turned to his staff officers, his eyebrows raised as if asking, *Can we make that happen?*

The G3 poured cold water on the idea: "Storms are coming in less than an hour, sir. The Air Force won't be able to do any precision bombing, at least not today."

Molloy said, "Then give me back the Aussie artillery...before my men collapse in their tracks from exhaustion. Finding that evidence of cannibalism gave them the will to fight like demons all night…but they're only human. They're burned out now."

"*Cannibalism?*" Freidenburg asked. "What are you talking about, Colonel?"

Molloy told the general and his staff the sordid tale.

The general seemed unconcerned. "War is hell, Colonel Molloy," he announced. "Simple as that."

"Some people's definition of hell is apparently a little different than mine, sir," Molloy replied.

Freidenburg shrugged. "Request for the artillery is denied, Colonel. The Aussies have just taken Gona. They're going to turn east and press toward Sanananda immediately. If I take their guns, they won't advance another inch, just for spite."

Molloy checked the map again. Gona had been a small Japanese outpost on the coast some eight miles west of Buna. No doubt, they defended it fiercely, but the Australians had the numbers, despite the toll exhaustion and jungle diseases had taken on them; and they still had those artillery pieces. It was just a matter of time before Gona fell. Sanananda lay between Buna and Gona; the fortifications there looked every bit as formidable as what his regiment was encountering around Buna.

The Aussies will need those guns, Dick Molloy told himself, *and a hell of a lot more*.

He was surprised to find the general now smiling at him. "Actually," Freidenburg said, "I'm very pleased I was finally able to light a fire under you and your men, Colonel. It's been a long time coming."

Dick Molloy stifled the rage that comment ignited. He asked, "So, General, I suppose there's no need now for your amphibious assault?"

A sardonic grin spread across Freidenburg's face as he replied, "Not unless your little freelancing stunt turns to shit and you fail to take Buna."

The general strolled over to the map and, without bothering to look Dick Molloy in the eye, added, "Don't ever fucking do something like this again, Molloy. Dismissed."

With Molloy gone, the G3 asked, "But sir, weren't you going to tell him about the tanks?"

"No," Freidenburg replied, "If I did that, they'd all just sit on their lazy asses until the damn things showed up."

The rain came as promised. Jock, with a squad from Able Company, trudged through the plantation to Charlie Company's position. Bogater Boudreau, the squad's leader, had been willing to wager they wouldn't run into any Japanese along the way. No one was willing to take him up on that bet.

"From what I hear," Boudreau said, "ol' Tom Hadley killed all the Japs fixing to flank us. We won't be seeing none of them until we meet up with Charlie Company."

Jock tried not to chuckle as he said, "That sounds like one hell of a war story, Corporal Boudreau. I can't wait to hear the version Hadley tells. I heard he doesn't see it quite that way."

"I don't know about that, sir...I don't see no Japs. Do you?"

"No...not yet."

"Then I'll say it again, sir...First Sergeant Hadley saved all our asses. If he don't get a big ol' medal for that, then I don't know what the heck a man has to do— short of dying—to get decorated around here."

Decorations were the last thing on the minds of Tom Hadley and his detachment. The rain had brought no respite from attacks by Japanese desperate to dislodge them. So far, though, no Jap had gotten close enough to hurl a grenade their way.

The GI manning one of the captured machine guns said, "Those Nips ain't so damn tough when they ain't in them bunkers." Raindrops sizzled on contact with the gun's hot barrel as he struggled to reload. "Piece of Jap shit...shoots slower than my grandma and it takes forever to seat one of these damn magazines. Give me a belt-loading thirty cal any day."

"You guys are doing just fine with those pieces of shit," Hadley replied, gazing into Buna Mission with binoculars. "Hey...I think I see one of their mortar pits."

He stopped to wipe the lenses dry and then took another look at his target.

"Shit," Hadley said, "they're fixing to hang one. You got line-of-sight on it?"

His eye squeezed against the mortar's sight, the gunner replied, "No dice, Top."

"All right then," Hadley said, "use the plotting board. Azimuth three-two-zero, range five hundred."

"We've only got three rounds left, Top," the mortar section chief said.

"I can fucking count, Corporal. Let 'er rip...get them before they get us, okay?"

The gunner's bloodshot eyes—strained, beyond tired—struggled to read the tiny numbers on the sight's knobs as he set the firing data. "I swear," he mumbled, "if I'm still alive when this is over, I'm gonna sleep for a week straight. I don't care if they court-martial my ass, either."

Bogater Boudreau would have cleaned up on his bet: they made it all the way inside Charlie Company's perimeter without seeing any Japanese. Lieutenant Lee Grossman filled Jock in on the current situation.

Pointing west, Grossman said, "Hadley and his boys are a couple of hundred yards over that way. They're shooting captured Jap weapons now and doing a hell of a lot of damage."

Jock asked Grossman, "What about bunkers in Buna Mission?"

"Hadley says there doesn't seem to be any between him and the Mission, sir. There are a few on the beach side, but they're all burned up and don't seem to be active."

"Good," Jock replied. "Here's what's going to happen: when the rain stops, the Air Force is going to bomb the hell out of Buna Mission and Buna Village. Then we're going to move in from the east, while Third Battalion comes in along the Girua River from the west."

Grossman seemed surprised: "You mean Third Battalion's actually going to do something constructive? That'd be a first."

"Yeah, tell me about it," Jock replied. "To continue, I'm going to have Able Company pass through your position here, Lee, and attack Buna Mission from the beach side. They'll be the ones to relieve Hadley, who can then join back up with you. Your company will attack straight ahead, while Baker Company will hook around and advance up Ango Trail to attack the southeast corner. They'll come up against bunkers, but I've got an idea how to get around them."

Grossman asked, "Are we getting any artillery support, sir?"

"Afraid not, Lee...but we're going to put all the battalion's mortars behind Baker Company—in open swamp country—where they'll have good fields of fire."

"Better than nothing, I guess," Grossman replied.

Jock turned to Bogater Boudreau. "Now, Corporal...you just walked the best route to get here and you know where First Sergeant Hadley's outpost is. I'll expect you to be Able Company's guide. Lieutenant Pop will be depending on you."

Boudreau replied, "Ain't no step for a stepper, sir."

It was mid-afternoon before Jock got back to his battalion's forward CP. The rain hadn't let up a bit. The makeshift CP was situated beneath a ground sheet strung between trees to keep out the rain. In the fierce downpour, though, the ground sheet had become a rain collector, about to collapse any second from the sheer weight of water. Three GIs were struggling to drain the cover and restore its slope so it wouldn't fill up again. They weren't having much luck; one field radio had already been doused with the runoff. Until the radio operators got a chance to dry it out, it would be as useless as if it had been thrown in a lake.

"You boys could fuck up a wet dream," Melvin Patchett fumed as he stepped in to provide direction to their hapless efforts. Pointing to the tallest of the GIs, he continued, "You, *Stretch*...poke the tarp right here with your rifle butt..."

When Patchett jerked his arms upward to lend a hand, the sleeves of his sodden, mildewed fatigue shirt separated at the shoulders. In a burst of rage, he ripped the sleeves clean off.

"Don't sweat it, Sergeant Major," Jock said, rubbing his hands over the many tears in his own sopping-wet uniform. "You're still the best-dressed son of a bitch in the outfit. And you can always draw the stripes on your bare arms with a grease pencil."

Patchett replied, "With all due respect, sir, that ain't fucking funny. Not a damn bit. It ain't bad enough them flyboys get their *three hots and a cot*, but I'm betting they get a new suit of clothes the minute a button pops off, too. At the rate we're going, them natives in their jock straps gonna be wearing more than us dogfaces real soon."

One of the radio operators handed Jock a message from Regiment. Its contents didn't seem to impress him at all.

As if a switch was thrown, Patchett was all business again: "So what's it say, sir?"

"It says we're to consolidate and hold our positions."

"Shit," Patchett scoffed, "you already had us doing that last night. You're way ahead of them brass hats, as usual, sir."

Java Queen, with her load of three Stuart tanks, was only a few miles from dropping anchor in Oro Bay when the tug, *Mieke*, making good speed back to Milne Bay, passed in the opposite direction. Beatrix Van Der Wegge scanned her cousin's vessel with binoculars: there was no sign of Jillian on board.

She grabbed the blinker light and flashed a message: *Where is Jillian?*

From *Mieke's* bridge, the answer flashed back: *Missing. Presumed drowned.*

Chapter Forty

The next sunrise brought clear skies—and the bombers of 5th Air Force. Jock and his men listened as they approached, encouraged and excited by what sounded like an aerial armada about to deal the first punch in their assault on Buna.

"Don't get your hopes up too much until you see where them eggs land," Melvin Patchett said. "We been down this road a few times already." The fact that the men of his command were close to the target area—in some cases, as little as a few hundred yards close—did little to bolster his confidence. He'd been on the receiving end of errant American bombs before.

"But it's a perfectly clear day, Sergeant Major," Lieutenant Tony Colletti, Baker Company's commander, said. "How the hell can they miss?"

Patchett's tight-lipped smile was his silent but respectful way of telling an officer exactly what he thought: *You dumb fuck. You got yourself a shitload to learn yet.*

In First Sergeant Hadley's position—the closest to the target area—he and his men burrowed deep into their fighting holes as the rumbling of aircraft engines grew louder. Tom Hadley peeked out from under the rim of his helmet just as the bombs began their plummet to the ground.

SHIT! They're going to land right on top of us!

He dropped to the bottom of the hole, yanking the helmet tight against his head. Right now, he wished his whole body could fit inside that steel pot.

The string of bombs landed, one right after the other, a series of explosions Hadley could only describe as *the footsteps of a giant on a double-time march.*

With each explosion, the ground in which the GIs lay shook as if attached to the planet by the thinnest of threads.

The sound of the impacts—those *giant's footsteps*—got closer and closer...

And then they stopped. The only sounds now were the distant *whoomps* of bombs impacting in Buna Village—and the pounding of their hearts.

Gingerly, Hadley and his men patted themselves all over.

They were all okay; *Close...but no cigar.*

But what about the Japanese?

Hadley slowly raised his head over the edge of the hole and brought the binoculars to his eyes.

"For fuck's sake," he said, "they tore the hell out of the beach, and that's about it. If anyone was taking a morning swim, they're dead about ten times over."

But the Japanese facing them in Buna Mission were still very much alive as they scurried from deep cover to man fighting positions once again.

"All right, guys," Hadley said, "be real careful now. Lieutenant Pop and his bunch are going to be coming soon. Let's try to shoot only the Japs, okay?"

Tony Colletti's Baker Company watched the bombing as they lay poised along Ango Trail. Much to their surprise, one bomb—at long last—scored a direct hit on a Japanese bunker, blowing it to smithereens.

For the first time in what seemed like an eternity, they had something to cheer about.

But after that brief celebration, it was time to get moving and launch their attack into the teeth of the remaining bunkers.

I need to be here with Colletti's company, Jock told himself. He had known that since the inception of this plan. Baker Company's roll would be the most difficult part of 1st Battalion's attack—and the most fragile.

But something was wrong right off the bat: along the trail, a platoon of GIs—not from Jock's battalion—had several dozen natives kneeling in a line, hands on head...

Like prisoners condemned to death.

A cocky sergeant strolled casually behind the line, laughing as he pressed the muzzle of his Thompson against the neck of each native in turn without pulling the trigger.

Standing to the side, a cluster of native women and children, all bewildered and crying, were being held at bay by American soldiers.

A young officer was in charge. Jock asked him, "What the fuck is going on here, Lieutenant?"

"We caught these Jap sympathizers manning one of the bunkers, sir," the lieutenant replied.

"What's your name, Lieutenant?"

"Lundsford, sir. James W."

"What on earth makes you think they're sympathizers, Lieutenant Lundsford?"

Before he could answer, one of Colletti's sergeants emerged from the bunker in question. "We cleaned this line of bunkers out yesterday, sir," the sergeant said. "There ain't a fucking weapon in there."

"Well, I'm pretty sure they shot at us, sir," Lundsford said, as if trying to convince himself. "They must have thrown the weapons in the swamp."

Colletti's men were muttering the same thing Jock was thinking: "Bullshit."

Jock asked, "What unit are you from, Lieutenant?"

"Love Company, sir...Third of the Eighty-First."

"You're Colonel Vann's men, then?"

"Yes, sir."

"Figures. I'll tell you what we're going to do, Lieutenant. First, release these people—"

"But sir, they must have been working for the Japs."

"And now they work for us. Do it now, Lieutenant."

Within seconds, the natives were on their feet, scurrying away from Buna as fast as they could.

"Very good," Jock said. "Now, you realize you're in the wrong place, don't you? Your battalion's boundary is Girua River."

The lieutenant looked confused. He pulled a map from inside his helmet and began to fumble with it.

Jock pointed west. "Don't bother, Lieutenant. It's that way, a good couple of hundred yards. I suggest you get over there immediately. They're probably wondering where the hell you are."

With Lundsford and his platoon gone, Jock settled into a secluded grove with Colletti's men. They needed to review the attack plan one last time.

"Through the swamp, fellows," Jock said, "it's the only way. While Third Platoon bluffs a frontal attack, the rest of us slide in through the wetlands and get behind the bunkers. When the Japs see us there—and they *will* see us—at least some of them will have to come out into the open and engage..."

Tony Colletti picked it up from there: "That's when we tell the mortars to let 'em have it."

"Exactly," Jock said. "Once we're behind the bunkers, you all know the drill..."

Jock paused, distracted by the sound of a jeep coming up the trail. A GI on the perimeter sounded the warning: *Big brass on the way.*

The jeep came to a halt just feet from Jock's briefing site. General Freidenburg stepped out.

So much for our concealed location, Jock told himself, cursing the sound of the jeep's engine. *Now every fucking Jap in Buna knows there's something to shoot at here.*

General Freidenburg stood in the middle of the trail, glistening stars and all, as if waiting for someone to salute him. Dozens of men would have been glad to offer that salute, if only it wouldn't make them a target for the snipers, too.

"Better step over here, sir." Jock urged the general toward the shelter of the trees. "This is a pretty hot area."

Freidenburg didn't move an inch, but the two staff officers riding with him—both colonels—inched steadily toward the cover of the trees. The general asked, "You're Miles, aren't you, Major?"

"Yes, sir. First of the Eighty-First C.O."

"I thought so. What are you waiting for, Major Miles? The air bombardment is over. Move your men up this trail on the double."

Up this trail—and become fodder for the bunkers' machine guns.

Half the company heard the general's order. Whatever hope the weak and weary GIs had held of surviving to see tomorrow was collapsing like a house of cards.

But then there was a most surprising and unlikely reshuffle of the deck. Unlike anything they had heard before in their military life, their battalion commander replied, "Negative, sir. We're not going to frontally assault bunkers. We learned that lesson a long time ago. We're going around them, through the swamp, and attack them from behind."

The GIs could not believe their ears. Sure, they'd heard men balk at orders before, but the man giving the order had usually been just a sergeant; the man resisting the order did it with the knowledge he was about to experience the full wrath of discipline that sergeant could cook up, be it guard duty, KP, or a trip behind the barracks to be beaten to a pulp.

But this was different—much different. They'd never seen an officer's order—much less a general's—refused by anyone, let alone another officer.

They had no idea where this standoff was going.

But Jock did. The cat was out of the bag now—and his mind was made up: as long as he was in command of this battalion, not one more man would be offered up to the slaughter of the bunkers.

If the general wants another frontal attack, he'll have to find someone stupid enough to lead it.

He fully expected the next words from General Freidenburg's mouth would be the ones relieving him of command.

But the general said nothing. He just kept glaring at Jock, as if waiting for him to crack—to come to his senses—and follow orders like a good soldier.

Jock said nothing, either. For the soldiers watching, the motionless silence of the two men became awkward and then frightening. The GIs were the pawns in this unlikely chess match, one in which the general had all the moves.

It would be *checkmate, Major Miles* any second, they were sure…

As soon as somebody said something.

That somebody was the general. He broke his glare at Jock, swept contemptuous eyes across the anxious troops, and said, "You're just yellow, Major, and I don't mean from the Atabrine, either."

Jock didn't reply. He betrayed no emotion at all.

But the GIs started to grumble; they didn't agree with the general's assessment.

They knew better.

"The Japs aren't near as tough as all you men think they are," Freidenburg said. "I'm betting there's no serious threat here. I'll decorate the first man who'll walk fifty yards down this trail toward Buna Village."

There were no volunteers.

"Some of us already got decorations, sir," a GI said. "They're called Purple Hearts, and we ain't begging for another one."

The general spit on the ground in disgust. "Like I said…you're yellow."

Then Jock said, "I'll tell you what, sir, I'll walk down that trail…if one of your staff officers would be kind enough to accompany me."

Freidenburg's two staff colonels were trying to make themselves invisible behind some trees. Neither was about to volunteer for anything.

"Well, I'm not seeing any takers, sir," Jock said, "so I'm guessing—"

His words were cut off by a *rumble-clank-clatter* of heavy machinery approaching. Everyone turned to see the olive drab outline of a Stuart tank, its treads throwing clods of mud into the air behind it as it chewed its way up the trail.

There was a man riding on top, standing behind the turret. Even from this distance, they could tell it was Sergeant Major Patchett.

The Stuart rattled to a stop beside the general's jeep. Patchett jumped down and said, "It followed me home, Daddy…can I keep it?"

General Freidenburg seemed annoyed by the tank's arrival.

"All right, then, Major," the general said, "maybe this is what you need to jack your courage up. All you people have been bellyaching about armor support ever since I got here. Well, here it is. Impress me."

The general and his colonels hopped in the jeep and made their escape down the trail toward *Double-Dare*.

Patchett gave Jock a curious glance and asked, "Still sucking up to the mucketymucks, eh, sir?"

"Get this," Jock replied. "The general wanted a frontal assault on the bunkers."

Patchett whistled like a bomb falling. "Well, fuck him and the jeep he rode in on. We're smarter than that now."

"Hey, Top…where *did* this tank come from, anyway?"

"A couple came up from Oro early this morning, sir. Supposed to be three, but one's broken down already. They said they got orders to go to Eighty-Third

Regiment down at *Double-Dare*, but they don't have the faintest fucking idea where that is, so I made them a little deal."

"What kind of deal, Top?"

"We'll guard their fuel reserves—a deuce-and-a-half with drums full of aviation gas—and they'll help us out. They're real touchy about that gas getting *appropriated*, especially with that airstrip at *Double-Dare* opening up for business."

"Who the hell is doing the guarding, Top? I thought we agreed every man not burning up with fever would be on the line in this attack."

"And they are, sir…they are. Don't you fret none. I've got some of those poor bastards from the Kapa Kapa doing the guard duty. They can do that job sitting on their sweet asses."

Jock wished he had bitten his tongue; as usual, Patchett had the details covered. But there was one more question: "You said *two* tanks, Top. Where's the other one?"

"I was just getting to that, sir. It's in the plantation, with Able Company."

Chapter Forty-One

It didn't take long for Corporal Bogater Boudreau to decide he wanted nothing to do with the Stuart tank given to Able Company. "It draws too much fire, Lieutenant," he told Theo Papadakis, "and it's slowing me down. Y'all can hide behind it if you like, but I'm gonna go find me Sergeant Hadley. Catch up when you can...if that's okay with you, sir."

Papadakis was beginning to feel the same way about the tank. The sergeant in command seemed much too cautious, almost timid: *He thinks there's a fucking sniper in every tree in this plantation, waiting to drop a grenade on him. And these tight rows of trees make its path kind of predictable for an anti-tank gunner.*

Still, it was nice to hide behind its comforting mass when the bullets were flying. The tank's main gun—though relatively puny at 37 millimeters—was the most firepower they'd had at their disposal since the loan of the Aussie artillery. The two extra machine guns it carried were nice to have, too, scattering the Japs before them like a giant steel broom.

And these damn Japs keep popping up everywhere...like they're crawling out of the ground five or six at a shot. It's like a firing range at a lunatic asylum. At least we ain't hit no fucking bunkers yet.

But the Stuart could only be one place at a time; Lieutenant Pop's company was spread thin, advancing in a line almost 200 yards wide. Corporal Boudreau and his squad were well in front of that line.

"Remember," Boudreau told his men, "Sergeant Hadley and his boys are firing Jap weapons now. Don't get fooled by their sound and do something you'll be real sorry about. We should be getting pretty close to them."

Two troopers on the right flank of the squad were certain they were *pretty close*. Twenty yards in front, they heard a Nambu firing toward Buna Mission, opposite their direction of approach.

"It's gotta be Hadley," one of the GIs whispered. "Otherwise, they'd be firing at us, right?"

The other GI agreed. Together, they low-crawled forward until they came to what looked like a freshly dug trench.

They slid in, expecting to be greeted like saviors—and found themselves face to face with three skeletal Japanese.

The gaunt Americans didn't look so great, either, but these Japanese might as well have been the walking dead.

The GIs tried to level their weapons—an M1 and a BAR—but they were too close.

Two of the Japanese soldiers already had iron grips on the muzzles, grappling them skyward despite the best struggle the GIs could muster.

These fucking Nips...they must weigh about forty pounds apiece. How can they be so fucking strong?

The panicked GIs fired several rounds, which streaked off to nowhere.

They were all locked in a struggle that would have appeared comical if it were not a matter of life and death: four men—exhausted and weakened by malarial fever before this joust even began—waltzing to and fro in the narrow trench to the rhythm of their mortal grunts.

The third Japanese soldier did his own hopping dance, trying to jab at the Americans from behind his comrades with a long bayonet.

But it wasn't long enough. Its point couldn't reach the GIs.

They danced on, for seconds that seemed endless, fueled only by adrenaline and the knowledge that to yield was to die.

The Nambu's sudden silence, followed by those strange, random shots of the GIs' weapons, caught Bogater Boudreau's attention. He crawled as fast as he could in their direction.

His worst fear: some of his men had found *Combat Team Hadley*...and killed them.

His greatest hope: any other scenario which resulted in no Americans dead or wounded.

What he found lay somewhere in the middle: a situation still in flux, like watching a feeble tug-of-war between geriatrics.

Bogater put a stop to the dance: from only feet away, he dispatched the Japanese clinging to his men's weapons with two shots from his Thompson.

The third Jap—the bayonet wielder—tried to run.

He'd only taken a few steps before Bogater's third shot found him.

"Y'all can thank me later," Boudreau told his panting, unnerved troopers. "Didn't crap your pants, did you?"

They shook their heads.

"That's real good. Now scoop up the Nambu and get moving. We ain't there yet."

A few moments more and they found Hadley. There was that same chatter of a Nambu as they approached, but this time Boudreau shouted the challenge word: *Laramie.*

Tom Hadley's voice called back the password: *Licorice.*

Turning to the two GIs who had waltzed with the Japs, Boudreau said, "You see? That's what the damn password's for, zipperheads. Now get down here and give those Charlie Company mutts a breather."

Boudreau's squad jumped down into the trench. They found themselves on a catwalk of dead Japanese.

Another five minutes and Theo Papadakis joined them in Hadley's trench. The Stuart idled 10 yards away.

Hadley, in awe of the metal monster, asked, "Where'd the tank come from?"

"The sergeant major gave it to us," Lieutenant Pop replied. "He gave another one to Baker Company."

Papadakis scanned Buna Mission with his binoculars. "So how do we get in there, First Sergeant?"

"I'm pretty sure there are no live bunkers on the beach side," Hadley began, "just scattered Japs in holes and buildings. I've been calling in the mortars on every position I can see. Just keep doing that and you won't have much trouble going in from this side."

Hadley pointed farther inland, toward Charlie Company's area of operation. "Charlie's going to have it rougher," Hadley continued. "They'll be up against bunkers, I'm pretty sure. We've been taking fire from over there, and we can't tell from exactly where. I've dropped mortars on them, but it didn't shut them up. I think there's a big open area, too. You see it? It's too bright to be in trees like we are here. It'd be perfect terrain for a tank."

Papadakis and Boudreau were thinking the same thing: *Nice as it would be to keep that tank, Charlie Company needs it a whole lot more.*

"Tom, I'm gonna give the tank to you guys," Papadakis told Hadley. "It wouldn't have a whole lot of room to maneuver on the beach, anyway. Tell Lieutenant Grossman that if I get in trouble, I might have to call for it back. But for now, it's yours."

Many loud *clanks*—every man's head went down as machine gun rounds bounced off the Stuart.

"See, I told you," Bogater Boudreau said. "You'd better be able to hide behind that damn thing because it draws fire like a son of a bitch. Better not be no anti-tank guns around here or the tankers' asses are gonna get fried."

***

First Battalion's battle for Buna Mission was at full throttle, for better or worse. Able Company pushed in from the beach in the north, Charlie Company from the plantation in the east, Baker Company from the swamps in the south. They could only pray Colonel Vann's 3rd Battalion was where it was supposed to be, covering the western flank.

The two tanks, hobbled as they were by terrain, were still making the difference everyone had hoped they would. The Stuart attacking with Baker Company dared not stray from the trail; it would promptly become mired in the muck of the swamp if it did. Protected from Japanese sappers by a squad of Lieutenant Colletti's GIs, it had done well from the trail, though, rumbling to less than 50 yards from the first bunker and pelting it with

37-millimeter shells. Aiming at a firing port but never managing to put one through, it took six shots from the Stuart's small-caliber main gun to partially collapse the bunker and pound it into silence.

Jock, with the rest of Baker Company, emerged from the swamp behind the bunker. "They're not all dead," Jock said, pointing at the dazed and battered Japanese stumbling out of its entryway.

Jock was right; most of the bunker's complement were quite alive.

The deafening racket of gunfire erupted.

So did the screaming of men at the top of their lungs.

The gunfire was over in 10 seconds.

The screaming was not.

GIs still in the thrall of combat cursed their enemy.

The wounded begged for help in two different languages.

The dead stared with vacant eyes into a realm no one wished to visit.

But this bunker finally belonged to the Americans, who wondered in fear how many more like it would have to be taken.

The GIs didn't have to wait long for an answer.

They were already drawing fire from another bunker.

Able Company raced along the groves rimming the beach and plunged into Buna Mission.

The terrifying noise, blinding smoke, and confusion of combat surrounded them as it had so many times before.

Kill or be killed once again became a doctrine not to be pondered but a mantra believed in with your heart and soul.

Rare was the GI not firing, hoping his refusal to participate in combat would somehow exempt him from its consequences.

You couldn't hide behind a battle line when there wasn't one—the enemy wasn't just somewhere in the distance before you; he seemed to be all around.

Theo Papadakis's one miscalculation: he forgot the mortars were almost two miles away. Once he called for fire over the walkie-talkie, his request relayed to the mortar section, and the rounds launched, it took over a minute for them to land on target—an eternity in close combat.

Caught in a murderous crossfire, he had to give up hard-won ground waiting for mortar rounds too long in coming.

That was my fuckup...and two good men died. I swear to God, I'll never stick our necks out like that again.

They were deep in Buna Mission now, a very different but no less dangerous battlefield. Rickety buildings still amazingly intact stood amidst the rubble of those flattened by 5th Air Force.

Bogater Boudreau took a practical view: "At least when you pitch a grenade here, it don't bounce off a tree and come right back at you."

He tossed one right through a hut's unshuttered window.

Its blast puffed fleeting clouds of dust and debris out every opening. The thatched roof fluttered like windblown hair.

The Japanese inside stopped shooting.

Motioning toward the hut, Boudreau tapped two GIs lying next to him and said, "It's y'all's turn…go finish them off."

The troopers didn't want to go. His voice trembling, one said, "You're crazy, Cajun. You really like this shit, don't you?"

"Don't matter none if I like it or not. I got no choice…and neither do you."

"But maybe the Japs in there are already dead."

"Then they won't mind you shooting them one little bit. Get your asses moving."

Tom Hadley was surprised to find what he thought was an open field was actually an airstrip not long abandoned by the Japanese. Drums of oil and fuel lined a trench covered with camouflage netting. Salvaged aircraft parts littered the field's periphery. There was a tattered windsock flying from a tall pole.

It made a perfect killing ground for machine guns, several of which opened up in an interlocking field of fire, crisscrossing the airstrip the moment the GIs appeared at its far end.

As most of Charlie Company sprawled on the ground for cover, a squad of GIs scrambled behind the Stuart as it rumbled toward the machine guns.

It was all over quickly. Two nests were wiped out, one blown to shreds by the tank's 37-millimeter gun at

30 yards, the other by its machine guns at point-blank range.

If there were more Japanese machine gunners, they had fled by the time the rest of Charlie Company crossed the airfield.

The GIs needed a break. Lee Grossman figured half of them were running fevers. As they sagged into a ragged defensive perimeter, he worried they might never have the energy to get up again.

Everywhere he looked, though, men were breaking off chunks of D bar—those bitter blocks of chocolate designed strictly to provide calories for energy—and popping them into their mouths.

At least they're giving it the old college try, Grossman told himself.

He'd seen troops that had thrown in the towel before.

His men hadn't.

He pulled out his pocket notebook: *I've got to make some notes for the after-action report—if I live long enough to write one.*

It fell open to a reminder he had written earlier that morning. He smiled when he read it: *Recommend Hadley for Medal of Honor.*

Lieutenant Colonel Horace Vann was suffering through another malaria attack. The *chill* phase was upon him, teeth chattering, wrapped in a blanket despite the sweltering heat of his CP tent. He'd tried to focus on his battalion's situation map but given up. His faltering concentration would only get worse when the chills passed and the fever kicked in.

A frantic staff captain burst into the tent. "Colonel," he said, "I've just been told there's a big gap in our lines."

"Show me," Vann replied, pointing to the map.

The captain hastily sketched a dismal picture: India and Love Companies had never established contact on their flanks, as were their orders. The resulting gap—rumored to be half a mile wide, maybe more—had become a causeway for Japanese fleeing 1st Battalion's push from the east, squirting enemy troops toward Sanananda or even the mountains inland.

"As we know, sir," the captain said, "the Japanese don't run away. They regroup to counterattack."

"Bullshit, Captain," Colonel Vann replied. "They ran away from Port Moresby. They've run away from a lot of places. They're not supermen...and they're not suicidal."

"But we're supposed to be the blocking force, sir." Pushing his finger into the map at the point of the gap, the captain added, "We're supposed to be stopping exactly what's happening right now."

"So...get those companies to close the gap, Captain."

"They tried, sir. They were beaten back...quite badly."

Vann wrenched his face into a look of disgust. "They never did have any backbone. Make them try again."

With great hesitation, the captain began, "Begging your pardon, sir...but many of your men are just as sick as you. I think this might be a time for you to make a command visit and...you know...*influence* the situation with your presence."

For a brief moment, Vann was full of piss and vinegar as he replied, "OH, DO YOU REALLY, CAPTAIN?"

But that spark burned out as quickly as it had flared. Colonel Vann slumped back into his camp chair like a man too exhausted to care. He tucked the blanket tight under his chin and muttered, "Just leave me in peace and go do *something*, will you, Captain?"

Charlie Company's break was over all too soon. They were up and moving forward again, leaving the abandoned Japanese airstrip behind.

They heard the gunfire and explosions from Buna Mission. Now, through the trees, they could see its buildings not far away.

Thinking out loud, Lee Grossman said, "It can't be this easy."

He was right.

The sound of machine gun fire seemed to be coming from everywhere at once.

The first rank of the lead platoon crumpled to the ground, mowed down like a bloody harvest.

Shit. Bunkers. One left, one right.
Where's the fucking tank?

The Stuart wasn't far behind. Its engine revved as it swerved through a row of trees.

The steady *CLANK* of bullets ricocheting off the metal beast was as unnerving to the GIs hugging the nearby ground as it was to the crew inside.

Lee Grossman and Tom Hadley, huddled behind a stout tree trunk, had figured out where the bunkers were.

The tank commander, buttoned up and half-blind in his turret, had not. His first shot from the main gun streaked above and past one of the bunkers.

He wasn't answering Hadley's radio calls, either.

"I've got to get him straightened out," Hadley called to Grossman.

Sprinting like a madman, the first sergeant hopped on the tank's rear deck. Huddled for cover against the turret, he saw why they'd lost radio communication:

The damn antenna's shot off.

He reached over the top and banged on the hatch with the butt end of his Thompson.

The hatch didn't open.

Can't blame the guy...I could be a Jap sitting up here. Got to get his attention.

Maybe this'll work...

He banged on the hatch with the Thompson again, but this time, he tapped out a rhythm: *thunk-thunkthunkthunkthunk-thunk-thunk*, to the tune *shave and a haircut, two bits.*

The hatch cracked open.

"YOU'RE TOO HIGH," Hadley said. "ONE BUNKER'S ONLY THIRTY YARDS DEAD IN FRONT OF YOU."

The tank commander shouted back, "THERE'S MORE THAN ONE?"

"THE OTHER ONE IS ABOUT TWENTY DEGREES LEFT AND A LITTLE FARTHER."

The tank's main gun fired.

Ducked down behind the turret, Hadley was disappointed: he hadn't felt a bit of recoil.

That gun feels a little on the weak side.

If a mortar can't crack one of those bunkers, how's this peashooter going to do it?

The main gun fired again.

And again.

Then the tank was moving, pivoting left slightly as the turret traversed in the same direction.

"YOU'VE GOT IT NOW," Hadley said. "I'M GETTING THE HELL OFF."

He slid from the tank to the ground.

The first bunker was still intact—but it was smoldering and silent now.

A platoon moved briskly to flank it and take it from behind. It only took seconds: three Japanese dead, one GI wounded.

When Hadley found Lee Grossman again, Jock Miles was there, too.

Jock asked, "How's the tank holding up?"

"So far, so good," Grossman replied. "Looks like it could use a bigger gun, though."

"Yeah," Jock replied, "I noticed that. Took six shots at damn near point-blank range to shut one up over in Baker Company...and even then, the bunker was still standing."

Hadley got his breath back and added, "Just so the sons of bitches inside get dazed for a minute, that's all we need."

Pointing toward the tank, Jock said, "Come on, let's see what's going on over there."

They scrambled to join the fight for the second bunker. Halfway there, the fire became so intense they had to drop to their bellies and low crawl the rest of the way.

The platoon sergeant facing that bunker told them, "That fucking thing gotta be made outta more than just dirt and wood...look!"

The tank had advanced to just yards from the bunker's front face, so close its machine gun couldn't depress enough to shoot through the narrow firing ports.

The main gun fired repeatedly—a dozen rounds in 10 seconds—and each shot resulted in nothing more than a cloud of dust and splinters as it glanced off the bunker's sloped roof.

"Sir," Jock's radio operator said, "I've got Regiment on the horn for you."

"Tell him to wait a minute," Jock replied. "We're a little busy here right now."

The Stuart's engine revved like it was at the starting gate of a race.

It lurched forward, its nose pointing skyward as it drove onto the bunker, until its chassis was perched nearly vertical, like a begging dog on its hind legs, its belly exposed to anyone on the far side.

The bunker didn't collapse; it didn't even shudder.

The platoon sergeant threw up his hands and said, "See? What'd I tell you? That fucking lump in the ground's made of iron or somethi—"

The shock wave came first.

Then they saw the flash of orange flames shooting from beneath the tank and heard the *WHOOMP* of the shell's impact.

A second more and they heard the distant *poom* of the gun that fired it.

High-octane gasoline began to flow from the Stuart like liquid fire, engulfing the bunker in its flames.

Two Japanese soldiers, ablaze from head to toe, stumbled outside to be shot dead—perhaps mercifully—by a host of GIs.

"Well," Hadley said, "that's one way to take out a bunker—drop a burning tank on it."

"We've got to get that crew out," Jock said. He stood up and started to sprint toward the spreading inferno.

He got to the commander's hatch. It was already ajar, two arms clinging to its rim.

Jock grabbed for the arms but Tom Hadley already had them in his grasp.

"This thing's going to cook off any second, sir," Hadley said, with startling calmness. "Here...I've got these guys. You go up front and try and get the driver out."

"No...no good," the tank commander mumbled. "All dead..."

Tom Hadley was amazed how easy it was to lift the man out. He seemed light as a feather.

Boy, I must be really pumping the old adrenaline. I'm strong as hell.

Then he saw why the man was so light: both his legs were gone.

Back down on the ground, they had no idea how they had gotten themselves and the legless man out of the flames.

Or how they had done it so quickly.

That speed had saved them: the second artillery round slammed into the tank's thin, exposed underbelly.

This time, the ammunition onboard did start to cook off, driving every man's head back to the ground once again.

Lee Grossman was already calling for fire from the battalion's mortars. Between transmissions, he told Jock, "I was looking for that artillery when it fired the second time. Saw the flash. Gotta take him out before he does any more damage."

Thirty seconds later, they heard the dull *crump* of mortar rounds impacting.

Binoculars still pressed to his eyes, Grossman said, "Yeah, that ought to do it."

Jock acknowledged Grossman with a nod; he was busy on his radio, finally able to have that conversation with Colonel Molloy at Regiment. While listening to the colonel, he watched as the medic shook his head and gently closed the tank commander's eyes.

The medic gave him a look that seemed to say, *Nice rescue, sir, but...*

Then he hurried off, toward the sounds of wailing men he might actually be able to save.

At first, Jock didn't know why Grossman and Hadley were staring at him with those worried looks. Then he realized his hand was shaking.

In fact, his whole body was shaking. All of a sudden, he was freezing cold, too.

What the hell's going on? Is this the fright just coming out now? Or...

He realized what it was:

Shit. Malaria.

Chapter Forty-Two

Melvin Patchett couldn't believe his eyes. "Begging your pardon, sir," he said to Jock, "but how the hell did you get malaria? You took your Atabrine real regular-like, didn't you? You must've—you're yellower than them Jap sons of bitches."

Jock shrugged, and then pulled the blanket tighter around his body. The chills were still with him.

"I was *pretty* good about taking it, I thought," Jock replied, "but Doc says it's not one hundred percent effective. Just my damn luck..."

"How high's the fever running?"

"Don't know, Top. I haven't had the fever part yet. But the chills haven't been too awful...so maybe the fever won't be, either."

"Let's hope so, sir," Patchett replied.

They both knew it was the fever that would make all the difference. Some of their men were fighting the Japanese right now with fevers of 103 degrees. Jock and Patchett had set that reading as the cutoff: any higher, a man was usually too weak and useless, a danger to himself and his buddies. He'd be pulled off the line and sent to the aid station.

"Do me a favor, Top...don't mention I'm sick to anyone, not even Colonel Molloy."

Patchett grimaced. "A little late for that, sir."

Dick Molloy was approaching, only a few yards away. He'd heard every word of Jock's last sentence.

Molloy asked, "Don't tell me what?"

Then he saw Jock huddled in the blanket; he didn't need an explanation.

"Shit," the colonel said, "you've got the bug, too. How bad?"

"Doesn't seem too bad so far, sir," Jock replied.

"That's good, because I've got a couple of things to tell you. It's not all good news, I'm afraid, Jock."

Patchett, not sure his presence was required, began to excuse himself. Molloy motioned for him to stay.

"I'm relieving Colonel Vann," Molloy said. "He left a hole big enough for half the Japanese Army to slip through. Your battalion has done a great job so far, Jock, but because of Vann dropping the ball again, some of those Japs you pushed back squirted right out the other side. We could have had them all trapped in Buna Village and let the Air Force pound them to dust, but now we'll have to fight them all over again. Worse, I've had to pull his lines back so his whole battalion doesn't get enveloped and destroyed."

Patchett asked, "Who's getting his job, sir?"

"Rudy Sontag. Just arrived from Australia. He's a damn good man. I think you both know him, right?"

They nodded approvingly.

Jock asked, "Anything we can do to help, sir?"

"Just keep doing what you're doing, Jock. Once all your units have moved through Buna Mission, consolidate your position on the far side and link up with Sontag on your left. Come tomorrow, we've got a tactical air unit moving into Dobodura airstrip. That'll give us continuous air support from sunup to sundown. We're going to get some Navy destroyers offshore by sunrise tomorrow, too. A naval shore group is coming up from Oro today to coordinate fire support."

Patchett whistled happily. "Them little five-inch guns on them boats will be better than nothing, even if it is swabbies doing the shooting," he said. "Why's the Navy suddenly so interested in coming way up here, sir?"

"Seems they just scored some big victory over the Japs north of Rabaul," Molloy replied. "The Solomon Sea isn't the sole property of the Imperial Japanese Navy anymore."

They could tell the colonel had something else to say but he looked hesitant, as if he couldn't find the words.

Molloy finally pulled a piece of paper from his pocket and said, "I've got this message here from Oro Bay...I figure it's meant for you. It's from a lady by the name of Beatrix Van Der Wegge. She's a freighter captain, I'm told. Do you know her?"

"Yeah," Jock replied, "I've heard the name. She sails with Jillian."

Words now failed Molloy completely. He handed over the sheet of paper.

Jock read it silently.

It was all there: how Jillian Forbes had personally led the *fireship* deception.

In other words, she'd gone and done exactly what I begged her not to do.

He couldn't tell if he was shaking from the malaria or the terse, life-shattering finality of those last four words: *She's missing, presumed drowned.*

Jock handed the message to Patchett.

After he read it, the sergeant major dismissed the message with a shake of his head. "*Presumed* my ass, sir," he said. "No way that lady's dead. She's too damn clever...and too damn tough."

Chapter Forty-Three

Night brought Jock's fever. The first thermometer reading: 102.6 degrees.

The medic started to say, "If it gets to over 103, he's—" but Patchett cut him off.

"We know the damn drill, Doc," the sergeant major said as he gave the medic the *bum's rush* out of the tent. "We wrote that rule, remember?"

"He keeps mumbling something, too," the medic added. "About some woman. If you ask me, he's getting delirious."

"No one's asking you nothing, son," Patchett replied. "We'll call you if we need you."

The medic gone, Patchett told Jock, "Try and get some shuteye, sir. I'll be in the CP if you need me."

As the sergeant major vanished into the shadows, Jock could feel himself being sucked down into that vacuum of despair again.

Does he really think I'm going to be able to sleep?
How can I?
It's my fault.
I told her not to go...
No, I begged her not to go.
She's not dead.
She can't be dead.
But if I really believed that, why do I have to tell myself over and over again?

It might have been the heartbreak; it might have been the fever.

Or maybe just the exhaustion they'd all lived with far too long.

Whatever it was, he collapsed into the emptiness inside him...

...and slept.

Dawn broke to strange, new sounds: the faint and distant roar of American aircraft taking to the air at *Double-Dare*; the much closer *CRUMP* of naval shells landing in Buna Village.

"Time to get up, *Sleeping Beauty*," Patchett said as he gently shook Jock. "You're gonna miss all the fun. How's the fever doing?"

Jock touched his hand to his forehead. "Feels like it's gone."

"Good to hear, sir, because we're fixing to carry you around like the Queen of Sheba if need be."

Struggling to focus, Jock asked, "Whose artillery is that?"

"The Navy's, sir. Lieutenant Pop's already got their fire support team up and running. Ol' Bogater Boudreau dragged those swabbie officers kicking and screaming right up to our front line. I tell you what...they weren't too thrilled about that, not one li'l bit. He even told them they ain't got a hair on their asses if they weren't close enough to eyeball the targets. None of this *we're going to do it by sound* shit. With all due respect, of course."

Jock had come around enough to visualize the scene Patchett described. He couldn't help but smile at the thought of the Cajun corporal goading naval officers to risk their necks *on land*.

Patchett continued, "The Navy's gonna be done in a couple of minutes, then it'll be the Air Force's turn.

We've got fire support coming out our asses all of a sudden."

"About fucking time," Jock said. "Is that tank still running, too?"

"Yeah. It's still with Baker Company. That okay with you, sir?"

"That'll be fine, Top."

Then he thought of Jillian...and the agony of losing her returned.

It took an entire day to fight their way into Buna Village. A rain squall in late morning had slowed things down considerably; the Air Force retreated to fairer skies, leaving only the guns of the Navy destroyers offshore to soften up what seemed a never-ending string of Japanese strong points.

The air support—now flying from the nearby airstrip at Dobodura—could spend much more time pounding any given target before it was chased off by weather or the need to refuel and rearm. "They're knocking the shit out of the Jap heavy weapons," Jock told Colonel Molloy, "but the troops do what they always did—they go underground until the planes leave. We're going to be digging them out of those holes for days."

"Good thing it's a small village, then," Molloy said. "What's your battalion's strength now, Jock?"

"Going down at a pretty good clip, sir. We're not really a battalion anymore...more like a very big company."

"I see," Molloy replied. "How're you holding up?" He hedged immediately, adding, "You know, being sick and all."

What Jock wanted to reply: *Malaria is the least of my problems. I feel dead inside...and unless I find her again, I'll probably feel this way for the rest of my life.*

Instead, he said, "I'll be okay, sir."

Jock was sure the colonel saw through this flimsy optimism to the lie festering beneath. It was what he needed to hear, though; they both had too much to do—with too much at stake—to flounder in the truth right now.

Later that evening, Tom Hadley and Bogater Boudreau asked to have a word. Jock knew it would be about Jillian; both had come to know her well during the ordeal on Cape York. Their respect and admiration for her was no secret.

"We all feel real bad about Miss Forbes, sir," Hadley said. "Hell, if it wasn't for her, we'd have all been dead last year on the Cape...not to mention right now, here at Buna."

Boudreau added, "So we want to volunteer, sir."

"Volunteer? For what, Bogater?"

"For the search party for Miss Forbes, sir," Boudreau replied. "She must've swum to shore somewhere around here, after she got the Japs' drawers all in a bunch with them *fireships.*"

Jock looked at the two earnest young men standing before him. Like Melvin Patchett, neither believed a little thing like being lost at sea could claim someone like Jillian. The doctrine of a combat commander loving his men had been a part of his being from his days at

West Point. But he had never felt that love more strongly than at this moment.

"I really appreciate that, guys," Jock said. "You don't know how much that means to me. But right now, I need you to do me an even bigger favor."

Hadley asked, "What's that, sir?"

"Just try to keep yourselves and your men alive, okay?"

The Japanese soldier was curled into a mudhole barely big enough for his withered frame. He could hardly see the notebook page inches from his nose. What little light there was filtered through voids in the rubble heaped above to conceal the hole.

He heard no American footsteps. It was time to put pen to paper.

> *I write my final entry for the hundredth time*
> *From a shelter that may well be my grave*
> *We who are left behind are human booby-*
> *traps*
> *Hundreds of us...maybe thousands*
> *Snipers at point-blank range*
> *Picking off Americans*
> *Exhausted men, like me*
> *Whose thoughts seemed a million miles away*
> *I killed five today, an unseen assassin*
> *How am I still alive?*
>
> *Once, we fought from ingenious shelters*
> *Marvels of practical engineering*
> *Which could withstand all but the mightiest*
> *blow*
> *Now we fight crouched in puddles*

With only frail scraps above our heads
While the airplanes fill the sky like flocks of
birds
Spreading their droppings of iron rain

When I am out of bullets I am to flee
But to where?
We are cornered in a room full of enemies
Some say they'll save their last bullet for
themselves
I will save my last bullet for a man in a group
At least I'll take one more of them with me
While his comrades free me from this hell

Chapter Forty-Four

Their first night inside Buna Village, Jock announced his decision: "I'm not going to keep trading one dead GI for one dead Jap in a hole, like General Freidenburg seems to want us to do. I don't think much of that equation at all. Neither does Colonel Molloy. So at first light, we're going to pull back a little and let the Air Force set fire to this whole damn place. And when those fires burn out, we're going to crush what's left with tanks."

His company commanders were relieved—but puzzled. Lee Grossman asked, "Tanks, sir? As in *plural*? Where the hell are we getting more tanks from?"

"The colonel just told me five more Stuarts are sitting at Oro now," Jock replied. "Assuming they all make the drive up here without breaking down, we'll get two more and the Aussies will get three."

As the briefing broke up, Melvin Patchett told Jock, "Good plan, sir. Real good plan."

But then he noticed Jock was shaking. "The malaria...it's coming over you again, ain't it, sir?"

"In spades, Top."

Late that night, as the chills rolled into fever, Jock had only one decision left to make: "Don't let the medic take my temperature, Top."

"Somebody's gotta do it, sir."

"Then you do it."

When Patchett took the thermometer from under his tongue, Jock didn't have to be a mind reader to know the number wasn't good.

"It's climbing. One-oh-four point three," Patchett said, like a jury foreman reading a *guilty* verdict. "We gotta get you to the sick ward."

Even though his voice was strained and shaky, Jock's words were emphatic: "The fuck you will, Top. I'm staying with my men."

Melvin Patchett laid a comforting hand on Jock's shoulder. There was no point trying to talk a feverish man out of something he had his heart set on.

Sure, he'll stay with his men...even if it kills him.

He sent a runner to fetch the medic.

The sun was high and the Air Force's firebombing well under way when Jock's fever finally broke. "He shouldn't even be here," the medic said to Patchett, who was pointedly ignoring him.

"You do realize, Sergeant Major, that we took four more men out of action during the night with the fever?"

Patchett bristled. "You trying to tell me my business, boy? Of course I fucking realize that."

Jock was still stirring, not quite awake yet. Nodding toward him, the medic added, "Well, then you know it should have been five."

He sprinted out of the tent before Patchett could unleash his wrath.

Jock gulped down the first canteen of water handed him, letting the last bit splash over his sweaty face. "The tanks," he said. "Did they get here?"

"Yep," Patchett replied. "Only one broke down and Colonel Molloy said to scratch it off the Aussie's allocation. I'm really starting to like that man."

"You see, Top? I told you he was a good man to work for. What else did I miss during the night?"

"Not a damn thing. We're all just waiting on the flyboys to finish up."

Jock tried to stand and nearly fell on his face. He would have if Patchett hadn't caught him.

"You know, sir...another bout of the fever like you had last night and you may not be with us much longer. And I'm not talking about a trip to the aid station, neither."

"Can't think about that right now, Top."

He found his feet this time. They headed out of the tent to watch Buna Village burn.

General Freidenburg was expecting gratitude from the Aussie commander, General Vasey. Instead, he was getting an earful.

"Two bloody tanks? That's all I get from you Yanks?"

"I think that's quite a fair allocation, General," Freidenburg replied. "You were doing quite well breaking through the Sanananda defenses without them. They're just icing on the cake for you now."

Vasey tried hard not to laugh in the American's face. "*Doing quite well*, General? If you call my horrendous casualty rates *doing quite well*, I don't want to know what *doing badly* entails."

Freidenburg paid no attention to the complaints. He had a few of his own.

"Looking at your situation map, General Vasey, you don't seem to be using the US Eighty-Second Regiment very effectively. Why aren't they in the main thrust of the attack with your boys, instead of just guarding your boundary with my Thirty-Second Division?"

"Because my men don't bloody trust them under fire, General. Neither do I. And since you Yanks have cocked up so badly, I need an entire regiment just to protect my flank from all those Japanese you let escape from Buna. I consider it poetic justice to call upon your Eighty-Second to provide me this service. Unfortunately, they don't seem very good at doing that, either."

"Now see here, General," Freidenburg said, "I will not tolerate—"

But Vasey kept right on talking. "Twice, I've had to rescue *their* flank from being enveloped by ragtag bunches of Nips. And another thing, General…can you tell me how many Japanese your Eighty-Second has killed or captured?"

Freidenburg was stumped for an answer.

"Then let me tell you, sir…a dozen. A bloody *dozen*. Thousands of Nips fleeing right through their lines to the hills—where, no doubt, we'll be fighting them all over again—and the best your lads can do is bag *a dozen*?"

Spitting fire, Freidenburg said, "I've listened to enough of your bullshit, General. Now I want a straight answer: when will you capture Sanananda?"

George Vasey wasn't in the least bit intimidated. His reply: "We'll capture it bloody well before you Yanks finish your mucking about in Buna."

The fires from the Air Force's incendiary raid on Buna were beginning to burn out. There was still plenty of daylight left to begin the task of finding—and finishing—any Japanese making a stand in the village. The engines of the Stuart tanks roared to life. A squad of men climbed on the back of each, doing their part in the symbiosis of infantry and armor: *You give us rolling cover and firepower, we'll keep the Jap sappers off you.*

Jock had been summoned to Regimental HQ just as the sweep into Buna Village began. He wasn't happy about it; he'd wanted to be with his men as they cleared the village inch by inch.

But maybe it's a blessing right now, he thought. *I'm about as wrung out as an old dishrag. I can tell by how everyone's staring at me that I look like warmed-over shit. Riding in this jeep is about as much exercise as I can handle at the moment. Maybe I should grab some chow up at Regiment...that might help.*

After nothing but K rations—and, when the sickness peaked, no food at all—the thought of a canned C ration entrée was making his mouth water.

He hadn't been in the HQ tent for a second when Colonel Molloy said, "Jock...listen to this."

An American voice was shrieking over the Division radio net, calling for immediate air support. The target: *Jap armored vehicles.*

They moved to the map to plot the given target coordinates. They couldn't believe where the pin fell.

"Impossible," Jock said. "That plots right on the edge of my zone, in Baker Company's area. It's bullshit...we haven't seen a Jap tank the whole time—"

He stopped cold. The realization of what was happening struck him—and everyone else in the tent—like a punch in the face.

Molloy asked, "That call's coming from Eighty-Second Regiment, isn't it? Over with the Aussies?"

"Affirmative, sir."

"They're looking across the Girua River, sir," Jock said, "right at my guys working with one of the Stuarts."

"Call off the fucking Air Force," Molloy commanded. "They're fixing to hit friendlies."

The Air Force liaison piped up and said, "We're not handling that call, sir. It's going through the Aussie net. They're relaying the Eighty-Second's support request."

"Break into the Aussie net, then," Molloy said.

"I'll try," the liaison said as he fumbled with the signal SOP book. "Gotta figure out what frequency they're on. But by the time we authenticate..."

Molloy was getting hot under the collar fast. "Then get Division on the fucking horn and have them do it. We don't have much time...there are planes in the air all over the place."

The colonel was right: there were planes all over the sky, just waiting for a target of opportunity like this—even if it was an American tank they'd be accidentally targeting.

But there wasn't enough time.

Lieutenant Tony Colletti, walking behind the Stuart with a squad of his men, heard the P-40 screaming toward them long before he saw her.

By the time the plane came into view, streaking at treetop level, it was too late...

He could see the big white stars under her wings plain as day.

For the pilot, who got nothing more than an instantaneous glimpse of his target, *a tank was a tank.*

Colletti's last thought: *Gee…nice to get air support when I didn't even ask for it.*

A hundred yards away, Melvin Patchett was an inadvertent witness as the mistake unfolded.

He heard the P-40 coming, too…and saw the bomb drop.

In the split second that followed, he was trapped within the silent bubble of excruciating pressure and pain as the blast's shock wave expanded at cosmic speed.

His ears too battered to hear the explosion, his body flung through space like a rag doll, Melvin Patchett felt like he had absorbed the blow of some giant sledgehammer.

When he finally struggled to his feet, aching but still alive, the Stuart was nothing but a smoldering shell, unrecognizable but for the severed tracks still dangling from drive sprockets.

Lieutenant Colletti and the men with him were gone, erased as if they had never existed.

Chapter Forty-Five

The close-in airstrip at *Double-Dare* made more than just close air support possible. Now, General Freidenburg could make regular trips to MacArthur's HQ in Port Moresby, flying there and back in the same day.

The current trip—five days and counting into 1st Battalion's clearing of Buna—was cursed with bad news for Freidenburg from the start. He had barely stepped from the airplane when informed his deputy commander, a brigadier general, had been shot and severely wounded by a sniper while attempting to *expedite* the clearing of Buna.

"It's a living hell in that village, sir," Freidenburg told MacArthur. "I've watched my men rooting Japanese soldiers out of the ground like they were pulling weeds."

An interesting analogy, but a lie: Freidenburg had yet to set foot in Buna Village and had no intention of doing so until it was completely pacified.

Adding insult to injury, the Australian command had upstaged the good news he came to announce: their radio message informing MacArthur they had conquered Sanananda had beat Freidenburg to Port Moresby by a good hour.

Looking none too pleased, MacArthur said, "And yet, despite your brilliant amphibious deception, Robert, we still struggle in Buna. How long until you're finished there?"

"Not much longer, sir…a matter of a few days. I've got the Japanese with their backs pinned against the Girua River. There's no place they can run now."

"Very fine. But one more thing, Robert. Those casualty rates—totally unacceptable. Washington is not pleased. I can't have any more Bunas. Is that understood?"

Freidenburg found the irony in MacArthur's words infuriating: *Suddenly he's worried about casualties? Isn't this the man who said, "Take Buna...or die trying?"*

Nonetheless, he replied, "Yes, sir. Absolutely, sir."

MacArthur finally cracked a smile. "But all in all, Robert, you've done an excellent job. I consider this campaign as good as closed."

Freidenburg wasn't out the door of the villa a minute before MacArthur had his message of *great success in Papua* on the airwaves to Washington.

Busy in the kitchen, Ginny Beech caught glimpses of the *Supreme Commander* standing before the drawing room mirror, preening like a schoolboy, practicing his victory speech.

"*His* victory, my bloody arse," she mumbled as she set out the general's fine china for supper. "His lads should be getting all the credit."

The table set, she returned to wondering if she'd ever again see the lad she cared about most: Melvin Patchett.

Nothing seemed *excellent* or *as good as closed* to the GIs clearing Buna Village. True, once they reached the Girua River—less than a half mile away—every square foot of this tropical graveyard would be secured. But in that distance, they could find themselves in any number of small but deadly battles with concealed Japanese.

One such battle had played itself out earlier that day. "That brigadier we ain't never seen before just walked smack into it," Bogater Boudreau told some GIs who'd missed the spectacle. "I guess them stars don't make you too smart. He was just standing there, tall as can be, telling us we was all *sissies*. Couldn't figure out why we was all crawling on our bellies, I reckon."

The tanks had been a godsend. As Tom Hadley put it, "Just think how fast we could have done this if we had those Stuarts from the very beginning...instead of the bullshit games we've been playing for the last month."

A few yards away, Jock sat on the hood of a jeep and watched the mop-up proceed. "Hey, Top," he called to Patchett, "those tanks are too close together. Spread them out...move one of them over to that creek bed with Able Company. That looks like trouble, don't you think?"

A few days ago, he would have had the strength to run over and correct the situation himself. Now, he was simply too weak: *I'd end up flat on my face in the mud after a couple of steps. That'd be inspiring as all hell to the men, wouldn't it? Those sick troopers still out here on the line...how the hell are they doing it?*

No sooner had the Stuart joined Able Company, the *POOM-POOM-POOM* of its main gun echoed through the burned-out rubble that was once a village. There was one hell of a fight going on at that creek bed. It was over in seconds.

Lieutenant Papadakis made the long walk back to Jock. Almost apologetically, he said, "Thanks for the tank, sir. We would've been in deep shit without it." His head hung down, he added, "I should've thought of it myself. That creek was a perfect ambush spot if there ever was one."

"Don't sweat it, Theo. Chalk it up to a lesson you'll never forget."

Moving like a man three times his age, Jock eased himself off the hood and settled into the jeep's right seat. "Let's get closer," he told his driver.

The Japanese soldier couldn't believe his good fortune. Some 30 yards away, centered in his field of fire, a jeep rolled to a stop. Several ragged Americans crowded around it immediately, their bodies slouched against the vehicle as if it was the only thing keeping them upright. They were all listening intently to the man in the passenger's seat.

He is their leader even if they do not bow to him. A fool could tell.

I have been given a supreme final gift.

Praying the faint *click-click* of the bolt wouldn't be heard over the murmur of the jeep's engine, the soldier checked the chamber of his Arisaka rifle—needless confirmation of a fact he knew all too well:

My last bullet.

But his shot at the leader wasn't clear.

Move out of the way, Yankee bastard!

He could feel his heartbeat pounding in his ears, a racing clock ticking off the last seconds of his life.

Hurry! Give me my moment. I am ready.

But the Yankees seemed in no great rush...

Until that one man moved…and the leader's cover evaporated.

The hunter locked eyes with his startled quarry.

He sees me! The eyes of a hawk!

The Americans became a blur, men scrambling to defend themselves, screaming like animals caught in the snare…

One by one finding their triggers.

I squeeze my trigger, too…

While the voices of my ancestors spirit me away.

Bogater Boudreau was keeping an exact count: this guy made the 27th dead Jap his squad would be pulling out of the ground since the assault on Buna Village began.

"Twenty-seven in five days," Boudreau said to no one in particular. "You'd think all the ruckus they stirred up, we'd be finding a lot more than that. If every squad in this battalion pulled out twenty-seven, that's…that's…"

"Nine hundred seventy-two, give or take," a private said, helping out his mathematically challenged squad leader. "Assuming, of course, all the squads actually have GIs in them…which they don't."

They kicked the last of the splintered, blood-spattered boards off the hole.

"Geez," the private said, "this guy's head got blown clean off."

His voice matter-of-fact, Boudreau replied, "Yep, that'll happen when half-a-dozen guys unload their

Thompsons all at once. Easy now…check him for booby traps."

"I hear Major Miles was the one who spotted the guy just in time."

"Heard the same thing," Boudreau said. "Too bad he had to get winged for his trouble."

"Winged? I heard he took it right in the chest."

"Nah…just the shoulder. He'll be okay."

"Funny, though," the private said, "when the medics hauled him off, he was shaking like a man scared out of his ever-loving mind."

"You don't know nothing, shithead. The major ain't scared. It's the sickness making him shake, that's all. He's got it real bad. You start spreading any bullshit rumors about him and it'll be your ass, you hear me?"

"Yeah, Corporal. I hear you."

"Good. Now give me a hand here."

They reached down, grabbed the dead man's belt, and pulled. The rotted fabric snapped in two.

"Son of a bitch," Boudreau said. "And we thought our duds were in lousy shape."

They grabbed his arms this time and pulled. The dead man didn't budge.

"Lord, we're getting weak," Boudreau said. "This guy gotta weigh about next to nothing."

It took four GIs to get the body out of the hole and carry it to the collection point. As they did, something fell from the dead man's pocket: a small notebook.

Bogater Boudreau picked it up. As he thumbed through the pages, a photograph fell out: a picture of a young Japanese woman.

"Well, darling," Bogater said, "better find yourself another lover boy."

The notebook's pages were full of neat writing. To Bogater's eye, it seemed to be structured like the verse he'd read as a child, except it was in some strange, unfathomable alphabet.

Boudreau slapped the book closed and said, "Don't look like there's no documents in here worth worrying our heads over."

He tossed the notebook into a burning pile of rubble.

It seemed anti-climactic when they reached the river bank, like the last play in a game decided long before the final whistle. A dozen Japanese soldiers huddled into a bunker little more than a child's sand castle fought to their last bullets. All but two were then crushed beneath the tracks of the Stuart tanks. One tried to escape—despite being so weak he could barely walk—by swimming the river, only to be dragged under by a crocodile after several futile strokes.

The last Japanese soldier emerged from a mangrove and tried to surrender to a startled GI who promptly shot him to death, emptying his M1's clip in the process.

Standing over the slain man, Patchett deadpanned, "Nice shot group, *Quick Draw*. Just remind me to never, ever sneak up on you."

As the echoes of those last gunshots faded and died, the survivors of 1st Battalion sagged to the ground as one, sitting and staring silently into the sunset. No one dared express relief or joy—they just wanted to be still, to rest for a moment, without wondering if that moment would be their last.

Those whose first campaign was Buna now knew what the veterans knew:

The taste of victory is not sweet.
It's bitter—a prized wine turned to vinegar.

The new dawn brought the sound of many trucks. The first thought in the head of every man in 1st Battalion: *They're bringing in hot chow!*

The trucks didn't come bearing food, though. They were carrying troops—men of the 41st Division, according to their shoulder patches. These men seemed *happy*—and they were much too clean and pressed to have been in Papua more than an hour or two. They certainly hadn't done a lick of fighting.

"These sons of bitches came straight from the airfield," Tom Hadley said, eyeing their spotless uniforms as he stood, filthy and unshaven, clad only in crumbling boots and tattered boxer shorts.

"Better than that," Melvin Patchett added. "I'm betting about forty-eight hours ago, every swinging dick was up to the hilt in some Queensland *sheila.*"

A spit-shined, cocksure captain strode up to Patchett. "I'm looking for the commanding officer, Sergeant. I'm told his name is Major Miles."

"The major's in the hospital, Captain." Pointing toward the latrine, Patchett added, "You need to speak with Lieutenant Grossman, he's ranking officer around here at the moment…but hang on a minute, sir."

He reached into his tent and produced several rolls of toilet paper. "Might want to bring these with you, sir…the lieutenant will sure appreciate it. Might want to keep a little for yourself, too."

Glaring at Patchett, the captain asked, "Is that some kind of joke, Sergeant?"

"No, sir. Ain't no joke at all."

Not quite sure this grizzled old sergeant wasn't trying to bullshit him, the captain set off smartly for the latrine. He had only taken a few steps when Patchett asked, "Begging your pardon, sir, but where the fuck y'all been?"

Chapter Forty-Six

C-47s were crammed into every available parking spot at the Dobodura airstrip. Waiting to board them were hundreds of GIs and Aussies. Some were wounded, some sick and feverish. A few, like Jock Miles, were unfortunate enough to fit both categories.

Up until a few minutes ago, he would have been considered one of the *walking wounded*, his arm in a sling which immobilized the collarbone fractured by the sniper's bullet. A painful wound, but not life-threatening. But now, the grip of malarial fever was setting back in. A medic scrambled to find Jock a stretcher for the plane ride to the big hospital at Port Moresby. Melvin Patchett found his commander by the loading door of *Nightingale 12*—a C-47 identified with a big *12* chalked on its fuselage.

Patchett took a sobering look at all the troops waiting to be evacuated. He recognized so many of them as his own—the men of 1st Battalion, 81st Infantry. "Maybe I should've had roll call right here this morning," the sergeant major said. "Damn sure looks like there's more of us on this airstrip than back at camp. How you holding up, sir?"

"I'll be okay, I guess, Top," Jock replied, his voice beginning to waver, sounding definitely *not* okay. "But the malaria...it's kicking my ass right now. The damn fever..."

"I know, sir...I know. You just take yourself a little time off in Port Moresby. You'll be good as new before you know it. And don't you worry about a thing. We've got everything under control here."

"I've been hearing the Forty-First showed up to relieve us, Top. That true?"

"Yeah, they're here...all full of piss and vinegar. They'll learn, I suppose...but not before they gotta haul some of their own off to Graves Registration."

Jock mustered a feeble laugh. "We all need that *cat-list*, don't we?"

Colonel Molloy made his way through the throng of waiting GIs, finally spying Jock and Patchett by *Nightingale 12*. "Glad I caught you before you shipped out, Jock," Molloy said.

He didn't bother to ask how Jock was feeling. One look told him all he needed to know: *This poor bastard's in bad shape. Don't make him lie to you again about how he'll be okay.*

"Actually, I'm glad you're both here," the colonel said. "Real quick question—what do you think we learned at Buna?"

Hurting though he was, Jock had an answer ready. "That's simple, sir," he said. "If I'm ever told to attack fortified positions without artillery and tanks again, I'm going to shoot myself in the foot right off the bat and be done with it."

Molloy and Patchett waited for his laugh but it never came. He looked dead serious.

Jock had one more thing to add: "And that isn't the fever talking, either, sir."

Chapter Forty-Seven

As the clouds thickened around her, *Nightingale 12* plodded east, searching for the low mountain pass that would take her to Papua's south coast and the final, western flight leg to Port Moresby. The C-47s of *Nightingale Flight* were strung out now—each flying on her own—to reduce the chances of colliding in the poor visibility. The mountains that towered somewhere off their starboard wingtips, hidden behind that harmless-looking white mask of clouds, were enough of a danger; the planes didn't need to be smacking into each other, too.

Jock's fever was, at last, doing the talking. Over and over, he was mumbling the same word. The lead flight medic asked his assistant, "What's he saying?"

"I don't know...sounds like some woman's name, like *Jill*, or *Jillian*, maybe."

"Take his temperature."

"But I did a half hour ago. It was one-oh-three. Typical...he's got malaria."

"Take it again."

This time, the thermometer read 105.3.

"Holy shit! This guy's on fire," the lead medic said. "Start sponging him down, Private, right fucking now."

As he worked the cool water over Jock's body, the assistant said, "Don't you dare die on us, Major. We'll get you there real soon, I promise."

The lieutenant barked the command: his sergeant sliced through the coarse rope with his sword. The prisoner—who had been tied, arms spread, to a bamboo pole, suspended like a crucified Christ in midair by that rope—crashed to the muddy ground. Aching arms now freed from the pole, the prisoner was dragged by soldiers back to the barbed-wire pen.

Only one of the other prisoners in the pen came to help, a young Dutch nurse who—as near as she could tell—had been held in this prison camp for over a year. The rest of the captives skulked away. They were afraid any association with this rebellious newcomer would only get them tortured, too.

The nurse gently cleaned the new prisoner's wounds with fresh coconut milk. With practiced hands, she checked for other injuries. When that was done, she whispered, "Did they rape you?"

In a strained voice, exhausted but still defiant, the prisoner replied, "No, and I'll bloody well find a way to kill them if they try."

The nurse sighed and shook her head sadly. She'd survived in this camp by making herself useful. This new prisoner seemed dedicated to the suicidal strategy of being a thorn in her captors' side, an insect asking to be swatted.

Stroking the prisoner's long hair tenderly, the nurse said, "Jillian Forbes, you silly girl…it's a miracle they haven't killed you already."

It was well past 1500 at Seven Mile Airfield outside Port Moresby. The planes of *Nightingale Flight* had come and gone—all but one.

In the Operations tent, the duty officer was running out of places to call, alternate landing fields where *Nightingale 12* might have set down. He held up a sheaf of radio messages for the squadron commander to see. "We know she didn't return to Dobodura, sir," the duty officer said, "and she's not at Fasari, Kokoda, or Milne Bay, either. We got Twenty Mile on the horn, too—no dice." He looked at the big map one more time and added, "And they sure as hell didn't fly to the Solomons...or back to Australia."

The squadron commander took a step outside the tent, taking a long, hard look at the afternoon storm clouds rolling off Astrolabe Mountain and the Owen Stanleys beyond. He shook his head— *Nightingale 12* would have returned to Earth somewhere by now: *She'd have been out of gas a while ago.*

"There aren't many choices left, then," the commander said. "She's either in the drink...or more than likely, she's down in the mountains somewhere. You never had any transmissions from her? Nothing at all?"

"No, sir. Not a damn word. It's like she just vanished."

***

More Novels by William Peter Grasso

Alternative history takes center stage as *Operation Long Jump,* the second book in the Jock Miles World War 2 adventure series, plunges us into the horrors of combat in the rainforests of Papua New Guinea. As a prelude to the Allied invasion, Jock Miles and his men seize the Japanese observation post on the mountain overlooking Port Moresby. The main invasion that follows quickly degenerates to a bloody stalemate, as the inexperienced, demoralized, and poorly led GIs struggle against the stubborn enemy. Seeking a way to crack the impenetrable Japanese defenses, infantry officer Jock finds himself in a new role—aerial observer. He's teamed with rookie pilot John Worth, in a prequel to his role as hero of Grasso's *East Wind Returns.* Together, they struggle to expose the Japanese defenses— while highly exposed themselves—in their slow and vulnerable spotter plane. The enemy is not the only thing troubling Jock: his Australian lover, Jillian

Forbes, has found a new and dangerous way to contribute to the war effort.

In this alternate history adventure set in WW2's early days, a crippled US military struggles to defend vulnerable Australia against the unstoppable Japanese forces. When a Japanese regiment lands on Australia's desolate and undefended Cape York Peninsula, Jock Miles, a US Army captain disgraced despite heroic actions at Pearl Harbor, is ordered to locate the enemy's elusive command post. Conceived in politics rather than sound tactics, the futile mission is a "show of faith" by the American war leaders meant to do little more than bolster their flagging Australian ally. For Jock Miles and the men of his patrol, it's a death sentence: their enemy is superior in men, material, firepower, and combat experience. Even if the Japanese don't kill them, the vast distances they must cover on foot in the treacherous natural realm of Cape York just might. When Jock joins forces with Jillian Forbes, an indomitable woman with her own checkered past who refused to evacuate in the face of the Japanese threat, the dim prospects of the Allied war effort begin to brighten in surprising ways.

Congressman. Presidential candidate. Murderer.

Leonard Pilcher is all of these things.

As an American pilot interned in Sweden during WWII, he kills one of his own crewmen and gets away with it. Two people have witnessed the murder—American airman Joe Gelardi and his secret Swedish lover, Pola Nilsson-MacLeish—but they cannot speak out without paying a devastating price. Tormented by their guilt and separated by a vast ocean after the war, Joe and Pola maintain the silence that haunts them both...until 1960, when Congressman Pilcher's campaign for his party's nomination for president gains momentum. As he dons the guise of war hero, one female reporter, anxious to break into the "boy's club" of TV news, fights to uncover the truth against the far-reaching power of the Pilcher family's wealth, power that can do any wrong it chooses—even kill—and remain unpunished. Just as the nomination seems within Pilcher's grasp, Pola reappears to enlist Joe's help in finally exposing Pilcher for the criminal he really is. As the passion of their wartime romance rekindles, they must struggle to bring Pilcher down before becoming his next victims.

A young but veteran photo recon pilot in WWII finds the fate of the greatest invasion in history--and the life of the nurse he loves--resting perilously on his shoulders.

"East Wind Returns" is a story of World War II set in July-November 1945 which explores a very different road to that conflict's historic conclusion. The American war leaders grapple with a crippling setback: Their secret atomic bomb does not work.

The invasion of Japan seems the only option to bring the war to a close. When those leaders suppress intelligence of a Japanese atomic weapon poised against the invasion forces, it falls to photo reconnaissance pilot John Worth to find the Japanese device. Political intrigue is mixed with passionate romance and exciting aerial action--the terror of enemy fighters, anti-aircraft fire, mechanical malfunctions, deadly weather, and the Kamikaze. When shot down by friendly fire over southern Japan during the American invasion, Worth leads the desperate mission that seeks to deactivate the device.

Made in the USA
Middletown, DE
07 December 2023